PRAISE FOR CB SAMET

Four-time award winning author

"… women engagingly contend with otherwordly entities and real-world danger, while also grappling with that most mysterious phenomena: the human heart. Samet's prose vacillates skillfully between various registers, expressing sensuality, suspense, and humor, as needed.

A collection of well-executed … tales of love and ghosts."

— KIRKUS REVIEWS (ON ROMANCING THE SPIRIT SERIES, NOVELLAS 1-6)

"Romancing the Spirit Series: a well written set of stories of romance, suspense, drama, paranormal, twists, and turns. I found it hard to put this set down. A must read set."

— BOOKSPROUT REVIEWER (ON NOVELLAS 1-6)

ROMANCING THE SPIRIT SERIES

PARANORMAL ROMANTIC SUSPENSE NOVELLA COLLECTION, BOOKS 7-12

CB SAMET

AVANTSTAR
PUBLISHING

CAROL'S CHRISTMAS

One night.
Two hearts. Three spirit.
A new twist on a Christmas classic.

CHAPTER 1

"She's going to die." Tony Olsen paced the small office in the back of the pawnshop.

Cold wind rattled the pawnshop window and its frame of green and red twinkling lights. A distant Salvation Army bell chimed.

"Relax, Tony boy. Everybody dies." Burke took a drag off of the cigarette that perpetually hung from his bottom lip. "I mean, look at the pair of us—a couple of nobody ghosts who don't want to move on."

Tony ran a hand through his gray hair. "But I've seen her death, Burke. Christmas morning. Bam!" He smacked his hands together. "Hit by a delivery truck. A truck!" Ghosts sometimes get glimpses of fate. Tony wished he hadn't been cursed with that particular talent.

He'd watched the vision of Carol's death in slow motion. She walked toward the curb, distracted and not checking traffic. She stepped off into the road, and the truck that hit her didn't have time to slow down, or even swerve.

"There's a lot of tragedy in this world, Tony. She's lived to be forty-two—that's a lot more than some people get." Burke leaned back in his chair which didn't move or squeak beneath his weight, and there was no noise even as he clumped his feet up onto the office desk.

"Besides," he continued in a gravelly voice, "from what you've told me about this woman, she don't got much of a life nowadays as it is."

Tony shoved his hands in his slacks—his Giorgio Armani suit pants. They were the very ones he'd been buried in when he'd died, five years earlier. Since his death, he'd been lingering as a spirit on earth, watching Carol Sullivan live the same life he'd had—making the same heartless, callous mistakes.

"Well, I'm partly to blame." Tony had never been kind to Carol. As a result of that—and other contributing factors from her past—she'd grown to become as cold and lonely as an iceberg, and drifting into an ever-melting, lifeless existence just the same.

"She can't even hear or see me," Tony continued. "How am I supposed to save her?"

Some living people had a gift—the ability to see and hear ghosts. The so-called mediums, however, were few and far between, and Carol wasn't one of them.

"She doesn't have any friends or family who can see ghosts. Without an intermediary, I can't reach out to her." Tony had been reduced to helplessly watching Carol ruin her life.

Burke pulled the cigarette out of his mouth and flicked nonexistent ashes off the glowing orange tip. He stared at one wall of the pawnshop where yellow paint was peeling from the plaster. Tony kept quiet. He recognized Burke's narrow-eyed gaze of contemplation.

Tony hadn't known Burke in life. He would never have associated with a pawnshop owner. In death, however, Burke had become his best friend. Tony wished he'd taken time to make friendships like this while he'd still been alive, but being a ghost was all about languishing in regret, wasn't it?

Burke scratched at his large belly.

"Save her, eh? Might be a way to—but not in the way you think."

"I'll try anything." Tony's voice cracked as he paced. He couldn't stomach the thought of a talented young surgeon like Carol dying before she recognized the opportunity to turn her life around.

"You can make your case to the Christmas Spirits."

"The Christmas Spirits? They really exist?"

"Of course. Some spirits can be seen by whomever they choose at certain times of the year. The Christmas trio is already *real* busy this time of year, though. They're probably booked up. Some people start booking them a year in advance."

"They could help me help Carol?" Tony stopped pacing. For the first time in years, something flickered in his chest—hope.

"They don't save lives. They save souls."

Tony's posture slumped. He wanted both for Carol—her life and her soul—and Christmas was only a week away. What were the chances his Christmas miracle could be worked into the busy schedules of the Christmas Spirits?

But he had to try—for Carol.

"So, is it like in the stories?" Tony asked. "The Christmas Spirits can save a soul in one night?" He sighed as he considered this. "They'd have to. She wouldn't have very long to live after that." He pressed the palms of his hands into his eyes, trying to block out the future image he'd seen of Carol getting hit by a truck on Christmas morning.

In his vision, she'd distractedly walked to the curb.

She'd stepped over the edge.

The end.

Burke shrugged, though his eyes looked at Tony with compassion.

"At least she'd have salvation. She can set things in motion to give her peace as a spirit. She wouldn't be lingering, like you—stuck wondering how to fix the cold-hearted deeds of her life."

Cold-hearted? Tony had seen Carol's tremble after she turned away from a patient's grieving family. She wasn't heartless—just frozen. She wasn't a monster, but closed off because of the hardships she'd faced. Maybe, a little holiday warmth and magic could melt the frost.

"Okay. I'll do it. Where can I find the Christmas Spirits?" Tony asked.

"This close to Christmas? They oughta be at Michigan Avenue, under the Chicago Christmas tree."

CHAPTER 2

Carol Sullivan carried a coffee in one hand and her phone in the other as she walked to the surgical intensive care unit. Her heels clicked on the linoleum floor, and her white coat gleamed beneath the fluorescent lights.

On her phone, she checked her email and her schedule. She had an OR case at 10 a.m. and maybe an hour break before two more surgeries. When Carol reached the work station, her physician assistant, John Baker, stood abruptly from where he'd been sitting.

He banged his knee against the countertop in his haste, and rubbed it as he stammered, "Good morning, Dr. Sullivan."

Carol Sullivan appraised Johnny's white coat, which was actually stained a dingy yellow and had frayed elbows. His shoes were the same scuffed, worn Burkenstocks she'd been staring at for years. She'd repeatedly told him to buy new apparel—so he could appear professional—but he'd ignored her request each and every time.

"What's the status?" she snapped.

Johnny handed her a single sheet of paper containing her patient list. "Mr. Smith is recovering nicely. We'll be pulling his chest tube today." Johnny glanced up at her briefly. "The patient was wondering if you'd stop by to see him today. He's day three post-op, and he said he hasn't seen you since his surgery."

Carol blinked irritably. "Johnny, do you know how much insurance pays for an inpatient post-op follow-up visit by a surgeon? Zero. Nada. Nothing. Zilch. That's why I have you. I do the surgeries; you see the patients while they're in the hospital. I get paid for one outpatient clinic follow-up visit—that's it."

It wasn't fair—to her or the patients—but she couldn't rewrite a broken system.

Disappointment seemed to ooze from the visible pores on Johnny's broad forehead and generously sized nose.

"I don't make the rules," Carol added, shrugging to cover the slight shake of her hands as she held the list.

Johnny pushed his glasses up on his nose and continued: "Mr. Johnson's family is asking what the next steps are. He's post-op day twenty-six. He's the one with..."

"...post-op pneumonia. Yes, I know. The plan is; he *can't* recover from his pneumonia—his lungs aren't strong enough. I warned him and his family that resecting his lung cancer was high risk."

"Oh, they understand that. They're not upset about his care, but they think he wouldn't want to be on life support the way he is now."

Carol's left eye twitched. "They want to pull life support?"

"Yes. If he's not going to survive, they want to stop it."

"Well, they can't." Her heart gave a small squeeze. "Not until he's post-op day thirty-one. Five days."

"But..."

"Stop gaping at me. You know how damaging thirty-day post-op mortality is to a surgeon and the hospital. Half the thoracic surgeons in the country would've turned down Mr. Johnson's case, but I chose to try to help him. My reward is to have his death increase my thirty-day mortality statistics? I don't think so. Again, I didn't make this rule, and all it does is damage those of us who are willing to be more aggressive. Other surgeons cherry-pick the healthiest cases." Sometimes she wondered whether she was saving lives or just feeding a machine that demanded more of her every year. She took high risk cases and risk getting penalized if complications happened.

Johnny hesitated. "But he's a patient, not a number."

"If only the national benchmarks we're judged by took that into account," Carol snapped back, irritated more at the unfortunate situation rather than Johnny.

"What do you want me to tell the patient?"

"It's Christmas Eve. They don't want him to die on Christmas and have that memory every year. Keep him alive until after Christmas and everyone's had a chance to enjoy the holidays."

Johnny nodded, but looked unconvinced.

Carol sipped her coffee before prompting the physician assistant. "Next patient?"

"The radiation oncologist wants to start Mr. Brown on radiation therapy, but we need to control his atrial fibrillation first."

"Good. Get him moved out of my ICU."

Johnny blinked at her.

Carol pursed her lips. "He's stage four. I can't fix him. I've taken care of his pleural effusion. Now, the intensivists can fix his atrial fibrillation."

"I know—it's just hard on patients to change teams."

"We've got three patients who are going to be post-op by the end of the day. I need those beds open." As if reading Johnny's expression, Carol admitted: "Yes, there's an assembly line to surgery—and, yes, it's impersonal." If she didn't move patients out of the surgical ICU, other high risk surgeries couldn't happen.

"Yes, ma'am."

Carol took a deep breath to rein in her frustration. She felt like she shouldn't have to justify all of her actions to Johnny the same way she'd had to justify them to herself when she started this career. She wasn't the one who'd made the system, and she wasn't the one who'd broken it.

Johnny knew how things functioned on the surgical service. Were his gushing emotions a direct result of the holiday season? Why did people get so sentimental during the period of a commercialized, staged event like Christmas?

A niggling memory of happier holidays tried to surface, but she shut it down. That way lay pain.

Carol glanced at her watch. "I need to scrub in." The busier she was during the holiday season, the less the loneliness crept in.

"Oh, and your office assistant called," Johnny added. "She said Mr. Forte is asking when he can schedule his lung volume reduction surgery."

Carol raised her hands in the air—phone in one, coffee in the other—indicating the situation was out of her control. "His insurance company won't approve it. If I do the procedure, I'm strapping him with a hefty bill for an elective procedure."

"His breathing is getting worse."

"Of course it is. His upper lobes are like Swiss cheese from emphysema."

"You could appeal the case."

"Did you know that insured people have more medical debt than the uninsured? That is how bad our medical care has gotten. It's unfathomable. People can't even afford deductibles—*deductibles*." She shook her head and left, stalking off toward the OR.

CAROL FINISHED HER PRE-OPERATIVE DOCUMENTATION. While waiting for the OR to open itself to her cases, she walked back to her office in the surgical services building.

"Carol!"

She stiffened—startled at the chipper voice. Then, with a scowl, she turned around.

"Hello, Mel."

Without invitation, Carol's younger sister wrapped her arms around her and squeezed. Melanie hugged her with the same warmth she always had. Carol envied her sister's ability to stay soft in a world that hardened everyone else.

Her sister was always cheerful, and Carol suspected pediatricians were all secretly dosed with antidepressants to maintain this state of perpetual happiness. How else could they be able to be all smiles around snot-nosed children, when their reimbursement rates were no better than those of a family doctor, or even a physician assistant?

The thought of such intangible happiness tightened Carol's throat.

Mel beamed a smile. "Did you get my text? Are you coming to our Christmas Eve party?"

Carol gestured at her scrubs. "Surgeries."

Melanie's smile remained undeterred. She wore a red knit cap with short curls protruding from beneath the edges. Her sweater was covered with tiny reindeer, set against a backdrop of green and red stripes.

"You should come by when you're done. Pike and I'll be up late celebrating."

Carol fought not to roll her eyes.

Celebrating? That meant gift-giving, junk food-eating, and excessive drinking—all the commercialized pursuits merchants wanted people to indulge in during the Christmas period. Spend. Spend. Spend. Meanwhile, credit card debt across the country soared.

Melanie shook her head. "All work and no play."

Carol pursed her lips. "The need for surgeries doesn't take a break just because the rest of the country does."

Melanie gave Carol a look of pity, even as she maintained her dimpled smile.

"Except it doesn't always have to be *you* doing the surgery, Carol— *every* holiday, *every* year."

Before Carol could protest, Melanie kissed her sister's cheek and bounded away down the hall, back toward the elevator.

CAROL FINISHED her final surgery for the day—a thoracic aortic aneurysm repair—and returned to the physician locker room. She should have felt satisfaction—another successful case—but the heaviness in her chest hadn't lifted all day.

At just four in the afternoon, most people had already left early because it was Christmas Eve. Apparently, most people were like her sister Melanie and wanted to spend the holidays with their families.

Carol didn't share that same sentimentality. Her life was entirely career oriented. She'd chosen between her career and a relationship—and while she felt she shouldn't have *had* to choose, she hadn't worked relentlessly every day and gotten into one of the best surgical residencies in the country, just to give it all up for a man.

Even if he'd been *the man*—the one for her in a way she knew she'd never have again. Carol hadn't been to a Christmas party since Liam walked out. She didn't see the point.

She changed out of her scrubs and back into her skirt suit. When she closed her locker, the lights above flickered.

Odd.

The metal doors of the lockers rattled on their hinges as the ambient temperature seemed to drop a few degrees.

Carol backed away from them. Was this an earthquake? Here in Chicago? Except, the rest of the room wasn't shaking; only the lockers shimmied.

Her heart raced. Was she hallucinating? She *had* drunk three cups of coffee today, on a still-empty stomach.

Suddenly, a man emerged from one end of the room.

Carol gasped. In a hoarse voice, she croaked: "This is the women's locker room!"

"Hello, Carol. You look well."

Carol squinted her eyes. "Tony?"

She blinked. "Tony… You—you can't be here."

Carol knew Tony—or *had* known Tony. They'd worked together. He'd died about five years earlier from a heart attack. Carol had even gone to his funeral.

Well, she'd sent flowers—or, maybe it was a wreath.

It didn't matter. She'd had too many cases. She couldn't have cancelled them all for the funeral of a coworker.

The figure of Carol's long-deceased thoracic surgery partner took a step forward.

"It's me, Carol—I'm here. But only for tonight, just this once." Tony walked closer.

He appeared to Carol just as she remembered him—in his seventies, with a full head of gray hair. However, he looked pale. No, more than pale. More than *deathly* pale.

In fact, he looked downright transparent.

"This isn't possible," Carol stammered, taking a step back from him.

"It *is* possible." Tony raised his hands reassuringly. "When you make your life only about you, *this* is possible." He gestured to his ghostly body—because Carol could now see that her former coworker *was* a ghost. "It's possible to be doomed to a spirit existence—a curse for my selfishness."

Carol shook her head, stepping nervously backwards from his shimmering, translucent figure. "W-what do you mean, selfish? You saved lives, Tony! You performed the most surgeries of any thoracic surgeon in the state."

While Carol could hardly claim to have been close to Dr. Tony Olsen, she wouldn't hesitate to admit that he'd been the best thoracic surgeon she'd ever trained under and worked with.

"Oh, I saved lives—just like you," he nodded. "Sure. I performed surgeries—but that was my *job*; and I performed my job with cold detachment. Those were people I was fixing—not cars."

"You can't get attached, Tony—you taught me that. You told me if you showed even the slightest hint of compassion, the medical system would suck the life out of you."

Was she really arguing with a hallucination?

"I was wrong, Carol—*dead* wrong." Tony shrugged. "Now, I'm just dead."

"What *are* you?" Carol's analytical mind was at work. A ghost? Specter? Wraith? What were the differences between them?

"I'm a spirit who can't move on. Don't become like me, Carol."

"Your stress," she countered, shaking her head. "I haven't been sleeping and eating well."

"Don't become like me, Carol," he implored.

Carol's temper suddenly flared white hot. "Since when did you give a damn about me?"

When Tony's expression faltered, she felt an unexpected sting in her chest.

"Since I died," Tony admitted. "Since I realized I trained you wrong. I emphasized the surgery, not the patient." He paused and then added, "And you're right to be angry—I was just as rotten to you as I was to my patients. I had you work too many long hours. Liam left you because I worked you too hard just like my wife left me."

Carol stood there, shaking. She hadn't realized Tony had known about Liam. She stiffened. It wasn't any of Tony's business. She wrapped her arms around her waist.

"You're not real." She needed to eat and hydrate, and then she'd stop seeing visions of her old mentor.

The lockers rattled again, and then the room seemed to close in all around her. Carol shrank back, tightening her arms around herself.

"Change, Carol!" Tony warned. "Don't become a lost spirit." He paused, raising a ghostly finger. "Tonight, you'll be visited by three ghosts."

"What? *No*." Despite her terror, Carol's cynicism rose to the forefront. "This is ludicrous."

"Three—" Tony repeated in a booming voice.

"—let me guess," she interrupted him. "The first one at 1 a.m.?"

Tony blinked. "Yes. How did you know that?"

She pinched the bridge of her nose. "No. Stop it, Tony. Whatever this is, you need to make it stop."

"Three ghosts!" Her deceased coworker warned, his voice growing supernaturally deep.

The lockers loomed closer over her, and terror overwhelmed her. She began to hyperventilate, her breath condensing in the ever colder air. Grated metal surrounded her—smothered her—until she closed her eyes and screamed in terror.

And then—nothing happened.

Moments later, when Carol dared to open her eyes again, she found the locker room restored to its usual condition—upright and immobile, with a bench in between each row of lockers.

She steadied herself on the nearest bench.

She didn't believe in ghosts.

She didn't believe in Christmas miracles.

CHAPTER 3

*C*arol hurried out of the hospital, intending to go directly home and have a large glass of Scotch—probably not ideal on an empty stomach but she didn't know how else to settle her nerves. She stomped down the street, hands in the pockets of her thick coat, and scarf flapping behind her in the breeze.

Yet, Carol didn't feel the biting cold. She didn't feel anything.

She plowed past Christmas trees, carolers, and stores decorated in green, red, and gold. She felt the joy in none of it. It was all sentimental commercialism designed to get people to overspend money they didn't have.

During residency, Carol had been forced to work the holidays. During surgery fellowship, she was the one without a spouse or children, so she'd always been coerced into covering the holiday schedule. Finally, when Carol had earned the clout to make someone *else* work Christmas, she figured—why bother?

Let the rest of them have their celebration and waste their money.

Carol paused at the corner. She had the choice of several paths home, but she always opted for the same one, which took her past the art gallery. She stopped there during her lunch breaks, or on her way home after stressful days.

She'd only intended to walk past The Stardust Gallery, but was instead surprised to find still open on Christmas Eve.

When she walked inside, the scent of cinnamon wafted toward her with the warm air, and she took a familiar path directly to her favorite painting. Three horses—black, white, and brown—ran through the frothy surf on a beach. Behind them, the setting sun lit the sky in vibrant orange. Something about the image of the glistening beach, wide ocean, and expansive horizon captured a sense of freedom. The horses were free to run—free from riders, free from the confines of a fence, and free from obligation.

She couldn't remember the last time she'd done anything without checking her schedule first.

She looked down at the signature in the bottom left corner: *L Charron.*

"Do you like it?" A man's voice sounded in her ear.

"I love it." Carol surprised herself with that confession. She turned to look at the man who'd asked her, standing beside her on the gallery floor.

"Liam?" Her eyes widened. "Oh, my gosh! *Liam!*"

Without even thinking about it, Carol reached out and embraced the artist. Her body instantly warmed to the familiar smell of his aftershave and feel of his chest. In the few seconds the hug lasted, the last conversation they'd had flooded into her mind.

Stiffening, she stepped back, regaining her composure and straightening her scarf. She was angry with herself. She'd had no right to hug Liam. That scare in the locker room must have affected her judgment.

"How are you, Carol?" Liam grinned.

He looked magnificent, wearing a sleekly tailored tuxedo. He was clean-shaven, and his wavy dark hair was brushed neatly back.

She stared at him. Had it really been five years? Liam looked every bit as good as the day he'd left her. His voice was the same soothing baritone.

"I'm good." She cleared her throat. "Really good." Her tongue felt thick with the lie.

She turned back to the painting. "Your work has always been breathtaking, Liam."

"Thank you." He chuckled softly. "I'm glad you like it. We're having a silent auction—a fund-raiser for the children's hospital."

Carol shook her head with a smile. Liam always gave so much of his hard work to charity. She remembered the many hours he'd spent painting and picking colors. He agonized over every brushstroke, but in the end, his creations always seemed magical.

"Since you like it so much," Liam added, "it would be remiss of me not to mention that it's for sale."

Carol said nothing.

Most days, she always found time to stop by The Stardust Gallery to see this particular painting. She'd never seen Liam here before, though. He didn't involve himself in the direct sale of his own work—except, of course, for fundraisers.

Carol stared at the painting. She'd grown so accustomed to seeing Liam's art, to having this small piece of him so close to where she worked, that the thought someone else might buy it annoyed her. She already considered the painting hers.

"The colors are so vibrant," she said, staring at the painting. "The brushstrokes capture the powerful muscles of the horses."

But she couldn't buy it. It was impractical. The colors matched nothing in her home, and she didn't have room for the enormity of it, in any case.

Liam had once told her he sought to create masterpieces that people would design a room around, rather than vice versa.

This was such a painting. A masterpiece.

"Did you ever start riding again?" Liam asked.

Still staring at the painting, Carol answered, "No."

She hadn't ridden horses since medical school. It had been a brief passion and a hobby of hers once, made possible by a friend who had let her ride his horses at no cost to her. But the eighty-hour work weeks during residency left no room for passions or hobbies.

At a loss at how to handle her emotions, she stood there stiffly. Although she was so close to Liam, with their shoulders nearly touching, she still felt like a great canyon divided them—a gorge filled with memories, regrets, and heartache.

She glanced down at his left hand. There was no ring, but that didn't mean he was single. Even if he was, it certainly did nothing to bridge the gaping divide between them.

A stocky, balding man came and stood on the other side of her and appraised the painting.

"It's *not* for sale," Carol snapped.

The man turned and looked up at her, eyes wide. Then, nervously, he moved to the next painting.

"Are you intending to buy it?" Liam asked with an amused tone.

"No." She paused. "I don't know. *He* can't have it."

Liam shook his head, expressing the disappointment she knew all too well. He stuck his hands into his pant pockets.

"Same old Carol. You can't bring yourself to indulge in the beauty and enjoyment of life."

Carol opened her mouth to criticize Liam, but his soft, sad eyes stole the fight from her. Instead, she felt the corners of her lips curl and surprised herself by teasing him. "Same old Liam—always trying to revive love in the world, one masterpiece at a time."

He gave her a smile that had her wanting to crawl back into his arms. He'd asked for one thing—a life that wasn't dictated by her pager—and she'd told him medicine came first. He'd believed her.

Instead, she pulled her coat tighter around her and snapped: "I should go." She paused, before adding, "I hope your auction does well."

"It was wonderful to see you again, Carol."

A lump formed in the back of her throat. "Goodbye, Liam."

A moment later, she stumbled back out onto the street where the cold that stung her eyes and the moisture that had welled beneath them. She stomped down the sidewalk, arms wrapped around herself.

How could her emotions for Liam still be so strong after five years?

How could he stand there and talk so civilly after everything that had happened?

He left me, she reminded herself.

Carol walked fast toward home, plowing through carolers and avoiding eye contact with all the people peddling for donations.

She wasn't hungry, but she stopped and ordered dumplings and egg-drop soup from a Chinese takeout restaurant one block from her brownstone anyway.

When she finally arrived home, she traded her skirt for cotton pajama bottoms and ate in the quiet stillness of her home in front of her computer.

While she ate, she reviewed labs and chest x-rays through the electronic healthcare record system. Then, she tossed her trash and moved from her couch to her bed, where she reviewed a few medical journals in her field followed by a final breeze through her email. Every click on the keyboard and turn of a page seemed to echo loudly in the empty room around her.

When she couldn't keep her eyes open any longer, she drifted into a deep sleep.

CAROL WOKE to the darkness of her bedroom and a scratching noise against one widow. When she turned her head and focused her eyes, she saw a clawed, gnarled hand scraping along the outside of her window.

Instantly awake, she bolted upright and blinked in terror. But it wasn't a hand scraping the window; it was just a bare, black branch with the moonlit sky serving as a backdrop. The wind had caused the tentacle-like twigs of the branch to rub against her window.

Heart still pounding, Carol reached for her phone as she tossed the blanket off.

1 a.m.

A shuffling noise suddenly emerged from her living room, and her heart beat faster. She sucked in a breath, quietly slipping out of bed and pulling her robe around her with shaking hands.

The shuffling noise continued. This wasn't her imagination—someone was out there!

Should she turn the light on? Wouldn't that make her as visible to her attacker as her attacker would be to her?

She looked around desperately for a weapon, but found only a shoe. She picked it up anyway, brandishing it like a weapon with the point of the heel facing out.

With the shoe extended in her trembling hand, Carol tiptoed out of her bedroom, down the hallway, and into the living room.

By the light of a gentle moon, she saw no dangerous figures standing in the darkness.

Heart still thudding, she scanned the shadows—but nothing threatening emerged.

Damn, Tony.

He'd gotten her worked up for nothing.

Distant music suddenly sounded. She turned, watching as the edges of her front door became framed in bright white light.

Was this a prank?

She trod closer to the door, trying to listen over the sound of her racing heart. What was that music? *Silent Night?*

Was it carolers? Out this late?

She wrenched the front door open, ready to scold whoever was waking her up in the middle of the night, only to find a small child standing on her doorstep—a child of perhaps seven or eight.

The chorus of singing dwindled to a stop. Carol stood there, looking down at a glowing halo of light surrounding the curly red hair of a little girl on her doorstep.

The girl looked angelic and had Carol gaping in awe, until stark terror suddenly struck her. Her eyes were too old, she cast no shadow, and her breath didn't condense in the cold air.

Three ghosts!

Carol wrenched her silk robe tighter around her, and in a breathless whisper demanded, "Are you the first?"

The little girl nodded softly. "I'm the Ghost of Christmas Past." Her voice was gentle and high-pitched.

Carol sucked in a breath. "What if I don't want to see the past?"

"Surely, you wouldn't close the door to your own chance at redemption, would you?"

"Redemption," Carol scoffed. "I help people every day. You're telling me that's not enough?"

"You do your job, and people are helped because of it. But you do what benefits you and your financial status. Your job is noble, but your tactics are not. Your intentions have become tainted."

Carol narrowed her eyes at the spirit. She might *look* like a child—with her red plaid skirt, black tights, and pine-green sweater—but she didn't *talk* like one.

She tightened her robe with a huff. "Okay. Let's get this over with, then."

The Ghost of Christmas Past extended her arm, and Carol dropped the shoe she'd forgotten she'd been holding. She took the small child's hand, pulling the door of her brownstone closed behind her.

Something that felt like a frightening leap of faith engulfed Carol. All around them, the Christmas decorations on the other brownstones glowed brighter and brighter, before finally blurring into great smears of green, red, and white.

Carol blinked several times, and when her vision cleared, she found herself outside a row of small townhouses. They were decorated with meager strings of Christmas lights, and the buildings looked faded and dingy. Small yards were closed in with chain-link fences.

A dark-haired girl was being dropped off by a school bus, and she lugged her backpack over to one of the townhouse doors. After pulling a key from around her neck, she unlocked the door and let herself inside.

The Ghost of Christmas Past followed the little girl, and Carol followed the ghost—in through the front door of her childhood home. This place she'd almost forgotten looked even more desolate than she'd remembered it.

Inside, all the rooms were tiny. Even the kitchen was so small that nobody could get access the refrigerator if someone else was cooking at the stove.

The walls were covered in peeling floral wallpaper—yellowed from time and stains. The smell of stale cigarettes hung in the air.

When the little girl crept quietly to her room, Carol and the ghost followed. Carol recalled how she'd had to be quiet whenever she came home from school, because her mother worked nights and didn't want Carol waking her up.

"You remember this place?" the ghost asked.

"I remember," Carol said flatly. "Mom worked nights. Dad worked days. They didn't see much of each other—or me."

The girl—Young Carol—flopped onto her bed in her tiny bedroom and opened a Nancy Drew book.

"You liked to read books," the ghost said. "You liked fiction."

"I liked escaping every afternoon into a book," Carol retorted. "I could enter a world in which I wasn't an unwanted child, a nuisance, and another mouth to feed."

Perhaps that was harsh. Carol's parents had always kept her and her sister fed, in school, and in a safe environment. They'd provided adequately for them—but Carol couldn't ever remember feeling truly cherished.

She watched her younger self turn the page of her book.

"It was in one of those adventures that I decided to pursue medicine." The ghost looked up at Carol, her red curls swaying from the motion. "*Nancy Drew. Case File number 35, Bad Medicine.*"

Carol chuckled. "That's right."

It was after reading that book that Carol had solidified how she'd wanted to help people—to better society. She'd planned to make a difference and be someone worthy of note—someone worthy of the affection of others.

Someone who was more than just an annoying kid with a key around their neck and an overactive imagination.

Carol did the math in her head. Her sister Melanie would still have been at daycare during the time of this memory. When Melanie was old enough for grade school, she became Carol's responsibility—a parent when they had no parents present. Carol had cooked for her and her sister and made sure Melanie did her homework.

When Carol had turned thirteen, her parents, who'd already lived practically separate lives beneath the same roof, finally divorced.

Despite her parent's unconcealed disinterest in each other, the separation had been a shock to young Carol. Melanie, five years younger, had taken it hard as well, and Carol had felt she'd have to put on a front of toughness for Melanie's sake.

Carol had spent her teen years only seeing her father on occasional weekends and holidays—all of which she'd had to arrange herself, since her parents only spoke to each other through their respective lawyers.

After Carol had finally left for college, many years after this memory had taken place, she hadn't bothered coming back home except to see Melanie.

"What happened to that child? The one who dreamed of making the world a better place?" The ghost blinked up at Carol.

"Reality," Carol replied, coldly, though the word tasted like ashes.

"Reality didn't change, Carol. You did."

CHAPTER 4

The house aged before Carol's eyes—the wallpaper peeling further and becoming a dingier yellow while the furniture shifted and changed as it was replaced over the years. She then found herself watching a twenty-year-old version of herself sneak into the house, carrying two glasses of eggnog and a gold, foil-wrapped present under her arm.

With the stealth of a mouse, twenty-year-old-Carol had slipped into Melanie's room.

Carol had been away at college at the time of this memory, but returned on this occasion to spend the holiday with her family—or rather Melanie, since their mother was working.

"Here you were taking care of others instead of just yourself," the Ghost of Christmas past said.

"Carol!" Melanie cried.

"Shhh. Merry Christmas." Carol handed Melanie a glass of eggnog and the wrapped gift. "It's after midnight, so I thought we'd celebrate together now."

"Why didn't you give this to me earlier tonight? When we did family gift exchange?" Melanie hugged her sister. "Besides, you already gave me a gift."

Young Carol took a sip of eggnog as she sat beside Melanie on the on the bed. A tiny green and red confetti tree sat on her dresser.

"Those were cheap decoy earrings," she explained. "This is the *real* gift. I can't give it to you in front of Mom. You know how she gets all huffy when we spend too much money on frivolous things."

"Oh? Something frivolous?" Melanie held the box next to hear ear and shook it with eager anticipation. Then, she dropped it into her lap before tearing off the paper with the ferocity of a groundhog clawing through dirt.

When she opened the gift, Melanie gasped.""It's the dress!"

She leapt out of bed and held the gown against her body. "Mom said I couldn't have it!"

"Well, Mom didn't buy it."

"But it was expensive!"

"Shhh." Carol shrugged. "I've been tutoring organic chemistry. Besides, you look gorgeous in it, and I know you want to go to prom."

Present-day Carol hugged herself as she watched the memory replay in front of her. "She did look beautiful that night."

"You doted on her like your mother never doted on you," the ghost responded.

"I sure did." Carol sighed. "Probably spoiled her rotten."

Except Carol knew Melanie was anything but rotten, and she'd gone on to become a pediatrician adored by both children and their parents. Carol was so proud of her.

But Melanie gave too much of herself. People took advantage— both of her time and her money. Melanie would never retire with the way she earned so little and spent so much—mostly on other people. Her sister's husband—a graphic designer—wasn't any more frugal than Melanie, but his heart was just as big and sappy as hers. Watching her younger self pour love into Melanie, she wondered when she'd stopped pouring anything into anyone. Carol wanted to reach out and hold on to the memory, but like everything else in life, it faded.

The room twisted and contorted around them again, until it finally morphed into a completely different location. This was an office—the walls decorated with numerous bookshelves, all stuffed with medical textbooks. Diplomas and plaques hung from the walls.

This was no Christmas memory.

Twenty-four year-old Carol had long hair flowing down her back. as she sat in the office across from a stony-faced man behind a desk.

Her stomach clenched as she remembered this man—this surgeon —all too well. He'd been in charge of the medical student surgical rotation, and he'd had the cruelest reputation for pimping students and belittling them on rounds. Surviving his wrath had been like surviving a hazing.

"Here you decided to armor up and become what they accused you of being," the ghost said.

"Dr. Sullivan," the stony-faced man began, looking down at the younger Carol over his long, curved nose, "you don't want to be a surgeon."

"I do, sir," Carol replied. "I'm here to ask you for a letter of recommendation for my ERAS, because that's exactly what I want to be."

She was applying for residency, and she needed a letter from a surgeon endorsing her qualifications for a surgical specialty.

"Women sometimes think they want to specialize in surgery," the doctor's tone was coolly patronizing, "but they truly don't."

"They don't?"

"A four-week surgical rotation in medical school doesn't open your eyes to the demands of a surgeon. There are no work hour restrictions in the *real* world. Women pick surgery, and then they either change course or back out completely when they decide it's too difficult or they want a family."

A family? What business was it of this man if Carol wanted a family? She didn't even know if *she* wanted one. How could *he* know?

But the man continued, "It's a waste to fill a surgical residency spot with a woman who won't have the commitment to complete it or the fortitude to become a dedicated surgeon."

Carol watched the eyes of her younger self grow wider, and her cheeks flush. She recalled being absolutely speechless at this humiliating encounter—a clear demonstration of sexual discrimination.

This man had known nothing of Carol's fortitude or dedication, but he had decided neither were sufficient based on her gender alone.

Present-day Carol paced the room and crossed her arms as the past version of herself sat in silent shock.

"Arrogant prick," Carol hissed. "*Save the spots for the men. They're better for the job.*" She sneered angrily. "How many women did this monster turn away from surgical residencies with this chauvinistic speech?"

The old surgeon folded his hands on his desk. "Why don't you take some time to think it over? You could consider pediatrics—or, with your excellent grades, you could go to a dermatology residency."

"I wished I'd had the courage to give that jerk a piece of my mind," Carol said, watching her twenty-four-year-old-self squirm in the chair.

"But you didn't," the Ghost of Christmas Past reminded her, "and he did write you that letter."

"Damn right he did." Carol blew out a huff of air.

"You showed him," the little red-headed ghost added.

"Yes, I did."

"You became the dedicated, ruthless surgeon working long hours and forsaking a family that he didn't think you capable of."

Carol shot the ghost a sharp look. Before she could reply, the stuffy office—three-sizes too small for the surgeon's ego—collapsed in on itself.

A new room coalesced around them—a workroom.

Carol instantly recognized the room, with computer stations lining two walls and a couch against another. In the middle of the room sat three rectangular plastic tables, each connected end-to-end to form a single, long table. This had been the workroom for surgical residents, and the night Carol and the Ghost of Christmas Past were visiting was Christmas Eve, some ten years earlier.

The tables were covered in plastic tablecloths, printed with bright poinsettias. Food was spread across the table, a mixture of essential Christmas nutrition, like ham, sweet potatoes, deviled eggs, bread rolls, baked mac n' cheese, stuffing, turkey, and more—all brought in by the residents and their spouses. Tinsel was stuck to various computer monitors, and a string of crooked lights ran along one wall. A half-dozen or so surgical residents were in the room, some working on computers and others playing computer games.

A younger Carol entered the room, wearing scrubs and looking worn. Her face brightened at the sight of the Christmas colors and the array of food. She walked to one end of the table and started making herself up a plate.

Clay was sitting in the workroom, too, with one foot propped up, stretching between the couch and the table and blocking young Carol's path. She scowled at her male counterpart. He was a tall, broad-shouldered blond man. When she scanned the room, she noticed none of the other female surgeons were in the room. Clay always timed his harassment for when other women weren't around.

"Only those who brought food get to dine," Clay said.

"I brought food," Carol retorted.

"Oh, yeah. What?"

"The pecan pie." Carol stepped over his leg.

"That was yours? Wasn't bad. It's store-bought though—the other girls brought homemade dishes."

Carol refrained from reminding Clay that his female colleagues were *women*, not girls. She looked at the table, noticing the even mixture of both store-bought and homemade dishes, so plenty of men must have brought store-bought food. With a sniff, she continued to prepare herself a plate of dinner.

"So," she began, as she loaded her plate, "because we're *women*, we're supposed to cook?"

Clay shrugged, and the gesture looked kind of like a 'yes'.

Present-day Carol pursed her lips, watching her younger self shoulder the abuse.

"He always made jabs like that." She remembered.

"Makes for a negative working environment," the ghost noted in her soft, child-like voice.

"Yes—and he stole cases. Our physician mentors loved Clay because he was charismatic—and *male*, like them."

"The male physicians weren't *all* like him."

Carol shook her head. "No, of course not. Clay was the exception, not the rule. I had many very good and genuinely caring coworkers."

"Still," the little girl considered, "it must have made working here feel more like a battleground."

"All the jabs—medical school, residency, and fellowship—were like death by a thousand paper cuts." Carol thought she'd formed a barrier around these toxic memories, but judging by her visceral reaction at watching her own past, she realized maybe she hadn't fully healed from these events.

Shouldn't she look back on the negativity of the past and realize how it had made her stronger? Shouldn't she reflect with quiet appreciation how these men had made her a better woman—and a better physician—because of their sexism?

Instead, she felt hollow.

The room hardened, transforming into a two-dimensional acrylic painting, before the textured brushstrokes cracked and burst, turning to fine, colored particles and blowing away to reveal a brand new scene beneath.

This time, it was of the Chicago cityscape bathed in the glow of streetlights beneath a navy night sky. Cheerful holiday decorations filled the shopfronts along the street, while exhaust fumes from the heavy traffic puffed into the cold air before being whisked away by the brutal Chicago breeze.

Looking around, Carol spotted the memory she was here to witness, watching herself emerge from the same hospital she worked at now.

Christmas. One year after the last memory she'd witnessed.

The younger version of Carol was shivering, pulling herself into a thick, woolen coat. She nestled her cream-colored hat over a head of long, dark hair and set off into the chill at a brisk pace.

Present-day Carol remembered this eventful night. She'd just finished a shift and was off for the rest of the night. Off for Christmas Eve—but back to work for Christmas night.

Young Carol walked past carolers and Christmas trees. Horse-drawn carriages, decorated with holly and blinking lights, jingled down the road carrying rosy-cheeked couples bundled together beneath blankets.

...and visions of sugarplums danced through their head.

Magic had been in the air this night—it was palpable. Carol heard one of her favorite Christmas songs: *Baby, It's Cold Outside.* She turned to see the source of the music.

The ghost said, "Here is when—"

"I know what this is," Carol said, unable to mask the breathlessness in her voice. She'd relived this moment a thousand times in her head, but seeing it now brought on a fresh wave of emotion.

A man was standing on the street corner, painting the enormous Christmas tree at Millennium Park on a large canvas. He'd set himself up with an easel and palette, and the work he was producing was exquisite. The artist had caught every detail of the glowing lights, reminiscent of a Thomas Kinkade painting, but still distinctly different to the man who'd been described as the Painter of Light.

Younger Carol approached the artist.

"It looks beautiful," she said to the backside of the painter, "but I'm surprised your paint isn't frozen stiff." She looked at his palette.

The man turned around and smiled at her.

She'd expected the painter to be someone older, but the man appeared to be only a few years older than she'd been at the time.

"Thank you." The artist rattled his pockets. "I keep a few tubes of acrylic in here, to keep them from solidifying."

Carol shivered. "It's a little chilly to be painting outside, isn't it?"

The artist rinsed his brush. "Actually, this is the warmest Christmas Eve Chicago has had in a decade. I couldn't miss the opportunity."

He gestured toward her scrubs. "Are you coming from work? Or going there?"

"Done with work."

"That's a blessing."

Was it? Carol never really understood that phrase, and "done with work" only meant until the next shift.

"Well, your tree is fantastic. Stay warm." Carol turned to leave.

"It's almost done," the artist rushed to say. "Wouldn't you like to wait and see the finished product?"

"These scrubs are paper thin," she shivered. "I need to get warm."

"Here." The artist pulled hand warmers from his pockets and gave them to her. "Give me ten minutes to finish. If you do, I'll buy you a hot meal in a warm restaurant."

Carol opened her mouth, about to object to this presumptuous dinner invitation from a complete stranger...

...but then, he smiled.

"I'm Liam."

Oh, that smile.

Young or present-day version, it didn't matter—neither Carol had ever seen something so warm and welcoming as Liam's smile. It was, in a word, *Christmas*. His smile was a radiant, festive gift.

"Carol." She smiled in return.

As Liam resumed painting, Carol noticed his expensive shoes and the fine, leather case for his painting supplies. This was no poor street artist, yet he'd still chosen to paint outdoors, on this cold, Christmas Eve.

When Liam finished, he let Carol take a photo of him beside his masterpiece—a masterpiece which he instantly dismissed as merely mediocre.

She shook her head. So far, the man's only flaw was his perfectionism.

Together, they packed his belongings into the leather luggage bag and secured the finished painting in a tote bag. Liam turned off the Christmas music playing on his phone and slid the device into his pocket. Then, he insisted they ride to a nearby restaurant in one of the horse-drawn carriages.

Carol balked at the over-priced impracticality.

"I've never ridden in one," Liam retorted, "and it's Christmas Eve. Relax. It'll be fun."

Liam pulled her into one of the carriages. His rough textured hands were warm.

Carol then watched her younger self get carried away in the carriage, sharing a blanket with a stranger who'd smelled like cinnamon and nutmeg. For once, she let herself do something simply because she wanted to, not because it made sense. The impulsive recklessness and romance of it washed freshly over her.

"We talked until the restaurant closed," Carol told the child ghost, standing there wistfully. "I shared everything with that man, and I'd never shared myself with anyone before."

No one before Liam, and no one since he'd left.

"You still love him," the ghost said matter-of-factly.

Carol sniffed and bundled her robe tighter around her body. She couldn't feel the frigid chill from the night of this memory, she'd never felt colder.

CHAPTER 5

$\mathcal{T}$he buildings and storefronts, adorned with their Christmas lights, blurred into a hazy Monet watercolor—before finally washing away completely to reveal bright, white lights.

As Carol blinked at the offending harsh light, an operating room came into focus around her, towering white walls and a sterile glow surrounding them. Beams of light concentrated on the exposed abdomen of a patient in the middle of surgery.

Carol watched a version of herself—this one in full sterile attire of gown, gloves, cap, and mask—assist a robust, older surgeon with a colon resection.

Present-day Carol's brain worked out from when this memory originated. She'd been a medical resident, not long after having met Liam. Young Carol was no longer a student who watched from a distance or held retractors. She directly contributed to this operation, moving intestines and suctioning blood. When the surgery eventually finished, Carol would be allowed to suture the abdomen shut.

The particular surgeon she'd been operating alongside that night was harsh. His hands moved fast with the practice of many years. He barked orders at Carol, and if she didn't move fast enough, he'd 'inadvertently' poke her with a needle and then blame her for it. Her first surgeries with this surgeon had landed her three needle sticks and a series of blood tests in the weeks that followed, all to make sure she hadn't contracted any diseases from the patients.

Every surgical resident—male and female—knew the hazard of working with this surgeon, but everyone was too afraid to report his behavior. In hindsight, she suspected that if a half-dozen surgical residents had banded together to report him, the medical center would have been forced to investigate. Maybe not, though, if the whistle-blowers had all been women.

"I hated him." Carol seethed as her chill from earlier was replaced by heated anger. Her blood practically boiled as she stood once again in the same OR as this egotistical, maniacal surgeon, watching her terrified younger self try to help, while avoiding injury.

Carol knew this painful trip down memory lane was supposed to be a lesson, so she pre-empted the Ghost of Christmas Past by clarifying: "I've never been, and never will be, anything like *him*."

How many times had this surgeon brought her to tears by making her feel inferior? Too slow. Too sloppy. How many times had he mumbled 'damn worthless surgeon' when they'd worked together?

Carol shook with rage at the memory of it.

"You're not like him," the ghost agreed. "Not yet."

The operating room faded to black.

A faint glow of green and red lit an entirely different room. A Christmas tree came into focus. Carol looked around and instantly recognized the room. Her heart gave a jolt at the apartment she'd once shared with Liam.

The small apartment had a tiny gas fireplace, lit specially for the occasion, and the tree stood in one corner. Above the fireplace, the television was set to play Christmas music on repeat.

It wasn't Christmas, exactly, Carol recalled. She'd had to work December 23 through to December 27, so she and Liam were celebrating on December 28 instead.

Her younger self danced around the room wearing a low-cut, red velvet pajama set. Liam wore candy cane-covered flannel pajama pants—and nothing else.

"I love it! I love it!" Carol—Santa Carol, in those pajamas—exclaimed happily.

She gazed on the Christmas present Liam had given her—a stunning painting of human lungs with Liam's signature, artistic flare. He'd rendered the airway branches to look like the boughs of a tree, and the image was vividly life-like with blue and green leaves and breathtaking depth and shadow.

The timing of the gift had coincided with her acceptance into cardiothoracic surgery fellowship. Tears spilled down Carol's cheeks—both past-Carol and present-day Carol. Liam took the Santa-adorned Carol into his arms and kissed her passionately.

He'd been so passionate.

His hands worked their way under her shirt as they kissed their way to the couch. She ran her hands along his bare chest as he laughed and tumbled on top of her.

"I love you, Liam."

Present-day Carol reached out a hand and covered the ghost child's eyes. The spirit might be centuries older than her ghostly appearance suggested, but she still didn't need to see what had happened next.

Eventually, Carol recalled, she and Liam had returned to gift giving, and Liam opened the new set of brushes she'd bought him.

Present-day Carol turned back to stare at Liam's painting of the lung-tree. She still had that painting to this day. Because it had become too painful to look at , she'd carefully wrapped it up and stored it in her closet. The beautiful painting was a reminder of what she'd lost—what she'd let go.

Objects shifted and shimmered around them, and then the same apartment went fast-forward two years into the future.

Young Carol and Liam were arguing.

With a wave of nausea, present-day Carol remembered this fight—their last fight. Ever. She'd already been crying from the last scene, and the tears kept coming.

With raised voices, the two of them had bickered about a familiar topic: Carol was spending too much time at work, and Liam was feeling neglected.

"You're never home, Carol."

"I have a job, Liam."

"A job that means more to you than I do!"

Present-day Carol tuned out the painful exchange of words. Regardless of the excuses she'd made—career advancement, being better than the competition, and being needed by patients—enough time had passed since this last fight for her to reflect, ruminate, and accept the truth behind the excuses.

"I don't want to see this," Carol told the ghost beside her. "I've already been through the pain of it once."

Like her memory of meeting Liam, she'd revisited this one thousand times also over the years. The truth was that no one had ever loved her as completely as Liam had, and she'd never been able to bring herself to feel as though she deserved him.

Carol never felt worthy of his beautiful love.

The truth was that no one had ever loved her as completely as Liam had, and she'd never been able to bring herself to feel as though she deserved him.

Carol never felt worthy of his love.

"You're smothering me!" Young Carol was shouting at Liam.

Carol cringed at the sound of her own words. When she saw the crushed look on Liam's face, her heart felt like it was breaking all over again. She collapsed to her knees, clutching her stomach.

"Stop," she begged the little girl. "Please, make it stop. Why are you showing me this? I can't change the past."

"The past cannot be changed," the redhead replied, "but it doesn't have to be repeated."

"I don't want to repeat it. That's why I never went back to him."

"There's another way," the voice of the small ghost trailed off, and then she vanished.

After a long, silent moment, Carol wiped away tears and looked up.

As she composed herself, she looked around. She was kneeling on the floor of her brownstone, surrounded by the familiar, soft gray walls. Her heart pounded with a dull ache.

In panicked haste, she reached for her phone and dialed Liam's number.

Did he even still have the same number?

The call went straight to voicemail.

"Liam, it's Carol," her words came out rushed. "I just…"

Her voice trailed off. What did she want? She just wanted to hear his voice, but that seemed like a ridiculous thing to say. Instead, Carol finished her message: "I just wanted to wish you a Merry Christmas. It was good to see you yesterday."

Still on the line, Carol forced herself to take a deep breath. As she did so, she looked up and caught sight of the clock on the wall.

1:45 a.m.

She bit back a groan of mortification. How inappropriate to call Liam so late! Could she delete the voicemail? Possibly, but he'd still see that she'd called.

"…and don't sell the horse painting—*please*."

With that, Carol disconnected the call.

She tossed the phone aside and deflated back to the floor. She felt empty, like her insides had been scooped out, and the little girl had been just the first of her scheduled supernatural visitors.

How much time until the next ghost arrived to further emotionally torture her?

Carol had thought she'd effectively buried the past, but now the memories were back—fresh and raw after the Ghost of Christmas Past had forced her to revisit them.

The pain now felt days old, rather than dulled by the passing years. Carol had forgotten how much she'd distanced herself from these memories, and that wasn't the only thing.

She thought of Melanie. She'd distanced herself from her sister, too. They'd been so close once.

And Liam. Carol had forgotten how hard she'd pushed him away. He'd been so loving that she'd felt inadequate in her reciprocation, but instead of trying harder, her response had been to distance herself from him.

Could she ever be the compassionate older sister that Melanie deserved? Or the doting companion in a balanced relationship? Could Carol rediscover that side of herself? Or was that a gorge too far to cross?

She stumbled to the bathroom and splashed cold water on her face. Staring at herself in the mirror, Carol brushed the tangles out of her dark, shoulder-length hair. In her reflection, her brown eyes looked tired and her cheekbones pale.

Taking deep breath, she stood up straight. With determination, she strode into the bedroom and changed into blue jeans and a forest green sweater. She might not have any choice about being dragged around Chicago by holiday ghosts, but she didn't have to be wearing a silk robe as she did so.

When Carol walked into the kitchen to get herself a glass of water, she froze.

A burly, bald man in torn overalls and stained work boots was standing there. A ring of keys hung on his belt. Were it not for his green sweater—with Rudolf sporting a flashing red nose on it—Carol might have thought this new arrival was a burglar. The ghostly stranger grinned at her, and she relaxed somewhat. A shaggy beard encased his smile, but it was warm and genuine.

"I'm the Ghost of Christmas Present."

"You look more like a janitor," she responded coolly. "I'm Carol, your next victim."

The ghost gave a hearty laugh, one that seemed to reverberate throughout the room as it shook his ring of keys. The warmth of his mirth even spread through Carol, dispelling the cold clinging to her after watching her wretched past.

"Shall we begin?" The spirit's voice was a deep baritone.

"Lead the way," she answered, devoid of enthusiasm.

The Ghost of Christmas Present unlocked a door, one that had materialized where her refrigerator had once been, and led her through.

She found herself standing in a tiny apartment, decorated festively with a small tree and a string of lights stretched across the border between the walls and ceiling. A bald-headed boy sat in front of the tree, beneath which lay a solitary present.

Carol walked forward, confident that the hairless boy couldn't see or hear her. She observed the paleness of his skin and the dark bruises on his arms.

"Cancer?"

"Unfortunately, yes," the Ghost of Christmas Present replied. "Leukemia."

Worry prickled her skin. "Whose son is he?"

"Corey, let's do this!" The answer came in the sound of a cheerful voice. Carol's physician assistant, Johnny, walked into the room wearing blue and white snowflake decorated cotton pajamas and black slippers. He looked ridiculous and Carol couldn't help but smile at his boisterous jubilation.

Johnny's wife entered the room, looking tired, but with a warm smile on her face at seeing her son by the tree. "Open it, Corey."

Johnny's wife entered the room, looking tired, but with a warm smile on her face at seeing her son by the tree. "Open it, Corey."

The boy tore into the present.

"Only one?" Carol asked.

The ghost didn't reply.

"An Xbox!" Corey's face lit with a smile. He stopped before opening the box. "But you said it would cost too much, because we needed to cover the cost of chemo."

Johnny rubbed the top of his head. "I got a bonus."

She choked at the lie. A lump of coal hit her stomach like a rock dropping into a well.

She didn't set Johnny's salary—that was done by the hospital—but she knew his wages were in the bottom third of the national average. Someone with his level of experience and dedication ought to make a lot more.

She glanced at the shoes by the door to the apartment. They were the same, worn loafers she'd been annoyed at day after day—hanging beneath the familiar, elbow-shredded white coat of her physician assistant.

Carol glanced at the Ghost of Christmas Present.

"I can talk to administration—argue for a raise." Her voice was a dry whisper.

"You said it yourself," the ghost responded, "the insured have the highest amount of medical debt. Johnny earns enough that he simultaneously doesn't qualify for medical financial assistance, but also can't cover the large deductible and out-of-pocket expenses for his son's treatment."

Carol gulped dryly. "I'll talk to administration about getting him a bonus, too."

The ghost nodded, stroking his beard.

The boy's mother came back into the small living room and handed Corey a mug of hot chocolate.

"Thanks, Mom. Thanks for the gift! I'm going to set it up!"

As Corey went to the television, Johnny and his wife—Penny— moved to the kitchen. Carol tried to remember if she'd ever actually met Penny. No, she decided. She knew the name from Johnny mentioning her, but Penny had never come to see her husband at work, at least not while Carol had been around.

"You didn't get a bonus," Penny snapped at him.

"I know," Johnny nodded. "I just wanted to make him happy."

"Ugh." Penny groaned. "It's that horrible woman you work for. You need to find a better job."

Johnny kept his voice low. "We've been over this. Corey's best medical care is here in Chicago, and I can't work anywhere else in the city with my noncompete clause."

Penny lowered her head and stepped into his arms. "I know. I'm sorry. Let's just make this the best Christmas we can for Corey."

Goosebumps prickled Carol's arms. Why the best? Had they been told this would be his last?

"Is Corey going to be okay?" Carol turned to the ghost, a pleading, shaky edge to her voice.

"I can't see the future," he replied dryly. "Only the present."

CHAPTER 6

*T*he lights on Johnny's Christmas tree blurred, and a new door appeared, adorned with a bright holiday wreath. The Ghost of Christmas Present, unlocked it, and they entered different living room, filled with a blue and white Christmas tree.

Melanie came into view, wearing the same festive colors from when Carol had seen her earlier, back when it had still been Christmas Eve. Carol stood in the living room of her younger sister's two-bedroomed loft.

The live Christmas tree was so plush that it filled one entire corner of the room and stretched so tall that the silver star brushed against the ceiling. Stockings hung over the gas-lit fireplace—four in all, each made from soft green and red velvet material. *Oh, Holy Night* played through a speaker system, while the couch was covered with Christmas pillows in vibrant gold and silver. Charles Dickens's *A Christmas Carol* sat in hardback on the mahogany coffee table.

As she stood there, Carol's sister held a framed photo, her expression uncharacteristically doleful. Melanie's husband, Pike, came into the room wearing red and green flannel pajamas. He towered over Melanie's small frame and wrapped gentle arms around her waist from behind.

Pike looked over Melanie's shoulder.

"The party was great. I'm sorry your sister didn't show."

"It was great." Melanie sighed. "I was hoping to give Carol her gift."

Carol peered closer at the framed photo in Melanie's hands.

A Christmas long ago was captured beneath the glass. In the picture, Carol was sixteen and had one arm slung over an eleven-year-old Melanie. They both wore Santa hats and broad smiles.

Carol swallowed and stepped back, watching Melanie gingerly tuck the photo in a decorative box and cushion it in white tissue paper.

"I wanted to tell her about…" Melanie's voice trailed off, and her hand lowered to her abdomen.

Carol looked back at the four stockings over the fireplace—one for Melanie, one for Pike, and one each for…

"Oh, Mel!" Carol's heart swelled with excitement for her little sister's expanding family. "She's pregnant!"

When Carol looked to the ghost for confirmation, he nodded.

"Twins?"

He laughed heartily. "Yes. Fortune has fallen upon them double-fold."

Carol smiled, but still felt an ache. Mel could have told her earlier, but held back even knowing Carol was unlikely to come to her party.

"Thank you for showing me this, Spirit. I want to be a part of their lives. I want to be the best aunt they'll ever have."

"You'll be the *only* aunt they'll ever have." His eyes twinkled.

She nudged him with her elbow playfully, surprised that she could physically touch this supernatural entity. "You know what I mean."

With a swell of excitement, Carol looked back at her sister.

A beeping of machines sounded, intruding on Carol's pleasant thoughts. The Ghost of Christmas Present unlocked a bland hospital room door as Melanie's apartment faded.

Carol stepped into a sterile ICU room. The beeping came from a monitor by a patient's bed, which showing a steady heartbeat and stable blood pressure. The ventilator supplied timed, incremental breaths through a breathing tube.

"Mr. Johnson." Carol let out an anguished sigh.

She looked at the ghost, whose bald head seemed to reflect the bright, fluorescent lights of the ICU room.

"I did what I could," Carol told him. "I tried to help him. He tolerated the surgery, but his lungs were too weak to come off the ventilator. Then, he contracted pneumonia."

The Ghost of Christmas Present dipped his head. "And his crime of failing to recover should doom him to being on life support? Which delays his inevitable death?"

"He isn't in pain," she replied. Mr. Johnson was comfortable on intravenous sedatives.

The large ghost motioned toward two women in the room, who sat in chairs watching over their loved one. Their drooping eyes and anguished expressions spoke volumes—a visual demonstration as to the extent of their suffering.

Carol raked her fingernails through her hair. "It's not my fault. Surgeons are graded based on their thirty-day mortality rate. If I pull the plug, I'm affecting my numbers—which, in the future, will only hurt other patients who…"

She stopped when she heard the quiet sobs of Mr. Johnson's wife.

Carol paced the room. "Okay, okay, I get it. These are people, not numbers. You've made your point, Spirit. Can we go now?"

The ghost hooked his thumbs through the straps of his overalls. Another door rippled into existence, this one brightly paint stained. Again, the ghost unlocked it and swung it open.

She followed him into a two-dimensional, vividly textured acrylic painting of a beach at sunset. When she stepped all the way through, she stood before the work of art where palm trees appeared so lifelike that a real breeze might have made the painted fronds move.

Carol didn't have to look at the artist's name to know whose work this was.

Liam.

She knew those brush strokes. She knew the hands that had crafted this masterpiece.

As Carol watched, she saw Liam standing there—beside an elderly man who leaned on a cane. They both wore tuxedos, and Carol recognized the room as part of the gallery she'd visited on Christmas Eve. Poinsettias adorned stands in corners, and empty champaign flutes rested on trays. Side by side, the two men stared at the shimmering water of the painting.

"Have you ever loved something you couldn't have?" The old man asked that of Liam without turning his gaze from the textured rendition of water.

"Indeed I have, Mr. Moretti."

"Sometimes, the pain of it feels like a trickling bleed," the old man mused. "An ache that slowly, subtly takes your life."

"You're not wrong, sir." Liam moved to clasp his hands behind his back. "This will be my last auction, Mr. Moretti."

Shock registered on Mr. Moretti's face. "But you've done so well, Liam! The fund raiser has been stupendous, year after year."

"My heart isn't in it anymore. I apologize."

"What will you do?"

"Perhaps I need time. Perhaps I need to find a way to stop the hemorrhaging."

"Oh, Liam." Carol wanted to reach for him—to comfort him—but stopped short. They were on such different paths now, weren't they? If she didn't think she deserved Liam *then*, she certainly didn't deserve him *now*.

"I don't know how to fix us," she told the spirit. "To fix *me*."

The Ghost of Christmas Present turned to her. "If he's the one giving the love, and you're the recipient of it, isn't it up to *him* to decide if you're worthy of his affection?"

Carol looked at the ghost through blurred eyes. Her temple began to throb. This was too much—just too much. She couldn't solve the problems of the medical community and mend all broken relationships. She was just one person.

Another painting of Liam's popped into her head. This one was a sphere of silver spinning on a lilac-colored lake beneath a teal sky. It was a painting he'd called *The Sphere of Influence*.

Everyone had their own sphere, Liam had explained to her—their own group of people, and their own environment, which they impacted both positively and negatively.

Whenever he got overwhelmed at all of the problems of the world, Liam had said he'd remind himself to scale his concerns down to his sphere of influence, who and what he could realistically improve without damaging or overwhelming his own psyche.

Maybe Carol could do that.

She couldn't change the dysfunctional, fractured medical system in this country, but she could change how she navigated through it. The system might reward delayed, assembly-line care, but she didn't have to conform to that. She could add her own compassion at no cost to her. She could have a positive impact in her sphere of influence, even if nowhere else.

"I think I can do it. I think I know how to change."

The ghost gave Carol a beaming smile, and then he began to fade from the gallery.

"Then, you're already on your way to success," his voice lingered after him.

"Thank you for showing me the present."

The ghost dipped his head as he vanished, keys jingling one last time.

CAROL FOUND herself alone in the art gallery.

She stepped forward, wandering through the gallery until she vaguely noticed the scenery change around her. She blinked, shaking her head and looking around the new location. In another apartment, she stood in a dark, unwelcoming living room.

In one corner, a towering figure, utterly unmoving and wearing a long, dark hood.

A chill ran down her spine and Carol shuddered at the sight of the Ghost of Christmas Future—Christmas Yet to Come.

He might as well be Death himself, or perhaps he was, because death was the inevitable outcome awaiting everyone.

Looking tentatively around the apartment again, she feared whose it might be—and what terrible future this ghost intended to show her.

Then, she saw them. Johnny and his wife, crying together as they held a photograph of Corey in their hands. Finally, Carol recognized the tiny apartment. It was theirs but devoid of Christmas decorations, unlike the last time she'd seen it.

Her chest tightened. Surely, this hadn't happened—or didn't *have* to happen. This was a vision of the future, after all, and the future hadn't happened yet.

Corey just needed appropriate and timely treatment, that was all.

"No, no, no."

Carol spun away from the heart-breaking scene—only to find herself back on the cold, dark streets of Chicago. This winter snow fell from a bleak sky, heavy with dark clouds.

She whirled around, back to face the Ghost of Christmas Yet to Come.

"Stop it! That won't happen. I won't *let* it happen."

The enormous cloaked figure said nothing but only pointed a long, bony finger. Carol's gaze followed the direction he indicated.

She wiped tears out of her eyes and focused on a scraggly, weather-beaten man huddled in an oversized, stained coat. He was leaning against the wall of an abandoned storefront, with an unshaven beard and dirt-caked fingernails. His eyes looked distant and destitute.

She shook her head. "That could be anyone."

Two women stopped to stare at him before continuing on their walk.

"I heard he was a famous painter, until he stopped painting one day." One of the women whispered to the other, her voice audible as the women passed where Carol was standing. "He traded his brushes for booze until he went broke…"

Carol shook her head, turning back to the homeless man. She recognized him through the dark beard—although not as the man she'd seen on Christmas Eve.

"No," Carol breathed. "Not Liam."

She turned back to the ghost, desperately grabbing hold of his abundant black robes. She looked up into the void of his faceless black hood.

"It doesn't have to be this way," Carol pleaded. "Let me fix it. I can save him—the way he saved me."

Carol turned toward the homeless man—her Liam.

She reached him, kneeling down to touch his bundled figure and, instead, falling straight through the now-intangible sidewalk.

Screaming, she plummeted into nothing. She fell through the darkness and landed roughly on her hands and knees, kneeling in soft dirt.

Heart pounding, she struggled up to her feet, spinning around to face walls of dirt in every direction. Then, she looked up—at the rim of the six-foot deep hole she'd fallen into.

Looming down above her, she saw a tombstone.

DR. CAROL SULLIVAN

Above her on one side stood the large, hooded figure.

On the other stood Johnny, dressed in a black suit with Penny beside him.

High above, a gray sky hung heavy with clouds. Down in the pit—her own grave—Carol felt frigid with fear.

"Why did we come here?" Penny asked, looming over Carol's grave.

"Somebody had to," Johnny replied. "After all, she was my boss. She was an excellent surgeon. She helped people."

"As long as she was helping herself."

Johnny didn't refute that. Instead, he looked down into the grave and murmured, "Goodbye, Carol."

The couple turned and walked away from her grave, leaving Carol alone in the darkness.

She wasn't alone for long. Someone else approached. Straining to look up, she saw her sister standing at the edge of the grave.

She gulped.

Melanie didn't look much older than she was now, which meant...

Carol turned and looked up at the looming, black figure of

Christmas Yet to Come. She longed to ask him, "When is this supposed to happen?"

But she knew he wouldn't answer her—and, in truth, she didn't need him to. She knew the answer.

Soon, apparently.

With tears in her eyes, Melanie dropped a single red rose into the grave. It fell, landing in the dirt at Carol's feet—the pedals scattering their crimson colors, in contrast to the black earth beneath them.

When Melanie left, someone began shoveling dirt into the grave.

Carol pressed herself against one wall of moist dirt as more cascaded down around her. Panic filled her as dirt hit her chest.

"Mel," she called up, out of the grave. "Mel, wait! Come back!"

Carol turned toward the other side of the grave, where the Ghost of Christmas Yet to Come and his shabby black cloak towered over her. She tried to claw her way out of the deep, dark hole, but she couldn't find purchase in the moist dirt.

"Wait!" she cried. "I know what I have to do! I know how to change! Please!" She slipped and fell, landing on her back with a thud.

The dirt kept coming. Shovel-load after shovel-load, scooped up with the grating of metal against dirt.

"No!" Carol screamed.

Then, all fell silent.

CHAPTER 7

Carol snapped her eyes open.

She was lying on her back in her bed, tangled in her bedsheets and still wearing her jeans and sweater.

I'm alive.

Flinging off the covers, she scrambled to the edge of the bed and snatched her phone off the charging station.

6 A.M. DECEMBER 25

Christmas day!

She stumbled out of bed and across the hallway into her home office. She had so much to do. There, she logged onto her computer. In rapid succession, she sent several emails. Then, she ordered pre-cooked entrees and sides to be delivered in the afternoon. Next, she found the gallery website where Liam's work was showcased.

After making her purchases, she dashed to the bathroom, feeling like she was floating on a cloud of elation. She was alive—so full of life—and she knew every step of what she needed to do.

In the bathroom, she baulked briefly at her appearance. A night without sleep and crying more in a few hours than she had in the last five years hadn't been kind to her face. After freshening up and adding makeup, she dressed in wool slacks and a sweater. Wrapped in her coat, she grabbed her purse and hospital badge.

At last, standing on the curb outside her brownstone, Carol inhaled crisp, chill air—the best kind, after a fresh snowfall. Church bells rang in the distance, and a neighbor brushed snow off his railing.

She caught a cab to the hospital.

En route, she called Jeff, one of the hospital financial officers.

"Carol, it's Christmas day." His voice crackled with irritation and exasperation. "Is there some financial crisis at the hospital?"

"Merry Christmas, Jeff."

"Uh, Merry Christmas," he replied uncertainly.

"I need a Christmas miracle," Carol said firmly. "Johnny has been my physician assistant for five years. He needs a Christmas bonus—a good one. That, and a raise—effective January 1st. He's underpaid, based on national averages, factoring in his experience and the cost of living for Chicago."

"You're telling me this now? Today?"

"A Christmas miracle, Jeff. I need you to make this happen."

"Carol..." he started to protest.

"Don't give me the company line about budget cuts and lean margins," Carol cut him off. "We've underpaid Johnny for far too long. Whenever he figures that out, he'll leave us for a job that pays him what he's worth. If I lose Johnny, my work productivity will fall by half until we hire and train a replacement. We both know that's a six to twelve-month endeavor, which is a much bigger loss than treating our employees as they ought to be treated."

"Okay, okay," Jeff sighed, "I can do the raise by January, but I can't release bonus funds on a holiday."

"I'll get him the bonus, and you can reimburse me," Carol replied. "I'm also doing one pro-bono case per month, starting in January."

"Carol..."

"Get behind it, Jeff. I'll get key administrators in a meeting after the holidays. They can spin it for marketing promotion if they want, but it's happening."

"What's gotten in to you, Carol? I thought you despised Christmas."

"I found the Christmas spirit I'd lost." She paused. "Oh, and I'm not working Christmas next year." Then, she hung up the phone, paid the cab fare, and bounded into the hospital.

With a happy heart, she passed nurses, aides, and other physicians —greeting them all with a "Merry Christmas!" Some stared in shock, while others smiled and returned the wish for a pleasant holiday.

Carol walked into Mr. Smith's room. He was sitting on the edge of his bed, eating breakfast in his faded blue hospital gown.

"Mr. Smith, you're looking well."

"Dr. Sullivan!" His unshaven face brightened. "Visiting on Christmas day?"

"I wanted to see how you're feeling. Your surgery went well, and I see your chest tube is out now. We should be able to get you home today."

"Today? That'd be a great Christmas present! The grandkids were hoping to visit this evening."

After a few minutes of socializing, Carol bid Mr. Smith a good day.

Next, she went to the ICU. When she reached Mr. Johnson's room, she found his family—wife and daughter—seated in his room. Carol pulled up a chair and sat in front of them.

"Dr. Sullivan?" the wife asked, startled.

Carol leaned forward looked deep into Mrs. Johnson's glistening eyes.

"I'm so sorry this happened to your husband."

"You told us pneumonia could happen."

"I know," Carol nodded, "but I wish this surgery would have worked for him."

"He hoped so, too, but he didn't want to live barely able to breathe. He'd rather die trying to get a better quality of life than live struggling the way he was."

Carol nodded. Mr. Johnson had told her the same thing before his operation, and she'd been honest about the risks of the surgery. For the first time, Carol wasn't thinking about metrics or mortality tables. She was thinking only of this woman's breaking heart — and the man who deserved dignity in his final hours.

"I'm sorry it didn't work," Carol repeated. "I'm sorry he didn't recover—that he won't recover."

"He didn't want to linger on life support."

"I know. Whenever you're ready, we'll let him pass comfortably."

Mrs. Johnson gave a pained sigh. "He's ready. Let's let the grandchildren say goodbye tomorrow. After Christmas—tomorrow."

"Tomorrow," Carol echoed. "I'll be here, and we'll do it together."

AFTER CAROL LEFT THE HOSPITAL, she grabbed a cab and stopped briefly at a department store on the way to Johnny's apartment.

With gift bag in hand, she slid out of the cab. "Keep the meter running," she called to the driver, before bounding up the stairs and knocking on Johnny's door.

Johnny answered the door in his pajamas, holding a cup of coffee. His eyes widened when he saw her. "Dr. Sullivan?"

"Merry Christmas, Johnny." She handed him the sparkling, silver bag.

"Johnny? Who's there?" Penny came to the door. At the sight of Carol, her expression darkened.

"Honey," Johnny said quickly, "Dr. Sullivan brought us a Christmas gift—isn't that *nice* of her?"

Penny's expression softened into confusion.

Carol extended a hand. "I'm Carol. We've never met, and that's inexcusable on my part."

Johnny pulled the card out of the bag and passed the bag to Penny.

"That's your bonus, Johnny," Carol explained, as he opened it. "That, and back payment on prior Christmas bonuses. There's also a letter in there, outlining your raise, effective January 1st."

Johnny stood there, eyes wide.

Carol turned to Penny.

"In the bag are a few Xbox games, and a gift card for more games for Corey. Penny, I bought you some scarves—because we don't know each other well enough for me to know what you like, but I hope to change that."

Johnny opened the envelope and gasped at the number on the check inside. "Penny, look at this."

He showed it to her. Her mouth fell open.

Carol backed away toward the door.

"I have to go—more deliveries to make—but I hope you'll come this evening to my house for Christmas dinner. The invitation should be in your email."

Carol then turned and scurried down the stairs. She nearly tripped on the bottom one, catching herself and laughing at her own clumsiness.

Once back in the cab, she directed the driver to Melanie's apartment.

The cab pulled up, and Carol paid the driver. She grabbed her bag and strode into the apartment complex.

When Carol knocked on the door to her sister's apartment, Pike answered—with disheveled morning hair and stubble on his jaw.

He scratched his chin. "Carol? This is a pleasant surprise. Come on in."

Carol stepped inside, dropping the gift bag on the floor. She hugged her brother-in-law, and his posture stiffened in surprise.

"Thank you for being so good to Mel," Carol breathed, pressing her head against his broad chest.

"Carol?" Melanie walked into the room, eyes widening.

"Mel!" Carol's heart soared to see her sister. She rushed to hug her, and, just as quickly, she spun around and picked up the gift bag, thrusting it toward her sister.

"I bought baby stuff," Carol explained. "All gender neutral—but it's a start." Her eyes sparkled. "And I bought two of everything."

Melanie's eyes widened even further. "But how could you *possibly* know?"

Carol didn't answer. Instead, she continued, "And if you're not otherwise engaged, come to my Christmas dinner tonight." Then, Carol hugged Melanie again. "It's so good to see you."

With that, Carol abruptly turned and headed toward the door. She had one more stop to make before going back to her house to prepare for Christmas dinner.

"Wait!" Melanie ran after her, snatching a small box from under her tree. "Take your gift, but we *will* see you later, too."

Carol graciously accepted the box, which she recognized instantly. She smiled but didn't open the gift.

"Thank you, Mel. It's one of my favorite photos. A perfect gift."

Leaving the couple pleasantly flabbergasted, Carol strode out of their apartment building and down the stairs to the street.

She pulled her coat tighter around her and breathed the air in deeply one more time. She'd go to The Stardust Gallery next, hoping to find Liam—*if* he checked his email and *if* he wanted to show up.

Ten minutes later, a cab dropped Carol outside the gallery. She walked up to the door, but could already see through the glass that the lights were off.

Well, it was mid-morning on Christmas, so perhaps Liam hadn't checked his email after all. Alternatively—and sadly, more probable— he just didn't want to see her.

She couldn't blame him.

Carol tested the door. Locked. She peered inside and saw no movement within.

Turning, Carol walked back toward the street, one foot in front of the other. She was within walking distance of her brownstone now, but the need to see Liam overwhelmed her.

There was so much to make up for. She didn't know if he'd ever forgive her but she needed to try.

Cars zipped up and down the street. Carol neared the curb.

She swallowed and resolved not to give up on what she and Liam had. She would check her email and see if he replied. Perhaps he had, and perhaps they could set up another rendezvous.

A low rumble in the distance grew louder.

She pulled her phone from her pocket, focused on the disappointment that she might not see Liam today.

She reached the curb and extended her right leg to step down…

"Carol!" A cheerful male voice called to her.

She paused mid-step, turning, and pulling her foot back.

A truck thundered past, slicing cold air across her coat.

As she pivoted toward Liam, he smiled, and she barely registered the gush of wind from the truck hurtling past her.

She walked toward him—resisting the urge to run into his arms.

He wore a cream-colored sweater and a fur-lined leather jacket. His dark hair was combed sleekly back, and his dark eyes twinkled with something like anticipation.

"Are you the 6 a.m. buyer, by any chance?"

"Yes," Carol grinned. "I *had* to have it."

In addition to sending several emails that morning, Carol had also finally purchased the horse painting—and a few others from the online store of The Stardust Gallery.

Liam smiled at her. "You lost sleep over it?"

She swallowed hard. If she didn't say it now, she might never be brave enough again. "I lost sleep over you." A sense of vulnerability closed around her. The way she'd treated him, Liam had every right to lash out at her now.

"Over *me*?"

"Over *us*," she amended, her voice shaky. "I never should have let you go, Liam. Can you forgive me?"

His lips parted in a welcoming smile. "Carol, I forgave you the moment I saw you desperate to open the gallery doors on Christmas morning."

She leaned closer, arched up, and kissed him.

The kiss was everything she remembered — warm, sweet, and utterly magical.

When they broke away, she no longer felt cold and her loneliness melted away.

"What changed?" Liam asked, tucking her into his arms.

"Everything."

TONY SAT on Carol's counter, unseen by all as he watched Christmas dinner unfold at her home. He'd only been granted that one moment to speak to her, when Carol had seen him on Christmas Eve. That would never happen again, according to the Christmas Spirits. Considering how badly he'd scared her, it was probably a good thing.

Tonight, he couldn't help but grin at the sight of so much holiday cheer. Carol's dining room was filled with green, red, and gold decorations—candles, miniature trees, and napkins. The table bowed beneath a Christmas turkey, green beans, mashed potatoes, buttered bread rolls, cranberry sauce, cornbread stuffing, and more. Tony wished he could smell all those delicious scents, mixed with the pumpkin pie baking in the oven.

Melanie, Pike, and Penny were busy bringing serving spoons to the table—while Johnny poured wine into waiting glasses. Corey snuck a bread roll into his mouth while no one was looking.

In the kitchen, Liam and Carol couldn't keep their hands off each other. Carol couldn't stop smiling. Tony had never seen her so happy.

"Mission accomplished," Burke said, shimmering into manifestation beside Tony.

"Better than that," Tony grinned. "She's happy, changed, *and* still alive."

"The spirit of Christmas wins again, thanks to the Christmas Spirits."

"I failed her in life, but I did right by her in death. I got my Christmas miracle," Tony beamed.

"That you did."

Tony looked down at his arms and legs. "Whoa! What's happening?" He was growing even more translucent than he already was.

"You're moving on, Tony," Burke smiled. "Your spirit is at peace."

"Oh? Great! Wait." Tony's eyes widened. "What about you?"

"I've got my own unfinished business. Don't worry about me."

"See you in the next world, Burke?"

"See you, Tony."

Outside, snow drifted past the window, soft and glowing—the quiet benediction of a Christmas well-saved.

ONE YEAR LATER

Carol fluffed the pillows and poured the wine, excited for Liam's arrival home. He was finishing up at the gallery charity auction and was due back at any moment. Christmas lights reflecting off the newly decorated living room. Snow drifted past the window in lazy spirals, and the fire beneath Liam's horse painting warmed the space she'd once considered merely functional.

Tonight, it felt like home.

Rediscovering their love had happened so seamlessly that they were already married come springtime. They'd honeymooned in Alaska. Carol had cut back her work hours to a reasonable, full-time load—and she now spent most weeknights and weekends with her husband. They sailed Lake Michigan, walked through the parks together, and kissed at every opportunity, as if they were teenagers, instead of in their forties.

Melanie had given birth to two adorable twin girls—and soon after, Carol had begun making time to give the new mom a regular weekend break, babysitting for a few hours so Melanie could indulge in some much-needed self-care.

Meanwhile, Pike spoiled the twins with every female superhero outfit and action figure he could find, which was a lot of them.

Corey had finished cancer treatments, and his last bone marrow biopsy showed complete remission. Johnny and Penny had dinner with Carol and Liam once a month. Usually, the men cooked while Carol and Penny had long discussions over what wine paired best with the food.

When Carol heard the door unlocking, she walked over to greet Liam. He entered with a flourish, spinning her in a circle with one hand wrapped around her waist, and a hungry kiss pressed against her lips. He pulled her against him as he spun her around, still kissing her senseless.

Sometimes she still marveled at how much her life had changed in a single Christmas—how much lighter her heart felt now that she'd allowed herself to love and be loved.

"Liam," she said breathlessly, between kisses, "what's in your other hand?"

Reluctantly, he pulled away.

"Your Christmas gift," he pulled his arm behind his back, "but I know when I give it to you, you're going to neglect me, so I had to get my affections in first."

"What is it?" She laughed, trying to peek around to see what he had hidden behind his back.

Liam surrendered and thrust a squirming ball of fur at her with a red jingle-bell collar.

"I'm not sure what he is—some type of mutt. He's a rescue, and the newest member of our family."

She sank both hands into the puppy's soft, golden fur. He waggled an excited tail.

"He's adorable!" She inspected him as she petted the squirming pup. "Definitely some Terrier. Maybe miniature Poodle and Schnauzer mix?"

Liam brought the puppy close to his face, and they nuzzled noses. "I think adorable covers it."

She took the puppy in her hands, and he licked them enthusiastically. "He's wonderful." She'd never imagined herself capable of balancing a demanding career, a husband, and a pet—but now the idea filled her with warmth rather than dread.

"What should we name him?"

"Something that's *us*," she pondered. "We met at Michigan Avenue —the Christmas tree."

"By Wrigley Square."

Carol smiled. "Wrigley!"

Liam grinned and leaned in for another kiss. "Wrigley? I like that."

"Come here, you." She tugged Liam closer—until there was no space between their bodies. "I'll never neglect you."

"Really? Let's have that glass of wine—and then you spend the night not neglecting me."

"I can do that."

Liam dipped his head for another kiss. "I love you."

"I love you, too."

Outside, soft snow began to fall again—quiet, gentle, and full of promise. The kind of snow that started on Christmas and seemed to bless everything it touched.

ALLISON'S ALIBI

A suspect with no alibi. A murder with unknown motive. And the killer is still on the loose.

CHAPTER 1

"So, you don't have an alibi?"

Spine straight in her desk chair, Allison arched an eyebrow. "If I'd known someone was going to murder my research colleague, I wouldn't have spent the night home alone."

"But you were alone Saturday night between the hours of ten pm and midnight?"

"Yes." Allison enunciated the word to make sure she was clear, because Detective LaGrange insisted on clarification of her initial answer as though trying to catch her in a lie.

Saturday had passed like any other. She'd worked a half-day at the lab and ridden her spin bike in her exercise room at home in the afternoon. Then, she'd spent the evening home alone and gone to bed alone.

"Do you know anyone who might have wanted Professor Baylon dead?"

Allison frowned. Wasn't that the million-dollar question? She'd been asking herself that question ever since learning of his death. "No. On an academic level, he worked well with others and stuck to his lab. I don't know much about his married life—married and kids are grown, both in careers now, I think. I seem to remember him showing me pictures of grandchildren—yes, new twins."

"Did the two of you socialize outside of work?" The detective's brown eyes scrutinized her, and his weathered skin suggested hard living, someone unafraid of getting his hands dirty and who didn't waste time on pleasantries.

Allison glanced at the other man in her office. Detective LaGrange had introduced him as Cash McCall, a psychic detective and police consultant. Rather than sit on the opposite side of her desk like LaGrange, Cash roamed her office, looking at her diplomas and collection of elephant figurines on her bookshelves.

In contrast to the wrinkled, ill-fitting suit Detective LaGrange wore, Cash sported tailored navy slacks and a pressed white shirt—to crisp for a cop. His black Oxfords were polished to a shine.

She turned back to Detective LaGrange. "We did not have a relationship outside work. I don't know much about his social life."

"But you knew him for five years."

"Yes, professionally."

"Five years working together and ya'll never went out for drinks? Shoot the shit or whatnot? Me and Cash, here, we've been professional colleagues for several years now. Closed over a dozen cases. We go out for drinks regularly." His voice was a slow but well-spoken and smooth Southern drawl.

Her gaze drifted to the consultant who stood near one of her bookshelves. He kept his hands tucked in his pockets as he perused the titles of textbooks. Sunlight from the window illuminated the faint, natural highlights in his thick hair.

Turning back to LaGrange, she said, "Well, perhaps murder investigations promote bonding better than petri dishes."

Cash chuckled, but she kept her eyes on LaGrange.

A knock came at the door before it was tentatively pushed open. Vera Myers stuck her head inside Allison's office. "Dr. Sloan, is it okay to go back to the lab now?"

Allison nodded to her research assistant. Not just hers. Vera had worked for Baylon too. The young grad student had already been questioned by the police. She dipped her head before leaving.

Detective LaGrange pulled out his phone, flicked through the screen, and then turned it for Allison to see.

She pulled her glasses onto her nose as she read what appeared to be a text message transcript.

I know what you've done.

"Care to explain the text message Professor Baylon sent you?" Detective LaGrange asked.

Allison suppressed a shudder at the eerie statement and kept her tone calm. As soon as she'd learned of Baylon's murder, she'd known his late night text would seem suspicious.

She needed to explain this to the detective the way she might talk to a belligerent patient—firm but don't piss him off. "I didn't see the text until Sunday morning because my phone is set on 'DO NOT DISTURB' from ten pm to seven am. When I saw it, I assumed he'd inadvertently texted the wrong person. I did my morning bike ride and thought I'd bring the text up when I saw him this morning at work."

LaGrange leaned back in the chair. "It all sounds so logical, doc. But lookin' at if from an investigative standpoint, I've got a vic who fingered you, and you've got no alibi to save your hide."

She slid her glasses off and let them dangle around her neck on the gold chain connecting the ends. If her father had taught her one thing, it was to keep her emotions bottled inside of her. The more emotional turmoil within—fear, pain, sadness—the more she was supposed to let those create an impassive shell on the outside.

Her stomach tightened, but her voice stayed cool. "Let's have another go at logic, shall we?" She steepled her fingers. "Now ... you haven't given the exact time of death—just ten to midnight for my whereabouts—but I do have this text message sent to me at 11:06. If I'm at the scene of the crime, murdering Baylon, why is he texting me?"

"I most certainly would like to know the same thing," Detective LaGrange replied, the sap in his voice growing stickier.

Allison resisted the urge to tell him to get out of her damn office with his judgmental stare, do his job, and find the real killer. She knew from her acclimation to Louisiana cultural nuisances that voices tended to grow sweeter as more venom was infused. Returning his acidity with her temper would only magnify her existing problem of his unspoken accusation.

She continued calmly, "There are two possibilities. Baylon could have texted me by mistake. My name starts with an 'A,' so I'm first on some peoples' contact lists. The other option is that the killer texted me from Baylon's phone."

"Why would the killer do that?"

Sensing her line of reasoning was one Detective LaGrange had also considered, she felt some consolation knowing he hadn't immediately jumped to her as the murderer.

Still silently listening, Cash leaned closer to one of her shelves, eyeing her green, gold, and purple Mardi Gras elephant figurine.

"Either a mis-text or misdirection," she said, pulling her gaze from Cash back to LaGrange.

"You're saying the killer wanted to throw suspicion onto you? Why?"

"I assume to keep suspicion off himself."

"Himself?"

"I needed to pick a pronoun. I have no idea if the killer is male or female."

"So how does the killer send a message on a password-protected phone?"

Annoyance rippled through her. Was this the detective's Matlock, play dumb routine, to get his perp to slip up?

"Although I've never tested it, I assume facial recognition or thumb prints on corpses still suffice to unlock phones."

"Yeah, I can't explain the text message either. But it's very concerning."

"I'm innocent, Detective LaGrange. You'll find none of my DNA at the crime scene, and my fingerprints won't be on the murder weapon."

"I'll let you know if that's the case when we find the murder weapon."

His eye contact lingered a few seconds. "Well." Detective LaGrange stood. "If you think of anything else." He extended a business card to her as he rubbed his balding head with his other hand.

Allison set the card down on top of her desk as she also stood. "Do you have any other suspects?"

"So far it's just you on my board, Dr. Sloan. Best you stay in town, yeah?"

CASH MCCALL STEPPED outside Dr. Sloan's office to speak with Detective LaGrange. "I'm going to hang back, Hyde. See if I can learn anything else." Dr. Sloan didn't have an alibi and didn't seem particularly distraught about her colleague's death, which piqued Cash's interest.

"Good luck. The ice queen in there is liable to eat you alive. Check in with me when you're done." Hyde plodded down the hallway.

Cash stepped back into Dr. Sloan's office where she stood behind her desk. She wore a baby-blue blouse, navy skirt, brown boots that rose over her calves, and an expression of wariness that the interview wasn't over yet.

"Why elephants?" he asked.

"What?"

"You have numerous elephant figurines. They must be of some significance to you."

"Elephants symbolize good luck." Her brisk answer suggested that might not be the real answer—or the complete one.

"They can also symbolize fertility, but you don't seem like the type of woman for frivolous superstition."

She crossed her arms as if to suggest he didn't know a damn thing about her.

"You don't have a Southern accent," he noted.

"I was a transplant to NOLA when I was in grade school."

"And then you left to attend college at Loyola followed by medical school at Johns Hopkins. Then, back to New Orleans five years ago."

"What do you do for the police exactly?" Dr. Sloan asked. She had an oval face and full lips with vibrant, youthful skin. Put her in blue jeans and a T-shirt, and she'd pass for a grad student like her lab assistant, Vera.

"I talk to spirits."

"Ah! Then you should be able to clear my name. Professor Baylon can tell you who killed him. And it won't be me."

Cash detected condescension in her tone, but it sounded forced. So, she was being defensive, which—combined with no alibi—was highly suspect.

He was accustomed to negative attitudes from skeptics about his medium ability. Instead of challenging her disbelief, he gave Dr. Sloan his most charming smile. "If only it worked that way. Sometimes it's that simple. But sometimes—as in the case with Professor Baylon— the victim doesn't linger as a spirit to resolve his own murder." Cash had spent time at the crime scene and encountered neither Baylon's ghost nor a ghost who'd witnessed the murder.

"Well, that's unfortunate." Her voice sounded genuinely disappointed. She brushed long, straight strands of mahogany hair off her shoulder.

"So, you didn't see Baylon socially. Were you hiding a romantic relationship?"

"He's twenty years my senior." She sounded insulted at Cash's insinuation.

Cash shrugged, slipping his hands back in his pockets. "He's a renowned researcher, and you're a beautiful woman. It wouldn't be the first time ..." he let his voice trail as he picked up a carved ebony elephant to inspect it.

Dr. Sloan walked to him, took the elephant, and reshelved it. Their fingers brushed briefly in the process, and Cash noted the smooth skin.

She glared at him. "The first time what, Mr. McCall? A woman slept her way to advance her career?"

"No, I—"

"Because I've published twenty papers and have my own NIH funding." She stood nose to nose with him, a feat made possible by the heels on her boots and pushing up on her toes like a ballet dancer. Without those extensions, she'd be about five-six. Her flushed cheeks enhanced a pair of livid blue eyes.

He liked the fire in her—hot and spicy like a crawfish boil—but he didn't like that he'd upset her. He usually didn't upset women until the third date—if they made it that far. Of course, suspects were entirely different.

"Dr. Sloan," he lowered his voice, balancing her anger with his calm, "I was trying to convey that you're beautiful enough to have any man you wanted, even tempt a married man in possession of a rational mind. I'm aware you are intelligent and successful on your own merit."

He'd read her online biographical sketch—college done by age twenty-one, medical school, residency, and fellowship done by age thirty, and now she had her own lab and research funding.

Her eyes roamed his face as if absorbing the sincerity of his words and expression. He noticed her eyes were a soft blue haloed by a silver moonlit glow.

"Okay." She rolled her shoulders. "I'm admittedly defensive after being accused of my colleague's murder. It's like I can't mourn him with this worry hanging over me." She moved away, leaned back against her desk, and crossed her arms.

Yeesh. She was wound tighter than a keening banshee. Yet, she'd finally displayed some emotion around Baylon's death.

"Not accused," Cash clarified. "Just a suspect."

She cocked her head to one side. "It's still unnerving. I'd like to mourn the loss of a colleague and scientist who contributed his expertise to the field of lung injury. Instead, Detective LaGrange has me wondering if I'll be publicly disgraced as he escorts me out of my office in shackles."

Cash noted the sincerity in her voice. Her initial stiff demeanor and lack of display of emotion about Professor Baylon's death while Hyde had interviewed her had made her seem suspicious, when in reality, she was hurting and worried. Perhaps all those years as a physician dealing with death had taught her how to quarantine her emotions.

Cash's casual demeanor and charm often caused suspects and witnesses to lower their guard and open up to him in a way they normally wouldn't to an officer of the law. In this case, Dr. Sloan's feelings worked in favor of exonerating her. Maybe.

"He won't cuff you and haul you into the police station. Not having an alibi isn't motive."

Did she have a motive? She wasn't sleeping with him, but what about professional jealousy or competition? Yet, Cash had researched her before this meeting. At thirty-two, she was a rising star in the research domain. She didn't need to eliminate anyone to maintain her upward trajectory. Self-defense perhaps? Did Baylon have a dark, dangerous side? If he did, it hadn't surfaced in any of Detective LaGrange's interviews thus far.

"She didn't do it," a baritone male voice said.

Cash looked toward the window of Dr. Sloan's office where an apparition of a man materialized. He looked to be in his late sixties with a full head of immaculately combed hair. He wore a three-piece suit and polished shoes.

The translucent ghost turned his gaze from the window to Dr. Sloan before landing on Cash.

Cash looked at Allison and gave a slight bow. "Will you excuse me?" Without waiting for a reply, he turned and left her office.

Cash walked through the hallways of the research building adjacent to the medical center. When he took the exit outside, he found a quiet quad with trees and a water fountain. A November breeze scattered the stiff fallen leaves of nearby magnolia trees.

Turning, Cash locked eyes with the ghost who'd followed him. "Dr. Allison Sloan's deceased father, I presume."

CHAPTER 2

Cash blinked under the morning sun streaming through live oaks dripping with Spanish moss. No one was within earshot of his conversation with the ghost.

"What gave it away?" The spirit asked. His voice was a slow, sad ebb. Another beat slower, and he could audition to be the next Eeyore voice over.

"The eyes," Cash replied.

"I'm not sure if that makes you extremely observant or if I need to be concerned about you being romantically interested in my daughter, Mr. McCall."

"I don't date suspects. I'm sure it's against my consulting contract somewhere."

"I just told you she's innocent, not a suspect."

"Are you giving me your blessing to pursue her romantically?"

"No."

Cash chuckled. There seemed to be no humor in this spirit. He suspected this was the man's normal behavior, and he wasn't so grave simply because he was beyond the grave.

"I'm not romantically after your daughter," Cash reassured him, resisting the urge to point out that Allison was over thirty and didn't need an overprotective father.

"Good. Because I couldn't help but notice you've dated a lot of women over the years."

"Hey, personal boundaries, counselor." Cash kept his tone light. He wasn't offended because he understood ghosts had the ability to glean information about people and events.

"I don't suppose you could use your supernatural powers of perception to tell me who killed Professor Baylon?" Cash asked.

Mr. Sloan frowned in disappointment. "No."

Disappointed in the situation or his inability to see the killer? The lawyer didn't strike Cash as the type to express disappointment in his own limitations.

"Well, perhaps you'll want to stick around in case you have insight that arises. Or just if you want to ensure I don't fondle your daughter."

The ghost scowled.

Cash suspected Sloan had been a man of power and prestige in his lifetime, and people hadn't conversed so casually with him.

"I'm joking. Lighten up, and help me solve a murder mystery."

Cash had one other mystery to solve—and that was what unfinished business with his daughter was keeping Mr. Sloan tethered to the world of the living.

ALLISON SANK BACK in her chair. Why had she let Cash McCall get under her skin? People rarely riled her. Sometimes, she was unflappable to the point of being called aloof. Between having had a no-nonsense lawyer for a father and working in a medical field that discouraged emotion, she'd learned to school her feelings.

She hadn't let the *real* detective see her frayed nerves, but the psychic detective—whatever that meant—had her boiling defensively one minute and nearly in tears the next. Maybe it was those golden eyes matching that thick, dirty blond hair. But what kind of charlatan consulted on murder cases under the auspices of talking to ghosts?

Her phone chimed with a reminder.

Right. Back to the lab. She had lungs to harvest.

After sweeping her hair up in a bun, she walked through winding hallways of bland linoleum, beige walls, and identical rows of wooden doors. She stopped at room 2042 and entered. She pulled on a lab coat hanging inside the room.

Vera Myers was standing over the research organoids. Her eyes looked puffy, and red splotches spotted her cheeks and neck.

"Are you okay?" Allison asked.

The lab assistant shook her head, blonde bob with frayed ends swaying. She sniffed. "I can't believe he's dead."

Allison nodded. According to news reports, Professor Baylon had been stabbed in an abandoned building downtown and discovered by a homeless person. Stabbed and left for dead. The single stab wound might not have been enough to kill just anyone, but Baylon had been on anticoagulation therapy to treat blood clots in his lungs he'd acquired after an overseas flight to a research conference.

Detective LaGrange had asked Allison if she knew why Baylon would be at an abandoned building. She had no idea.

"Do they know who did it?" Vera asked.

Allison put on her reading glasses and slipped on a pair of vinyl gloves with steady hands. She was reeling on the inside but portrayed calm on the outside—a long-standing habit.

"They do not," she replied. And if suspecting her was any indication, the police were clueless.

Vera reached for a pair of vinyl gloves from the cardboard box with shaky hands.

"Why don't you take a few days off." It wasn't a question. The poor girl didn't need to be trying to do lab work after the death of her mentor.

"But there's so much to do," Vera protested.

"I'll take care of it. I'm not working in the ICU this week."

"Okay." Vera hung her lab coat by the door as she left.

Allison moved the piece of lung tissue from one container to the next to prepare it for slicing and making slides for staining.

"Dr. Sloan?"

Allison looked up to see Cash McCall standing in her lab. She sighed, suddenly wishing she hadn't dismissed Vera so the extra body would be a buffer against his interrogation.

"Yes, Mr. McCall? You won't find any elephants in here." She continued her work.

He chuckled, a damn infuriating sound she actually enjoyed.

"Call me Cash."

She paused with her hands in midair and looked up at him. Something in his demeanor had changed since she'd seen him only fifteen minutes ago. Had he decided she wasn't a suspect, or was this his way of luring her into a false sense of ease to garner an inadvertent confession? She had nothing to confess, but she'd keep her walls up, nonetheless.

"What can I do for you, Cash?"

He grinned as he leaned against the counter. His playful eyes seemed to be considering her question in a way that had nothing to do with the investigation.

Confused, she turned her attention back to the lung samples in front of her as she waited for an answer.

Cash watched Allison work. Since seeing her in the office, she'd pulled her hair up in a loose bun and put her reading glasses back on.

"Always working," her father's ghost said. "She works too much. That's my fault. I'm proud of her accomplishments, but I wish I'd taught her to enjoy life more."

Cash wondered about Allison's relationship with her father, but he wouldn't talk to the ghost in front of Allison. Cash had become adept over the years at listening to ghosts, while interacting with the living who remained unaware of a paranormal presence just five feet away.

"What's your work?" Cash asked the physician.

When he'd tried to skim content from her publications in preparation for the interview with Detective LaGrange, he might as well have been reading hieroglyphics.

Allison talked as she worked. "These are organoids—small lung replicas. We're … I'm studying the effects of acute lung injury. I expose the tissue to irritants and study the damage on a cellular and molecular level."

"Irritants?"

"Any number of things—lipopolysaccharides, which are released during sepsis and cause acute respiratory distress syndrome, diacetyl which is in e-cigarettes and can cause popcorn lung, molds which can cause hypersensitivity pneumonitis, and the list goes on." She explained with enthusiasm and not as though she was trying to talk over Cash's head.

He didn't understand most of what she said, but liked listening to her talk.

"Did you say 'popcorn lung'?"

"Yes. In the 1990s, some workers in microwave popcorn manufacturing plants were suffering from bronchiolitis obliterans—an inflammatory lung injury from the airborne diacetyl. Hence, 'popcorn lung'." She hesitated. "Named for how it was discovered and not because the lungs turn into anything resembling popcorn."

"Ah. So you injure your miniature organs and then study them. Then what?"

She looked up at him with a slight smile as though pleased at someone's interest in her work. "We figure out how to reverse it. It's all in a petri dish, so to speak, but cures start with bench work."

"Have you had any breakthroughs? Anything that might make a competitive researcher upset?"

Allison stiffened. "Upset enough to kill Baylon? No. Believe me, if I knew who to cast suspicion on to alleviate your suspicion of me, I'd send you in their direction."

"I don't suspect you."

She shot him a disbelieving glance. "What changed?" Bending back down, she continued her work.

"A ghost vindicated you."

Allison gave a brittle laugh, but her eyes betrayed relief. "Okay, well, put in a good word for me with Detective LaGrange."

"I'll do that," Cash said.

When she glanced at him again, disbelief in her expression, he kept unwavering eye contact until she broke it.

Cash took a step forward. "The problem is that if you're innocent and this murder is research-related, you could be in danger."

"That's my concern as well," her father said. "I don't know who the killer is, but I know it's somehow connected to the research."

"I'm sure there must be other possibilities." Allison sealed her samples in plastic cases and snapped off her gloves.

Cash shrugged. "No bad debt. No jealous lover. No terminal illness. No family discord."

"A theft turned violent?" she asked.

"Nothing valuable missing on his body."

She leaned one hand on the counter and took off her glasses. "Shouldn't you be with Detective LaGrange … detecting?"

"I don't have to be with him to be working the case."

"I thought you didn't suspect me anymore."

"I don't, but I still think the murder is related to Baylon's research."

Mr. Sloan huffed. "Stop inching your way closer to my daughter. What are you playing at?"

What was Cash playing at? Allison didn't like him, didn't trust him, and took his medium abilities to be a joke. So why did he want to win her over? Because he liked a challenge. And because of an unexpected and probably misplaced masculine desire to keep Allison safe.

"Why don't you show me the research Professor Baylon was working on? Explain it to me. Maybe something will emerge."

Allison raised her arms. "You're looking at it. This is our workspace. There's no secret underground lab."

"What about his work computer?"

"In his office."

"Can you show me?"

"I don't know his password."

"I'd still like to see it."

She narrowed her eyes at him but didn't back down. "Is this the part where I'm supposed to ask for a warrant?"

Cash noticed she was so close, he could reach out and snag her by the white collar of her lab coat.

He tucked his hands in his pockets. "If you want to obstruct the case and look like you're hiding something, sure."

"Okay. Let's go snoop." She turned and walked away, hanging her lab coat on a hook near the door.

Cash followed her out of the lab, hoping her father didn't see Cash looking at her backside and the gap of skin showing between where her skirt ended and the top of her boots began.

"Are these your days?" he asked. "You go back and forth to your lab?"

"I'm seventy percent funded, which means I do my research seventy percent of the time. The remaining time, I'm an intensivist."

"Sounds intense." He hadn't a clue what type of specialist that made her.

She glanced at him with a quirk of her lips. "An intensivist is someone who works in the ICU—an intensive care unit."

He considered the proximity of the hospital just across the quad from the research offices. "Hmm. So, outside of the lab, you're actually saving lives in real time."

"It's not so dramatic as you make it sound."

"Reality or humility?"

Instead of answering him, Allison reached a door and tested the knob. Locked. The name plaque on the wall read: *Prof. Allen Baylon*

After withdrawing her phone, she punched in a quick number. "Hi. This is Dr. Sloan. I'm in the Charter Building. I'm here with Detective McCall who's with the police department investigating Professor Baylon's death. He would like to enter the professor's office ... Yes, okay. Thank you." She disconnected the call and turned to Cash. "Security will come open the door. Let's see if he was hiding something."

CHAPTER 3

llison had data to analyze, papers to write, and emails piling up, but she knew all of that would have to wait until Baylon's murder was solved.

Could there be a link between his research and his death? It seemed improbable. They weren't curing cancer. While their research in acute lung injury was important, it wasn't worth dying over.

She could settle the matter with this police consultant by showing him how benign all of Baylon's files were.

Probably.

She leaned against the wall as they waited for the security staff to arrive. "So, where is the mysteriousness in the psychic consulting you do? Other than mentioning ghosts, you haven't put on much of a show."

Cash leaned on the wall opposite her, bracing himself with one knee bent, foot on the wall. His demeanor seemed so casual, like he could lure a villain into forgetting he was actively hunting a killer. "I'm not a showy guy."

Allison chortled. "I doubt that." From what she'd seen, he was smug and probably knew women found him attractive.

"Is it me you don't trust or men in general?"

"I'm a woman of science, Cash. I don't mix well with a man earning a paycheck by claiming to see ghosts."

He'd smiled when she'd used his first name in addressing him.

"Does that unwavering reliance on logic stem from having a rigorously rational father?"

Her jaw tensed, but she didn't reply.

Cash softened his voice further. "Perhaps even a joyless man like that would tell you to relax and have a little faith in the inexplicable."

"I highly doubt that."

When the medical center security guard arrived, Allison showed him her badge, and he let her inside Baylon's office. The security guard nodded and left.

Cash proceeded to do exactly what he'd done in her office—explore the shelves with framed photos and rows upon rows of journals in chronological order.

Allison watched him circle the room, waiting to see if he'd start touching objects, close his eyes, and claim to be "connecting with the other side."

Instead, he remained a silent observer, absorbing his surroundings. He moved with ease and a certain relaxed stealth, making her wonder what sort of work he did prior to becoming a police consultant. Dust motes drifted in the narrow beam of light from the single window, turning Baylon's office into a museum of paper and stale coffee.

"Allison?"

Had he asked a question while she was watching him move?

She swallowed. "Yes?"

"I'm going to log in to his computer now." Cash sat at Professor Baylon's desk in front of his desktop computer.

"I don't know his password."

"I do. Your fa—phantom told me."

Allison walked around to stand behind Cash. No way he'd be able to guess the password. The password requirements at the medical center mandated uppercase and lowercase letters, several characters, and numbers. She couldn't remember her own password for a week after she was forced to change it every three months.

"Rockstar_PhD70," he spoke as he typed.

"That's ridiculous."

No sooner were the words out of her mouth than the computer desktop appeared.

Cash began systematically opening files.

"How'd you do that?" No point in denying her shock.

"A spirit—though not Professor Baylon's—has agreed to help the case. Sometimes spirits can glean information. In this instance, he was able to tell me Professor Baylon's password. I'm not often so lucky."

"He? You're saying there is a male ghost helping you as we speak?"

"Yes." Cash continued scanning files, seemingly unperturbed by her tone drenched in skepticism. "He perhaps has his own agenda, but our objectives align for now."

"Does he have a name?"

"Um. T.S."

"Do you not know his name or not want to share it?"

"I don't want to share it."

"Last name Eliot? Are you going to start spewing poetry?"

"No. But you're welcome to keep guessing."

She shook her head. What did she care if he wanted to keep his ghost's name a secret? She didn't believe Cash anyway. There had to be some other explanation for the password. Perhaps Baylon's wife had told Detective LaGrange who'd told Cash.

The psychic consultant opened Baylon's email and logged in. Allison leaned forward to watch, feeling an uncomfortable sensation of voyeurism in looking at a colleague's email. She couldn't turn her gaze away from it.

Yet, forty minutes later, she thought she might fall asleep while staring at the mundane contents of it all—committee meetings, mandatory continuing education, manuscript edited with track changes, travel arrangements for the next medical conference, and the list went on. His email was as dull as hers.

Allison slipped her glasses off and rubbed her eyes. "I'm going to leave you to this tedious work and go for an afternoon caffeine pick me up."

"That sounds wonderful." Cash pushed himself up from the desk.

She took a step back and faltered. Nothing in her statement had been an invitation for Cash to join her, but that hadn't deterred him. How was she to rid herself of this man?

After leaving Baylon's office, she stopped by her own, Cash following. She picked up her purse and checked briefly to make sure her inhaler was inside.

"Medication?" Cash asked.

"If Mother Nature invented it, there's a fifty-fifty chance I'm allergic to it. I don't go anywhere without my inhaler or my Epi-pen."

"You have asthma?"

She nodded. "Allergic asthma since childhood."

"Must've made outside playdates difficult."

"True. I did dance and gymnastics instead of outdoor sports growing up."

He kept pace with her through the hallways and down the stairs to the main floor.

"You bristled at the mention of your father. Tell me about him."

She never talked about her father, but Cash's request was so straightforward, as if he was asking directions, that the words were leaving her mouth before she could stop herself. "He was a great lawyer—so they say. I never saw much of him. Most of my memories are of a busy, hardened man who didn't make time for the family he created. You've heard the Harry Chapin song "Cats in the Cradle"? He was that father—always promising and never delivering. I have those elephants he gave me but not much in the way of memories of quality time together. After fellowship, I returned to New Orleans to spend more time with him, but fate and an aneurysm decided otherwise."

When they reached the coffee stand, Allison ordered two Café Cubanos. She didn't ask Cash what he wanted, but since she was paying and answering all of his questions, she didn't think it rude to order for him in hopes of accelerating the uncomfortable encounter.

Was it uncomfortable, though? The words about her father had flowed with uncharacteristic ease. Perhaps that was Cash McCall's true supernatural power—creating an environment where people dropped their walls and talked about themselves. After all, who'd suspect judgment from a man claiming to see ghosts?

"And like the song, now you're leading a busy life." Cash sipped his coffee.

"I suppose so. I think my father tried a few times to reconnect with me in fellowship, but I had grants to write and twelve-hour shifts to work."

"Is that why you're thirty-two and single?"

She led Cash outside to the quad where the fresh air did more to revive her than the coffee.

"Is my personal life relevant to the investigation?"

"Everything is relevant," he deadpanned.

She arched an eyebrow of doubt, but answered his question anyway. "I'm still single because I work long hours and no man wants that—except maybe soldiers and pilots. But I move in different circles, so I'm unlikely to meet those men. I never started a family because it's not fair subjecting a family to my lifestyle."

"You think you'll be a disengaged parent like your father was?"

They walked the perimeter around the quad. The November air was cool, but the heat from his shoulder just inches from hers made her acutely aware of his nearness.

"It wouldn't be fair to pursue a relationship if I couldn't know the outcome."

"Come now, doctor. No one knows the outcome with any certainty. And as a researcher, surely you know that experimentation is the only route to finding your desired outcome."

"Is that how you justify promiscuity? Experimentation?"

"Why would you call me promiscuous?"

"You give off that vibe." She drank her Café Cubano.

He shook his head in baffled amusement. "What vibe? You and your father really are cut from the same cloth."

"What do you mean by that?"

"What vibe?" he countered.

"A flirtatious, no-woman-can-pass-this-up vibe. Do people really fall for that?"

"I'll have you know many women find both me and my psychic detective abilities alluring."

"Well, I guess there's that. The world is full of gullible fools to take advantage of."

CASH WALKED BESIDE ALLISON, feeling the icy prickle of her words.

"You deserved that," her father said. "You made her confide in you about me. If you're going to dig up painful memories, you'd better be prepared for the backlash."

"Duly noted." But Cash wasn't deterred. He looked at Allison. "I've helped the police solve over a dozen cases—*without* taking advantage of anyone. And I assure you that none of the women I've spent time with ever felt taken advantage of."

Allison kept silent.

Remorse or reproach? Cash wondered.

Cash normally wasn't fazed by unbelievers. He didn't waste time trying to convince them spirits existed and that he was one of the few people who could see them. The people in his life who mattered believed him—his parents, his sister, and Detective LaGrange.

Cash's dilemma was that Allison's father still roamed the world of the living, and if Cash was going to help the ghost move on, he suspected he'd need Allison's cooperation. He'd need to make her a believer eventually.

"Over a dozen cases?" Her tone had transformed from cool distaste to warm curiosity bordering on awe.

"Yes."

"How?"

"Since you don't believe in ghosts, there isn't much point in describing the process to you," he teased. "Besides, the process has been different for each case. Sometimes the apparitions are the victims, sometimes friends or family of either the victim or the killer. And sometimes the family of a future victim."

Cash glanced over at Mr. Sloan who glided beside his daughter, listening intently to their conversation.

"Only once did the victim outright tell me who killed him, but obviously that won't hold up in a court of law. The onus is still on Detective LaGrange to prove it, but it helps if he can focus his efforts."

"Detective LaGrange believes in ghosts?"

"I don't think he'd agree to that. But he believe in me. I helped him solve a campus murder case—at a university his niece was attending. That went a long way in building rapport."

"How did you get started on something like this? I don't imagine 'psychic detective' is listed on job boards."

Cash tried to gauge if Allison was being sincere and was surprised to find she was.

"After my criminal justice degree, I started working as a private investigator. Ghosts are harbingers of secrets—or have access to them. But not always the ones you want. Sometimes my cases overlapped with police investigations. I gave Detective LaGrange key information to nail a career-making case for him when I could have claimed solving the case as my own. During the next case he struggled with, he asked me to come on board and help. We signed a consulting contract."

"Do you still do PI work, too?" She rotated her wrist, remixing the contents of her coffee.

"Yes, but I have enough business and a good reputation that I can be selective about what I agree to do. I don't do cheating spouses."

"What's your favorite type of case?" she asked.

"Missing persons. They don't always have a happy ending, but giving people closure is rewarding."

"Yeah." She smiled, eyes brimming with surprised delight. "I can relate to that. Sometimes, my greatest accomplishment in the ICU is helping families let go of their loved one and honor the patient's wishes. The ultimate outcome is someone's death, but when it's done correctly, I'm ending the patient's suffering, giving them death with dignity, and shortening the dying process—giving everyone closure."

Cash stopped and turned to regard Allison. Despite her skepticism about his medium abilities, she was trying to connect with him on a personal level. Her reaction was vastly different from most women. In his experience, a dichotomy existed: women were either intrigued by his paranormal abilities and it became a topic of every interaction in a brief yet mutually satisfying relationship, or women were repulsed by his exploitive career preying on those fool enough to give credence to a man claiming to talk to spirits.

Enter Allison Sloan at stage right who fit neither category, and he couldn't read her enough to know if the connection she was attempting to bridge represented an interest in him.

"Are you okay?" Allison asked.

"He's damn smitten is what he is," her father grumbled.

No one had ever asked Cash his favorite type of case, and certainly no one had ever made an attempt to relate to his type of work.

"Yes, I'm good," Cash finally answered, ignoring her father. "I find I'm enjoying myself more than I should, and I'm keeping you from your work."

"Oh, okay."

"Thank you for the coffee and the company." He began a backward retreat.

She raised her Café Cubano in salute. "You'll let me know when you find the culprit?"

"Yes, of course." Cash turned and walked away.

"Well, you can't just leave her unprotected," Sloan protested.

"You want me to protect her or stop ogling her? You can't have it both ways," Cash hissed.

"And why not?"

A man in scrubs passing Cash glanced warily at Cash seeming to talk to himself. Cash sighed and pulled out his phone.

"Who are you calling?" Sloan asked.

Cash put the phone up to his ear as he continued walking toward the parking lot. "No one. I'm pretending to talk on the phone while talking to you so as not to look like I'm having a psychotic break."

"You're still walking in the wrong direction."

"I'm going to my car."

"But Allison—"

"Allison has the security of her lab. So unless you can tell me there's some imminent danger, I'm going to take a minute and collect my thoughts about this case. I also need to check in with Detective LaGrange."

Sloan frowned. "No, nothing imminent."

"How about *you* stay and keep an eye on your daughter? If anything concerns you, let me know, and I'll come back. Also, let me know if you glean anything helpful to the case."

"Okay. I agree to your plan." His voice oozed reluctance. "And then you'll be back? By the time she gets off work?"

Cash reached his car and stopped to stare at the translucent, needy lawyer as he continued to hold the phone to his ear. "You want me to chaperone your daughter?"

"Like a protection detail," Sloan clarified, straightening his already impeccably straight tie.

Cash dropped the phone into his pocket. "You realize I'm neither a cop nor am I armed. And even if I tell the detective that a ghost wants protective surveillance on Dr. Sloan, he can't submit the request based on the statement of a psychic consultant."

"Just you." Sloan had morphed into the bargaining lawyer. "An attacker would be much less likely to try anything with you by Allison's side."

"So I come back, and then what? I invite myself to her house for dinner?"

Sloan scoffed. "Please. I'm sure a dedicated bachelor like yourself knows exactly how to invite himself into a woman's home. Except this time, you'll have a clean conscience because you're putting yourself between her and danger and not between her sheets."

Cash jerked the car door open. "First of all, my conscience is clean. Secondly, I don't put myself anywhere I'm not wanted. Lastly, how about you turn that ghostly power of perception off me and try to find out who the killer is so you can clear your daughter's name?"

Cash sat down in the car. He didn't need a judgmental ghost, and his personal life was his own. He certainly didn't need the spirit of the father of a woman he'd never laid hands on looking down his nose at Cash's life choices.

Closing his eyes, he exhaled. He could drive away and pretend this was just another case. Or he could admit the truth; he was going back —for the ghost, for the case, and, God help him, for Allison Sloan.

CHAPTER 4

Allison walked back to the lab with mixed emotions about Cash's abrupt departure. One minute they were unexpectedly connecting on a professional and personal level, and the next moment he'd made a clean getaway. Perhaps he'd been enjoying himself more than he should for her position as a suspect in his case. Probably, so was she.

She told herself she was grateful for the distance, but her chest felt oddly hollow walking back to the lab alone.

It was good that he left. Those friendly eyes and warm smiles were easy to lose herself in, and she had work to do. He shouldn't have looked so thoughtful when he'd talked about missing persons. His behavior made it harder to write him off as a smug fraud.

When she arrived back at her office, she checked the clock, Three in the afternoon. Barring no further distractions, she hoped to put the finishing touches on one of her manuscripts and upload it for submission.

An hour and fifteen minutes later, Allison pressed the SUBMIT button. She leaned back in her chair and rolled her shoulders several times.

The little mail icon on her desktop monitor stared at her. She knew her inbox would be overflowing with emails from the day, as she hadn't yet looked at it. But she also knew once she started in on it, the rabbit hole of e-mails would devour the rest of her day.

She could go back to the lab and work with the organoids some more.

The lab.

Her joint working space with Professor Baylon. Now, the lab belonged only to her because someone had murdered her collaborator.

Murdered.

Allison shuddered.

And Cash McCall was concerned Baylon's death might be research related. What possible connection could there be? Nothing had revealed itself on his computer or email.

His lab notebook, maybe?

Baylon was always scribbling in a little black book. Allison assumed they were notes about his research, but it could be étouffée recipes for all she knew. She'd never felt inclined to snoop through any of his notes.

Until this very moment.

After walking back to the lab, she searched for the notebook. She'd opened and closed these drawers hundreds of times, but today she did so while snooping, and it felt oddly intrusive.

She found nothing suspicious in the lab. And no notebook, which wasn't unusual—he might simply have taken it home with him.

Or it might be in his office.

Allison walked back to Baylon's office, winding through hallways perpetually lit by long fluorescent ceiling lights. The building was quiet except for the hum of those lights. The lab techs who worked within these walls usually clocked out by four pm because they typically started their days early.

The slight squeak of her boots on the linoleum created an eerie sound. The noise had never seemed unnerving before now, but she'd never been walking alone after the murder of a colleague as she contemplated the possibility his murder could be related to his research. The speculative link brought her own personal safety into question.

When she reached Baylon's office, the door was still unlocked from her trip there earlier with Cash.

Cash McCall—who had her on edge now thinking about murder motives buried in a little black book.

She sat down in Baylon's office chair and swiveled aimlessly.

Were you hiding something, Allen?

If he was and it was research related, why wouldn't he tell her?

Because he was *Rockstar PhD*?

Arrogance wouldn't bring him back from the grave.

AFTER LEAVING ALLISON, Cash pulled his car into the parking lot of Audubon Park. As it was Monday, the zoo was closed, and there wasn't much foot traffic in the area.

Whenever he needed to clear his head during a case, he would find a place to park and walk. Today, it was the park outside the zoo.

He phoned Detective Hyde LaGrange.

"What the hell, Cash? You abandoning me to work the case alone while sweet-talkin' that dynamite doctor?"

"No. I've been working the case, too," he calmly replied.

"A'right now, don't get all snippy on me. She shoot you down, is that why you sound like you swallowed a wasp?"

"I don't hit on suspects."

"Yeah, yeah, I know. But usually when I rib you about being a ladies' man, you play along. What's different?"

Cash walked the trail of the park under a late afternoon sun. He ran a hand through his hair. LaGrange was right—Allison and her father's ghost had Cash off his game. He wasn't supposed to be thinking about the way she'd smiled when she talked about giving families closure or how amazing she'd smelled leaning over his shoulder in Baylon's office.

"I'm hearing some spiritual concerns that Dr. Sloan may be in danger."

"Did a ghost tell you that?" Hyde asked.

"Her father's ghost."

"Huh."

"Yeah. We were discussing the possibility of the murder being research-related. Nothing turned up in an hour of searching the professor's office and desktop files. But I'll keep digging."

"Do you think Dr. Sloan is hiding something?"

"No, and neither does her father."

Hyde snorted. "'Cause daddy'd never cover for his bébé girl. Mm-hmm."

"I've never known a ghost to lie. I suppose he could be withholding information, but his concern for her safety seems genuine. Can you put a watch on her?"

"Because you say her daddy's ghost got the jitters? Non. You bring me somethin' real, then we talk."

Cash kicked a fallen twig from a live oak off the paved path. "What'd you discover while I was at the research lab?"

"Tech has scoured Professor Baylon's home computer and cell phone. No affairs. His finances aren't great though."

"Oh?"

"He's been living beyond his means—college tuition for kids, big mortgage, BMWs, country club membership."

"Anyone take out a new life insurance policy on him?"

"No, but the existing one would cover all of that plus funeral expenses."

"So, his wife is a suspect." Cash continued to walk.

"Always … except for her solid alibi of being out of town with one of the kids. But there's more. On a chat app, the professor was conversing with someone named Techy25. Most of the conversation was deleted, but our guys found a snippet where the professor says he's going to back out of a deal."

"What deal?"

"Dunno. It doesn't specify, but then Techy25 says, 'we need to meet.'"

"Sounds ominous." It also worked in Allison's favor. Cash didn't think she'd refer to herself as a Techy.

"It does. It could also be nothing more than turning down a contractor for a kitchen remodeling. But the fact that it's a semi-hidden chat room with no real names seems sketchy."

"Definitely sketchy," Cash agreed.

Hyde sighed. "You wanna run that by your new ghost sidekick and see if he gets any vibes from it?"

"Uh, yes. He's currently with his daughter, though." Cash didn't think Sloan would take kindly to being referred to as a sidekick. Cash was more apt to call him a pain in the—

"Oh, *pauvre toi*—looks like you gotta haul yourself right back to that pretty doctor. Well, when you see her again, find out if Techy25 has any meaning to her, but not in a way that might tip her off."

"Got it."

"And watch your back, *mon ami*. If she's our killer, her daddy's ghost sure ain't gonna pull her off you."

In Cash's experience, ghosts couldn't do much to affect the physical world, but that didn't matter in this case. "It's not her."

"Oh? You sure enough to bet your life on that?"

Cash bit his lip, thinking of the message Baylon had sent.

'I know what you've done.'

And Allison had no alibi.

Hyde let out a chuckle. "That's what I thought. Back to work, *Romeo*. And call me with updates." Hyde clicked off.

After the call with Hyde ended, Cash continued to walk through the park, thinking about the case.

Sloan appeared. "Are you coming back to protect Allison?"

Cash could tell by the sluggish tone of Sloan's voice that there was no immediate danger attached to his question.

"I will."

Stopping, Cash sat on top of a wooden picnic table. He and Mr. Sloan were alone in this part of the park. Cash looked expectantly at the man.

"My daughter was home alone when the murder happened, just as she said."

"Well, you can't be her alibi, so you'll have to give me more than that."

Sloan's brow furrowed. "Like what?"

"Whodunit."

"I don't know who killed Professor Baylon."

"Did he have enemies?"

"Everyone has enemies."

"Strike and move to rephrase. Who were his enemies?" Cash asked.

"I don't know."

"Did he ever argue with anyone?"

"Not that I saw."

"Have you seen anything suspicious?"

"No."

"What exactly do you do with your time here on Earth?" Cash had to ask, because clearly Sloan was not particularly observant about his daughter's environment.

"I check on Allison from time to time." The ghost's voice held an edge as if challenging Cash to harass him about watching his daughter.

"Easy, counselor. This isn't a court of law, and you're not on trial." Cash suspected the 'from time to time' meant several times a day. Had he been following his daughter aimlessly since his death?

"But Allison could end up on trial, and she's innocent," Sloan said.

"Why—*if* she's innocent—was she defensive and prickly in her office toward the detective?" Cash asked.

"That's what you're supposed to do under pressure. The more emotion you feel, the tighter you control it. It's called being professional."

Cash ignored the derogatory tone insinuating that he wasn't

professional. "Maybe in a court of law, but not if you want to convey innocence in the murder of a colleague."

"You're suggesting Allison melt into a hysterical puddle?"

"Nothing so extreme. Just a little sadness. A few tears. They worked together for several years."

Sloan crossed his arms. "Well, I didn't teach her to be a sap. She's a strong woman—accelerated college degree, top of her class in medical school, research grants right out of fellowship."

"Her resume is very impressive." Cash dipped his head slightly.

Sloan gave a curt nod of approval for Cash's sincere compliment.

"Makes for a lonely life, though," Cash added gently.

Allison's father's eyes flashed before he seemed to realize Cash's demeanor wasn't judgmental.

Sloan deflated slightly as his shoulders sagged. "I suppose I taught her that, too—not making time for relationships." The regret in his voice was thick and sticky as molasses.

Cash hopped up from the picnic table. "Let's solve a murder, and you'll feel better."

"I'll go check on Allison." Sloan nodded before vanishing.

Cash strode to his car, slid inside, and headed back to the hospital.

He needed to figure out how to explain not only arriving back a few hours after leaving—perhaps he could brainstorm more questions about the investigation—but also how to stay attached to Allison. He really didn't want stay awake all night on some stake out watching her home from a parked car. And he was certain her father wouldn't settle for her spending a night unprotected until the killer was caught.

IN BAYLON'S OFFICE, Allison opened drawers and ruffled through papers, receipts, business cards, printed protocols, drafts, and notes. Nothing caught her eye, not that she would know what suspicious documentation looked like. She also didn't see Baylon's notebook.

Standing and stretching, she decided to abandon her fruitless search. The police would find the killer.

"Oh, Dr. Sloan."

Allison turned to see Vera Myers standing in the doorway. "Hi, Vera. I thought you went home."

"I did, but then I remembered I needed to process the surfactant from yesterday."

"Okay."

"Did the police learn anything else?"

"I'm sure if they did, Detective LaGrange wouldn't share it with me. Besides, it's only been a few hours."

Allison wouldn't tell Vera the police suspected her last living superior of murder. Vera seemed worried enough without adding that piece of information.

"It's still scary to think his killer is out there somewhere," Vera said.

Scary, yes. But Vera didn't need Allison substantiating her fears. She already looked like a terrified rabbit ready to jump out of her skin.

"You're safe," Allison reassured her despite her own discomfort walking down the hallway in isolation only a half hour ago. "There's security here, and they'll escort you to the parking garage if you want."

"Yeah. I'll do that. Okay. I'll just be a few minutes in the lab, and then head back home. Are you heading out soon?"

"I just have a few things to wrap up. And, Vera?"

The lab assistant turned back toward her. "Hmm?"

"Take a few days off. If there's anything that needs follow-up in the lab, just make me a list, and I'll take care of it."

When Vera left, Allison took one last look around Baylon's office. Her gaze fell on the peace lily by the window, lit by the setting sun. Baylon loved that plant—watered it, repotted it. She'd even caught him talking to it on occasion. Maybe she could take care of it for him. It would be a way to keep his spirit alive on campus.

Ugh. Not alive in the sense that might resonate with Cash McCall. Cash.

The thought of him and his warm, infuriating smile snuck in

again. She shook it off, annoyed that he could haunt her thoughts the way ghosts supposedly haunted him.

He was an intelligent and attractive man who could make a great living without discrediting himself by claiming to see ghosts. So why did he? Did he like the reactions people had when meeting a medium?

Allison had spent a great deal of time as an ICU physician dealing with death and dying, and never had she suspected anyone of turning into a ghost.

Her fingers ran over the smooth veins of the leaves on the lily as she thought of Cash's alluring smile. Shaking off images of him, her focus landed back on the plant. When she nudged the pot to rotate it, something dark behind the ceramic caught her eye—a small black rectangle tucked where only someone looking closely would see.

Allison chewed her lip. Well, it hadn't made it there by accident and certainly appeared to have been stashed in a hiding spot—not terribly stealthy, but not readily apparent to the casual observer.

Such secrecy might mean nothing. Baylon could have been guarding his research notes—or that award-winning étouffée recipe— and not hiding the identity of his killer. Or a motive for murder.

So why was her heart pounding as she reached out and grabbed the book?

Her heart stumbled. That little black book—Baylon's constant companion—had a weight in her hand that felt heavier than paper and ink.

After opening it, she skimmed the notes, most of which looked related to his lab work and some of their shared projects. Her fingers touched something harder. A card stuck between pages. The thick stock paper was folded in half like a Thank You card or Birthday card, but the front was an abstract design of swirling colors with no words.

She unfolded it.

Ali,

Baylon always called her Ali.

I owe you an explanation. Let me begin with, I'm sorry. I've made a terrible mistake. I—

The note ended abruptly.

Mistake?

If there had been a lab error, he wouldn't have gone through the trouble of writing a note. He would have just walked down the hall to her office. What was so awful that he would hand write a note? Lost grant funding? A breach of institutional board review protocol? Did he publish a shared project without including her in the authorship?

I'm sorry.

Had the man ever apologized for anything?

She looked back at the book in her white-knuckled grip with her fingers pressed to the leather.

Fingerprints.

She had no alibi for the murder of Baylon Saturday night. Someone texted her on his phone around the time of his death. And now, she held a card written by the murder victim apologizing to her for something. And her fingerprints tainted his most prized possession.

If she didn't find the real killer—and fast—Hyde LaGrange's next visit wouldn't be for questions. It'd be for cuffs.

CHAPTER 5

Cash flashed his police consultant badge to the young security guard who let him back into the research building after hours.

"I can find my way back to Dr. Sloan's office. Thanks." Cash waved as he left the guard behind.

"You came back." Mr. Sloan's ghost—prim and proper, but wearing an expression less despondent than usual—appeared beside Cash.

"Reporting for guard duty, sir."

"Don't mock me."

"Lighten up. How is she?" Cash strode down the hallway. He couldn't imagine being confined to such a dreary building filled with laboratories, but then Allison had said she alternated this work with working in the ICU, so perhaps it was another change of pace. Plus, she could escape to the quad for fresh air when the south Louisiana weather cooperated.

"She's fine," Sloan said.

Cash reached Allison's office and peeked inside the room. "*Where is she?*"

"Professor Baylon's office."

"Oh? That's not suspicious at all," Cash teased.

Allison's father scowled.

Grinning, Cash turned and walked toward Baylon's office. When he angled to enter, Allison ran into him. A flutter of paper filled the air in a flurry.

"Oh, my gosh, Cash. I'm sorry." She dropped to her knees and began scooping up the leaflets filled with handwritten notes. Her hair looked disheveled and her cheeks flushed.

Cash turned back to the ghost with a smirk to emphasize how awfully strange Allison was acting for an innocent woman.

The crease between Sloan's eyes deepened.

Cash chuckled. "It's fine." He bent and helped her stuff papers back into a small black, leather-bound notebook.

"I'm glad you're here," she said, still breathless. After standing, she smoothed her shirt. "I have to tell you something."

"Okay. Take a deep breath. You look like you've just run a hundred-yard dash."

She put one hand up to her heart as if to feel how fast it raced. Nodding, she took two deep breaths but didn't yet appear at ease.

Cash took her gently by the elbow and led her back to her office before asking, "Did you find something?"

After they entered her workspace, Allison closed the door. She reached into her purse, withdrew her inhaler, and took two puffs of the medication back to back.

Cash leaned against her desk, worried about her present state. Was she at risk of a full asthma attack? Did he need to be prepared to call for an ambulance?

She paced, occasionally rising to her tiptoes. Ballet. She mentioned being a dancer as a child; she must have done ballet. He briefly imagined waltzing on a dance floor with lean, graceful Allison in his arms. As she paced the room, presumably letting the medicine take effect, Cash watched strands of hair wave around her face.

"I did find a clue." Steadier now, she set the little notebook on her desk but kept hold of a small greeting card. "The problem is ... the problem ... " She hesitated, stopped pacing, and stared at him. "Why are you back?"

Cash considered her question.

The truth: *I wanted to see you again.*

What her father thought: *To protect you from a killer at large.*

What Cash actually said: "I'm still following leads. Now, what clue?"

Allison fidgeted with the card. "I want to tell you because I think I trust you—weird ghost issues aside."

"Why in the world would she trust *you*?" her father piped in.

Cash wanted to point out to the uptight attorney that he obviously also trusted him. Why else would Sloan want him watching over his daughter?

"I'm trustworthy," Cash added casually.

"The problem," Allison restarted, "is that the clue … well, here. Read it." She thrust the small card at him.

Cash opened it and read it twice before asking, "What's he sorry for?"

"I don't know." Her voice sounded pleading. "But it looks like motive, doesn't it? Like I had a reason to want Baylon dead?"

"Do you?"

"No!" Her blue eyes flashed as she threw her hands up in the air. "But I've no alibi and now this."

"Where did you find the note?"

"In his research notebook in his office."

"Why'd you go back to his office?"

She flopped into her desk chair and ran her hands through her long, brown hair, tugging out what remained of her bun. "After you left, you had me contemplating your theory that his death might be research related. I figured the best place to find out would be his notebook. He carried it everywhere, and he was always writing in it."

"Did you learn anything from it?" Cash walked to her mini-fridge in one corner, pulled out a small bottle of chilled water, and set it before her.

She looked like she needed something stronger, but water would have to suffice.

"No." She took a gulp with a look of gratitude. "I found that note and panicked. Maybe if I have time to go through each page, I'll find something."

"Okay. Let's do that."

She lifted her head and looked into his eyes with something like surprise and adoration. "You're not going to call Detective LaGrange to haul me downtown?"

"Should I?"

"No." Her voice was all exasperation as her brow furrowed in a cute expression of disapproval.

"Well, you happen to have a ghost who put in a good word on behalf of your innocence," —which Cash felt was a much better reason than *'I think you're innocent because I'm attracted to you.'*

"Okay, well, please thank him for me."

Cash sat in the chair across the desk from Allison. "Are you saying you're a believer?"

"No. But if your ghost tells you I'm innocent, then I'm going to thank him."

Cash wouldn't tell Allison that the ghost actually belonged to her. Not yet, anyway.

He put his elbows on her desk and leaned across. "I'm hungry. Let's grab a bite to eat and go through the notebook. Then, I'm your proof that you didn't tamper with anything."

She hesitated.

"Will you get in trouble for that?" she asked.

Cash leaned back with a shrug. "We aren't withholding evidence because we have yet to determine if it's evidence. Besides, if I solve LaGrange's case, all will be forgiven."

Her expression brimmed with gratitude, causing Cash to wonder if he could earn more than just dinner with her. But as soon as the thought crossed his mind, he dismissed it. They were chaperoned by her father's ghost, and she was a suspect in a murder investigation.

ALLISON DROVE Cash to Clancy's Restaurant on Annunciation Street. There were no available tables, so they took seats at the far end of the bar. Allison set her purse and the notebook down on the marble countertop.

She couldn't believe she'd confessed everything to Cash. When she turned to leave Baylon's office, she'd vowed to tell no one. She planned to solve the case alone. Then, as soon as she saw Cash, she knew she couldn't keep it from him. She wouldn't be able to look him in the eye and keep her composure as she had with LaGrange.

And why was that?

She could maintain her composure during an ICU cardiac arrest and deliver tragic news calmly, but Cash McCall walks in and she turns into a bumbling fool. Her crumbling must have been caused by all the worry about being accused of murder. It had nothing to do with his friendly eyes or slight upward curl of a full set of lips.

A man with whom she was oddly attracted, and who provoked a strange emotional vulnerability in her, wanted dinner. Taking a moment, she reminded herself this was not a date.

"Penny for your thoughts?" Cash asked.

Allison cleared her throat and opened the notebook. "I should start looking for clues."

He placed a hand on hers, stopping her from turning pages. "And we will, but go ahead and order first."

The bartender arrived, and Allison ordered a water and comfort food—seafood gumbo. Cash ordered iced tea and blackened catfish.

After the bartender poured their drinks and moved to other patrons, Allison opened the notebook to examine it with detached objectivity. She pulled her glasses from around her neck and rested them on her nose.

Cash's calm demeanor and belief in her innocence infused her like a cool tincture, soothing her angst. Her calm composure wrestled her frayed nerves and won.

He scooted his barstool closer to look at the book with her and grunted. "Huh. A doctor with neat handwriting."

"Rockstar Baylon was very meticulous. His attention to detail was one of the many reasons he was so successful."

Was successful.

Until someone snuffed out his life.

"It's clearly legible," Cash said, "but I don't understand any of it."

She turned the pages after each inspection and gave Cash the Cliff Notes version. "Meeting notes. Inflammatory cascade. Proteins, immunoglobulins, and markers he's testing or wants to test. Here's a batch of tissue samples he tested for different inflammatory markers." She continued to flip as she sipped the water the bartender had poured, all the while keenly aware of Cash's shoulder touching hers and his smell of cedar.

By the time the food arrived, they'd worked their way through half of Baylon's little black book.

With the smell of seafood and sassafras wafting in the air, Allison felt ravenous. "I haven't eaten all day. I rode my indoor spin bike, came to work, heard the news about Baylon, and met with Detective LaGrange. After you left, I worked." She took a spoonful of gumbo into her mouth.

"Can't survive on Café Cubano alone. You need to make more time to care for yourself."

"I biked."

"Yes, but everything else about your day seems hectic and rushed. And I get the impression, despite the tragedy, the workflow you described is more normal than not."

She narrowed her eyes at him as she chewed another bite. How was this man so perceptive? That must be his "paranormal" skill—the power of perception. Maybe his uncanny ability to read people made him seem psychic. Perhaps he was more *mentalist* than *medium.*

"So, *you* lead a balanced life?" she asked.

"I'm very balanced—elliptical machine for cardio, yoga, fasting, meditation."

A tall blonde in a short skirt approached the bar. "Cash McCall, you never called me back." The woman's voice was part seduction, part pout, and all silky Southern drawl.

"Loretta, good evening." He stood politely and kissed the cheek she thrust at him. Without acknowledging the woman's blatant feelings of rebuff, Cash turned and introduced Loretta to Allison. "Loretta, this is Allison. Allison, Loretta."

Allison pondered at what point they had become Allison and Cash to each other and no longer Dr. Sloan and Mr. McCall. The transition has seemed comfortable and effortless.

Loretta, feigning surprise as though she hadn't noticed a woman accompanied Cash, managed a smile and wave.

"This is a business meeting," Allison assured Loretta, who visibly relaxed. "Cash is ruling me out as a murder suspect—he's still deciding."

Allison suppressed a grin when Cash narrowed his eyes at her. Perhaps she'd finally riled him the way he'd been riling her.

Loretta blinked rapidly and took a step back. "Oh. Well. Cash, you have my number."

When Loretta left, Cash sat back down. "What was that for?"

"What?"

"I already explained I no longer think you're a suspect."

Oh, cher—it's nice to hear him repeat that.

Allison shrugged. "Well, this way, Loretta isn't under the misconception that you and I are here together. You're free to call her back."

"I won't call her back."

The firmness in his voice surprised Allison, but she wouldn't press for clarification because it was none of her business.

Cash explained anyway. "Loretta and I had a nice night together. I'm straightforward with the women I spend the night with. If I'm looking for a lasting relationship, they would know it." His tone held a level of irritation, Allison hadn't heard before now. "She came over here, knowing you and I were having dinner, and probably suspected something more, which means she came to upset at least one of us."

Allison stirred her gumbo lazily, mixing rice, roux, and shrimp. "I'm not upset, and she didn't interrupt anything. So, what's the problem?"

"Her intentions were malicious. That's a character flaw I don't like."

"Hmm," Allison mused. She pointed the tip of her spoon in his direction. "Do you suppose if you'd dated her before sleeping with her, you might have picked up on undesirable character flaws?"

Cash gave her a crooked grin as he took a bite of his catfish. "Where's the fun in that?"

She groaned with an eye roll to avoid a laugh that might encourage him.

CASH FINISHED his meal as Allison opened Baylon's notebook again. Cash wanted to tell Allison how much he enjoyed her company, but it seemed inappropriate under the circumstances.

He also wanted to have a private conversation about her father and why he was still following her around five years after his death. Such a discussion might stir unwanted memories. He didn't want to cause her pain. But could he ease it?

No. Too soon.

First, he needed to gain her trust.

Cash leaned closer once again. He liked the proximity to her, even if she'd insinuated he was a promiscuous bachelor. Because she didn't move away or squirm, he suspected she didn't mind his closeness.

"You don't have to sit so near to her," Sloan grumbled. He stood on the opposite side of the bar counter, looking out of place in a backdrop of hundreds of bottles of booze. "You said yourself, you can't read what's written."

Cash leaned in and read from the page Allison skimmed. "Malignant organoid matrix." He glanced up and winked at Sloan who pursed his lips in aggravation.

"Yes," Allison drew the word out in a perplexed tone. "But that's my project. Baylon wasn't working on this with me."

"What was the project?"

"An oncologist who specializes in lung cancer approached me about using our lung organoids to propagate tumors."

"Meaning?"

She pulled off her glasses, dropped them around her neck, and looked at Cash, their faces close. "The oncologist arranges for us to get samples of tumor cells—either from a biopsy or resection of the cancer. We inject it into our lung organoid and let it grow. Then, the oncologist has as much malignant material as he wants for testing. Mostly, this was a feasibility study. Meaning, can we do it on a handful of cases and will the tumors stay viable?"

He tried to grasp the significance of what she was saying, but it eluded him.

She must have interpreted his expression, because she continued. "There's a practical implication. Let's say a patient has a biopsy and they're not a candidate for curative surgery. They get first-line chemotherapy and immunotherapy. What if they fail that treatment or can't tolerate it, but the pathology sample is all used up from initial testing?"

"They'd have to have another biopsy."

"Right. Which isn't lacking risk or expense. Meanwhile, if the patient's tumor from their initial biopsy or surgery had been stored and growing on an organoid matrix, then the patient's own cancer cells could be tested and retested for mutations to determine the next line of therapy."

"Like backing up a hard drive."

When she smiled at him, he felt a giddy rush like he'd earned an A on a science quiz.

"Yes," she said.

"Why would Baylon take notes on your research?"

Allison slipped her glasses back on and scanned the page. "I don't know. He has notes on tumor types, genetic markers—" she turned the page "—DNA extraction, environmental temperature. He shouldn't have been recording any of this. He's not on the research protocol."

"What if the oncologist working with you found out? Could he have been angry enough to commit murder?"

"No way. Preston is the nicest guy. Look," she turned her gaze back up to Cash, "even if I'm a terrible judge of character and wrong about the oncologist. If he wanted to ruin Baylon, all he'd have to do is present this evidence to the institutional review board. Baylon would face disciplinary action and disgrace."

"What if the oncologist found out about it but didn't have proof? After all, you're the one who found Baylon's book."

"Preston would have come to me about it."

"Preston?"

"Preston Waters."

Cash pulled out his phone.

"What are you doing?" she asked.

"Calling Detective LaGrange. He needs to interview Dr. Waters in light of this information. We should also get that notebook to him."

"Can I copy it first? These pages are my work, too."

"Sure."

Cash slipped off his barstool, glancing back at Allison as he walked away. She closed the book and strummed long fingers along the black leather cover.

"She's been betrayed," her father said, following Cash as he walked outside Clancy's Restaurant.

Cash nodded.

Sloan sighed. "Baylon's theft of her work is one more piece that makes her look guilty. And even if you believe her, how is the word of a psychic detective going to redeem her before a jury of her peers?"

Cash didn't have a satisfactory answer. Allison was in a quicksand of trouble.

No alibi.

An accusatory text message.

An incriminating handwritten note.

And now motive.

CHAPTER 6

Cash called Hyde and updated him on the notebook and Allison's research.

"Baylon stealing research only makes Dr. Sloan look more guilty," Hyde pointed out the obvious.

"Except, she was genuinely surprised and crushed five minutes ago when she discovered his deviousness." Cash paced the entryway outside the restaurant lobby. He suddenly remembered he hadn't asked Allison if she knew who Techy25 could be.

"And she just happened to *discover* the espionage in your presence?"

"I haven't given Allison much space today." Literally.

At the bar, she hadn't seemed uncomfortable when he'd scooted closer—all in the interest of the investigation. Oh, but she smelled like warm vanilla.

"Can't imagine why," Hyde said.

"Because I'm investigating."

"The murder, or something else about the doctor?"

Cash chose not to dignify that with an answer. "Where are you at on your end?"

"I went back to talk to the wife because we found some suggestive text messages."

"Suggestive of murder?" Cash asked.

"Suggestive of her having an affair."

"Oh?"

"Yeah. She swears it was all only over the phone and internet and nothing physical. But then she got very defensive. She said she suspected Dr. Sloan of having an affair with her husband."

"Based on what?"

"Woman's intuition that Dr. Sloan wanted her husband."

"So, no proof."

"No."

Cash rolled his shoulders. "So, basically, she's pointing the finger at Allison because she's a younger, attractive female and Mrs. Baylon wants to cast suspicion off herself."

"Seems that way. But it's another strike against your girl. If this goes to a jury, they're going to eat that up."

"Not my girl." The denial came out too fast, even to his own ears.

"You've spent all day with her, you're on a first-name basis, and you claim her father's ghost is talking to you. What do you want me to call her?"

"I'll get back to you on that. For now, she's not my girl and not a suspect."

"She's a suspect to me. Get me that notebook first thing in the morning." Hyde clicked off.

"She's not your girl," Allison's father stated.

Cash kept the phone to his ear as he scowled at the apparition. "Yes, I'm aware of that. But right now I'm the only one looking out for her, so how about you hold your judgmental stares and condescending tone."

Sloan opened his mouth in what looked to be a moment of protest before closing it. He looked in the direction where his daughter sat and then back to Cash. "You're right. Thank you, Mr. McCall, for looking out for her."

. . .

ALLISON SAT at the bar while Cash talked on the phone.

She knew her predicament grew gloomier by the hour. If the case against her continued to mount, she'd need a lawyer by this time tomorrow.

Her father would've been perfect for the job. And if she was his client, he might actually treat her with some importance in his life. With her career on the line, he'd have sufficient motivation to help. She'd worked so hard in her career to achieve in part to impress her father—every nod of approval at good grades, every small acknowledgement to his work colleagues about his daughter being pre-med, his daughter in medical school, his daughter the doctor.

So much work for such tiny morsels of recognition.

Now, her father was gone.

And what did she have to show for her years of hard work? A career that could be ruined at any moment and a lifetime of loneliness stretching out as long as a double-stranded helix.

She opened her wallet and signaled the bartender for the bill.

It wasn't in her nature to wallow in self-pity. She made a difference in patients' lives, and her critical care staff were a cohesive group of colleagues. She had a different type of family with them.

Even if she was taken into questioning by Detective LaGrange, NOPD only had circumstantial evidence on a crime she didn't commit.

Of course, a jury needed only to be convinced beyond a reasonable doubt.

WHEN CASH REJOINED ALLISON, she'd already paid for the food and was standing, hoisting her purse onto her shoulder as he approached. He was impressed she'd just quietly handled the bill, but perhaps her actions were a statement rather than a courtesy: this was business, not a date.

"Ready to go?" she asked.

No.

He wanted to stay, set the book aside, and share a bottle of

Cabernet over conversation. Then, they could make plans to go out dancing like there wasn't a killer on the loose.

"Yes, absolutely." He forced out the words.

They walked to her car on the curb under a starry night surrounded by the familiar smell of mossy trees, old wood, and brackish water.

Allison unlocked the car, and they climbed inside.

"I'll take you back to the medical center visitor parking to get your car." She started the engine.

Sloan cleared his throat from the back seat.

"How about we get you safely home? I can take a ride share back to my car after that," Cash said.

Sloan said, "You need to find a way to stay with her." Her father's tone was uncharacteristically pleading until he added, "In a gentlemanly fashion."

"I'm always a gentleman."

"Are you?" Allison mused, oblivious to the rest of the conversation.

"Always."

As they drove, Cash felt at a loss for words. If he was trying to seduce her, he'd be charming his way into her home—gentlemanly-like. But he wouldn't mislead Allison. He liked women, and liked spending time with them, but all interested parties knew what the expectations were.

The expectations with Allison were … undefined. He wouldn't finagle his way into her bed, both because she was a suspect to Hyde and because Cash didn't want a one-night stand.

He wanted—

Hell, he didn't know. But their relationship was already more complicated than a name in his contacts and a pleasant memory. For starters, he wanted to find Baylon's killer so their opposing roles of suspect and psychic detective could be removed from the equation.

Conversation thinned as the city lights blurred past, and the silence between them seemed louder than the jazz on the radio.

Allison drove into the Garden District before pulling into the driveway of a two-story white brick home with a decorative balcony supported by white pillars. Based on the number of windows, it was probably at least four bedrooms. Small yellow floodlights lit a white porch. The house sat on about a quarter acre of manicured land.

"That's a lot of house for one person."

"It was my father's home." Her tone held an element of loneliness Cash wanted to explore. She exited the car and shut her door.

He took a deep breath as he opened the passenger side door, deciding he'd tell her the truth now about her father and why he needed to stay with her.

"Danger!" The single word spoken by the ghost of Timothy Sloan had Cash out of the car and sprinting around the back of it at lightning speed.

"You killed him!" A gray-haired woman screamed from the end of the driveway as she raised an extended arm and fired a gun.

CHAPTER 7

Cash dove, tackling Allison to the lawn as the gunshot rang
out. He spun with her in his arms, trying to take the brunt of
the force of the fall. The impact knocked the breath out of him, and
his heart raced from the adrenaline. While looking over his shoulder,
he kept himself between Allison and the assailant.

The short woman screamed again—pale-faced and wide-eyed—
before getting into a car parked on the road. Tires squealing, she took
off down the road.

"Allison, are you okay?"

"I'm okay. I'm okay."

Her breathing was quick, and Cash could feel her rabbit-fast heart
rate beating against his chest.

"Mrs. Baylon dove off the deep end. I need to phone this in." That
meant letting go of Allison, which he didn't want to do until he was
certain she was okay.

She closed her eyes for a moment as she leaned her head against
his chest, panting. Cash smelled grass and her shampoo, and for a
heartbeat the world was nothing but her breath stuttering against his
ribs.

"Do you need your inhaler?"

She shook her head. "No, I'm okay."

When her breathing slowed and she sat up, he let go of her and pulled out his phone. Before he dialed, he exchanged a look with Sloan who stood with his mouth agape, probably realizing how close his daughter had come to joining him in the afterlife.

When the detective answered, Cash said, "Hyde, we have a situation."

~

AN HOUR LATER, Cash paced Allison's driveway.

She sat on her front porch looking devastated as her father's ghost sat beside her, unable to offer physical or emotional support.

In the yard, police walked the perimeter while crime scene investigators combed for evidence—the bullet, the casing, the tire marks.

"Is Baylon's wife in custody?" Cash asked.

Hyde stood still with his arms crossed over a protuberant belly. "Yeah, she is. This doesn't exonerate Dr. Sloan."

Cash knew that, even though it infuriated him. Dispassionately, he understood Mrs. Baylon's actions didn't make her her husband's killer. Why attempt to kill another woman if Mrs. Baylon was the killer? If she wanted to throw off suspicion, a public confrontation would make more sense. Shooting at Allison—ambushing her when she thought she'd be alone—wouldn't cast more suspicion on Allison.

Also, the murder weapons were different. If Mrs. Baylon was going to kill her husband over a supposed affair in a fit of rage— which she'd demonstrated she possessed—why hadn't she used the same gun to do so? Why a knife instead?

Hyde shifted his weight as calculating eyes watched Allison. "Maybe Dr. Sloan should stay in a hotel tonight. She might feel safer after what happened here."

Cash stopped pacing. "Don't insult my intelligence, Hyde. You don't give a damn about Allison's safety. You want to make sure she doesn't have the opportunity here at her home to hide evidence while you're busy getting your search warrant."

Hyde pulled his shoulders back and turned a hard expression on Cash. "Don't let this case get between us, Cash. We work well together."

"Then show me a little faith."

Hyde stepped closer. "Trusting you doesn't exempt me from doing my job. I trust that you're on the level and not getting defensive because you want to sleep with her. Aside from that, I need proof." Hyde turned and began walking away from Cash.

"I thought it was innocent until proven guilty. Not the other way around," Cash called after him.

"And I want that little black book," Hyde tossed back over his shoulder.

Cash walked over to the porch, letting his frustration with the situation seep out of him. Allison didn't need his negative emotions spilling onto her.

He sat beside her, saying softly, "They're almost done here."

"I can't believe she shot at me. I can't believe she thinks I'm capable of killing anyone. Three people have suspected me of murder."

"Just two now."

"Well, judging by Detective LaGrange's grumpy glares, he thinks I coerced you or seduced you into thinking I'm innocent."

"Seduced?" Cash put his elbows on the stairs behind him and stretched out his legs. "I could be so lucky."

He waited for her father to chide him, but Sloan said nothing. He was probably still shell-shocked from his daughter being shot at.

Cash sighed. "Look. You've had a bad scare. Why don't you pack an overnight bag? I've got a spare bedroom." Before she could object, he added, "But I'm trusting you not to seduce me. I've a reputation to uphold."

She choked out a laugh. "Your chastity is safe with me."

"Well, that's a damn shame. But I'll manage." He pushed to his feet. "How about that go-bag?"

He extended a hand and helped her stand. She grimaced slightly. Cash suspected she suffered some bruising from getting tackled by a man, though she wasn't openly complaining. He'd tried to cushion her as much as he could, but his primary concern had been moving her out of the trajectory of the bullet.

Allison walked inside and disappeared up the stairs.

"I haven't seen her comfortable around men the way she's comfortable around you."

"Careful, counselor. That almost sounded like approval."

Sloan cracked a smile. "Maybe with your charisma, you should've been a lawyer."

"I like what I do."

"You're good at it."

"Okay, now you're just buttering me up for something."

Sloan raised his hands in mock surrender. "No ulterior motive. Though saving my daughter's life has modified my perception of you."

"Oh?" Cash raised his eyebrows hopefully.

"Not enough for that."

Cash chuckled.

"Do you often save lives during your cases?"

"No." Cash rubbed the back of his neck. "That's a first."

"What's a first?"

Cash turned back to the porch to see Allison at the door. She'd packed fast, and he wondered if that was a product of pulling call nights for the ICU.

"First time fighting with Detective LaGrange." Truthfully, this case represented many firsts for Cash—protecting a suspect, dodging bullets, an overprotective father, and a woman he was connecting with on a personal, yet not intimate, level.

"Are you all set?" Cash asked.

"Yes."

ALLISON LEANED against the passenger side door as Cash drove her car to his place. If she wasn't so exhausted, she might contemplate how twelve hours ago she hadn't liked the man. Since then, they'd found common ground, made efforts toward solving a murder, and had dinner together. All of that had been followed by his saving her life.

Before the police had arrived at the house, Cash had tried to downplay the event, saying Baylon's wife would've had to be a good shot to hit a target at night at the end of the driveway. He even showed Allison how the trajectory of the bullet didn't align with where she'd been standing. By Allison's own calculations, the bullet wasn't far off, and Cash sprinting toward the woman's target probably threw off her aim.

So, either way, he still saved her from being shot.

And how had he known? Allison hadn't seen the woman approaching up the driveway until she screamed, but Cash had already been dashing toward Allison before Mrs. Baylon unleashed her battle cry and revealed her presence.

Had the ghost warned Cash?

T.S.

The same ghost who told Cash that Allison was innocent. The same ghost who knew Baylon's computer password. And Allison had heard part of a one-sided conversation between Cash and his ghost on her porch.

She listened to the steady hum of the tires on the road. She couldn't work through everything now. Her brain needed to power down for the night.

What if Cash's ghostly interactions were a manifestation of a medical condition? What if a brain tumor was causing him to hallucinate? That wouldn't explain the password and the dodging of bullets. She'd have to table this puzzle so she could process it logically another day.

Closing her eyes, she saw visions of Baylon's wife aiming a gun at her. Allison shuddered.

Cash moved his hand from the steering wheel, as if to take her hand, but redirected it to adjust the rearview mirror. "Tell me about the elephants."

"The elephants?" She sat straighter.

"In your office. They're very beautiful."

"My father bought them for me, usually for birthdays and Christmas. When I was six, we took a trip to Thailand, and I fell in love with elephants after I got to pet and ride them."

Cash smiled as if pleased he'd learned the true meaning of the many elephants in her office.

She added, "They are good luck also. The raised trunk signifies the showering of luck." She frowned. "I haven't felt very lucky these last twelve hours. Lucky to have you looking out for me, I suppose."

He reached and took her hand in his. Warm reassurance spread through her.

"You're from Louisiana, so you know what *lagniappe* is?" she asked.

"Extra."

"You're my *lagniappe*. Lucky *lagniappe*."

Like crème filling in a King Cake or beignets at Cafe du Monde, Allison thought. Cash was something rich and sweet and splurge-worthy. He was something extra in life. Maybe the something extra Allison had been missing—the something extra worth rearranging the rigidity in her life to enjoy. She'd been thinking that even before the attack. When she'd stepped out of the car before Cash tackled her, she'd been considering asking him inside

When they reached his condominium, he parked the car. They walked through card-access security to enter the building. A friendly front desk clerk waved and greeted Cash as "Mr. McCall". Allison followed Cash to the elevator.

Once on the fifth floor, they entered his two-bedroom condo. The space was tidy and warmed with potted plants by every window. A bookshelf brimmed with titles of psychology, criminal justice, and ghost lore.

"This is nice," she commented.

Cash closed the door, clicked the deadbolt, and walked to the kitchen where he poured two glasses of water. He handed her one. "Why don't you shower, and that will give me time to make up the bed in the spare room?"

Nodding, she thanked him and took her bag and water to the bathroom. There, she enjoyed a hot shower and lingered after she'd washed until she stopped shaking. After toweling off, she slipped into yoga pants and a T-shirt. She left her hair towel-dried.

She found Cash in the kitchen explaining to no one that, "Chamomile tea will help Allison relax."

She cleared her throat.

Cash turned to her, a smile lighting his face. If he kept looking at her that way, she might stop caring that he talked to himself.

"I made tea." He set the mug down on the counter across from the stove.

"Chamomile. I heard. Thank you." She leaned on the counter, wrapped her hands around the cup, and smelled the light aroma. She wasn't used to someone tending to her, and the gesture softened something within her.

"Yes, well, ghosts *aren't* like vampires who can only be *invited* inside someone's home." Cash took a sip of his tea as he shot a menacing glare at nothing but the refrigerator to his right. "And sometimes, they linger incessantly even when you've assured them you're protecting the person they're looking out for."

Allison cocked her head to one side. "Why do I get the feeling most of what you just said wasn't directed at me?"

"Your ghost is a bit overprotective of you."

"Oh? So T.S. is *my* ghost now?" Allison chuckled.

"He's always been your ghost. And he's the one who alerted me to the danger at your house."

"But you're the one who risked your life."

Cash stared at his mug, dipping his teabag up and down.

She shook her head. "I'm still replaying the shooting. How on earth did it come to this? I was always cordial with Mrs. Baylon. And for her to think me capable of ..." her voice trailed as she lifted the tea to her lips and drank the soothing liquid.

"She's hurting and obviously more than a little unstable," he offered. "She probably replayed events in her mind—times her husband worked late with you, times maybe the two of you traveled to work-related events together. You shared a side of him she wasn't a part of. Maybe Mrs. Baylon's feelings had been festering for a while, and maybe her husband dismissed them or overlooked them entirely."

Allison let the logic of Cash's words sink in and offer comfort. Perhaps Baylon's wife suspected something and felt the murder was confirmation of her feelings.

Setting down her cup, Allison shuddered. "And the *real* murderer is still out there."

Cash came around the counter and took her hands. "And you're safe here. We'll investigate more tomorrow."

The warmth from Cash's touch spread up her arms. His gentle gaze roamed her face, gaining a new heat and desire the longer his eyes lingered on hers.

"Allison, I really want to kiss you right now. My only hesitation is the awkwardness of having this moment in front of your ghost."

My ghost?

She swallowed. "Well, I can't see him, and he isn't bothering me, so don't lose your chance."

Cash leaned forward, sealing his lips to hers. Heat surged through her, melting her fatigue and shattering all worried thoughts unrelated to being close to Cash.

She stepped closer to him, wrapping her arms around him as they deepened the kiss. He kept his hands unmoving on her hips, and she sensed restrained desire in his body language.

When the kiss ended, Allison took a step back, even though she wanted another kiss ... and probably more.

"So much for not seducing you." She licked her lips. "I'm going to stop there. I didn't mean to make you violate a code of conduct you probably have as an investigator. That, or make you wonder if I'm somehow manipulating you. And I certainly wouldn't want you to attribute it to some sense of obligation on my part for saving my life. For what it's worth, I've never kissed a man I've known less than three dates, much less one I've never dated."

Cash tugged her back to him, but instead of another kiss, he touched his forehead to hers. "There are a lot of violations I want to commit with you right now. But we don't need to rush anything. We'll start with sleep, solving the case, and then you and I can see how far we want to take these sparks." He ran a hand over her hair. "If and when we take that plunge, you won't sense any reluctance on my part."

Tomorrow she would face the police again. Tonight, she faced desire—and both felt equally dangerous.

"I like your plan." Using every ounce of her willpower, she stepped back. "Goodnight, Cash McCall."

CHAPTER 8

*C*ash took a cold shower.

Allison Sloan was a passionate woman under her cool, professional exterior.

Fortunately, she'd been able to access her rational brain in the heat of the moment—unlike Cash who'd been teetering on the edge of losing control through the entire kiss. If she'd asked for more, he'd have given it to her—consequences be damned.

Instead, she'd listed the reasons why a passionate night together would be a bad idea. None of which was because she didn't want him. He took that as a good sign. But she'd missed one reason. Cash didn't want a hookup or anything fleeting. And he wouldn't get intimate until that expectation was clear.

He dried off, wrapped the towel around his waist, and walked to the bedroom.

"My daughter is not a one-night stand."

Cash startled. "*Sonofaspirit!* Don't you respect personal boundaries?" Cash scolded Sloan in a harsh whisper, not wanting to wake Allison in the other room. Part of him suspected he deserve the scare; he had, after all, kissed his daughter in front of him, but he hadn't wanted to miss the opportunity.

Sloan crossed his arms, his semi-transparent form standing in front of a lamp, not casting a shadow. "She's not a one-night stand," he repeated.

"I heard you, and I agree with you."

"Because if you think … wait? What?"

Cash pulled on a shirt. "She isn't, and that's not what I want."

"But you only just met her, and your track record …" Sloan protested.

Is none of your business, Cash wanted to say. But that wouldn't shorten this conversation.

"The McCalls have a long history of settling down later in life. We also don't take commitment lightly. So if you're wondering why I'm thirty-eight and never married, it's because I only intend to do it once." He grabbed boxers and shorts, walked into the bathroom, and closed the door two-thirds of the way. "And before you get any ideas, I'm not saying I want to marry your daughter. I'm saying I want a go at something with substance."

"Well, what does that mean?"

"It means I've known her less than twenty-four hours, so who knows what will happen." He emerged from the bathroom dressed for bed. "Besides, we have a murder to solve. You should be more worried about the threat the murderer poses to your daughter than the one posed by me."

The corners of Sloan's mouth fell. "I am. But you're the only one who can see and hear me, so I'm lashing out where I can."

Cash pulled the covers down on his bed. "Apology accepted. Now, your daughter is safe here, and I'm not going to sneak into her room like some insatiable teenager. So, I need you and your sixth ghost sense to go spy while we get some rest."

"Spy?" Sloan looked mortified, as though Cash had asked him to scrub public toilets.

"Yes, spy." Cash climbed into bed. "Flitter back and forth between the lab, the offices, and the police station. See what turns up."

"I don't flit."

"Transport then."

"You want me to spy on Detective LaGrange's work?"

"If you want me to stay one step ahead of the investigation into your daughter, yes. Hyde thinks I'm compromised because I like your daughter—and he's not wrong. But he won't share details with me now."

"He never said that."

"He didn't have to. But I can't solve the case if I'm missing pieces."

Sloan crossed his arms, looking more like an insolent toddler than a respected lawyer. "Fine. I'll spy." His mouth puckered in distaste.

"Thank you, counselor." Cash turned out the light and relaxed into the softness of his bed.

"If you're serious about dating my daughter," Sloan's voice dropped a conspiratorial octave, "how are you going to get past the ghost thing? She'll never trust you as long as you claim to see the supernatural."

"I don't know how to overcome that obstacle. But I won't lie to her, and I won't lie about my gift."

THE NEXT MORNING, Cash brewed coffee and tiptoed around his kitchen so as not to wake Allison. It occurred to him as he was falling asleep last night that he'd never brought a woman to his home. Nights with other women usually involved their place. It was one way he ensured they weren't lying about being married and enabled him to avoid awkward morning-after moments.

Her father returned from his spying escapade.

"Any news?" Cash asked.

"Allison's research assistant was sneaking around the lab last night."

"Curious. What'd Vera do after that?"

"I don't know. You said to watch the lab, the offices, and the police station. I didn't tail anyone."

"That smells amazing." Allison walked into the kitchen with her hair a tangled mess and still in her yoga pants and t-shirt. Their fitted design hugged her chest and hips.

Cash's only source of dissatisfaction was that he hadn't been the one to do that to her hair. But they'd made the responsible decision last night. Dammit.

He poured Allison a cup of coffee and passed it along. "Sleep okay?"

"Yes. I thought I'd struggle with everything going on, but exhaustion took over."

"Breakfast?"

"Coffee is my breakfast." She took a sip and gave a moan of delight that had him wondering if he could elicit such sounds from her.

She caught a glimpse of herself in the reflection of the microwave door. "Ugh. Well, there isn't a side of me you haven't seen now—composed in my office, working in my lab, falling to pieces as a suspect, taking my inhaler to avoid an asthma attack, nearly in tears after being shot at, and now this."

Cash smiled. "All the facets that make you, you. Perpetually polished people don't exist. And you're beautiful in all of those roles."

She eyed him, disbelieving, over the rim of her mug. He considered showing her the attraction was genuine, but a murder case still loomed between them.

"Do you need to finish that cup, or can I start talking shop?"

"Start talking," she replied.

"Is there any reason Vera, your grad student, would be at the research lab in the middle of the night?"

"No."

"No experiments on any timed cycle that would fall late?"

"No. Why?"

"Your fa—phantom saw her at the lab last night."

"Maybe she left personal effects and had to come back for them," Allison suggested.

"No," Sloan interjected, "the researcher was definitely searching for something."

Cash relayed to Allison, "T.S. seems to think Vera's activities were dubious. Like she was searching for something."

"You think she was looking for the little black book?" Allison asked.

"If she wanted to steal Baylon's work, she couldn't do it with you there. It'd have to be after hours."

Allison bit her lip, hands wrapped around her coffee cup.

Cash arched an eyebrow. "You aren't defending her, which means you think she might be capable of stealing."

"No. I mean … it's just." Allison sighed. "Vera is at the lab all the time. Could Baylon have been documenting work on my tumor specimens without her knowledge? I find that hard to believe." Allison took another sip of coffee as Cash watched her mind churn with questions and possibilities.

He waited for her to continue.

"I wonder—did she know he was taking notes on my work and was too afraid to upset Rockstar PhD, or was she in cahoots with him?"

"Cahoots?"

"That's the term, right?"

He nodded with a grin. Her detective mind was adorable. He also wouldn't mention that she hadn't yet dismissed Vera being in the lab late at night as unsubstantiated hogwash from Cash's imaginary ghost.

"Yeah." He scratched the stubble on his jaw. "So, Vera's behavior last night sounds more like cahoots."

"What do we do about it? Now that I have copies of the notebook, and she has nothing, she can't steal my work. I'm not sure how to get proof enough to fire her, though."

"Allison." He blinked at her several times. "Finish your coffee. You're missing the bigger picture here."

She gave Cash a puzzled look as she took another gulp.

He leaned forward on the counter. "If Vera was working with Baylon, she may have a motive for murder."

"What? Not Vera."

"Does the name Techy25 mean anything to you?"

Allison rubbed an ear. "Not the entire name, but Vera went to Louisiana Tech and calls herself a 'techy' sometimes. I can't say definitively that username is or isn't hers. Why?"

"Baylon was texting someone by that name in a private chat room the night he was murdered. If he and Vera were stealing your work, maybe Vera found out Baylon was going to apologize, and he threatened to tell you everything—effectively ending her career before it began. Maybe Vera got cold feet, and *she* threatened to tell you. Except nothing at the crime scene looked like self-defense on the part of the murderer."

Allison added, "And the apology note Baylon started suggests he was the one growing a conscience."

Cash took Allison's empty mug. "Why don't you get dressed, and we'll go talk to Detective LaGrange?"

ALLISON FLEW through her bathroom routine and pulled on jeans, a pink blouse, and her brown boots. Her mind was reeling. No way Vera could hurt anyone. She'd even said in her interview that she wanted to work in a lab that didn't torture and kill mice in the name of science.

Allison had refrained from pointing out that mice research had advanced science in cancer therapy, understanding immune deficiency, and malaria treatments—to name a few. Mice research bore seventeen Nobel prizes and had saved millions of lives.

Furthermore, if Vera had stabbed Baylon, she'd have been doing so knowing he was taking blood thinners and therefore knowing his risk of a fatal injury was high.

With the morning sun streaming between concrete slats, Allison and Cash walked through the parking deck to Allison's car.

"What the heck?" Her car was lopsided where someone had slashed her driver's side rear tire.

Cash bent down to inspect the damage. "Baylon's wife is in police custody, so this is someone else."

"People really hate me." She pressed the key fob to unlock the trunk. "I've got a spare tire."

"Wait, Allison."

She opened the trunk and gasped at the sight of a knife covered in blood. She leaned closer as a faint buzzing sounded from the trunk. "Is that the murder weapon?"

Beside the knife, lay an empty, open jar she didn't recognize. The buzzing noise grew louder as a dozen bees flew out of the trunk. Allison screamed, backing up and turning, but too late. She felt the stings of several bees.

No, no, no.

She didn't have much time. She needed her epipen, and she always kept one in her purse. Heart rate spiking, she grabbed for her purse on her shoulder even as she felt her body's reaction to the bee venom. She knew the inflammatory cascade all too well—an IgE mediated response of histamine. Blood pressure drop, throat swelling, asphyxiation.

Cash was beside her. "Allison, what can I do?"

But already she couldn't speak. She dug in her purse but couldn't find the Epi-pen. It was always there. She checked every month. Had someone moved it?

"This was a trap," Cash said.

She felt herself falling. Cash's strong arms helped lower her to the ground as he pleaded for her to tell him how to help her.

She couldn't breathe.

Then, she was floating—a shapeless, bodiless form looking down at her own pale, limp body.

Cash gripped her shoulders. "Sloan, tell me what to do."

A man's baritone voice said, "Her back-up epinephrine injection is in the glove compartment."

That voice! Allison knew that voice!

In seconds, Cash had dashed to the car, retrieved the Epi-pen, and removed the cap. He plunged it into her bicep, but she registered no pain and her limp body didn't flinch.

"C'mon, baby. Come back to me. Is it working?"

"Yes, but she needs rescue breaths."

Allison looked in the direction of the helping voice to see her father standing and looking down at Cash and her body.

T.S.

All this time, Timothy Sloan had been helping Cash. And Cash hadn't told her because he knew she'd never believe him.

Allison would've called out to both of them, but she had no voice.

Cash pinched her nose, tilted her head, and breathed. Between breaths, he pulled out his phone and dialed 9-1-1. Between breaths, he gave the operator his location.

"Stay with me, Allison."

With each breath, Allison felt herself tugged back into her body until she was resting peacefully, and all went dark and silent.

CASH ADMINISTERED rescue breaths to an unconscious Allison. He'd taken basic life support classes every few years, so he knew the mechanics of how to perform resuscitation.

Knowing the motions didn't keep fear from securing a vice-like grip around his gut. But Allison's chest rose and fell, so her throat hadn't completely closed off—thanks to the epinephrine. Her skin color reperfused, and her pulse—which she'd never lost—strengthened.

"Vera's here."

Sloan's words sent spikes of ice down Cash's spine. Without leaving Allison's side, he glanced around but didn't see anyone else in the garage.

"Where?" Cash gave Allison another breath.

"Lurking beside a car a ways behind you—too far for her to hear what you're saying. She's trying to decide if she's going to risk coming after you to steal the book."

Cash glanced at Baylon's little black book, which had spilled onto the floor near Allison's purse.

"Is she armed?" He gave another breath.

"Tire iron from the trunk."

At least it wasn't a gun. His odds were better against a striking weapon, and he had the element of surprise. But he couldn't be detained fighting a vicious woman while Allison suffocated.

"Okay, Sloan. You're going to watch Vera like a hawk while I breathe for Allison. When that monster gets within three feet of us, I'm counting on you to let me know."

"I can do that." His tone grew an even sharper, anxious edge.

Cash continued to breathe for Allison, using all his willpower to trust Sloan to alert him to Vera. If he turned around too soon, he'd either scare her off and she'd get away or he'd be drawn into a much longer confrontation—which Allison couldn't afford. If he turned around too late, well, he wouldn't be much good to Allison unconscious from a blow to the head.

"Now!" Sloan shouted.

Cash spun and lashed out a leg as Vera stood with the tire iron drawn back above her, looking as though she'd planned to come down on his head like an ax to wood. His foot struck her knee with a sickening crunch.

Vera cried out as she crumbled to the floor, dropping the crowbar and clutching at her bent joint. Cash kicked the crowbar out of reach before turning back to Allison and giving another breath.

He positioned himself on the other side of Allison so he could keep watch on Vera. The woman sobbed on the ground for a full minute before composing herself and trying to pull herself along the concrete away from the crime scene.

She didn't get far before a black and white appeared, followed by an ambulance.

"What's going on here?" the officers demanded.

"My name is Cash McCall. I'm a psychic detective with the NOPD. You can confirm that through Detective Hyde LaGrange. This is a crime scene. That woman attacked Allison Sloan who I'm trying to keep alive."

One officer stood watch over Vera as the other called Detective LaGrange.

When the paramedics climbed out of the ambulance with their medic bags, they assessed Allison and used a mask attached to a bag and oxygen to breathe for her. Following another dose of epinephrine, she was breathing on her own.

After starting an IV and running fluids into her vein, the paramedics loaded her onto the stretcher and then into the ambulance. One took her ID from her purse while the other checked her blood pressure again.

Cash started to join Allison in the back of the ambulance, but the paramedic beside her held up a hand.

"Are you family?"

"No."

"I'm sorry. We can't take you with us."

The sobering words reminded Cash that he needed to stay with the evidence anyway.

Allison's father glided into the back of the ambulance, his expression somber. "You're family to me. I'll stay with her," Sloan consoled Cash.

The second paramedic shut the back doors and climbed up front. The ambulance drove off.

Cash scrubbed his face and wiped tears from his eyes. He didn't have time to fall apart. He pulled out his phone and called Hyde.

Sitting in Allison's driver seat with his feet on the concrete floor of the parking garage, Cash put his head in one hand and held his phone to his ear with the other.

"I'm on my way," Hyde said, background noise suggesting he was in his vehicle.

Cash relayed the events to Hyde.

"I've got a forensics unit en route over there to process the knife. Nobody touched it?"

"No." Cash pushed himself out of the seat and looked around. The officers had Vera cuffed in the back of their cruiser now. "There are security cameras. We might catch Vera Myers in the act of planting the knife and bees."

Hyde gave a grunt. "She had a time-stamped club pass as an alibi, but apparently that was by design. How is Dr. Sloan?"

"When you get here, I'm going to the hospital to check on her. You'll keep me posted?"

"Will do."

*C*ash stood on the other side of the one-way glass, watching Vera Myers await interrogation.

He'd gone to the hospital where Allison had been in the ER getting medical attention and would be sent to the ICU for monitoring. Since he wasn't family, he wasn't allowed to see her or be informed of her condition. When he explained to the staff that she didn't have any immediate family, they assured him that she was one of their own and was in good hands.

Annoyed at the circumstances, Cash brought his nervous energy to the police station and asked Sloan's ghost to give him updates about his daughter.

Detective LaGrange entered the interview room and thanked a red-eyed, disheveled Vera for coming to the station. She glowered at him. Hyde went on to explain how she'd been caught on security camera planting the knife and bees in Dr. Sloan's car. While that was technically true, Cash had seen the dark footage with Hyde, and Vera's hoodie might make it difficult to convince a jury beyond a reasonable doubt that the perpetrator was her. Her downfall had been staying at the crime scene with the same clothes when she attacked him—all of that also on camera.

Hyde—seeking a confession, not a trial—explained how the evidence proved Vera's guilt. They didn't need a perfect case yet. They needed enough for Hyde to squeeze the truth out while Vera still thought she had options.

Allison's father materialized beside Cash. "Allison is doing well, under the circumstances. The doctors gave her fluids, steroids, and something called an H-two blocker. In the ICU, she'll be taken care of by health care providers who know her and care about her."

Cash nodded, hands in his pockets, while keeping his gaze forward on the interview.

Sloan's voice had that familiar slow, sad ebb. "I guess Vera moved the Epi-pen from Allison's purse sometime yesterday when Allison was in the lab or Baylon's office. As for the trunk, Vera could have stolen a spare key from Allison's house. She house sat for Allison on occasion—watering her plants—when she was away on conferences, so she knew the hidden outside key location." Sloan gave a laborious sigh. "If I'd tailed her, I would've seen her plant the bees."

"You stayed lookout at the lab, which is what I asked you to do. Sneaking around a lab does not a murderer make," Cash consoled him.

"You would've known what to do. You're a good judge of character."

Cash didn't have a cheeky comeback so he simply said, "Thank you."

In the interrogation room, Vera began to sob, mascara streaking and hands trembling. It was an ugly scene that didn't invoke an ounce of sympathy from Cash. She'd tried to kill a woman he cared about.

"We had an agreement," she snapped, her mood transitioning from sad to angry. "The professor agreed we were going to sell the lung organoids and the sustainable matrix for them. And then he backed out!" She shook her head, frayed blonde tips swinging. "We were going to miss out on millions of dollars because he grew a conscience."

"What's a company want pieces of fake lung for?"

Vera snorted at Hyde's apparent ignorance. "We had the ideal environment for implanting tumor cells. Once it was purchased and mass-produced, samples from all over the country could be implanted and grown—each paying patient with their own mini-lung and preserved tumor. People would pay to have their tumor stored indefinitely so that molecular mutations could be tested at any time to determine future treatments."

"Market that big for lung cancer, really?" Hyde asked.

Vera gave him an incredulous red-eyed stare. "It's the leading cancer in the United States. Lung cancer kills more people than breast, colon, prostate, and pancreas cancer combined."

"We talkin' real big money, then?" Hyde asked calmly.

She rolled her eyes and crossed her arms.

"So you off the professor, but without his lil' black notebook, you got nothin' to hawk, *cher*. That about right?."

"He hid his notebook, and Dr. Sloan found it."

"So, you went after Dr. Sloan? You planted them bees, knowin' she's deathly allergic. That's how it went, yeah?"

Vera sniffed indignantly. "You have the footage, don't you?"

"I do. But lemme tell you somethin'—folks sleep easier when they get it off their chest. Start from the top, and tell me how you killed Professor Baylon and attempted to kill Dr. Sloan."

"I want a lawyer."

Hyde leaned back with a fatherly smile. "No problem." As he slowly stood, he pushed a legal pad and pen to her. "People usually feel better when they write things down—gets it off their chest. I'll leave this here in case you want to do that before that lawyer gets here."

Sloan, who'd stood beside Cash listening to Vera's questioning, vanished.

Hyde left the interrogation room and walked around to the room where Cash stood. "Another one in the books," Hyde said, clapping Cash on the shoulder. "Good work, mon ami."

Vera stared at the paper before picking up the pen and starting to write.

A hollow sensation loomed in the pit of his stomach. He wouldn't feel the success of this case until he saw Allison's healthy glow again.

Hyde frowned. "Any word on the doctor?"

"Her father says she's stable in the ICU."

"You like her, huh?"

Cash turned toward Hyde. "Yeah, I like her."

Allison's father reappeared. "She's asking for you."

Cash straightened as a knot in his chest loosened and was replaced by an elation in his belly. "I gotta go, Hyde."

"You leavin' already? You never skip the big confession scene, *Romeo*."

But Cash was already out the door and bounding down the hallway.

ALLISON LOOKED around her hospital room at greeting cards and flowers from the staff. They'd amassed a collection in under a few hours. How strange it felt to be a patient in her own ICU. More than anything though, she was grateful to be alive.

Her body felt so exhausted, as if she'd danced the entire Nutcracker. Meanwhile, the steroids they'd pumped into her had her wanting to crawl out of her own skin.

When she'd woken, she'd asked about Cash, but none of the ICU staff knew who or where he was other than the news that he'd saved her life. She suspected he had a murderer to help catch.

Vera.

Sweet, studious Vera. Young, vibrant, and apparently deadly. The betrayal ached more than the bee stings.

Vera was one of the few people who knew of Allison's bee venom allergy.

Allison flopped her head back on the bed. She wanted to see Cash, but had no way of reaching him. Even if she had her phone, she didn't have his number.

"Dad?" She swallowed and blinked back tears. "If you're here, can you ask Cash to come see me?"

. . .

Twenty minutes later, Allison heard a knock at her door.

A nurse poked his head into the room. "Dr. Sloan, you have a visitor. Says he's with the police department. Name's Cash McCall."

"Yes, Dan. Please let him in and add him to the visitor list." Allison sat up straighter. She patted uselessly at her tangled mess of hair, acutely aware of how frightful she must be look.

Two minutes later, Cash strode into the room, his smile lighting her world.

He bent over and kissed her cheek. "So good to see you breathing on your own." He pulled up a chair beside the bed and took her hand, careful not to disrupt her IV.

He kept his gaze on their hands as his cadence was fast and voice tight. "Vera is confessing. Everything will be wrapped up by the end of the day in terms of her arrest. She wanted to sell your lung organoids to a company that would cultivate people's tumors for a price." He rubbed his thumb along the back of her hand.

"Cash?"

He didn't look up at first. Then, he slowly raised his eyes to meet hers.

"Thank you for saving my life. And I'm infinitely grateful my father was there to tell you what to do."

Cash's eyes widened. "You know?" he stammered. "You saw?"

"I've had the rare near-death patient tell me they were looking down at themselves during a code—watching their own resuscitation —and now I know what they were referring to. I sort of hovered— bodiless and speechless. I saw you and me. Then I *heard* my father's voice talking to you."

"He's been looking out for you."

"He's the one who told you I was innocent?"

"Among other things." Cash gave her a wry grin.

"I was pretty harsh on you about being a charlatan."

"Comes with the territory. Besides, I took it as a challenge." Cash's eyes sparkled. "I was winning you over, despite your disbelief."

Allison chuckled. "Yes, you were."

He laid his head on her shoulder, saying nothing. She waited for him to share what was on his mind, but he remained uncharacteristically silent.

She stroked a hand delicately through his hair. "I can't tell if you're praying, sleeping, or communing with spirits."

"I'm taking a moment to let the relief wash over me at seeing you well." He lifted his head. "I know you must be exhausted and need rest." He started to stand, but reluctance slowed his motion.

"Cash?" She gripped his hand before it slipped away. "Now that I'm no longer a murder suspect ..." her nerve faltered. She didn't want him to leave without knowing how she felt. But was the ICU after a nearly fatal event really the time to ask him out?

Cash sat back down with an amused curve of his lips. "I'd like to date you, Allison. And not that I have any way to prove it to you, but your father says he thinks he could tolerate me in your life."

Allison laughed. "That sounds like him."

She had no idea how she was going to navigate a future that included a psychic boyfriend and a ghost for a chaperone—but for the first time in days, the idea of "future" didn't feel so fragile.

CHAPTER 10

12 MONTHS LATER

Cash stood beneath the arch of ivory roses, unable to breathe for a heartbeat as Allison stepped into view. White silk flowed over her gorgeous figure. The sparkling embroidered top seemed to enhance her sapphire eyes. She wore her rich brown hair in an updo with teasing curls framing her face.

Her gaze never left his.

"She's a dream come true," Cash whispered—meant for Timothy Sloan, though the priest beside him gave a soft nod as if in agreement.

"You deserve each other," Sloan said, wiping at his eyes as his figure shimmered near where Allison would soon stand. "I'm delighted she found her match."

Her father had insisted on remaining a lingering spirit long enough to see them wed. He promised he would move on after their happy day. Over the last year, Cash had been the intermediary between Sloan and his daughter, helping repair the father-daughter relationship. But it was time for her father to let go. And Allison needed closure, too.

Vera Myers was doing time upstate. Baylon's wife was charged with a misdemeanor. When Vera's confession went public, Baylon's wife sent Allison a letter of apology. All the same, Allison filed a restraining order against her.

Allison had looked into the company wanting to buy her lung organoids to grow tumor cells. She sold her organoid patent with a clause that a percentage of the proceeds the company made from use of the design would go toward lung cancer research. She kept the rights to use her own cellular microenvironment to further research in the field.

Cash scanned the crowd of wedding attendees. His family and friends watched in silent awe as Allison walked down the aisle. Hyde LaGrange was in the second row on the groom's side. Allison had coworkers and friends filling her side of the church.

His bride reached him at the altar with a radiant smile.

Cash took Allison's hands. "You know, if you'd had an alibi that day, I might never have stayed long enough to get to know you."

"I'm glad I didn't have an alibi."

The priest cleared his throat and projected his voice. "Dearly beloved, we are gathered here today—"

"I do," Allison interrupted.

"I do, too," Cash said.

Sloan gave a watery chuckle. "You are supposed to wait until the question is asked."

Cash turned toward the ghost—toward the man who had once glared at him—and nodded.

"Thank you," Cash said quietly, "for trusting me."

Sloan's edges softened, a glow washing through him.

"I can go now," he whispered. "She isn't alone anymore."

Allison blinked as if sensing something shifting in the air.

Cash cupped her jaw. "You'll never be alone again."

As Sloan's form dissolved into light—finally at peace—Cash leaned in and kissed his wife.

<<<>>>

MICHELLE'S MIRACLE

A medium who guards her heart. A man who's finally picked up the pieces of his own. And the ghost determined to bring them together.

CHAPTER 1

*M*ichelle walked for an hour through New York City blocks to get from her apartment in Park Slope to the commercial building for her appointment. The cool spring air chilled her cheeks, but her brisk pace, overcoat, and hat kept her core warm.

When she arrived at her destination, she took the stairs to the fourth floor and walked the corridor to find her new accountant.

She came to the office with the business name on the door:

CONNOR ROSS, CPA

She knocked and slowly entered the office.

A man about her age, mid-thirties, stood and came out from behind his oak desk. "Ms. Barcella, you're very punctual."

The man had dark brown hair and an immaculately trimmed beard just long enough to be a beard rather than stubble. The room and his appearance conveyed professionalism.

She shook the hand he offered as she glanced around the small office appraisingly. The furniture was tasteful—darkly stained wood against light gray walls. A painting of a frosted mountain peak hung on the wall opposite the desk.

"I'm Connor Ross."

"Oh." She dropped her hand. She thought this younger man was the office manager or receptionist. "I was expecting someone older and maybe balding. That's incredibly stereotypical of me."

He shrugged and grinned. "Another twenty or thirty years and you might be right. Although, my father still has a full head of hair, so I've got that in my favor."

He walked around his desk and slipped on a pair of reading glasses. "Are you ready to get started? If you'd like, I can get you a cup of coffee, a soda, or bottled water."

Behind Connor and off to the wall by the window, the faint shimmer of a woman dressed in blue jeans and a pink sweater rippled into view. She stood, staring out the window.

Please, not here ... not today.

Michelle bit back a groan. She just wanted someone to help her with money management—not someone haunted by a ghost. "Maybe this was a bad idea."

"I'm sorry?" Connor's expression turned confused.

"You're obviously busy. I shouldn't take up your time."

"You have an appointment," he reminded her with a bemused expression.

"Right." She glanced at the brunette near the window and back at Connor. Maybe if the woman stayed over there, Michelle could get through this appointment. "It would be rude of me to leave. I'll stay." She handed him her folder containing the documents outlining her assets. She had an electronic version she could send but wanted to meet the person who might manage her accounts before sending personal information.

"Please, have a seat."

He waited patiently as she carefully took off her hat and coat and set them down in the client chair beside her. He settled into his leather chair across from her at the large desk.

The ghost by the window turned her attention to the two of them. Michelle concentrated on not making eye contact with her so the ghost wouldn't know she could see her.

"Oh, Connor," the woman said in a pitying voice. "When a pretty woman like that enters your office, you need to take her coat for her." She sighed. "How are you ever going to remarry?"

Connor, oblivious to the woman's gentle chiding, looked intently over Michelle's documents.

Michelle's gaze fell on a photograph on his desk. The woman, who was now a ghost, looked very alive in the photo as she smiled and pressed one rosy cheek against Connor's cheek. He wore a delighted smile.

"What did you have in mind?" Connor asked.

"Hmm? Oh. I'd like to set up some accounts with the money from my parents' life insurance policy. I was thinking of investing in a variety—bonds, stocks, and real estate. A sum should be safely earning interest that will create a monthly stipend for me. And a certain amount would need to be set aside for retirement."

"Both of your parents passed?" He set down his glasses, looked at her, and folded his arms on his desk.

"Plane crash a year ago. I'm finally getting around to making financial decisions."

"I'm sorry for your loss. I know what it's like to lose a loved one."

"Your wife." Michelle regretted the words the instant they were out of her mouth.

"Um, yes. Leukemia. How did you know?"

"You have a picture of the two of you here, but you're not wearing a wedding ring."

And I can see her spirit by the window, she didn't add.

Michelle had dodged enough questions around the knowledge she inadvertently learned by seeing and talking to ghosts that she could think fast on her feet to provide alternative explanations. Except now, Connor was probably wondering why Michelle was noticing the absence of a wedding ring. At least that was perhaps less creepy than the conclusion people sometimes drew—that she'd cyber-stalked them and learned personal information online.

"I'm sorry," she told him. "What was her name?"

Connor looked at the picture frame on his desk. "Penny." He

dropped his head back down, placing his glasses back on, and looked at Michelle's finances.

"Oh, Connor." Penny shook her head sadly. "You've got a gorgeous woman—who checked out your appearance and noted you're single—in your office and you can't even *see* her."

Michelle bristled and pursed her lips tight to avoid the temptation to correct Penny. Michelle was not "checking him out."

Penny continued, talking to her husband even though he couldn't hear her. "She's single," she sing-songed. "Oh! And she's an artist."

Michelle leaned back and crossed her legs. She gave Connor a disarming smile to cover her strange behavior. Ghosts had an irritating ability to glean personal information from people. She wanted to tell Penny that the best thing she could do for her husband was to move on and let him have peace. However, she kept silent because if she spoke to the ghost, her medium abilities would be revealed.

Connor adjusted his glasses. "We can definitely do a retirement account and investments. I'll need to know what your monthly budget is, including recurring payment amounts—house, car, student loans."

"No debt. I can send my monthly expenses to you in an email."

"Okay. I'll pull the paperwork together for you to give me proxy to set these accounts up. We'll arrange a day and time for you to come back and sign them."

Come back?

Perhaps everything could be done from email from now on, enabling Michelle to avoid Penny. She could provide her signature through online applications. Michelle felt bad for the ghost and empathized with Connor's loss, but ghosts had a tendency to fixate on ideas and make themselves a nuisance to those who could see them.

"Yes," Penny cheered. "She'll be back, which means you'll have a second chance to make a first impression."

Michelle shot Penny a glowering look as she reached for her coat and hat. She wasn't some ghost's plaything.

Penny blinked in shock.

Oh, no.

Standing, Michelle tugged her coat off the chair and turned to

Connor. She needed to make a fast exit, though she found the man attractive and might have considered staying longer if not for the ghost.

"Okay. Thank you for your time. You have my contact info."

Connor stood when she stood, taking off his glasses and tapping them on his chin as he watched her fumble to pull on her jacket. He stepped forward and held the coat up so she could find the other arm hole.

"Thank you." Slipping it on, she turned to leave, but Connor was standing between her and the door. And he was close, apparently baffled into immobility by her rush to leave.

When she looked up at him, he gave a slight smile. She smiled in return and began to regret needing to make a hasty retreat. He didn't move, as if her presence short-circuited his logic. She wasn't sure she minded.

"You saw me!" Penny declared. "You can hear me!"

Michelle straightened her collar and side-stepped the accountant. After hastily yanking open the door, she walked toward the stairs.

Connor stepped after her into the hall. "I'll email you."

"Sounds perfect." She forced cheer into her voice as she waved without turning around. "Thank you!" she called over her shoulder.

The ghost was hot on her heels. "Wait. I've never been seen by the living. How can you do that?"

Michelle reached the stairwell. "It's a curse."

"It's a miracle!" Penny glided effortlessly beside Michelle as she rushed down the stairs.

"No. It really isn't." Michelle had had some good relationships and had helped other ghosts move on, but some were needy and clingy. She sensed the ghost of a young woman, who lingered to watch her husband's every day activities, was in no frame of mind to consider moving on.

"It's fate," Penny added.

"Not really. You need to move on and stop haunting your husband."

"I just want him to be happy. He needs to find someone."

"Happiness is intrinsic. It doesn't come from a person."

"We all need love," Penny countered.

Michelle stopped abruptly at the bottom of the stairwell and looked at Penny. "Well, I can't argue with that."

Penny smiled sweetly.

CONNOR STOOD IN HIS OFFICE, trying to remember what was next on his agenda after Ms. Barcella. He tried to recall the last time a beautiful woman around his age was in his office.

Probably not since Penny.

Michelle was beautiful and … strange. Her expressions varied from congenial to flashes of irritation that didn't seem directed at him. She was obviously distracted, which explained why she hadn't used but a fraction of the one-hour consultation she'd scheduled.

Then his eyes fell on the hat on the floor. It must have fallen when she hurried to stand and don her coat.

He picked it up, walked to the elevator, and took it to the ground floor. Gaze scanning the tiny lobby, he didn't see her. Well, he could give it to her when she came back to sign the papers.

From the stairwell, he heard Michelle's voice. She pushed through the door and startled at Connor's appearance. When she looked up at him, there was that smile again. Confident and genuine.

"Ms. Barcella, you forgot your hat." He extended it to her.

"Thanks. And please, call me Michelle." She took the hat, their fingers brushing for only a moment.

"Michelle," he said dryly, taking a step back, because the proximity and touch did something strange to his body. "Who were you talking to?"

Her smile widened, eyes sparkling. "One of the eccentricities of being an only child and an artist is talking to yourself."

He suddenly felt foolish, rushing after her to return her hat with nothing else to say. "I noticed you didn't take the elevator. You don't like elevators?"

She chuckled. "I was trapped inside an elevator once with a wailing banshee for twenty-three minutes. Never again."

Connor pictured a hysterical woman's claustrophobic anxiety clashing with Michelle's calm demeanor. Still, it seemed an odd reason to avoid elevators. Surely the chances of a strange encounter like that happening twice would be rare.

"What type of art do you do?" He struggled to keep the conversation going, though couldn't say why he wasn't ready to let her leave.

"Acrylic mostly, but I like to sketch with charcoal."

"Wow. And the paintings—are they portraits or landscapes or abstract?"

"Mostly landscapes but I'm adding abstract. I like to recreate the landscape of places I've traveled. However, I haven't traveled much and certainly haven't flown since my parents' death, so I've done less landscaping lately."

"Understandable." Loss of a loved one in a plane crash seemed a plausible way to develop a fear of flying. "Do you have a gallery or display in town?"

"Not yet. Putting your artwork on display is a bit like baring your soul. I'm not ready for that type of exposure."

Connor shifted his weight. "Well, I don't have a critical eye, and I enjoy most art, so I can offer encouraging appraisal with the absence of judgment."

"Are you asking for a private viewing?"

"Um. No. Well, I don't know." He'd been attempting friendly conversation, but he had no idea what a private viewing involved. It sounded far too intimate.

Michelle did that thing again where she glanced to one side as though an irritating fly buzzed nearby.

"Thanks for the hat." She fitted it back over impossibly long strands of dark, silky hair before walking out of the building.

Connor stood there feeling like a fool. He was trying to be friendly, but the interaction had dissolved into … something. Or had it escalated to something? He wasn't sure.

Probably best he just let that one go. The few dates he'd had since

Penny's death often deteriorated into him talking about his wife and the other women talking about their ex-husbands or ex-boyfriends. Younger women were disappointed by his robust work ethic that didn't include weekend parties, and the older ones were embarking on new or second careers post-divorce and didn't have time for the activities he enjoyed.

With his hands in his pockets, he took the elevator back up to his office. Work was his comfort zone, and wilderness hiking was his passion. Neither required an abundance of interpersonal relationship skills.

"Michelle," he murmured, unsettled and intrigued. "Who are you?"

CHAPTER 2

Michelle walked back to her brownstone, wishing the sounds of street traffic would drown out Penny's relentless questions.

"Do you like him? Because he definitely liked you. And don't pretend you didn't notice—your smile gave you away. Were you intentionally try to intimidate him with the private viewing invitation?"

Michelle jammed her ear pods into her ears more forcefully than necessary and held her phone in one hand.

"Well, that's just rude," Penny said. "We were having a conversation."

"We *are* having a conversation. The ear pods are so I don't look like I'm talking to myself. As for the private viewing—that's not licentious. It's a term for someone getting a personal view of an artist's work."

"You flustered him." Penny hesitated. "Well, maybe that's good for him. He needs to break out of his shell. All he does is work, work, work—Monday through Friday. Then, he hikes alone on the weekends."

"Sounds like a responsible adult."

"He needs social interaction."

"So, go find a guy to pester into being his buddy."

"You're the first person who's been able to see me as a ghost. I am *not* letting go of you."

"Swell," Michelle complained.

"Just get to know him," Penny pleaded. "He's a likable guy. Oh! And he cooks. He does this chicken and brie dish that's to die for."

"Oh, yeah? Well, I can make mac n' cheese."

"You do? Gourmet? I had gourmet mac n' cheese once made with gouda. It was soooo good."

"Not gourmet. Add water and cheese powder and mix."

"Ugh. Gross. But that just means the two of you will be a good fit. He cooks, you don't. You're artistic, he's not. You're confident in your social skills, he's introverted. Yin and yang."

Michelle climbed the stairs to her brownstone and punched the key code. "Penny, you seem very nice, and I'm sorry for your loss and Connor's. I truly am only in need of an accountant, and I'm not letting the wife-ghost of a man set me up with her husband."

"I'm not giving up." Penny floated closer.

Michelle stepped back over her threshold.

Penny involuntarily stopped in her tracks. "What the—?"

Mo, an oversized tabby, wound his way between Michelle's ankles, meowing and welcoming her home.

"Cats keep spirits away," Michelle explained. She learned that pleasant tidbit from Egyptian folklore.

Penny pouted, "That's not fair."

"It's how I keep my sanity. You're not the first ghost to follow me home. You won't be the last. Goodbye, Penny." The moment the door clicked shut, relief washed over her—followed immediately by guilt thick enough to taste.

As she fed Larry, Curly, and Mo, she shook off the feelings of remorse. She couldn't help all ghosts, and she'd learned to draw boundaries. She needed her personal space. She certainly couldn't be a fill-in bride just because Penny didn't want her husband to be lonely anymore.

Michelle stripped off her day clothes and donned her painting overalls and slippers. After tucking away her hair under a hat, she stepped into her artist's room where a dozen works in progress surrounded her. She turned her attention to the forest at sunset—barren black trees stretching to the sky against a backdrop of vibrant pinks, purples, and oranges. Today, she'd finish this painting. Maybe tonight she'd get Chinese takeout from Double Dragon and watch Sherlock Holmes as she ate in peace, alone.

PENNY WATCHED Connor's usual routine—office work until after dark, takeout pad thai, unwind watching old MASH episodes, and then off to bed. In the morning, he'd be up at five am for his weightlifting and treadmill routing.

She ached for him, wanting him to have greater fulfillment.

As Connor slept, Penny rewound the encounter with Michelle over and over in her mind. Had Penny pushed too hard or not hard enough? She wasn't sure, but she wasn't giving up. Michelle wouldn't stay inside her house forever, and when she did venture out, there'd be no cats to keep Penny away.

Before she could ponder whether her plans to be persistent made her some type of paranormal stalker, she felt herself being pulled into cold darkness. Icy tentacles snaked around her so tight and cold, it hurt. She found herself on a hard, icy surface, pulling her body into her clothes like a turtle into its shell, trying to preserve warmth. Where was she?

No. Not her. She peered at her hands and clothing, barely visible in the blanket of night and gray clouds. She was in Connor's body. But where was he?

Not in his bed where she'd left him. Hiking clothes. On a mountain then. Freezing, dehydrated, and trapped.

And how far in the future was this terrible event?

CONNOR SAT OUTSIDE on his friend Jeff's back porch with his feet propped up near the small propane fire pit as he watched the dancing flames. "I felt like a buffoon. I took your advice and tried to engage with a beautiful woman in conversation, and it fell flat."

Except, Michelle had smiled—something warm but a hint of mischievousness, the way a woman does when she knows a secret you don't.

Jeff adjusted the volume on the baby monitor. He rolled a small bag of frozen breastmilk between his hands to help it thaw. "You're out of practice a little, but it couldn't have been *that* bad."

"Flaming disaster," Connor bemoaned as he raised his glass of gin and tonic and sipped.

"The more you practice, the better you'll get. If a woman is put off because you're flustered as a result of being a little rusty, then she's not the one for you anyway. What'd she look like?"

"Soft, slightly tan skin, curves in all the right places. Long, chocolate-brown hair. Like, *really* long brown hair. She was all around classy. But she's an artist, and I could totally envision her wearing a white smock and covered from head to toe in colorful splashes of paint."

"Nice imagery."

"Smart too. She already had a half-dozen different ideas for savvy financial investment."

"Wait. What? Did you ask out a client?"

Connor bristled. "I certainly did not. All I tried to do was strike up friendly conversation."

"Right. But if that had been well received, was your next action going to be asking the client out?"

"I hadn't actually thought that far ahead. But I don't go out to bars, so when you told me to strike up conversations with a woman, I wasn't sure what other situation to do that in."

Jeff scratched the back of his head as he considered Connor's dilemma. "Well, it's not exactly like I can take you out and be your wing man." He gestured at the baby monitor. "Oh, by the way, Katrina does have about three different women she's interested in setting you up with."

Connor choked on his next sip of gin and tonic. "I'm not sure about that. I'm trying to get better at simple conversation. I'm not sure I'm ready for another blind date."

A small, whimpering cry crackled through the baby monitor.

Jeff pushed up from his seat. "Well, that's the end of that. Gotta go, Daddy duty calls."

Connor followed Jeff inside his friend's house. Katrina worked as a nurse three nights a week, which put Jeff on dad duty. Connor knew Jeff liked the solo time with his kids.

Jeff poured the thawed milk to a warm bottle and shook it.

"Daddy, I had a nightmare."

Both men turned to see Jeff's oldest child clutching a teddy bear and standing at the bottom of the stairs. Connor saw Jeff's dilemma—comfort the four-year-old or feed a crying baby.

Connor set his drink on the counter. "You take care of the baby. I'll chase away the nightmares."

"You sure?"

"Yeah. It'll be fun."

"Thanks, man."

MICHELLE SAT at her kitchen table eating a bowl of granola and yogurt as she skimmed through the news on her laptop. Her email beeped in announcement of an incoming message.

Connor notified her that the papers were ready to be signed.

"He's up early." She took her computer to the couch where Mo leapt into her lap to compete for her attention.

She pet the cat with one hand as she pecked out a response with the other. "What do you think, Mo? I say we just have him send it via courier at my expense and we'll skip seeing Connor's ghost. Maybe if we stay here another day, Penny will forget all about me."

Mo purred, which was clearly an indication of agreement. Michelle continued petting and typing.

SEND.

She had plenty to keep her occupied at home—her artwork, the cats, her endless internet search for a gallery in the perfect location. She would search, find a half-dozen worthy places for rent and then pick them apart for some minute flaws, all the while knowing that her true reluctance was putting her creations on display. The only person holding Michelle back was Michelle herself.

Three days passed uneventfully, and by the next morning, she needed to get out of her brownstone. She walked two blocks away to a coffee shop and parked in a chair with her laptop, a bagel, and a cup of Earl Gray.

"This place is cozy." Penny appeared in the chair opposite her.

Michelle looked over her cup at the ghost with unconcealed irritation. She sipped her tea before replacing the cup on the saucer. Next, she opened her laptop and began typing.

"Well, that's rude." Penny crossed her arms.

Michelle raised her eyebrows before gesturing at her computer screen.

"Oh!" Penny hopped up. "You're doing that incognito communication thing." She came around to stand beside Michelle and read the words on the screen aloud: *"What do you want?"* Penny cocked her head to one side. "Connor needs your signature, so you need to come back to the office."

Michelle shook her head as she typed, *No. He's going to send it via courier, and I'll send it back.*

"Well that seems impersonal," Penny retorted.

Michelle typed again, *He's my Financial Advisor. We don't need personal.*

"Okay. Let me challenge you on that. Is this how you interact with all your business associates or only the ones with ghosts?"

In answer, Michelle took a bite of her bagel and began chewing.

"Right." Penny rolled her eyes. "I'm going to take that as a 'no' which means the only reason you're not being personal is because I'm scaring you away."

Michelle shrugged. Penny wasn't wrong. Michelle didn't want to be a weird third wheel.

"I'll take that as a 'yes.' Now, imagine if you'd met Connor with no wife-ghost. You might have had chemistry—"

Michelle frowned.

"—or just a friendly conversation." Penny backed down. "I'd settle for friendly conversation."

Michelle typed, *But you'll be there.*

"I don't have to be. I can give you privacy."

Like now?

Penny huffed. "You're being unreasonable."

Michelle shifted her weight in her seat and bit her lip before typing, *I don't want to hurt your feelings, but have you considered that the best thing you can do for your husband is to move on?*

Penny took a shaky breath. "I can't."

Can't or won't? Michelle sat back, drinking her tea and waiting for Penny to elaborate.

"I get these visions—dark and ominous." Penny's normally energetic tone turned eerily hushed. "Like there's danger on the periphery of Connor's life. I can't leave knowing something's out there is going to get him."

Something?

Penny sighed. "Something. I don't know what."

Michelle dipped her tea bag up and down, avoiding eye contact with the ghost. She tried to think of words of comfort. No one wanted to think of their loved one in danger, and ghosts could sometimes glimpse the future. But the suggestion of danger didn't mean harm would definitely fall on Connor. And a dark and ominous feeling could be nothing more than Connor dying of old age. What's more— if Connor was in some form of danger, Penny couldn't do anything about it.

"Do you have any more information?" Michelle asked aloud.

When one of the patrons turned to look at her, Michelle sent him a sweet smile as she slipped in her earpieces.

"Cold," Penny said with a shudder.

Michelle snapped her laptop shut and packed her belongings in her bag. She slung it over her shoulder and left the cafe.

Penny kept pace, floating beside her. "Cold and fear and pain."

"Frightening. But, Penny, it's so vague. It could be something that happens tomorrow or twenty years from now."

Penny fidgeted with the fringe on the sleeve of her pink sweater. "You're right."

"Unless you know more, it's probably not something either one of us can change."

Death was inevitable. Michelle knew this fact all too well. Of the top three causes, some could be delayed and some couldn't. Heart disease could be sudden or slow. Cancer, number two, was often an extended process. And number three, the one Michelle was most familiar with, was more abrupt and shocking—unintentional, unexpected accidents with life-threatening consequences. While motor vehicle crashes topped the leading cause of death from trauma, Michelle's loss had come from a plane crash. One minute her parents were alive—riding a single engine plane to Martha's Vineyard. The next minute they were gone forever.

"Are you okay?" Penny asked.

Michelle stopped on the sidewalk outside the entrance to the Sunset Park. "I can't help Connor, Penny. I don't have the power to prevent death or injury. If I did, my parents wouldn't have died in a plane crash a year ago. I'm still putting my own life back together."

"I'm not asking you to be his savior. Just be his friend."

Michelle was certain Penny wouldn't settle for the relationship remaining a friendship. She would pester and persist rather than do what she needed to do, which was move on from lingering as a spirit.

Disinclined to agree to Penny's wishes, Michelle opted for another tactic. Maybe she could help her move on another way.

"Tell me about your life." Michelle turned right and began a long walk through the serene park trails.

Penny's smile faltered. "Where should I start? The day I died...or the day Connor will if you don't help him?"

CHAPTER 3

Sunrise yoga invigorated Michelle. When the weather was warmer, she'd be able to go out on the back porch. For now, she sat near a window and faced the golden sun rays. She finished the routine with deep breathing as Larry and Mo tumbled through the room chasing a ball stuffed with bells and cotton.

She followed yoga with a trip to her art room to work on last week's landscape painting. It had three overgrown pheasants looking back at a red-tailed hawk perched on a tree limb at the edge of a forest. With a chill, Michelle realized the hawk symbolized one gifted in helping others emotionally. She backed away from her painting.

After deciding she'd lost her creative rhythm for the day, she showered and dressed—boots, jeans, sweater, and her favorite coat and cap. She ventured back out to the cafe.

"Connor has questions," Penny appeared beside her.

Michelle didn't slow her walking. Despite a long conversation with Penny the other day, she was still lurking in the world of the living. Unfortunately, the more time she spent with Penny, the more she enjoyed her company. However, she didn't want to be roped into seeing Connor.

"He can ask me via email," Michelle said.

"And he needs your signature."

"Again? I just told him to send it via courier."

"He never got the email."

Michelle stopped and turned to stare at Penny. "And why is that?"

"I might have disrupted Connor's email inbox after you sent it."

Michelle frowned. "So you've discovered your ability to malfunction electrical equipment."

"Is that a normal ghost thing?" Penny asked as though discovering a superpower.

"There's nothing normal about ghosts, but yes, most can screw up electronics at will. Really powerful ones can cause a breeze or move objects."

"Spooky."

Michelle resumed walking.

"Where are you going?" Penny asked, following closely.

"Apparently I'm going to my financial advisor's office to sign papers and answer emails." Since only Michelle could interact with Penny, the ghost couldn't pester Connor into initiating a relationship the way she did Michelle. As long as Penny could only access one person in this relationship she wanted to forge, Michelle only needed to remain professional to avoid entanglement.

"It's almost lunch time," Penny said.

"Is it?" Michelle continued her brisk pace.

"There's a sandwich place close to his office."

"I'm not hungry."

"Connor is."

Michelle stopped and stared at Penny. "What's next? You want me to pick up his dry cleaning on my way?"

Penny chuckled in a don't-be-ridiculous manner. "Oh, no. But he is almost out of black ink on his printer cartridge and the chain general store on the corner carries his brand."

Michelle blinked at her. "Unbelievable."

~

CONNOR POURED his second cup of coffee for the day. He finished rebalancing two investment portfolios, opened a Roth IRA, and added to a client's college fund. Next, he had a pro-bono tax project for a nonprofit leukemia charity foundation. The work was a tribute to Penny.

By the time he finished the taxes, it would be about time to break for lunch. That would be followed by a meeting with the CEO of Schulster and Morgan Law Firm. If the meeting went well, they would put him in charge of their employees' retirement fund accounts.

Connor's mobile phone rang. "Hi, Jeff."

"Hey, you got plans tonight?"

"No." Connor was up for 'guys' night'. If Katrina was working, he'd help Jeff with the kids. If she was off work, maybe they could shoot pool at the bar near Connor's apartment.

The long hesitation before Jeff spoke gave Connor pause.

"Katrina's got a blind date for you." Jeff rushed to add, "she's real sweet and works with Katrina. I told Katrina you didn't want her setting you up, but she's on a mission. Just try this once more, and she promises that'll be the end of it."

Connor leaned forward and rested his forehead on the edge of his desk and staring down at his shoes. That wouldn't be the end of it. The last nurse Katrina had set him up with had spent the entire evening comparing Penny's illness to her old patients. She'd meant well, but he'd gone home feeling like a case report, not a person.

"Connor?"

"Yeah, okay. Text me the time and place."

No. Why didn't I just say 'no'?

"Thanks, man. You won't regret it."

"Famous last words."

"It won't be as bad as last time."

"Sure."

"Okay. See you then." Jeff clicked off.

Connor set his phone down, but didn't lift his forehead from his desk. His mind raced with schemes on how to un-commit to tonight's blind date—late work, financial crisis, hit by a bus. Jeff wouldn't let him off the hook for any of those things.

Connor closed his eyes and imagined for a moment he was hiking the Great Smoky Mountains. He could almost smell the fresh air and feel the mountain breeze. Zero electronic devices and no connection to the bustle of everyday life. Man and nature. Maybe he could do a small rejuvenating day hike this Saturday.

He needed to keep building endurance for his upcoming trip to Superior Hiking Trail.

After standing, he stretched and grabbed his tie off the coat rack. He worked it under his collar before smoothing it down.

A knock sounded at his office door. He wasn't expecting company, but walk-in clients were always welcome. When he opened the door, he was surprised to see Michelle standing before him. Her face was framed in long, dark hair, and she wore the same tan coat and gray hat.

"Ms. Barcella, this is a pleasant surprise."

"Michelle. And I understand you wanted to review some things. If now isn't a good time, I can come back—or just email."

"No, no. Now is good. Please, come inside." He stepped aside and motioned for her to enter, noticing the brown bag she carried and recognizing the logo of his favorite sandwich shop. His stomach responded with an eager growl.

"I brought lunch. By the sound of it, perhaps we should eat first."

Connor took the bag, set it aside, and helped her out of her coat. He hung it on a rack near the door. "Actually, this will only take a few minutes. If we get business out of the way first, we can better enjoy lunch."

"Okay. Business first."

MERCIFULLY, Michelle was able to focus on Connor's explanation of each financial document she signed as Penny kept quiet by the window. She'd worried Penny would distract her, but she was surprised to find her own thoughts disrupting her concentration.

Along with discussions of diversifying her portfolio, Michelle caught herself noticing the richness of Connor's dark eyes and long length of his eyelashes. Was his hair as thick as it looked?

She glanced at Penny who silently observed the two of them at Connor's desk. Scheming little trickster. But Michelle couldn't really be upset at Penny wanting companionship for someone she cared about, even though she was misguided in thinking Michelle was that companion.

Connor moved his mouse and clicked it several times. "I'll print a copy off for your records."

"Right. Printer." She stood, walked to her coat, and dug in her pocket. "I bought this for you."

Connor accepted the ink cartridge with a puzzled look. "You bought me ink? And you got the exact cartridge matching my printer?" He walked over to where her documents were printing and looked at the faded image. "You're giving this to me just as I ran out of ink?"

"Call it women's intuition." Dang. She should have considered the ramifications of buying him an ink cartridge. "Lunch?"

"Lunch," Connor agreed with a skeptical tone.

Finally, the financial planning ended, and they were reaching for sandwiches. Michelle could focus on eating instead of Connor. As she unrolled the paper around the sandwich, she tried to remember what she'd ordered. Two of the same. She'd distractedly rattled off whatever Penny had recommended while in a hurry to get the food, get the ink, and get the meeting over with.

Connor inspected his sandwich. "You got me a Philly cheese steak, no onions, extra peppers."

Michelle looked at her own sandwich. So she did. "Is that a bad thing?"

"It's my favorite sandwich."

Michelle shot Penny a look. "Imagine that." The petite woman shrugged as if innocent.

Biting into her sandwich, she tasted the savory meat, provolone cheese, and burst of sweet peppers. "That's pretty good."

"You've never eaten from this place before?"

"Nope."

"But how did you—?"

"A friend recommended the place and the Philly. It's not that strange. Don't make it a thing."

"But no onions?"

Michelle shrugged. "Who wants onions in the middle of the day? You might have clients. You might have a hot date later. Who knows?"

Penny laughed.

Michelle felt her cheeks flush. Those words sounded all wrong spoken aloud.

Connor swallowed the bite he'd taken. "No hot date, although my friend has set me up with a blind date."

"Oh?"

Hope springs eternal.

Penny broke in, "Ugh. It's not going to go well. She's going to ask about me and then launch into a tirade about her ex."

Connor continued, "Apparently, according to my best friend and his wife, the world is going to pass me by if I don't start dating again." He took a bite of his sandwich.

"You need to set your own pace."

Swallowing, he smiled. "Right? That's what I try to tell them."

And that's what I try to tell your wife.

Connor's phone buzzed. "That's Jeff right now giving me the where and when."

"Can you politely decline?"

"Jeff is tenacious, only slightly less so than his match-making wife. They'd only let me off the hook if I had a better offer."

For several moments, only the sound of their chewing filled the room. Michelle didn't dare look at Penny. The ghost was most certainly staring her down, silently willing her to make Connor a better offer. When at last Michelle glanced in her direction, the expression was unmistakable—don't let Connor go to dinner and suffer through a woman talking about her ex.

Michelle roughly set her half-eaten sandwich down on the wrapper. "Fine."

Connor startled. "Fine?"

Michelle's words had been directed at Penny, but he didn't know that.

"Private artwork viewing. My place. Six PM." She snatched pen and paper and wrote down her address.

"No, you misunderstand. I was making conversation not fishing for—"

"I know. But I'm giving you a better offer. Take it or leave it."

Connor stood. "I'll take it."

"You can think about it first." She walked toward her coat, but he beat her to it and held it out for her.

"Do you always rush out of people's offices?"

"Only when they're haunted," she said under her breath.

"Haunted?" he asked.

"Never mind." She turned, and he helped her into her coat.

When she turned back around, he did that thing again where he didn't step back. She thought about that thick hair and what it would feel like between her fingers. As her arms moved up of their own volition, she diverted them to his tie. She straightened it and snugged it tighter before smoothing his shirt, her hands lingering slightly longer than necessary.

She took two steps back before looking into his eyes to see a mixture of heat and confusion.

"You can think about it first," she repeated.

"I'll be there. I'm excited to see your work."

His sincere tone gave her a little thrill, followed by worry. She hadn't shown her recent work to anyone.

Hesitantly, he mimicked her and straightened the collar of her coat. Her mouth went dry at the accidental brush of his hand along her jaw line.

"Thank you for lunch." He hesitated as his brow slightly furrowed. "And ... the printer cartridge."

His words reminded her that Penny was watching. The ghost kept her distance and kept quiet, but Michelle could feel her intense stare.

She reached the stairwell, pushed the door open, and stepped inside. She leaned against the wall, waiting for her thudding heart to subside.

Penny rubbed at her earlobe. "You're upset with me?"

Michelle pulled off her hat and raked fingers through her hair. "You've got me all discombobulated. I feel like I know him because you've told me about him, but we aren't actually even connected on a friendship level. Meanwhile, I'm adjusting his tie like I know him—like I have a right to touch him. He must think I'm crazy. Of course, I talk to ghosts, so maybe I am. I really am." Michelle started down the stairs.

"He wasn't looking at you like he thought you were crazy."

"And you," Michelle whirled pointing a finger at the spirit, "having me bring his favorite sandwich. What are you playing at?"

Penny crossed her arms. "I haven't disguised my intentions."

Michelle resumed her descent, slower now. "I invited him to my house. And at dinnertime. I am not cooking him dinner—that's the wrong message."

"What message?"

"I invited him over to spare him an awkward evening, not to seduce him."

Penny chortled.

"That's funny?" Michelle reached the last stair and slipped in her ear pods before opening the door.

"You are so far removed from anything close to seducing him. You could cook a three course meal, and Connor wouldn't mistake that for seducing him based on the rest of your behavior."

"My behavior? You mean the part where I stared into his eyes."

"That's attraction, not seduction."

"Ah, hah." Michelle wagged a finger at Penny. "But is the attraction real, or am I attracted to him because you instigated this?" Michelle turned and walked quickly down the street.

With crossed arms, Penny glided beside her. "I instigated nothing.

I merely made suggestions. You're both single. And I think your different personalities complement each other. You're artistic and introspective. Connor is conservative and constrained."

"Yes, but we're supposed to discover that together not through someone else."

Penny shrugged. "I'm like a dating app. People use them all the time to find compatibility. Besides, tonight, you're going to be in your cat infested house, so there'll be no prying Penny to blame for anything."

Michelle considered this carefully. Penny pried, but her presence also meant that Michelle would keep her own actions in check. What if Penny wasn't there, and Michelle didn't stop at fixing his tie? Then, she could hardly blame her attraction on Penny's meddling.

Art. Connor was coming over to look at her paintings, nothing more. Michelle would talk about artwork and keep her hands to herself.

"I need to figure out dinner."

"Do you like Indian? There's this great Indian restaurant—Tikka Indian Grill on Fifth Avenue. You can send for take-out. The tikka masala is to die for."

Art. Connor was coming over to look at her paintings, nothing more. Michelle would talk about art and keep her hands to herself.

CHAPTER 4

Connor stood in his office staring at the door after Michelle left. He felt pleasantly bamboozled and tried to shake off the butterflies that danced in his stomach at the prospect of a date. Was it a date? It was a private viewing of her art collection, which could be entirely platonic. Connor decided that he didn't care. It would be quality time spent with a beautiful and delightfully perplexing woman.

He picked his phone up off his desk and texted Jeff, *I have a better offer for tonight.*

Jeff's reply was almost instantaneous, *It had better be a woman.*

Her name is Michelle.

That's all I get?

Connor chuckled as he typed in Michelle's work web address. Her website not only had her portfolio of artwork, but also her picture. Connor had pursued the website after he'd met Michelle the first time and found an ABOUT THE AUTHOR page with a picture of her posed on a rock with a background of spruce trees. Since she looked to be trail hiking, Connor had instantly liked the picture. He sent the link to Jeff.

Several minutes later, Jeff's reply came, *Wow. She's a looker. Artists can be eccentric, you know?*

And that she was, Connor thought.

But he also realized the comparison Jeff was making. Penny had been sweet and as mild-mannered and conservative as Connor. The two women were quite in contrast. Yet they were both kind, and a kind heart was the most appealing trait in Connor's mind.

Jeff texted again, *I expect the full details this weekend.*

Connor rolled his eyes even though Jeff couldn't see the motion. *It's only an informal viewing of her artwork.*

Something better, Connor thought with a smile.

DETAILS, Jeff replied back.

Connor set down the phone. He needed to get back to work and prepare for his afternoon meeting. He re-wrapped their half-eaten sandwiches, placed them back in the bag, and sat down at his desk.

Promptly at six, Connor rang the doorbell of her brownstone.

After the sound of light footfalls, Michelle opened the door dressed in baggy, worn and torn blue jeans and a teal T-shirt with ART IS LIFE smeared in bright, bold letters. Her hair was back in a messy braid. He felt more confident in his selection of khakis and sleeves rolled on his blue button-down shirt. No tie—though he wouldn't have minded her straightening it again.

"You're on time." Her voice was slightly breathless.

"You aren't ready yet. Sorry."

She waved a hand. "No, it's fine. This way I don't have to stand in front of the closet for an hour trying to decide what to wear."

Connor wondered if clothing selection usually took Michelle an hour or only would have in this instance because she considered it a special event.

At her motions, he followed her inside her home. The moment he entered, he took in the cozy charm of her brownstone—sunlit hardwood floors, shelves crowded with art books and plants, and a faint scent of paint mingling with lavender. It felt like a place someone truly lived, not just slept.

"I invited a guest without first considering that I haven't had a guest over since … well, since I moved in. Cleaning was in order."

"You didn't have to clean on my account."

"Oh, yes, I did. I've seen your tidy office."

"Clients come to my office. It has to be tidy."

"Uh, huh." She walked to the kitchen where she had two glasses beside a cutting board with cucumber slices. "I dare you to look me in the eye and tell me your place isn't just as tidy."

He looked into those golden-flaked hazel eyes. "I'm tidy," he confessed with a wry grin. "But the only reason you'd feel the need to clean is if you wanted to impress me."

She poured simple syrup and gin in a stainless steel container before shaking them together in ice. "Of course I want to impress you. You're about to judge my art."

Two cats bolted through the kitchen. A light gray one ran and skidded around the corner while a dark gray one stopped at Connor's legs and brushed forcefully against them, demanding attention. He bent down to caress the soft fur.

"I should've warned you in case you're allergic."

"I'm not," he said.

"That's Mo. The other is Larry. And Curly is a calico, but he's shy so you may or may not see him tonight."

"You've got a lot of cats."

She dropped a cucumber on the rim of each glass before handing his to him. "They keep spirits away."

He took his drink and waited for her to elaborate.

Instead, she raised her glass to his. "What are we toasting to?"

"I'm an accountant. We have lame toasts like to a fiscally responsible year."

She clinked her glass to his. "Practical. Not lame."

They both drank. Connor tasted the refreshing cocktail. Cucumber gimlet. What were the odds she'd prepare one of his top three favorite mixed drinks?

"Your turn. What do you want to toast to?"

"World peace. Smaller carbon footprints. New friendships."

They tipped glasses again, but Connor drank distractedly. Friendship. Was that a good sign she considered them friends and they could building on the friendship from there? Or was she drawing a line in the sand—we can be friends and nothing more?

"Shall we look at the art?" he asked.

She took another drink and set it down on the kitchen counter. "Nope. Rule of showing is you feed first. That way your viewers are in the right frame of mind for enjoying your art." She looked into her glass as she spoke and knocked the cucumber into the ice and alcohol. She had long, slender fingers with neatly trimmed, bare nails.

Artist's hands, Connor decided.

"You're worried I won't like your art?" He took a step closer and set his drink on the counter.

She straightened and looked into his eyes. "You're the first to see most of these in person."

"But you'll have your own gallery soon."

"I'm still looking. I've been looking for six months."

"Haven't found the right space, or are you afraid of showing your art?"

"Showing your art is baring part of your soul." A lovely flush spread up her neck and into her cheeks.

Connor had the sudden, ridiculous urge to promise he'd be careful with whatever part of her soul she showed him. "I'm sure they're beautiful. The ones I saw on your website are breathtaking."

"You checked out my website? Taking a sneak peek?"

He grinned, enjoying the proximity to her and his own brazen boldness to stand close. He was in no rush to do anything other than enjoy her company, but something in the sparkle in her eye had him wondering if a kiss could be worked into tonight's agenda.

The doorbell rang, breaking the spell of the moment.

"Dinner," Michelle announced.

She left and returned from the front door with a sack of food and began to unload it.

"You've gone all out. Can I help with anything?" he asked

"All out would have been me cooking. But I wanted you to have an enjoyable time which does not include eating something I attempted to cook. You can carry them to the table and dish out servings."

He did so, smelling the flavorful tikka masala, cumin, and garlic naan. When he'd fixed the plates, he returned to the kitchen and inspected the bag. "I love this place."

"You do?" her voice sounded alarmed. She gave a calculating scowl at the bag with the restaurant logo. "Of course you do."

He couldn't gauge her. She'd ordered his favorite sub and favorite Indian, but appeared to have neither conspired to do so nor taken pleasure in the serendipity of it.

Puzzling. But he'd be more troubled if she'd somehow researched and schemed to woo him on the premise that the way into a man's heart was through his stomach.

He reflexively glanced at his ring finger. Penny had always advocated that mantra. But it had been her peppy personality and adoring glances which had stolen his heart.

"Are you okay?" Michelle stood before him, handing his drink to him so they could sit and start dinner.

"Yes, sorry." He took the drink.

Michelle shifted her weight. "I'll make you a deal. You don't apologize for anything about dinner with a woman that makes you think about your wife, and I won't apologize if I tear-up showing you artwork that my parents will never see."

Connor reached up and stroked a thumb along Michelle's jaw. "I accept."

A ball of fur leapt into Connor's chair.

"Larry! Get down." Michelle shooed the cat away.

Connor smiled. "Are you ready to eat dinner?"

"Dinner."

MICHELLE RELAXED into a comfortable dinner with conversation. They talked about how Connor became a CPA and how she developed a love of art. They briefly touched on the loss in their lives—her parents in a plane crash with Michelle's new fear of flying and Penny's short battle with leukemia.

The conversation moved from there to favorites—food, drink, entertainment, and hobbies. They liked similar things, though their favorites varied. She liked painting nature, and he enjoyed hiking in it.

Tonight felt so good, conversing with a handsome man genuinely interested in who she was as a person. He had a deep, warm smile that lit up his brown eyes.

Their differences seemed like opportunities to try new things rather than barriers to a relationship. As they talked, they cleared the table, followed by entering her art studio.

Michelle watched Connor taking in the wall-to-wall paintings in various stages of incompleteness. Another wall contained a rack of completed works.

She took him through the scenes one-by-one—ocean views at different times: sunrise, day, evening in a storm; horses running on a beach; a lighthouse; forests during all four seasons: lush to barren, autumn leaves to fallen snow. Connor had something nice to say about each one of them.

"That one." Connor pointed.

Michelle looked at the forest with a hiking trail leading through it. She'd drawn a mixture of spruce, aspen, and oak.

"The way you capture the light streaming through the trails. It looks magical."

"I'm glad you like it."

"I love it. How much?"

She blinked at him.

"This is my private viewing, right? Don't I get to purchase one?"

"No."

"No?"

She swatted a hand playfully at his shoulder with a laugh. "No, because you had three cucumber gimlets and no one needs to spend a thousand dollars on an alcohol-induced impulse buy."

"I had three drinks over the course of three hours. I assure you, it's metabolized enough it's not affecting my judgment."

"The other reason is that I don't want you to purchase my painting as a way to buy my affection."

Connor frowned. "I suppose we don't know each other well enough for you to know I'd never do that. But I think I already have some of your affection, and so far, you've bought me lunch and dinner." He grinned and tapped his chin as he gazed up to the ceiling. "In fact, I could claim you've been trying to buy my affections."

"I would never!"

Connor laughed, picked her up, and spun her in a circle. Just as unexpectedly, he set her back down again as if he'd surprised himself too, and turned to the next painting a beat too briskly

She smoothed her shirt. "That's Old Faithful. Yellowstone was the last trip I took with my parents."

"Amazing colors."

"Thermophilic bacteria. I learned they make the rich greens and blues."

Connor turned toward her. "Would you like to take a hike with me Saturday? It would mean spending a half day at Dater Mountain. I'd call it leisurely, but I need to do it with my full pack on as part of my training for a week long trek in Minnesota, but it'd be leisurely for you."

A flicker of unease skated down Michelle's spine—uninvited and irrational. Cold, Penny had said, and pain. She pushed the thought aside. This was a pleasant evening, not a premonition.

She considered his offer. In the confines of her home, Penny couldn't enter, but on a hiking trail, she'd be watching them. Michelle tried to take the ghost out of the equation. If Penny weren't lurking, would she want to take a hike with Connor?

"Yes."

"Yes?" He gave her a skeptical look. "That took a lot of contemplation and evidence of internal debate on your part. I was starting to wonder if we'd had that brief connection a moment ago or if I'd imagined it."

"Yes, I want to go hiking. And yes, we had a moment. I usually weigh the pros and cons before any decision. I don't agree to anything on a whim. My hesitation is a personality trait and shouldn't be mistaken for reluctance."

"Nothing on a whim?" he asked.

She hooked her arm through his. "If you're looking for an artist with spontaneity, I'm not it. I like creativity and I like activity. I'm a woman in motion, but my actions are by design."

"I don't have a preconceived notion of what I want in a woman. If I had to pick three characteristics, I'd say kind, honest, and true to herself. Although standing in this room, I'm tempted to add artistic to the list. These truly are spectacular."

"See, food and alcohol first. Works every time."

"No, I'm serious. You need to get that gallery open. People need to see these."

His sincere declaration stroked her ego. She had become accustomed to getting critiques on her art from teachers during her college days so she'd naturally braced herself for the same harsh reviews from everyone else. Tonight, she dared to think maybe her creations were worth a public display.

Tonight, she dared to think maybe her creations—and her heart—were worth a public display.

CHAPTER 5

Michelle sat on a bench at Sunset Park, still replaying events from last night—conversation that seldom lagged and Connor's raptured interest in her.

"You're glowing." Penny appeared and glided beside her.

"I knew you wouldn't stay away long."

"How could I? Connor has a spring in his step, and you're grinning like a schoolgirl. The evening went well?"

"A lady never kisses and tells."

Penny clasped her hands together. "You kissed?"

"No. I think we were close just as he was leaving, but Curly decided to streak through the living room and barreled into Connor's leg."

Penny scowled. "I liked cats when I was alive, but as a spirit, I think I despise them."

Michelle chuckled.

"Still," Penny continued, "there was romance in the air?"

"Yes. And my looming secret."

"What secret?"

"You!"

"Connor doesn't need to know you talk to me."

"Eventually, he needs to know I talk to spirits," Michelle said. Even voicing it made her stomach tighten. Telling someone always risked losing them.

Penny waved a dismissive hand. "Sure. Eventually. You haven't even kissed yet. Supernatural revelations come *way* later in the relationship."

"Do they now?" Michelle wanted to ask Penny when she became an expert in all things paranormal.

"Yeah, they do. Everybody has their little crazy side. We all have those strange behaviors or beliefs we keep under cover until we're ready to reveal them to people close to us—even then, we usually start in small doses. You're being cautious—not manipulative—by not telling Connor yet."

"Oh, yeah? What's your crazy?" Michelle cocked her head to one side.

"I couldn't hold my alcohol. More than a half a glass and I had no inhibition. I didn't even dare drink during the first six months Connor and I dated."

"And then?"

"And then we went to this big Christmas party—friends and clients of the firm he used to work for. I got tipsy and started doing the *Riverdance* on the dance floor."

"*Riverdance?*"

"You know the Irish dance and music show."

Michelle shook her head. "Nope. Never heard of it."

"Really?"

She moved her head slowly from side to side. "You'll have to show me."

Penny straightened her spine and began kicking her legs. Michelle tried to picture her doing such a lively dance in a room full of conservative people.

Michelle pursed her lips together until she couldn't contain her amusement any longer, and laugher burst forth.

The ghost swatted a hand at Michelle. "You big jerk! You knew what I was talking about."

"I did. I just wanted to see if you'd dance."

"Well, now you've seen it."

"So, what did Connor do at the party?"

"He very sweetly—and with crimson cheeks—escorted me off the dance floor."

Michelle enjoyed the story and understood the point Penny was trying to make. Yet, she doubted quirky dance moves were as damaging to a relationship as claiming to see ghosts would be. In fact, she could see Penny's inebriated liveliness endearing her to Connor rather than serving as a deterrent.

MICHELLE WALKED beside Connor as they hiked Dater Mountain in mid-afternoon.

"This is beautiful."

Connor adjusted his heavy-appearing pack. He looked like he was taking a week-long hike instead of a three hour trek. She only had her small messenger bag over her shoulder with water and her sketchpad.

"Yes. You should see the place blossoming in the spring and compare it to the vibrant fall changes. The beech, oak, and aspen are breathtaking those times of years."

"You said you're training for Minnesota?"

He nodded. "I'm doing part of the Superior Hiking Trail. It runs along Lake Superior. It's going to be fantastic. I also want to trek more of the Appalachian trail and out west to the Rocky Mountains— Mount Elbert is the highest peak in Colorado. Forget the nightlife of Vegas, I want to go there to hike Zion National Park."

"Such an adventurer."

"You could go with me." He wore an expression that said he'd surprised himself with the offer.

Way too soon, she thought.

"I appreciate the invite. I truly do. I'm not ready to fly yet. The last flight I tried, I panicked and couldn't get on the plane. I only developed this fear after my parents' death. I know it's psychological, and I've read that I need about six months of behavioral modification and then I'll be fine to fly again. I haven't taken the time to go to therapy."

They reached a rocky ledge where Connor sat on a huge, textured stone after unloading his pack. "Well, there are plenty of gorgeous trails within driving distance of New York. We can start with those."

"I'd like that."

He tugged on her pant leg. She took the cue and sat beside him, shoulder-to-shoulder.

Yes, she could envision trips like this every weekend with Connor. His smooth, easy demeanor was a constant comfort. She glanced at his profile against the blue sky. She could get used to seeing him regularly, too. But the same question plagued her now as with every early blooming relationship she'd had—how to get past the issue of her seeing ghosts with a man who, upon learning her secret, would want to have her committed to a psychiatric ward?

She'd posed that question to her mother who had assured her the right man at the right time would be a believer and supporter of her gift. So far, Michelle hadn't met anyone she felt comfortable divulging her secret to. As time passed, she doubted she ever would.

She had the sudden urge to kiss Connor—something passionate which would convey where she dared to want this relationship to go.

Instead, she pushed off the rock and pulled out her sketchpad. "Will you let me sketch you?"

"Oh, um. Okay."

"No, no. Don't move. You're perfect right there."

He froze.

"Look at the horizon, just like you were a moment ago."

She sat cross-legged, charcoal pencil in hand, and got to work. If her fears were true and this misadventure with a man and his ghost wife was short lived, at least she'd take this moment with her forever.

When she stood, he stood.

"Can I see it?" he asked.

Michelle bit her lip. "I don't know."

"Come on."

He walked to her, but she tucked the sketchpad behind her back. He wrapped both arms around her, pinning her gently and touching the notebook but not retrieving it.

He looked down at her. "Well, when we're tangled up like this, I'm not so interested in untangling to see the sketch."

She grinned. "Is that so?"

"I'd like to kiss you."

"I'm not stopping you."

When he leaned closer, she met him halfway. His warmth radiated through her as he released the pad, wrapped his arms around her, and deepened the kiss. Despite all her paranormal encounters, kissing Connor felt like the single most sublime supernatural experience she'd ever had. She was simultaneously lighter than air and grounded in his strength.

When they pulled away, he stared down at her. "Wow." He reached up and touched strands of hair over her shoulder. "I'm going to brunch at a friend's house tomorrow. Will you join me?"

"I'd like that." She would have liked to keep kissing him, too, but other hikers starting milling about the rocky ledge.

He slid his hand down and held hers. "It's a date."

CONNOR HELD JEFF'S BABY, Arthur, as Katrina and Jeff set the table.

"Is she coming?" Jeff asked.

Connor glanced at the grandfather clock in the dining room. Michelle was ten minutes late, but this was brunch, not an office meeting. He'd offered to pick her up but she'd politely declined. Perhaps she'd gotten lost, except that was hard to do in the era of global positioning satellite.

He bounced Arthur as he held a soft toy for the baby. "She's coming."

Connor's confidence stemmed from the great experience they'd had yesterday hiking and the difficulty they'd had saying goodbye outside her brownstone. He hadn't mentally prepared himself to take such an emotional plunge with this woman. He'd had to force himself down her steps to put distance between them before he took a physical plunge he wasn't anticipating.

When the doorbell rang, Katrina beat Connor to open the door.

"Hello!" Katrina declared, smile beaming. "Michelle, it's great to meet you." She ushered Michelle inside while glancing at the plastic container of store bought strawberry shortcake.

Connor admired that she was the type of guest who didn't arrive empty handed to a host's house.

Katrina took the dessert. "Thank you. I'm Katrina. My husband, Jeff, is over there. My oldest, Nancy, is drawing at the table, and Connor is entertaining our little Arthur."

"This is a lovely home." Michelle greeted Connor with a kiss on the cheek before exchanging handshakes with Jeff.

The brush of her lips sent a warm spark straight through Connor. He hoped no one noticed the way his breath hitched.

Next, she walked over to Nancy. "Oh. You're drawing a rainbow. It is very beautiful. Is that your house beneath it?"

"Uh, huh." Nancy remained focused on her coloring.

"I like drawing too. Once a month, I go to the children's hospital at Mount Sinai just so I can color with the kids there."

"You color with kids?"

"Yeah. We use crayons and charcoal and water color."

"I want to do water color."

"Well, it can be messy, so you have to get parental permission."

"What's that mean?" Nancy asked.

"Your mom has to say it's okay."

"Mom, can I do water color?"

"We can look at getting you water colors," Katrina said.

Connor watched the exchange in awe. Michelle conversed as easily with children as she did with adults, and her smile carried an instant charisma. Katrina was already looking at her with the adoring eyes of a mother appreciating kindness to her child.

"I didn't know you went to Mount Sinai." Of course, there were probably many details about her he had yet to learn.

Michelle went to the kitchen and helped Katrina pour mimosas. "I volunteer there once a month. The kids love it. We bring these big easels and paints. They leave their artwork hanging on display for a few weeks."

Jeff laid out utensils. "Connor tells us you're shopping for a gallery to rent."

"Yes. In fact, I'm meeting a rental agent this afternoon, so I'll have to leave a few minutes early."

Katrina gasped. "Oh, I hope you do a grand opening. We'd love to go. And Jeff runs a catering company if you're including that sort of thing."

"Honey, don't market to Connor's girlfriend."

"Actually, I'd love help with that. I have no cooking expertise, and it would be nice to serve hors d'oeuvres at the event. Truthfully though, I have commitment issues. This is the thirteenth gallery I've toured, and I haven't agreed to rent any of them." She softly laughed at herself.

"She's worried about public judgment," Connor said, hoping he was contributing and not overstepping.

Katrina shook her head. "Connor says your work is amazing."

"I'm not sure his opinion can be validated because I fed him delicious takeout and alcohol before his viewing."

"A strategic move on your part," Jeff said.

"Of course."

Katrina carried a plate of crepes to the table. "Connor gave your artwork glowing accolades. That's good enough for me."

As they sat and passed plates of food, the conversation continued about everyone's careers. The meal gave Connor a blissful sense of normalcy. Michelle engaged easily in conversation and had none of the initial awkward moments they'd shared in his office. Although she'd been hesitant to start a friendship with him, there was no reluctance on her part since their dinner the other night.

~

Connor helped Jeff clean up the table and wash the dishes while Katrina rocked the baby in her arms. Michelle had left to meet the realtor for the gallery tour.

"Michelle seems very nice," Jeff said.

"I really like her," Katrina added. "I think she contrasts you enough to add a little spice to your life, but you two are both gentle, amicable souls who also complement each other."

Jeff rinsed soap off a platter and handed it to Connor to dry. "I would've liked to learn more about her, but I was afraid of asking too many questions which would inevitably lead toward her having to talk about her parents' death. I didn't want to bring up a sad subject."

Connor nodded. "It's painful for her. And under the circumstances, she's not sure she'll ever fly again. She said she tried once but was frozen in fear and had to leave the airport … and lose the cost of a ticket."

"But you both like hiking," Katrina offered.

"Yes, we had a great time yesterday on a hike."

Connor noticed the exchange of looks between Katrina and Jeff. It was something wistfully conspiratorial but no doubt hopeful on his behalf. And as much as he was wishing his friendship with Michelle would blossom into something more, he couldn't criticize their behavior.

"Don't you have a trip coming up?"

"Yes, but it's a flight to Minnesota, so I'll be solo on that one."

"Other than a fear of flying, I don't really see any fault," Katrina said.

"She does have three cats," Connor said.

"Three?"

"She said one was hers, and she picked up the others as strays. She also said she keeps cats around because they repel spirits." Connor chuckled, but something about the way she'd said it—too casually, too quickly—lingered in his mind. He thought about the banshee on the elevator comment and the other about something being haunted.

Jeff shrugged, "Everybody has quirky superstitions. Katrina always throws salt over her shoulder if anyone knocks over the shaker."

"I don't want any bad luck in this household," Katrina fired back.

Connor chuckled.

"Well, I say keep dating her and see where it goes." Jeff turned off the water and dried his hands.

Connor's lips quirked. "Thanks for the unsolicited advice on something I plan to do anyway." And for once, the idea didn't fill him with dread—only anticipation.

PENNY HAD BEEN WATCHING the relationship growing without making her presence known to Michelle. She congratulated herself on the budding relationship she'd helped propagate. Michelle and Connor had a certain magical sizzle—a genuine attraction on a physical and emotional level.

Maybe Penny could hang a sign and open for business as a ghost dating app. Surely a single success story was enough to launch a business.

She sat on the highest ledge of the Empire State Building, looking out over New York City. There was no new entrepreneurship in her future. Like Michelle had told her when they first met—Penny needed to move on. She could feel the pull to the other side. A gentle tug at her core. A soft calling song. The transition would be easy and effortless.

Suddenly, a harsh wave of cold rolled over her. She gasped as she was knocked from her perch. She tumbled through the night sky until she dropped onto a ledge. Stumbling in the darkness, she felt cold stone beneath her.

Cold and pain.

Connor's future.

Surely, the only reason she would have the power to see such a terrible thing was if she was meant to change it. Pairing up Michelle and Connor evidently didn't alter the fact that Connor would die alone—on a ledge. Penny had more work to do. She needed to take a deep dive into the future and find more details about this ominous, dark event.

She had one purpose left. One last act before she surrendered to the light.

She would not let Connor die.

CHAPTER 6

onnor mapped his trip. Since Penny's death, he'd worn down boots on trails across the country—sections of the Appalachian Trail, upstate New York ridges, long Midwestern treks.

This hike would be thirty-eight miles on the Minnesota Superior Hiking Trail which ran up the coast of the beautiful lake. He looked forward to hiking a varied terrain of cliffs and canyons, rivers and bogs.

With the hectic tax season behind him, late April was the perfect time to enjoy the outdoors. He expected the hike would take four days and would require a day on each end for travel. For a six day vacation off the grid, he needed to make sure everything at work was in order —calls forwarded to a paid answering service, projects at or near completion, and accounts reconciled.

And then there was Michelle. He was deeply enjoying her company. She was graced with easy social skills and didn't seem to take herself too seriously. She could laugh at her inability to commit to a gallery and admit that her flying phobia was a weakness she intended to resolve.

If she didn't have a fear of flying, she might have agreed to come. He was certain he'd enjoy her company, and she'd likely enjoy the scenery.

Perhaps she would have found something new to paint. The thought made him smile. How relaxing would it be to have a new painting of a place he'd hiked overlooking Lake Superior on a wall in his office?

Perhaps hiking alone was better. He and Michelle were still in the infancy of their relationship, and a six-day trip was a long time to spend isolated with another person. Except it wouldn't be just any person—he'd be with Michelle. Vibrant, beautiful Michelle.

He leaned back in his chair and stared at his hiking checklist.

Time.

The two of them had time to discover if the relationship was a right fit for both of them. In the meantime, he could hike and reflect on the delightful changes Michelle would add to his life.

MICHELLE WAS SUCKED INTO A COLD, dark void. Icy air cocooned her, so frigid it sank into the heavy pants and coat she wore. Her bones and joints were so cold they ached. She shivered, which made the pain worse. The pain didn't sit right in her bones—wrong height, wrong angle, like she was wearing someone else's body. Her leg felt swollen like it had been injured, maybe even broken.

She huddled in a ball, terrified and surrounded by darkness. When she tried to look, she could barely make out a wall of jagged obsidian rock. She was sitting on hard stone. Opposite the rock wall was open and vast nothingness. Isolation and cold filled her with a destitute and foreboding sense that she would die alone on this rock.

Jolting upright in her own bed, her lungs dragged in air like she'd been underwater. Bundling herself in a warm sweater and cotton hat, she tried to rid herself of the aching pain from the dream as it wore off.

In her bathroom, she lit a white candle and stood before the mirror. The tiny flame flickered. Using pink lipstick, she drew an eye then a closed circle around it.

"Penny Ross, I summon thee."

Penny's ghostly image appeared in the circle of lipstick on the mirror. She looked around. "Whoa, how'd you do that?"

"Did you give me this dream?"

"Did I? Was it about Connor? I was trying to show you the future I sense for him. Did it work?"

As heat and frustration boiled through her, Michelle tore off her hat and tossed it aside.

Penny startled.

"Did it work? *Did it work?* You just gave me one of the worst nightmares of my life."

Penny shrank back from the mirror. "Sorry. I didn't know what would happen."

"Never again. Promise me that."

The ghost nodded vigorously. "Never."

"He leaves in two days, right?"

"Yes."

"I'll talk to him before he leaves."

"When?"

"Penny, it's four o'clock in the morning. I need to first recover from this fright you've given me. I'll go to his place later this morning." Michelle suspected this was a conversation best had with Connor face-to-face.

WAITING, her stomach took a series of nervous tumbling flips.

Connor opened the door. "Michelle?"

She stood before him, panting from the effort up the stairs. "Can I come in?"

"Of course. How do you know where I live? Are you okay?"

She nodded as she took in his apartment—neat and tidy, just as she'd expected. The walls were a light green which complemented slate colored furniture. The living room was straight ahead, the kitchen to her right, and the bedroom to her left. She could see through his open bedroom door that he was packing for his hiking trip.

"Did you change your mind? Do you want to go with me?" Connor asked.

"No. But I need to ask you not to take this trip." She walked over to the backpack beside organized containers laid out on the bed.

His brow furrowed. "Why would I not go?"

"It's not safe."

"Not safe? Are you saying this because you're worried about me flying?"

"Yes," Penny said. "Tell him, yes, that you don't want him to go because you're afraid of him flying."

Michelle shook her head. She wasn't going to lie to Connor. And how would such a statement play out in the future? Would she tell him he could never fly anywhere?

"That's not it," Michelle said, feeling a cold sweat down her spine. "There's a storm that'll hit Minnesota and the mountains you'll be hiking along. You're in danger." She ran a hand along some of the clothing and the pockets of his backpack.

"I checked the weather, Michelle. I always check before I go. I'll get a little bit of sleet and maybe some wind, but I'll be fine. I do a lot of hiking, and I know how to manage in the wilderness." His tone was warm and gentle, as though she just needed patient reassurance and she'd stop worrying.

His patience and attempt at reassurance were admirable, but she'd felt his suffering. She couldn't back down.

"I'm asking you not to go. It's not safe."

Connor's expression shifted to pursed lips in what looked to be a mix of not wanting to disrespect her but also having no intention of indulging her paranoia. "I value our relationship. I would really like for us to become something more. But I can't drop my plans based on unsubstantiated worries. I'm flattered you're worried about me, but I won't set the precedent that I stay home so that nothing bad ever happens to me. That's not a healthy relationship for either of us."

Michelle leaned against one wall, frustrated at the situation but also understanding Connor's point of view. He was under the misconception that her fear on his behalf related to losing her parents—as such, it was 'unsubstantiated' and not to be encouraged.

She'd have to try a different approach. If he didn't believe her, she would lose a chance at a relationship with him, but if he died on that ledge, that chance would be gone anyway. "The reason why—"

"Don't do it," Penny cautioned.

Michelle hesitated, took a breath, and decided to ignore Penny's warning. They had discussed the possibility that Michelle would tell him the truth. This was the moment. "The reason why I know it isn't safe is because Penny told me."

"What?" Alarm and something dangerous flashed in Connor's eyes.

"I can see ghosts. Penny is here. She's been here all along. She's the one who told me to pick up Philly cheesesteaks and tikka masala and make cucumber gimlets. She told me your printer cartridge was going to run out of ink and what model to buy. She told me your address and door code. And she told me that this weather front is going to turn into a nasty storm, and you won't survive it."

All of the color drained from Connor's face. His mouth fell in a look of shock and revulsion.

Michelle had feared that look all her life. The look when someone realizes a person they care about was broken beyond repair. Penny had been right, Michelle shouldn't have told him. Still, she'd have had to eventually. She wouldn't lie to him.

"This isn't funny," Connor snapped in a tone she'd never heard.

"It never is. It's never funny living a life where ghosts speak to you and sometimes tell you what the future holds." Michelle's heart sank. She could see in his eyes that nothing of the joy and friendship they shared over the last few weeks could conquer doubt when faced with the illogical, improbable supernatural.

Never more than this moment had Michelle hated her gift with such intense contempt. Her curse. She'd helped some ghosts and some people over the years because she was a medium, but did it save her parents' lives? Did any ghosts offer up information before the plane crash? No. And now that one had given her the opportunity to save the man she cared about, she couldn't save him anyway because he didn't believe her.

A useless gift really was nothing more than a curse.

She felt tears stinging her eyes. But she wouldn't stand there and cry before Connor like a hysterical mental patient. She told him what she came here to tell him. She could do nothing more than warn him.

She headed toward the door, Connor still too stunned by the revelation of her insanity that he didn't move to stop her.

"Don't let him go," Penny pleaded.

Michelle turned to the ghost. "You asked me to warn him, I warned him. I sacrificed the relationship we could have had to do it. That's all I can do." She pulled open the door and gave one last look at Connor's lost stare. She cast her gaze down to the floor. "When the storm hits, find shelter. If you end up cold and alone on the rock, call for your wife. Ghosts can bring comfort at the end."

With a bleeding heart and tears threatening to unleash a cascade, Michelle pulled the door shut behind her as she left.

WHEN MICHELLE GOT HOME, she poured a glass of Merlot, dressed in her painting smock, and threw herself into her art.

She pulled out her largest canvas, six feet tall, and set it against one wall. She chose a mix of bright and dark colors. The reds and oranges were harsh and vibrant—anger and heartbreak. The blues and greens were deep and rich—sorrow and pain.

What use was a supernatural gift if she couldn't save the people she loved? Her parents were the only other people who'd known about her seeing ghosts. And the only reason she maintained her sanity in a world where she walked the line between the normal and paranormal was because her mother had had the gift as well. Michelle had the benefit of a loving parent with knowledge about how to interact with ghosts and the living when no one else saw what she saw.

Michelle had told Connor in the desperate hope that even if he couldn't become an instant believer in her abilities, he could believe in her sincerity and her feelings for him. She'd hoped that up until that point, their interactions would prove meaningful enough to enable him to at least consider the possibility of ghosts. But he hadn't. His dumbfounded reaction reminded her of the night five years ago when she'd told her neighbor about a potential fall off his ladder or when she warned an old high school classmate not to get her in boyfriend's car Friday night. Sharing her secret never went well.

Perhaps her fault this time had been mentioning Penny. She could have just left it vague—she sees ghosts, or even vaguer, that she had a premonition.

Regardless, Michelle was alone, painting herself into oblivion while Connor took the trip that would send him to join Penny.

When Michelle was done drinking and crying and painting, she sobered up with a shower and several glasses of water.

Before bed that night, she put on a necklace made of Navajo Cedar Berry beads to repel any chance that Penny could worm her way into her dreams. Perhaps when Connor joined her in spirit, both of them would have peace.

A FEW DAYS LATER, Michelle watched the weather front move across Minnesota and toward Lake Superior on The Weather Channel. The screen showed clouds in various colors representing snow and sleet mixed in an image that was visually appealing. But she knew what was actually happening in those mountains. Somewhere out there was a man who would lose his way and fall to a rocky ledge under a dark sky on a cold night.

She hadn't spoken to Penny since her falling out with Connor. Wearing the Navajo necklace had kept the ghost away. Of course, knowing Penny, she probably followed Connor to the mountain to remain by his side.

Still, Michelle felt guilty. Maybe she should let Penny have the opportunity to say goodbye to her. Michelle took off the necklace, left it on her coffee table, and exited her brownstone. She walked a few blocks to the familiar coffee shop. She ordered a small cappuccino and took it with her outside to walk the block.

"Oh, thank heavens I found you!" Penny declared, her usual neat hair looking windswept around wide and frantic eyes.

"How is he?" Michelle asked, spine rigid as she braced for bad news.

"Fine at present. The storm is getting closer. But I know a way you can help him. I've seen a way. You can save Connor."

Michelle's heart skipped a beat. "How?"

Penny grimaced. "You'll have to fly to Minneapolis. There, you'll have to wait till the storm passes. Then, you'll need to rent a helicopter and fly to the exact location I tell you. Because there won't be a logical or electronic way to track him, mountain rescue won't believe you, and they won't take you up. You'll have to pay for a private chopper, show them where Connor is, and then take that information to a rescue chopper."

Michelle took a shaky breath. Penny had put a lot of thought into this elaborate plan, except for one key point ...

That's a lot of flying.

Her knees nearly gave out. Turning, Michelle walked back to her brownstone. Although she didn't know how'd she manage the flying, she said, "I'll start packing."

For Connor, she'd do the one thing she'd sworn she'd never do again—get on a plane.

CHAPTER 7

On the taxi ride to JFK airport, Michelle arranged for pet sitters to come out and take care of her cats. She arrived at the airport with one carry-on bag and enough nervous energy to fill a hot air balloon.

After she got through airport security, she paced in the terminal until it was time to board. She didn't wait in line. There was no point sitting in the confined space until everyone else was boarded and the plane was closest to takeoff. Until then, she could walk the terminal and convince her body she was not about to board a large casket.

"I don't think I can ride up there with you," Penny said. "Are you going to be okay?"

The last thing Michelle wanted to consider was that a spirit in-flight could instigate an electrical malfunction in the airplane and cause an abrupt drop from 10,000 feet. "I'll be okay," she lied.

Michelle watched the flight attendant scan her ticket, and then she boarded the plane. For Connor, she could do this for Connor.

"I'll see you when you land." Penny slowly dissolved from view.

As the flight attendant went through her preflight check and safety instructions, Michelle strapped in, pulled out her notepad, and started sketching in charcoal. From the memory of the dream she had, she

197

drew the images of Connor on that narrow, rocky ledge. He was huddled near the wall, looking out over the long, deadly drop. His jaw was firm, and his gaze was hard.

Behind him, the obsidian rocks were jagged and slick with moisture. The sky above revealed the trail of storm clouds passing.

She sketched Connor and the landscape throughout the entire plane flight. With her mind distracted, focusing on the details of his eyes and the sharp edges of the rocks around him, she didn't think about her fear of flying.

BY THE TIME Michelle had finished her drawing, the plane began its descent. Mercifully, she hadn't been incapacitated by her fear. Focusing on the man she cared about had distracted her and given her strength.

After the plane landed and she deboarded, Penny waited for her at the gate. A look of relief spread across the spirit's face when she saw Michelle walk with determination toward her.

Michelle slipped in her ear pods. "What's my next move?" She was putting a ridiculous amount of faith in Penny's planned. If she failed, Michelle would be emotionally crushed. She pushed those thoughts aside.

"The storm is just over Connor now. It has to pass through before you can even rent a chopper."

"No," Michelle corrected her, "it has to pass before we can take flight, but I can rent it now."

Penny gave Michelle a grateful look, and for a moment, she thought the ghost might try to hug her.

"So, who is the pilot that will agree to fly me to my specified destination for a price?"

"Mountain View Chopper Tours. Two days-worth of customers canceled because of the storm. The pilot, Harry Harper, has a grandson on the way, he wouldn't mind a little extra money to throw the mother's direction."

"You've done your homework."

"Yes, well, while you were getting over your fear of flying, I had three hours to investigate my paranormal abilities and invade the personal life of the multiple chopper tourist venues."

CONNOR'S HIKE wasn't as relaxing as he'd hoped it would be. Michelle's strange behavior before he left was troublesome. There was such finality to her behavior, like she truly believed he wouldn't come back alive. And he didn't know what to make of her claims to see his dead wife. That pained him as much as unsettled him. It felt manipulative, yet he didn't think Michelle was capable of manipulating anyone.

A claim to see ghosts was bizarre enough, but why would she go as far as claiming to see Penny? Michelle only stood to lose in a tactic like that. He didn't have an explanation for how she knew his favorite foods. Perhaps there was some evidence of that on social media somewhere, but he couldn't envision Michelle scheming in such a way.

He tried to push those thoughts from his mind so he could enjoy the clean breeze, the scent of pine and oak, the crunch of packed snow and dirt beneath his boots, and the scurrying of birds and squirrels around him. When he got back home, he could talk to Michelle in more depth about the things she'd said.

The wind through the trees came on swiftly and sharply. The air was colder than he'd expected. Dark clouds closed in overhead.

Just a little wind and rain, that's all.

If the weather stranded him, he had a satellite phone. He was only six miles from the nearest town and had food supplies well enough for three days. If the storm turned into something severe, he would be able to wait it out.

By the time the sleet hit, Connor had covered himself in his poncho and continued to trudge through the wind. Still not too bad. Even though darkness crept in, there was little point in striking up a tent because in this wind it would become a kite. He opted to just stick to the trail and stay the course until he reached a shelter.

As the ground became slick with ice, the narrow trail became more difficult to discern. When he realized he'd gotten off track, he decided to double back. The ground became rock, jagged and hazardously slippery with moisture.

Despite wearing his rubber-soled boots, Connor had difficulty with traction. He planted his feet firmly, pulled off his pack, and dug out his phone. He needed a little GPS guidance in the dark to get back on track. He couldn't be more than a few miles from civilization.

A gust of wind tugged at him as he unlocked his phone with one hand and held his pack with the other. When he went to adjust the pack, his footing slipped. He momentarily caught himself by holding a sapling, but when the forty-pound backpack shifted further, the momentum caused him to fall.

He rolled a few feet and thought he'd come to a halt all together, but the rock beneath him disappeared, and he fell, clutching his open backpack as fear coursed through him. When he struck a hard surface, pain shot through his leg, and darkness closed around him.

MICHELLE RENTED a car at the Minneapolis airport and drove north to Duluth and Mountain View Chopper Tours. She realized that she hadn't driven a vehicle in over a year—probably not the best time to get behind the wheel when she was nervous about Connor and driving through sleet. Her fingers cramped on the steering wheel. This was a spectacular time to rediscover both driving and black ice. Since her parents' death, she had stayed in Park Slope, always walking or taking a ride share to her destination. She didn't even own a car.

"Left here," Penny told her.

Michelle took the left and drove up a steep gravel incline. At the top of the driveway, a sign along a wooden fence read:

MOUNTAIN VIEW CHOPPER TOURS

"You're quite the GPS," Michelle remarked.

Penny stared up at the darkening sky as sheets of rain and snow fell. "Storm's here."

That meant Connor was in the thick of it.

Michelle exited the car and dashed through the precipitation to a small log cabin. Behind the building, she could see the helicopter. Was she definitely doing this? Was she going to pay money to go up in the air in that tiny metal contraption?

She looked back at Penny who stood under the open sky, letting the moisture flow through her. Michelle thought of her dream and her sketch and a man on a ledge.

Yup. Bird bound.

She knocked on the door and entered. A man slouching in a chair behind a counter cluttered in brochures sat up straighter.

"I don't have a reservation, Mr. Harper, but when this storm passes, I'd like to rent a flight."

He looked around her. "Just you?"

"Just me."

"Well," he pulled out a brochure and opened it for her, "we've got a few different route and length options. Longer of course is more expensive. It'd be cheaper if you had a group of people to join."

"Just me," she repeated, smiling. "There's a vertical cliff I'd like to see." She pulled out her sketchpad and showed him the man on the ledge.

"Well, that could be the stretch along Tettegouche State Park. It's probably a forty-five minute flight one way." He tapped his finger on the price and scratched at graying sprigs of hair on the top of his head with the other.

She pulled out a credit card. "Can we leave as soon as the weather clears?"

He nodded. "It won't pass until late tonight though. Obviously, the other mandatory condition is daylight."

"Right. How soon in the morning can we take off?"

"Shop opens at eight."

"I'll double your fee if we leave at sunrise."

. . .

AFTER MICHELLE PAID for the flight, she drove to a nearby bed and breakfast the pilot recommended. She rented a room and closed herself inside it.

"We're all set," she told Penny, although the ghost had been hovering over he shoulder during the entire exchange with the pilot.

"I won't be able to go up in the helicopter with you."

"It's okay. I'll find him. Look, all I can do for the next few hours is get some rest. Why don't you spend the night with Connor? Sometimes people feel spirits in times of emotional or physical distress. You might be able to bring him some comfort."

"That sounds good. I'll do that." Her eyes glistened with ghost tears. "Oh, Michelle, we're so lucky to have found you. Not only have you put up with me, but you've come all this way to help Connor."

"Hey, we're friends, right?"

"We are." Penny sniffed. "I wish we could have been friends while I was alive."

Michelle chuckled and smiled. She refrained from pointing out to the ghost how a friendship with Penny when she was alive would have been awkward since Michelle was embarking on a romantic relationship with Connor. Or, she had been, until she'd told him her secret.

THE FIRST ITEM Connor reached for was his flashlight. The second was his satellite phone in his backpack. Unfortunately, he lost half the contents of his pack when he fell—phone included.

Connor found his hand warmers, but they were barely enough to keep his hands warm, much less any other parts of his body. If he could move around, he could get warm, but he couldn't climb with his injured leg.

He ate a protein bar and washed it down with water. Next, he dug in the side pocket of his backpack which contained his flare. He'd need to save it until he saw boats on Lake Superior or heard hikers or saw aircraft. In addition to the plastic cylinder of the flare, he felt paper.

He pulled it out and shone his flashlight on what looked to be a letter. The envelope had his name on it. He recognized Michelle's handwriting from the documents she'd signed in his office. He remembered her running hands along his backpack. Is that when she'd planted it?

Dear Connor,

I know we already said our goodbyes. I guess I had a hard time letting go. Perhaps my presence as a spirit has made moving on more difficult for you.

I'm so proud you ventured to start your own business, and it has been a success. And you've made time for hiking—my favorite was the Smoky Mountains. Of course the views on your Superior hike are spectacular, but because this particular hike lands you stranded on a cliff with a broken body part, it isn't my favorite.

You're wondering how Michelle and I knew you'd be on a cliff and find this letter. I'll let you in on a little ghost secret—apparently, we can see bits of the future. I can't tell you what stocks to invest in … yet. If only I had this ability in life, I would have discovered which student was putting gum under my desk.

Since becoming a ghost, I've been quite alone—until Michelle. She was the first person who could see and hear me. She's been a miracle. (She argued with me about the miracle bit, but I convinced her to leave it in the letter.) You should know that her odd behavior has been my fault (well, not all of her behavior; she is an artist, after all!).

Anyway, I think the two of you are a great fit. She doesn't think I should say that because she thinks you won't believe she transcribed this letter for me. She's afraid you'll think she's being manipulative, but I think you'll read this with new clarity. A new perspective.

If I am right, hold this letter to your heart and think of me. I'll do whatever I can spiritually to let you know I'm here. You're not alone on this cliff.

Your Adoring Wife,

Penny

Connor reread the letter several times. The vernacular unmistakably belonged to Penny. The farewell was her signature sign off. He felt the memory of her loss again—raw and hard. The pain eased when he thought of her watching over him. Then Penny had connected with Michelle who'd seen Penny in his office that first day and tried to rush out. He thought of Michelle's surprise and irritation that she'd bought his favorite foods.

Penny.

Penny had definitely manipulated Michelle but not in a negative way. In her way of trying to act in the interest of all people involved. Just like Penny—the schoolteacher who tried to include all of her students. The wife who wanted to do everything she could to bring him happiness.

And she had.

But Connor had crushed it. He recalled the look in Michelle's eyes when he didn't believe her—not even a little. Was there any fixing that?

"I miss you, Penny." He pressed the letter to his heart. "And I'm sorry I didn't believe Michelle. I'll win her back. Can I win her back?"

Warmth.

It started at his chest where the paper rested, then ran along his ribs like a slow, gentle tide. Hypothermia? Hallucination? Or Penny, just once more?

"I love you. I love both of you. If I live through this, I'll fix it."

Somewhere above the howl of the wind, he thought he heard a distant thrum. Or maybe that was just his heart refusing to give up.

CHAPTER 8

When Michelle exited her rental car, the thudding sound of rotor blades echoed from behind the cabin. Her stomach lurched, confirming she'd made the right decision to skip breakfast. She forced her legs forward, one step at a time.

Determination.

Perseverance.

"Looks like you're fired up and ready to go," Michelle said to Harper.

"It's an odd request—a lone tourist wanting to fly first thing in the morning. There's some urgency in you that I don't understand, and I suppose you'd tell me if you thought it was my business. But I can use the money, and I don't mind taking in a sunrise over the lake. So here we are."

"Seems like I picked the perfect pilot."

"She's warmed up and ready when you are." Harper gestured toward his helicopter.

"I'm ready," Michelle lied.

As she boarded the helicopter and strapped in, she looked around the landscape. No Penny. She hadn't seen the ghost since they'd parted last night in her hotel room. Good. She was with Connor, where she needed to be.

Michelle slipped on the headset the pilot handed her and then clutched her sketchpad as the helicopter rose into the air. The tiny contraption shuddered as the roaring blades reverberated through her entire body. The harness felt too tight, the metal too thin. The world looked terrifyingly small through the curved glass.

For a moment, she was distracted by the breathtaking landscape. Bare poplar and aspen mixed with green pine and spruce. The mountaintops were caked in pure, white snow. The lake to the right was a clear, sky blue and stretched so far into the distance to meet the horizon that it looked more like an ocean than a lake. The sun glinted off the surface, winking at her.

When they flew near the cliff's face, worry filled Michelle. It was so vast and steep, she wondered how they would spot Connor. [more description of cliffs]

Then magic and fireworks burst in an orange light. Connor had set off a flare. He must've heard the helicopter.

"What the—?" Harper startled.

"There!" Michelle cried.

The pilot banked toward the flare. He flipped on his radio. "Search and rescue this is Mountain View Chopper oh-nine-five. I've got a stranded hiker on a rock face." The pilot rattled off his location.

As they neared the rock wall, Michelle saw Connor seated on the cliff face waving his hands at the chopper.

The pilot glanced warily at her. "Why do I get the feeling you knew that man was on that cliff. And if you knew he was there, why didn't you just alert the search and rescue team to begin with?"

"There are policies and procedures a rescue team has to follow. I'm not a family member of this man. I'm a friend. If I'd shown up saying my friend was stranded in a storm and stuck on a cliff, they'd want proof. They'd check hotels, shelters, rental records. Hours—maybe days. Meanwhile he's freezing on a ledge with no way to move. But if we 'happened' to find him on a tour? That's immediate proof. No red tape."

"But if he didn't call you, how did you know where he'd gotten himself stranded?"

"The answer, Mr. Harper, is not for the faint of heart. It's better to accept that you'll end your day having saved a man's life, which is more important than how fate led me to you."

MICHELLE WATCHED as the orange and white rescue helicopter arrived. She wondered if they'd do an aerial rescue or land and repel down the face of the cliff. They seemed to be in a state of indecision as they hovered near the rock wall. Perhaps they debated the safest way to retrieve Connor from the ledge. The icy rocks would make repelling slick, but she suspected rappelling straight down from the helicopter had its own set of risks.

At last, the team seemed to have made their decision. A man in a harness attached to a rope from the helicopter was slowly lowered down as the helicopter hovered. Michelle was thankful the air was still and quiet after the storm. The man was hanging like a yo-yo, and she worried that a strong gust or sudden movement of the helicopter would thrust him into the rock wall.

When he reached the ledge, he fastened Connor into a harness and secured the two of them together. When they rode into the air tethered to the helicopter, Michelle finally breathed a sigh of relief.

Harper turned the tourist chopper southbound. "I suspect your sightseeing is complete."

"Yes, thank you."

"Well, your friend might go to St. Luke's in Duluth. If not, there's a dozen hospitals in Minneapolis."

Michelle's mind whirled with a mix of emotions—passion, longing, tenderness, and fear. The strongest being fear. Did she want to check in on him? Did Connor want her to check in on him? They hadn't parted on good terms. And she wasn't sure how he'd react to her rescuing him. Except, he wouldn't know she'd been involved in the rescue. She didn't think Harper had flown the helicopter close enough for Connor to identify the passengers.

If he didn't know, Michelle would never have to answer a barrage of questions about her abilities. She didn't want to face his skepticism and confusion again. Even if the traumatic event led him to consider the possibility of ghosts, and if he believed Penny's letter, what rational reaction would there be to his eyes opened to a supernatural part of the world he couldn't see, other than fear? Who could possibly want to live a life with a partner who sees ghosts?

Her father had. She wished she'd thought to ask him how he'd managed it with her mom.

AFTER CLIMBING off the helicopter and thanking Harper, Michelle drove back to the bed and breakfast, packed her belongings, and started her car. She had a return flight to JFK from Minneapolis.

As she put the car in drive, Penny appeared beside her. "Thank you for helping Connor. You saved his life. He's on his way to HCMC. They're going to have to fix his leg."

"Good. He's getting medical care. He'll be back home in no time."

"You're not going to go see him in the hospital?"

"Penny, he doesn't believe me."

"But you rescued him. And he read the letter we wrote. It's all different now."

"Do you know that for sure? Did any of this really change his mind? Besides, he doesn't know I was on that chopper."

"Well, he would if you stop being so stubborn and go visit him in the hospital. Wouldn't you want to see a familiar face if you were stranded on a cliff and then had to go into surgery alone?"

"I got search and rescue out there, what more do you want from me?" She couldn't stand the thought of another rejection from him.

"I want you to suck up your pride and your fear and go see him in the hospital and let him know you love him."

"None of that guarantees a different outcome."

"No, it doesn't. But if you fly back to New York, you're not even giving him a chance to prove that he might be able to trust the paranormal abilities you have."

"The curse," Michelle scoffed.

"The *miracle*."

"You don't know what it feels like to have someone you care about look at you like you're not the person they thought you were."

"No. But I know loneliness."

"You can't fix his loneliness."

"You assume he's the only one I don't want to see lonely. You and I are friends, Michelle. We talk, we laugh, we joke. You're an incredible woman and artist. Sure, I started on a mission to help Connor, but I want to see you happy, too. I know, I know. Happiness comes from within. But it also comes from love. I think the two of you have that special spark, but you're both going to have to trust each other to make it work. No one ever said love was easy."

Michelle sighed in resignation and took I-35 South toward Minneapolis.

MICHELLE WAITED to be allowed to see Connor. Because she wasn't family, the medical staff had to ask his permission first.

At last, she was allowed back to his hospital room.

She stood, leaning on the doorway. If she stepped forward and he rejected her again, she wasn't sure she could survive it. "Are you okay?"

"Better," he said, adjusting the covers on his hospital bed. "Because I didn't notify anyone I was in the hospital, I'm guessing Penny told you."

As she entered, she noticed his color seemed a little pale, and his lower leg was in a cast. "She did." Michelle held her hat in her hands and fidgeted with the rim. The lump in her throat seemed to expanded.

"Is she here now?" He glanced around the room.

"No. She wanted to give us a minute." Michelle couldn't tell if Connor was asking her because he believed her or because he wanted to see if she was standing firm on her assertion that she could see ghosts.

"Michelle—"

"Well, I wanted to make sure you were okay. I'll let you get some rest."

"Michelle."

She hesitated by the door.

"Please, come inside, take a seat, and let me apologize for not listening to you," he said.

"It's okay. I know how it sounded—desperate, clingy, needy."

"You are none of those things. Please, sit. I'd like to hear more about how your abilities work. You saved my life. I'd like to at least thank you for that."

She couldn't seem to move from the spot where she stood. Was he saying he believed her?

Her gaze rose to meet his. "I didn't—"

"I'd know that hat anywhere. You were on the chopper that found me. Please sit."

Michelle surrendered. She pulled the chair in the room up beside his bed and sat. When he offered her his hand to hold, she clasped it.

Connor squeezed her hand. "When you told me those things before my trip, I didn't know what to think. Then, when I was alone on that ledge with Penny's letter, I understood. Or, at least, I understood that I needed to talk to you more about it." He scrubbed his other hand across his face. "I felt her out there in the cold with me. And she helped you find me, didn't she?"

Michelle swallowed. "She loves you very much."

"I love her, too. But, I also love you. I'm sorry if it's too soon to say something like that, but it's true. When you're freezing on a cliff," he said softly, "everything unnecessary falls away. And what's left ... is the truth."

Speechless, Michelle brought his hand to her lips and kissed it.

"And maybe I don't understand or comprehend the extent of your ability to communicate with ghosts, but it's obviously part of who you are. I have no intention of changing any part of who you are."

Michelle sniffed.

"So, can we still be together?" he asked.

"We can still be together."

~

~~ 3 MONTHS LATER~~

MICHELLE HAD FOUND a gallery she liked and rented it. She'd hired an art major finishing his last semester of college to work part time to help set up the show floor. Between painting and preparations, Michelle had continued to date Connor as he transitioned from crutches to a boot to walking normally.

Tonight, though, wasn't about art. Tonight, Penny would move on. Michelle sat on the floor of her unfinished gallery with Connor inside a circle of yellow candles. In the center of the circle burned frankincense, emitting a sweet scent. Penny hovered in the wisp of smoke released from the incense.

"Are you ready?" Michelle asked Penny.

"Ready."

Penny didn't need a special ceremony to shift from this world to the next, but Michelle and Connor did. They both needed different types of closure. Penny had become a friend and had helped Michelle through her self-imposed isolation.

"Connor," Penny began, "I'm so grateful you found Michelle. She's a wonderful match for you and you for her. I wish you a lifetime of happiness."

Michelle relayed the message to Connor.

Connor stared at the twirling, fragrant smoke. "Thank you, Penny, for helping us come together. I wish you peace. Rest knowing I'm happy."

"I'll miss you," Michelle said.

"I'm glad I had a friend in you," Penny said.

Then, she simply faded from view in light and smoke—like silk in the wind—happy and content.

EPILOGUE

Opening night at Barcella Gallery was magical. Michelle had her favorite works on display, each painting with its own spotlight. Twinkling golden LED lights canopied the tall ceiling. Waiters walked through with trays, dispensing hors d'ouerves catered by Connor's best friend's company. Michelle's art student handled sales so she was free to talk about colors, mood, and her inspiration.

Michelle paused in front of one painting—one of her few portraits. Penny in her pink sweater, gazing out Connor's office window as though still watching over them. A week after returning from Minnesota, Michelle had painted it in one breathless rush, unable to sleep until Penny's presence lived somewhere permanent. It wasn't for sale. This artwork would stay in the gallery.

Connor put an arm around Michelle. "Your night was a success." His broken leg had fully healed, and they had a day hike planned for the next weekend.

Michelle looked around as people filed out of the gallery at closing time. Jeff and Katrina, having secured babysitters, stayed longer. They stood arm-in-arm, looking at her painting of Lake Superior but casting glances in Connor's direction with oddly expectant expressions.

Michelle kissed Connor on the cheek. "I couldn't be happier with how it turned out, and I don't even know if I sold anything."

Connor's smile warmed her, but there was something else in his eyes tonight—an intensity she couldn't quite place.

"Yes, I did."

"Maybe, you're in the mood to make someone else's dream come true?"

She gave him a quizzical look before he dropped to one knee and raised a ring before her. Her heart throbbed with excitement.

"You're my miracle, Michelle. Every moment I spend with you is a gift I treasure. Will you marry me and let me treasure you for as long as I live?"

"Yes!"

He rose to his feet, wrapped his arms around her, and spun her around once. As he set her back on her feet, he pressed his lips to hers in a soft, succulent kiss.

For the first time in years, Michelle felt completely whole—seen, loved, and no longer burdened by her gift. Penny had led them to each other. Love would carry them forward.dd9

GRACELYNN'S GENIE

A kidnapping in the depths of the Colombian jungle. A genie with an agenda. And a rescue mission gone awry.

CHAPTER 1

"*I* wish for an adventure." Grace hung upside-down, muscles trembling, sweat sliding toward her hairline. Her abs burned.

"Are you sure, Darling? This is your third and final wish."

Grace twisted to face her ghost-genie, watching those penciled brows arch. "I know the score, Constance. It's time."

Constance rippled, translucent in a haze of blue smoke. Her voice was a deep baritone—although rouge covered her thick lips. "But your life is already an adventure, Darling." She protested as she waved a hazy hand through the air. "You travel the world on your medical expeditions—South America, Africa, Eastern Europe." Masculine eyebrows had been replaced by a thin, penciled line with a feminine arch. Her eyes were framed by impossibly long, dark eyelashes.

Grace frowned as she strained to curl her body. Perhaps her life had once been an adventure. Now, though, it felt like a hollow, endless search for …

Something.

"Adventure, Constance. What can you find for me?" She didn't want her genie ghost talking her out of her request.

Ten years ago, Grace had bought a bronze lamp during a medical mission. Like Aladdin in the fairytale, she'd unwittingly unleashed what she'd at first thought to be a trapped genie from within—in the form of the deep-voiced, shimmering Constance. Over time, Grace had learned that Constance was actually a ghost who spent her spiritual existence pretending to be a genie. Because she was a ghost, few people could see or hear her.

Two of Grace's three wishes had been used. Those wishes had brought her some of the best and worst times of her life. They were cursed wishes.

Misleading to even call them wishes, Grace thought bitterly, but she'd put off using the final wish long enough.

"Adventure," Grace repeated, and Constance pouted.

"You don't want an adventure. You want something reckless. Just like the reckless behavior that keeps launching you head-first into dangerous countries to volunteer medical care."

"Adventurous *and* reckless," Grace grinned. "Yes, let's do that."

After grasping the bar above her, she released her feet with the press of a button. When her legs swung down, she began a series of intense pull-ups.

"You know—" Constance fidgeted with the decorative silver coins on her blue pantaloons "—there are people in *this* country who need medical care. You don't have to travel to third-world countries to find people in need."

"I tried a free clinic here," Grace countered, breathless from her pull-ups. "We were robbed. And then we were sued." She shook her head and strained to pull herself up for her tenth pull-up. "Who sues a free clinic? Only Americans." The clinic won the case, but the ordeal had been so draining, Grace closed the clinic anyway.

"Getting yourself killed won't bring Daniel back," Constance murmured.

Although the words were spoken softly, Grace felt like a knife had been driven into her back. She dropped to the floor and shook out her aching arms.

"I'm sorry, Darling," Constance frowned. "That was uncalled for."

"*Wish*," Grace demanded flatly as she walked over to the quadriceps machine. She sat and began her leg extensions.

"Okay, okay," Constance sighed. "When do you want to leave?"

"The sooner the better." She hadn't traveled in over a month and was starting to go stir crazy in her large, empty home. "I just need enough notice to give the pilot time to file a flight plan."

Wherever they were going, the local pilot could get her to a major airport.

Constance narrowed her thickly lashed eyes. "So ... somewhere remote?"

"You know I like remote."

Constance chewed the ends of her blue, flashy nails. "And dangerous?"

"I eat danger for breakfast," she quipped, feeling the strain in her legs from the machine.

"Something heroic?"

"That's optional. I'm not so much looking for fame and glory." Grace wanted something to take her mind off being alone—a state in which she perpetually kept herself.

"Don't I know it." Constance's lips drew down. "It's maddening. I've advised sultans and kings—I've *made* sultans and kings, elevated from mere paupers on the street. You could be sensational with me by your side, if only you changed your wish to, say—"

"*Adventure*, Constance," Grace snapped though with no malice in her voice. "Work your genie mojo."

"Fine." Constance huffed. Then, she brightened. "Oh, I may have just the thing brewing. Let me focus."

Grace narrowed her eyes at the ghost's glowing apparition. Constance schemed behind those rippling blue eyes, but Grace wasn't unduly concerned. Whatever the future held, her third and final wish couldn't put her through as much suffering as the first two wishes had.

～

WADE RAWLINGS HIT the hard ground with a thud, jarring every muscle in his body. Gasping, he coughed moist dirt out of his mouth. As he looked around at his surroundings, he took a shaky breath. A circular prison—a dirt pit in God-knows-where, Colombia, South America—enveloped him.

He'd been dragged past a row of similar pits before finally being dumped into this one. Did other people languish in the neighboring holes—and, if so, how long had they been there?

This was not how he'd envisioned the end of his trip to South America. He'd left the Amazon rainforest after taking amazing footage of the rich vegetation, wildlife, and forest fires. Beauty and devastation, yin and yang. His photos and videos were intended to raise awareness of the blaze back in the United States and to be used for fundraising efforts to stop the fires. As his trip had wound to an end, Wade had planned an add-on shoot in Neiva, Colombia.

He'd never made it there.

Somewhere between Bogotá and Neiva, the bus he'd been riding in had been hijacked. Wade's crew of two other men—locals he'd hired to help navigate the countryside—were killed instantly when they'd tried to resist. Wade hadn't made that mistake—but he'd still been beaten, tied, and finally dumped here … in a pit.

Of particular interest was how the bus driver had simply driven away from the hijacking, unhurried after Wade and his hired help had been forced off the bus. Had the driver been paid to inform the Colombian guerrilla fighters whenever foreigners boarded his bus?

Deep in the pit, Wade curled his knees up and clutched his side, feeling the tender bruises. The abductors had knocked him to the ground and kicked him when he'd initially moved with too much hesitation.

Now, he had to wonder how long his captors would keep him. As long as it took them to realize he had no influential connections or wealth back in the States. Sure, his pack had contained expensive photography and filming equipment—but that had been the extent of his wealth. Wade was certain that when his kidnappers discovered he wasn't ransom-worthy, they'd simply let him rot in this dirt prison.

Above him, darkness descended. All around, the noises of the jungle filled the air. Despair ebbed into his bones.

GRACE'S athletic figure moved lithely as she worked her way through routines on each of her exercise machines. While the woman was physically fit enough for any conceivable adventure—up to and including climbing Kilimanjaro if she so desired—Constance questioned the fitness of Grace's mental health for the task ahead.

Since Daniel's death two years earlier, Grace had grown increasingly reckless about her own safety. She might have saved many lives as a physician, but each new mission came at high risk, putting her in peril. Grace's behavior wasn't promoting her own longevity.

But the woman's escalating recklessness was at least partly Constance's fault. The wishes she'd granted Grace weren't wishes in the truest sense of the word. Constance couldn't perform instantaneous magic, but she *could* follow a hypothetical course of action in her mind's eye and see the potential outcome.

She'd possessed the ability to see into the future ever since becoming a ghost, millennia ago, but the gift had limitations. For example, Constance couldn't foresee *all* the ramifications a course of action might set in motion, because numerous and multiplying external factors played into a person's future over time.

This time, though …

"Eureka!" Constance exclaimed.

Grace blinked at her, stopping her countless repetitions on the monotonous machine at the sound of Constance's startling exclamation.

"Picture this," Constance spread her arms wide and jiggled her body, until the shining coins on her pantaloons jingled loudly, "the Colombian jungle."

Grace cocked her head to one side. "You've piqued my interest."

"There's an American man held captive there—an innocent man!

The clock is ticking until his inevitable execution, but *you* can save him."

"Can I?" With skepticism in her eyes, Grace drew back.

Honestly, sometimes Constance felt her dramatic flair when entirely unappreciated. "Yes! I can guide you there. *We* can save him."

"What's involved?"

"Obviously the plane rides there. You'll have to land on a remote airstrip in a small plane—and have a quick turnaround time to get back to the plane before you lose your opportunity to leave. That means one or two nights in the jungle—tops."

Grace started a round of upper body presses as she seemed to consider Constance's proposal.

"It'll be too risky for the plane to sit there and wait for us. What if I parachute in instead? Then we could have a plane fly in for a scheduled pick-up?"

Constance strangled back her opposition to Grace jumping out of a plane. She wanted to help Grace, but would this trip be a step toward healing? Or just a short reprieve before her next downward spiral?

"That could work," she said hesitantly, biting her lip.

Oblivious to Constance's concerns, Grace finished her set and finally stood, scrubbing a towel across her face. "How much time do we have?"

A glimpse of hope flashed through Constance. Maybe Constance's scheming could help Grace turn her life around. Maybe saving someone was what Grace needed to save herself.

CHAPTER 2

Constance cringed as Grace jumped out of a perfectly functional airplane. The genie didn't want to think about the seemingly countless number of things that could go wrong during an attempted parachute descent into the teeming jungle below. She couldn't comprehend this thrill seeking behavior when life was such a fleeting, precious gift. And yet, to feel alive, she'd witnessed people engage in activity that threatened death.

As Grace plummeted through the air, she clutched the heavy pack she wore across her chest—backwards, so her chute could deploy behind her. Fortunately, there was no wind or rain to make this ludicrous risk-taking even more dangerous than it already was.

If something went wrong, Constance could do nothing to intervene—a big fat *nothing*. Her apparition couldn't catch anything other than a drift.

Constance tried to reassure herself as Grace soared through the air that the woman *had* been fully trained in the suicide—er, *art*—of parachuting. She'd packed her own parachute, and she'd jumped two dozen times previously ... and it hadn't killed her yet.

But those had been controlled jumps, over flat land, and in ideal conditions. Constance kept her nervous thoughts to herself, first and foremost because showing fear was unbecoming of a mystical being like herself. Secondly, because she didn't want to distract Grace as she sheared through nothing toward the looming jungle canopy below. And lastly, because the woman probably couldn't hear anything but the roaring wind right now.

At twenty-five hundred feet, Grace pulled her ripcord and the dark green silk deployed perfectly. The parachute billowed out and sharply slowed Grace's descent. Now, floating smoothly, she neared the jungle canopy. As she descended, she maneuvered away from the rocks and ravines beneath her—but that left the only other option for a landing: trees.

Grimacing, Constance squeezed one eye shut, not wanting to watch but unable to look away.

Grace tucked in her hands and feet as she speared through the treetops. She passed through the branches and boughs—and only when her parachute snagged on the tree limbs above her did her descent come to an abrupt stop.

She grunted in pain. "Ow! Whiplash."

"You've got bigger problems," Constance warned, floating down alongside her.

Following Constance's gaze downward, Grace gulped. "I'm a bit higher off the ground than I'd hoped for." She couldn't simply unhook her harness and drop to the jungle floor below—not at this height. At least, not without breaking a leg. Instead, she worked the heavy pack slung across her chest loose.

Removing the thick coils of rope that had been wrapped around it, she released the heavy pack. It plummeted down before falling on the floor of the jungle with a heavy thud.

Constance gasped. "Be gentle, you brute! My lamp is in that pack."

Free of the heavy pack, Grace had more mobility. She wriggled and maneuvered, swinging back and forth from the straps of her parachute.

"It's fine," she grunted. "There are clothes around it. The only things that probably broke were my MREs."

As she hung from the parachute, she looked up at the state of it.

"I'm won't be able to keep the chute. It would take too long to untangle it."

Using the rope she'd grabbed, she tied herself to a tree, connecting the rope to her parachute harness and then looping it over a thick branch. Next, she unhooked her parachute from the harness, dropping free, only to be caught by the thick rope she'd secured. Face red with the strain, she began lowering herself down to the ground below.

When her feet were finally on solid ground, Grace wasted no time recoiling the rope and retrieving her backpack, which she slung over her shoulders the way it was meant to be worn.

At last, Constance breathed a sigh of relief.

"Ready?" Grace asked, as if they were about to take a walk in the park, not trek toward danger.

Constance gave Grace a disapproving once over. She was dressed for the occasion, at least. Grace wore khaki pants with multiple pockets, sporting a pocketknife and a flashlight. Her tank top left her shoulders and arms bare, and the skin shined with the coat of bug-spray she'd applied to avoid insect bites—and the diseases they carried.

Her blonde hair had originally been in a braid, but the leap from the plane and the death spiral toward the Earth had replaced that with a hairstyle that could only be described as 'dashingly wind-blown.'

Yes, Constance's plan might just work.

GRACE ADJUSTED her backpack as she hiked through the jungle, following the path Constance led her through. Exhilaration after the plane jump had her blood pumping and her feet moving swiftly.

Everything leading up to this moment had happened so quickly. The journey to the Colombian jungle had been condensed—a flight from upstate New York to JFK, followed by the flight from JFK to Bogotá, followed by renting a single-engine plane to drop her roughly ten miles from her intended destination.

Maybe if Constance had been a *real* genie, the trip could have been taken on a magic carpet, instead of airplanes and a parachute—but at least the travel time had enabled Grace to plan.

Grace needed enough food and water for two people for the extraction trip and had packed accordingly—plus she'd packed flashlights, flares, a lightweight tent, a blanket, meals-ready-to-eat, water filters, bug spray, netting, changes of clothing, and a compass. In addition to packing it, Grace had coated herself with so much bug-spray she imagined she'd probably glow in the dark.

That final item—the compass—Constance had been affronted by, because, in her opinion, Grace had her to serve as a ghostly guide and wouldn't need a compass. But 'always prepared' was Grace's motto.

On one of the connecting flights to Colombia, Grace and Constance had reviewed the layout of the camp where this American was being held prisoner. The genie had given Grace more details than a drone could have delivered.

Too bad Grace couldn't go to the authorities and ask them to extract the American prisoner; to do so, she'd have to explain that her inside information source was a ghost. Such a claim was unlikely to pass muster, even if such information could be used to prevent future kidnappings.

As she trekked, the quiet jungle hike reminded her of the time she'd once hiked the Appalachian trail—not long after Daniel's death. Nature and remoteness brought her comfort, and the labor of setting a brisk pace—not to mention the thirty-pound backpack on her shoulders—kept her from dwelling on her internal pain.

Constance floated ahead of her, a blue beacon out of place in a jungle … then again, only Grace could see her.

"How much farther to the camp?" Grace asked, which was an entirely different question than 'are we there yet?'.

"In my prime, as Jinn Constantine to Memed II, who ruled the Ottoman Empire for thirty years and conquered Constantinople—I would have said two leagues. We called them *fersah*—but to you, I will say seven miles."

"You'll let me know of any danger?"

"I'll let you know about wires, mines, sentries, lions, tigers, and bears."

Grace snorted. "Does that make you the Tin Man?"

Her voice dropped a playful octave. "Darling, I'm the all-seeing Oz."

"Oh, begging your pardon," Grace quipped.

"If this doesn't go well, you've got bigger problems than flying monkeys."

She grunted her reply to Constance. The genie worried, but Grace had faith in her ability to find the path to safety in a tough spot.

The crunch of her boots on the path beneath her and the clamoring of the birds and squirrels distracted her from the danger lurking around her.

"See those green and red flowers?" Grace pointed toward petals that were vibrant with a waxy sheen. "Those are heliconia species."

They walked past Colombian oaks, Pekea-nut trees, and the Yopo tree with its fern-like leaves. The view was lovely, and the temperature wasn't unbearably steamy, either—although the humidity caused her to sweat straight through her shirt. She'd opted for long pants made of ninety-seven percent nylon, because they were protective, breathable, lightweight, and fast drying.

Although she enjoyed the hike, she hoped it wouldn't rain. Rain would soak her pack and add even more weight to it. That weight, and the rain-slick ground, would slow down the entire rescue trip. Because it was September, the rainy season was supposed to still be a few weeks away—but that didn't mean Grace wouldn't get wet.

In front of her, a yellow frog hopped from one emerald-colored leaf of an Aphelandra to another.

"Cute little thing," Grace noted, knowing full well that one kept one's hands to oneself around wildlife in foreign territory.

Constance floated in front of Grace, looking like she thought the jungle might come alive and swallow them both. "The golden poisonous frog," she breathed reverently. "That 'cute little thing' has enough poison to kill a dozen people."

"Oh!" Grace's eyes widened. "Is that the frog that native tribes use to make their poison darts?"

Constance swatted uselessly at a spiderweb, her hand passing right through it. "I don't share your enthusiasm—but, yes. Darts and arrows. Tribesmen hold the frogs over a fire and collect the toxins sweated from their skin."

"Well, let's not upset any indigenous tribes, shall we?"

Constance shot her a look over her shoulder as her lips twitched. "No raiding sacred temples, then."

Grace chuckled. "Look at you with your pop-culture references. I think that Indiana Jones scene was actually set in the Peruvian jungle —but, hey, that's not too far from here."

Grace continued her hike—step by step, hour by hour. She and Constance lapsed into comfortable silence, and Grace sensed—by Constance's escalating nervousness—that stealth was becoming paramount.

An hour before nightfall, Grace found herself a tree large enough to call home for the night.

After pulling on gloves, she made the arduous climb into the boughs of the towering tree. Once secure, she pulled her pack up after her, into the tree, and tied it off. Then, she tied off her rope to her harness—the same one she'd worn when she parachuted out of the plane that same morning. Next, she secured her hammock, stretching it across the space between two opposing branches. Finally, she draped mosquito netting over the hammock.

After grabbing water and a protein bar from her pack, she crawled inside her nest and pulled the mosquito netting closed behind her. Looking down at the jungle below, Grace surveyed the scene. At twenty feet above the ground, with foliage between her and the jungle floor beneath, she wouldn't be impossible to spot from the ground, but someone passing by in the dark probably wouldn't notice her.

Up in the tree, she was reminded of when she and Daniel had once gone zip-lining in Costa Rica. She'd been in medical school, and Daniel had been a practicing internist at the time. They'd been married for only a year at that point, and their love of travel had been one commonality that had brought them together in the first place—that, and a foolish wish.

She settled into the hammock, the netting whispering shut around her. The jungle murmured all around her, alive and indifferent. Her weary muscles tugged her tired body. Tomorrow, she'd attempt something she'd never tried before—a rescue mission.

Miles away, a man waited in a hole.

Sleep beckoned her, but she fought it long enough to whisper, "Hold on."

Whether she meant the stranger … or herself … she wasn't entirely sure.

CHAPTER 3

Hovering in the canopy of foliage, Constance watched over Grace as she slept—as she'd done during the physician's many dangerous trips, and as she'd done for sultans, kings, and queens over the centuries.

Perhaps time and experience should have made Constance a formidable advisor, but the longer she "granted wishes"—peering into the future and picking a course of action which would make a person's wish come true—the less certain she became that she could accurately fulfill such wishes. While Constance had once heralded herself as a mighty jinn—twisting fate and turning the tides of war— her actions after the ebb and flow of centuries seemed a meddlesome sort of arrogance.

Following a dormant eighty-five years, Constance's lamp was discovered by the young and carefree Grace—a refreshing woman, full of life. She and Grace had become fast friends, and Grace, who'd been content to be enamored by having a genie in a lamp, had let a full year pass before even asking for her first wish. And what a simple wish it had been. The college girl had wanted love.

Constance had set her on the path to love, but also, unfortunately, heartbreak.

When the inhabitants of the jungle—birds, monkeys, frogs, and big bugs—began squawking their early morning ruckus, Constance brought her attention back to the present.

Grace stirred. Her long blonde hair had curled at the ends in the jungle humidity, and her oval face had lightly tanned overnight from yesterday's sun exposure. Bright green eyes flickered open, and she instantly looked at Constance's expression.

"Trouble?" Grace asked.

"No trouble, Darling."

Reassured, Grace stretched. The hammock swayed with her motions. She sat up carefully and brushed away the long bangs covering her forehead.

Within twenty minutes, she had everything packed away and repelled back down the tree. She coiled the rope back around her backpack, picked up the harness, and readjusted everything as she secured it around her.

"Is our timing still good?" Grace asked.

So efficient, so driven. So devoid of enjoyment.

Because now was not the time to mention any of this, Constance only nodded. "You can sneak a note to the captive when we get to the camp. Then, we'll come back an hour later when the rebels are away from camp. That's when we'll make the rescue."

"Okay. Let's go save a life." She started walking.

Constance followed with a frown. This last act would fulfill Grace's three wishes, which meant Constance would be free to leave her. Except Constance had always been free to go, or free to stay.

The 'wish' limitation had been something of her own creation—a rule she'd put in place a long time ago to limit how much time she'd have to spend with people who might try to abuse her ability to see into the future.

So, even after this 'wish' was provided, Constance thought perhaps she'd stay with Grace just a little while longer. They were friends, after all—and Grace hadn't stabilized herself after losing Daniel.

But as disastrous as her first two wishes had been, Grace might be eager to be rid of Constance. Perhaps that's why she'd made this third and 'final' wish.

Grace had everything money could buy, but money couldn't buy happiness. Could adventure? Constance was taking a gamble that she could transform Grace's wish for adventure into something more. Constance was, after all, a self-professed meddlesome genie—and she couldn't change her nature any more than she could really grant wishes.

~

WADE'S STOMACH RUMBLED, and he licked his dry, cracked lips. He simultaneously longed for raindrops to fall on his face and whet his thirst—and for no rain at all. Rain would turn his dirt pit into a mud pit.

A faint shuffling noise above had him raising his eyes. From up above, he spotted someone peering down at him—someone with a flash of blonde bangs.

A woman?

As quickly as her face appeared, it disappeared again. Then, the lattice roof of his caged pit lifted, and a bag tumbled down toward him. Before it landed in the dirt, Wade grabbed and fumbled with it, barely catching it. Glancing back up, he saw no one so he opened the delivery. The bundle contained a canteen, a protein bar, a harness, and a note.

> *Eat, drink, and put on the harness. I'll be back to hoist you out in an hour. Be ready to run. —Grace*

Wade stared at the neat, compact handwriting. Someone knew he was here. Someone had a plan. His throat tightened. He almost called out—*Hey! Wait!*—but clamped his mouth shut. No point advertising that his miracle had arrived.

But how did anyone know where to find him? And who'd be

footing the bill for rescuing a nobody photographer from deep in the Colombian jungle?

He could worry about that later. For now, Wade committed to being ready for when this mysterious cavalry returned. With gratitude, Wade followed the instructions on the note—quenching his thirst and satisfying his hunger.

When he finished, he reread the note.

Cavalry? Or just one person?

Grace.

Amazing Grace.

'How precious did that grace appear.'

Surely, an entire team of operatives was needed to successfully infiltrate this camp. The Colombian guerrillas were ruthless, and Wade had already witnessed how they had no reservations in using either the butt or the bullet-firing end of their AK-47s against anyone who stood against them.

In his lifetime, Wade had seen violence and death first-hand—but yesterday's killing had been especially cold-blooded and terrifying.

Maybe 'Grace' was a code name or team name. *Team Grace.*

It could be—except it wasn't a very fearsome team name.

Still, the lyrics of Amazing Grace—*'I once was lost, but now I'm found'*—gave him hope.

After strapping on the harness, Wade began stretching his arms and legs. He suspected he'd only get one chance at escape.

Be ready to run.

GRACE CROUCHED BEHIND A TREE. Of the six pits in front of her, only one was occupied. Having only one person to rescue increased her likelihood of success. Soon, the Colombian rebels would leave the camp to go on another raid, according to Constance, and then Grace would be ready for action.

The guerrillas' cabins were several hundred yards from the pits, and she wondered if that was by design so they didn't have to hear their captives screaming for help throughout the night. After trekking ten miles through the jungle, Grace knew screaming out here would be useless, but perhaps the guerillas' victims wouldn't realize that if they were in a pit, desperate for help.

She used the time to create a decoy escape trail—making deep footprints in the dirt and mud and snapping off shrub and fern branches, heading off in the opposite direction to the one she intended to lead her rescued prisoner. Her fake trail would misdirect the Colombians once they noticed their captive was missing. When they began their search, they'd hopefully be thrown off course.

Grace couldn't take credit for the clever plan. One additional advantage to befriending a ghost familiar with all forms of battle strategy—learned over the course of thousands of years—was that Constance could coach Grace through various techniques of self-preservation, including misdirection.

In the distance, the sound of diesel engines roared.

"It's time," Constance said.

The lions are leaving their den.

Grace looped her rope around the tree nearest the pits before tossing aside the lattice roof of the makeshift prison. She lowered the other end of the rope—the one with the carabiner—down into the prisoner's pit.

After pulling on her leather gloves, she heaved the rope toward her, hand over hand, one after the other. Something heavy weighed on the other end of the rope, which she assumed to be the kidnapped photographer. All those repetitions in her exercise room paid off. Grace hefted up the heavy man, and when she felt the weight on the rope finally slacken, she peered at the edge of the pit and saw him pulling himself up and over.

Releasing the rope, she shook out the burning muscles of her arms as she strode forward and grabbed the man by the harness. She pulled until his entire body was free and away from the pit the rest of the way out, pulling on his harness until he was finally free.

As soon as he was on his feet, he stripped out of the harness and wrapped the rope up for storage, not saying a word. Grace watched, trying to get a measure of him. He wore mud-plastered khaki pants and a light blue button shirt rolled up at the sleeves. His wavy black hair matched a pair of intense dark blue eyes and three-days of accumulated stubble.

She swallowed. Even half-covered in dirt, the prisoner looked good—*and* he was clearly cool under pressure. She gave a narrow-eyed glare at Constance, who'd apparently neglected to mention that the man she'd led Grace to rescue was almost exactly Grace's age, very attractive, and … *not* wearing a wedding ring.

Constance, hovering just over the man's shoulder, gave Grace a sheepish grin.

Irritation flashing through her, Grace turned, scooped her pack off the ground, and slung it back over her shoulders. This was meant to be an adventure—not a matchmaking service. A mission. Not speed dating with AK47s in the background.

Well, Grace could ensure it *only* remained adventurous.

"This way," she barked, heading north.

The man dutifully followed her. "Thank you," he called after her, still carrying the harness and rope. He kept effortless pace with her, despite Grace's fast stride. "I'm Wade Rawlings."

"Gracelynn Kowalski," she responded curtly. "And don't thank me yet. We're not out of danger—not until we're on the getaway plane."

"We have a getaway plane?" The awe in his voice was palpable, but did nothing to soften her mood.

"Yes."

"Is it just you?"

"Me—and my genie."

The genie she wanted to chastise, but now wasn't the time.

"Is that a metaphor for something? Like… inner compass, gut instinct?"

"Nope."

Grace could sense Wade's confusion, but she didn't pause or turn around to look at him. She continued the hike, keeping a brisk pace.

"How'd you find me?" he asked.

"Spiritual guidance. With attitude." She could certainly derail

Constance's scheming if Wade thought she was crazy. But he wouldn't be interested in her anyway. She was broken, and he probably had a girlfriend.

"How did you find me so soon?" he asked, tone mild as though unruffled by her curt behavior. "I didn't think we'd even be reported missing yet."

We?

Crap. Had she left someone behind? For a second, Grace's mind returned to what she'd thought earlier—*he probably had a girlfriend.*

But then, with a stab of guilt, she remembered his crew. Constance had told Grace that Wade's crew hadn't survived.

"I'm sorry about your team," Grace stammered. "Also, all of your equipment was in the main camp. I wasn't about to risk rescuing it."

His cameras, data, and video footage were all irretrievable.

"I'm just grateful you got me out."

"Don't—"

"—thank you until we're in flight. Yes, got it."

Despite herself, Grace grinned—but fortunately, with her back to him, he couldn't see it.

"So, you were getting footage of the Amazon rainforest?" she asked.

"The rainforest is being devastated by forest fires." Wade's breath deepened as he kept pace with her. "Over thirteen hundred square miles have been destroyed this year. I've been in South America for a month taking photos and video of the wildlife, as well as of the fires. My work was supposed to be used to promote save-the-rainforest efforts in the States."

Grace asked, "Is anything being done about the fires now?"

"Some money is being thrown at it, but not enough." Wade pushed aside a low-hanging branch. "Did Dixon send you?"

"Dixon? I don't know who that is."

"National Geographic," Wade replied. "He fronted me some money for the trip, in exchange for photos. He's the only one I know with the funds and connections to pull off a rescue, not that I'm complaining."

He paused before asking, "So, is this something you do? Rescue hostages?"

"You're my first." She wouldn't explain that rescuing him was intended as a distraction from her own pitiful life. "I'm a physician. I usually do medical missions. This is … a side project." Her voice held false cheer as she shot a menacing look at Constance—the traitorous genie who'd put her in a jungle with a handsome man with a good heart. With her back to her as she floated ahead, Constance missed Grace's glare.

"Like Doctors Without Borders? I did a shoot with them once."

"Yes, like that."

"Dr. Kowalski," he said, as if testing out the sound of the name.

"Just Grace is fine."

"So, do you have a clinic somewhere in Colombia, Grace?" The way he'd said her name sent shuttering delight along her spine—a foreign sensation she hadn't experienced in ages.

Stopping, she turned and finally looked at him.

Wade came to an abrupt halt, almost running into her because he'd been watching his foot placement instead of where he was going—or, maybe, he was too busy asking questions to focus on his surroundings.

She peered up at him, trying to get her bearings with his body close to hers. "No clinic here, Wade," she said coolly. "A spirit friend told me how to rescue you, so I did."

For a heartbeat, only the sounds of the jungle swirled around them.

CHAPTER 4

W ade blinked down at Grace. Her loose blonde hair was frayed at the ends. A pair of dark, green eyes—partially obscured by her chunky bangs—stared back at him. She had full lips and a slender neck. Her tank top exposed fit biceps, glistening with sweat, and the neckline revealed the swell of her bosom. He kept his eyes up though, out of respect. This woman was compact, agile, and not overly muscular—but she'd still probably give him a run for his money in an arm-wrestling match … or dropkick him if she caught him ogling her.

"Spirit friend?" He raised an eyebrow. "Are you on some type of spiritual journey?"

"I suppose I am." After cocking her head to one side, she spun away and resumed walking.

He admired her backside as she walked ahead of him—at least, until he tripped on a root and barely caught himself before falling. Brave, formidable, and gorgeous.

Too bad she's crazy, he thought.

But if crazy got him out of this jungle, he would graciously accept it.

"Does your spirit friend have a name?" he asked, curious how deep the crazy ran.

"Constance."

"Can you see her? How does she guide you?"

Grace glanced back at him, as though puzzled by his line of questioning.

He was used to receiving that look. In fact, Wade's sister had always accused him of asking too many questions. Told him he should've been a reporter rather than a photographer.

"I can see her *and* hear her," Grace eventually answered. "I read somewhere that less than one percent of the population can see and/or hear ghosts."

Where did she read that? The National Inquirer? Wade wondered.

"Is she here now?" he asked.

"Yes, I'm following her back to the rendezvous site."

"What does she look like?"

"A transgender genie in a blue silk jumpsuit."

"Oh." His eyes widened. "That's fairly specific. Does she pop out of a lamp?"

"Sort of," Grace nodded with her back to him. "Spirits can be tied to physical objects if those objects held significance to them during their life. While Constance is anchored to her lamp, she doesn't poof out of it, or live inside it."

Again, Wade thought, *oddly specific.*

Perhaps under any other circumstances, the conversation would have been disturbing—the woman saving him talking about seeing and hearing a ghost, and all—but as they fled through the jungle, the strange topic helped distract Wade from his fear and fatigue.

"How long has she been a spirit?"

"Before Christ."

"Wow. I bet she's handy in Trivial Pursuit."

Grace paused, looked back at him, and finally laughed. She'd been so serious up until this moment that the unexpected laugh made him smile. He liked the musical sound and the way her entire face softened when she was amused.

"How long have you known her?"

Continuing onward, Grace moved a branch aside for him. "Ten years now."

"Oh! So, not a brief spiritual encounter then?"

"No—we're good friends. Perhaps *too* good of friends."

Because the comment didn't seem directed him, Wade didn't ask her to elaborate. Instead, he asked playfully, "You called her a genie. Does she grant wishes?"

Grace's shoulders tightened. "She grants trouble." She continued to press forward, her demeanor returning to the iciness of earlier.

Had his tone or his words set her off?

In a detached, clinical tone, she said, "We're going to be hiking until dusk. You might want to save your energy."

By not talking?

Wade didn't consider conversation an energy expenditure. He'd heard introverts did, though. Perhaps Grace was an introvert who'd rather speak to an imaginary genie than a real person. None of his business—except, he wanted to know more.

Juan Landa stared at the empty pit. Around him, his men took off into the jungle, following tracks left by the man who was supposed to still be in the hole below him.

Impossible!

No one could climb out of the pits.

Based on a second set of smaller footprints, the American had help. But how was that possible? No outsiders knew about this camp. Even satellites couldn't spot it through the dense foliage.

Perhaps a heat signature drone could, Juan mused—but who had the money for one of those? Nobody who cared enough to find their camp, hidden within half a million square kilometers of jungle. Had the photographer been wearing a tracking device?

If a military force had infiltrated, they would have destroyed the camp and not simply rescued a single captive. Besides, how could a rescue team have arrived so fast? Had someone witnessed the kidnapping? That would be the only explanation.

"*Culicagado*," Juan swore.

He *needed* that American—and whatever ransom he was worth. Everyone had someone willing to pay for his or her life.

Juan allocated his money to a worthy cause. His outfit was one of five guerrilla cells in the jungle, each working off the grid to save money for the coming revolution. Colombia's puppet government needed to be replaced by patriots. Because of greedy politicians who cared more about their suits than their people, foreign businesses were stripping the country of its resources—resources that needed to be nationalized for the sake of Colombia's indigenous people.

Juan's phone rang. He snatched it from his pocket. "Hello?"

"I have a sweet proposition for you."

"I'm a little preoccupied, Sal."

"Too busy for a rich American?"

I lost my last one, Juan thought.

Unless his *compatriota*, Sal, referred to the one he'd just lost.

"I'm listening."

"An American woman—a physician—parachuted out of my plane yesterday. I'm supposed to pick her up tomorrow at one of the landing sites."

Juan raised an eyebrow. "Why was she parachuting into the jungle?"

A lone American parachuted into the depths of the Colombian jungle? At the exact moment Juan held another in captivity?

These events were too coincidental for him to dismiss.

"She said she wanted to go sightseeing," Sal grunted. "Anyway— she's a doctor, *and* she had enough money to rent my plane solo. I figure she'd be worth twice my usual fee."

Juan lit a cigarette and took a drag. Phone clasped to his ear, he walked back to his tent. This American woman would be worth twice Sal's fee—*if* Juan captured both her *and* the man who'd escaped.

"Okay," Juan agreed, "but you only get paid when we have her in custody."

"No, I get a finder's fee."

Juan flicked cigarette ash onto the ground as he looked around his tent. He couldn't put together that much cash fast, so he'd have to have something valuable to offer the pilot instead.

His gaze landed on the pile of cameras and video equipment they'd confiscated from the photographer. Probably worth a few thousand American dollars—and the pilot could sell it in any major city.

"Okay," Juan growled. "I'll bring you a finder's fee. Which landing site?"

"*Serpiente verde.*"

"What time do I need to be there tomorrow?" Juan would continue his search for the photographer with his soldiers, right up until the rendezvous time. If his men found the man *and* the woman first, Juan wouldn't have to pay Sal anything.

CHAPTER 5

*C*onstance glided through the air as Grace and Wade slogged through the jungle in silence. The infuriating woman wasn't even trying to be friendly—and Constance knew Grace was fully capable of amicable behavior. She'd had forged many friendships during her medical missions.

Today, though, the exasperating woman seemed to be deliberately thwarting the development of any kind of friendship with the man she'd rescued—perhaps because she suspected Constance of attempting to matchmake the two of them… which, in her defense, Constance *was*.

But Grace needn't be so stubborn about it!

In any event, saving Wade's life should go a long way toward counterbalancing her 'crazy talk' about conversing with ghosts.

Grace almost never talked about seeing ghosts. Today, she wouldn't shut up about it.

Constance knew why. The more unhinged Grace sounded, the farther this handsome photographer would stay from her heart.

"You could ask questions about him," Constance prompted. "Maybe seem interested?"

"I'm not," Grace snapped back.

"Not what?" Wade asked. Because he couldn't see Constance, he'd naturally assumed the comment had been directed at him.

Grace corrected herself. "I'm not, um, sure the weather is going to cooperate. Feels like rain."

Feels like rain?

Constance looked up at the sky.

Oh, my!

It *was* going to rain, and a downpour would have a disastrous impact on their ability to reach the rendezvous point by tomorrow afternoon. Constance began exploring different possible outcomes, focusing her ability to see into the future.

One truth soon became apparent: If Grace and Wade were going to survive, they'd have to take a detour—and Grace wouldn't like it.

GLIDING IN FRONT OF GRACE, Constance took a sharp, southbound turn. Grace followed Constance, and Wade followed her.

"You're right about the rain," the ghost explained. "We need to make a detour."

"How do you keep your bearings in this place?" Wade asked. "The canopy is so thick. I can't even tell what time of day it is." He raised his bare wrist. "Plus, they stole my watch."

"I'm following the ghost," Grace replied curtly, feeling a little guilty that he was forced to put all his trust in her while she projected her frustration with Constance toward him. If she wasn't deliberately undermining Constance's efforts at matchmaking, Grace would have had the decency to lie and comfort him.

Wade cleared his throat. "So, you're telling me that my entire fate —from you finding me in that pit in the first place, to us reaching the plane to escape—relies on the help of a ghost named Constance?"

"She prefers to be called a genie—or jinn, or ginnaye," Grace corrected him. "Besides, she's gotten me this far. I've done ten medical missions—and avoided capture or death three times."

He scoffed, but somehow the sound of disbelief was more humor than irritation. "I've been in and out of war zones taking photographs, and avoided a similar fate more times than that, but I've never claimed spirits were involved."

In and out of war zones? Risking his life? Grace took a moment to absorb that tidbit. Constance had told Grace that Wade had been in more than one tight spot before, so he wouldn't be in pieces when she pulled him from the pit.

"What was your third wish?" Wade asked, changing the subject.

She stopped, and for a moment the jungle sounds seemed louder than his voice. Turning slightly, she cast soft words over her shoulder. "You've heard the saying *be careful what you wish for*? Well, it's true."

"Grace—"

She turned back and continued walking, not letting Wade finish his sentence.

That would be the end of it, she was sure. The photographer, who risked his life for impactful images to change the world, had now seen her spirits—*and* seen her broken. There'd be no burgeoning friendship between them, and Constance's matchmaking efforts would fizzle into oblivion—where they belonged.

Raindrops began to fall, tapping out a gentle melody on the canopy of trees.

"Should we set up something to collect rainwater for drinking later?" Wade asked.

"I've got a Life Straw filter," Grace called back. "It'll remove bacteria and protozoa from any water source and make it drinkable. But I don't want to stop until dusk."

"Can I at least carry something? I've only got the harness and rope. You've got all the weight in your pack."

Constance turned her head, floated in front of Grace, and scowled. "Let him carry something. It can't be any heavier than the mound of misery you insist on carrying with you wherever you go."

Grace rolled her eyes and replied to both of them by snapping, "When we stop for camp for the night, we'll sort out how to divide it up. No stopping before then—we don't have time."

Constance's words wriggled under Grace's skin, though.

The misery you insist on carrying.

Choosing to cling to her grief was voluntary. Grace knew that, even if hearing it was hard. Daniel had been gone for two years now, and Grace still hadn't let it go. She would never let the emotions go—but she knew she didn't have to wear them like a shield, or like shackles. Daniel wouldn't have wanted that anyway.

"I bet the kids love you on road trips," Wade said as he followed her through the dense jungle, oblivious to her inner turmoil. "Do you allow bathroom breaks?"

"They have to pee in a cup," Grace said—and then, sensing his shock, reluctantly added, "I'm kidding. I don't have any children. You?"

"No children," Wade replied. "I was married once, but she decided she didn't like my working environment. Said she felt like she'd married a soldier—one who may or may not return from each tour of duty." He sighed. "I'm mostly to blame, I guess. I didn't make enough effort, and we were both young."

Grace hadn't expected Wade to open up like that. She certainly hadn't planned on doing the same, but his sharing caused a nagging sense of obligation to well up inside her.

"My first marriage—also too young," Grace reluctantly offered, "ended when we discovered we were incompatible in all the nuances of life: hobbies, travel, money management, and even monogamy." She sighed. "The first ended badly. The second was amazing. He died in a bike accident … "

"That's terrible." His voice sounded thick and empathetic. "How long ago?"

"Two years."

Sometimes, the ache is still so raw it feels like two days.

"I guess spirits are safer relationships," Grace continued. "Maybe that's why I kept Constance around so long. She doesn't cheat, lie, or steal. And she can't die on me."

Constance glanced briefly back at her, eyes full of compassion.

Wade said, "But you're living your life, at least. I've seen a lot of people simply exist instead of living. You haven't shut out the world, despite your suffering."

"I became a physician to help people," Grace said quietly. "I have no intention of stopping that." She paused before asking, "Are you normally this positive and encouraging? Or only toward people who rescue you?"

"Probably mostly the rescue."

When she glanced back, Wade grinned at her. The rain had drawn his dark waves into curls, and drops of moisture ran down his cheeks. The drops had become a downpour.

"Water break?" he asked.

She stopped, unhooked the canteen, and handed it to him.

He took a long drink. "Do your parents know you venture into jungles and save complete strangers?"

"I always let them know which country I'm going to, and for how long—but they don't know the details." She chuckled. "Better for my dad's blood pressure that way. I'm sure they assumed this was another medical mission trip."

"Are you close to them?" He took another drink before handing the canteen back to her.

"We don't live close, but we talk every week. My parents live in Nashville." She reattached the canteen and took her own drink from the straw attached to the water pouch tucked into her backpack. From the side pocket, she pulled out a packet of trail mix and handed him the bag.

"Nashville? Is that where the name Gracelynn comes from?" He munched a handful of trail mix.

"Yes, actually. My dad is a huge Elvis fan. Apparently, if I'd been a boy, I would have been Elvis. He had to settle for Grace."

"I like Grace."

"Well, much to my mom's chagrin, my dad still calls me Elvis. Drives her crazy. Of course, that's probably part of the reason he calls me that."

Wade chuckled. "Well, you look much more like a Grace than an Elvis."

"Thank you. Thank you very much."

"Not a bad impersonation." He grinned, an expression that warmed something inside her.

Grace winked. "You should see me in my blue suede shoes."

Her face grew hot despite the cool raindrops. Was she actually flirting? In a jungle? With a man she barely knew?

Ugh—she must've come across as *so* lame. At least Constance was only eavesdropping and not adding her own commentary right now.

She needed to focus on the rescue. They'd escaped the camp and put distance between themselves and the rebels, but safety wasn't guaranteed until they were out of the country.

She didn't want her first rescue mission to be her last.

CHAPTER 6

*W*ade couldn't help but admire Grace's red cheeks, framed by the blonde hair clinging to the side of her face and neck. The unflappable jungle doctor on a mission blushed when she flirted, transforming the prickly front she'd put on initially. He appreciated the flirting, but it made him notice how her soaked shirt clung tightly to the curves of her athletic body.

He forced his eyes back to hers, saying, "The rain is probably a good thing. It'll wash away our tracks."

She nodded, adjusting her backpack.

"Here—I'll take it." He approached and began hoisting the heavy pack off her shoulders.

When she turned, her footing slipped in the mud. He tried to catch her, but his feet were swept out from under him as well. They both landed in a tangled heap, and their bodies began a rapid descent through the slick mud.

They were cascading down the jungle slopes, like they were riding a log flume, and all Wade could do was cling tighter to her to avoid being separated. A thick root nearly clotheslined them.

As they slid through the mud, Wade desperately wondered if he could angle his body in front of hers in order to absorb the brunt of their landing whenever it came.

Suddenly, the bottom fell out from beneath them, and they plummeted through the air. When Grace unleashed a panicked gasp, he realized that was the first sign of fear he'd seen or heard from her.

Looking down, a flash of shimmering sapphire greeted him seconds before water engulfed them. The river hit like a fist. Cold closed over his head.

He fought the heavy drag of his wet clothes, fumbling for the backpack. Grace's fingers were locked around one strap, knuckles white. Tugging the backpack close to him, he kicked hard, hauling them both upward with the pack keeping the two of them tethered.

As their heads broke the surface, he took a gasping breath. The fast-flowing river they'd plummeted into carried them swiftly north.

"There!" Wade cried, indicating a bank where they could both swim.

"It's on the wrong side of the river to get to the rendezvous point!" Grace shouted, splashing and spluttering. "And Constance says there's a coral snake in the tree by the edge!"

The icy chill that instantly shuddered through Wade had nothing to do with the temperature of the water. "Let's *not* go there!"

Snakes. He'd been so excited about escaping that he hadn't been thinking about jungle snakes. What were the rules about stripes and danger?

Red touches black, no worries for Jack. Red touches yellow, dangerous fellow.

He mostly hoped he'd never get close enough to see red touching *anything*. He might not believe in ghosts and genies, but if one was warning him about snakes, then he would listen.

He and Grace swam toward the bank on the opposite side of the fast-flowing river. They struggled to pull themselves out of the water by clawing through the mud and tree roots. Eventually flopping onto the safety of the rain-soaked bank, they gasped desperately for breath.

After a moment to compose themselves, he struggled up—shaking out the sodden backpack. Beside him, Grace squeezed water out of the front of her shirt.

"You okay?" he asked.

"Shaken, not stirred," she snorted. "Dang. Now I want a martini."

As he pulled the backpack on, Wade winced, feeling a sharp pain in his side.

Her voice was filled with concern. "What is it?"

"Probably just bruising." He grunted. "The kidnappers had a little fun softening the toes of their boots on my ribs."

"Let me see." She leaned closer.

Although he liked her concern and the idea of her hand on him, he shook his head. "Let's just finish getting where we're going for the night." He might not be a physician, but even he knew not much could be done if he had broken ribs—not here in the jungle.

As they resumed walking, wet clothing and soaked shoes weighed him down, but each step took them both closer to escaping the jungle.

After fifteen minutes, they finally pushed between fanning ferns and found themselves in a small clearing. The clouds overhead had parted, and sun streamed through the tree leaves. Light sparkled off the surface of a small waterfall cascading down onto a stone ledge before emptying into a shallow pond.

"Oh, Wade." Grace's voice filled with astonishment as she stared at the view. Then, she shook her head, as if listening to a voice he couldn't hear. "Right—thank you, Constance."

He looked at her, raising an eyebrow. "This seems like a good place to rest for the night."

"And to take a shower," Grace added, voice all eager anticipation..

Spinning in a slow circle, he gauged the clearing. A tent would fit nicely off to one side.

When he came back full circle, he discovered Grace tugging off her shirt, presenting her back to him.

"Whoa! What are you doing?"

She stopped and turned to look over her bare shoulder at him.

"I told you I was taking a shower—and then you turned around! I thought we were on the same page."

He averted his eyes. "Okay, okay—sorry. I didn't realize you meant *right* now." He turned his back to her, shrugged off the heavy back-pack, and busied himself unloading the contents they needed.

When he finally had the inventory arranged, he peeled off his wet socks, boots, and shirt, and grabbed the small bottle of soap he'd found in the backpack.

"Soap?" he offered.

"Yes—and there's a blanket in there we can use as a towel."

He side-stepped over to Grace, extending his hand to pass her the soap—and catching a glimpse of her bare, toned legs.

There was no place close to the waterfall to hang the blanket for her, so he stood there instead—blanket in hand, staring at a red *Passiflora* that bore vibrant, slender petals.

"Thanks." She lifted the blanket from his hand and walked past him, towel wrapped around her.

"My turn."

After peeling off his sodden pants, he carried them, along with his shirt and socks, to the waterfall. He left on his boxers—which, to his mind, was the equivalent of a swimsuit. He had no intention of clinging to modesty in the middle of a jungle.

He stepped beneath the cascading waterfall and closed his eyes—letting the water wash away the coat of mud on him. Then, he scrubbed dirt out of his hair and off the rest of his body. Finally, he washed his clothes, hanging them to dry on a marmalade bush.

Grace, now dressed again, handed him the blanket. For a second, he thought he'd caught her staring at his bare chest, and he felt heat in his cheeks as he dried off.

Now who's blushing, Wade?

When he finished, she handed him a wad of spare clothes with a toothbrush on top.

"You brought me a change of clothes?"

She shrugged. "When Constance told me you were being held at the bottom of a pit, I figured you'd want clean clothing."

He checked the tags. "You even got my size!"

"Courtesy of Constance," Grace nodded. "She mentioned a few things about you—" she shot an annoyed look to her right—as if to somebody Wade couldn't see "—and neglected to mention a few others."

He raised an eyebrow. "What other thing?"

"Never mind. We need to make camp."

"I thought that spot over there would make even ground for a tent."

Grace bit her lip, placing her hands on her hips. She gazed upward. "No. It might rain again, and this area is prone to flash floods. We need to camp up in the tree."

"*In* the tree?" Wade rubbed the back of his neck. "I've slept in some strange places, but never in a tree before. This'll be a first for me. Do we strap ourselves to the branches or something?"

More importantly—would there be snakes up there?

Grace stepped into the harness and pulled it on. "Not exactly."

Overhead, thunder rolled again. Somewhere in the distance, something howled.

Tonight they'd sleep in the trees. Tomorrow they'd find out if the jungle planned to let them leave.

CONSTANCE HOVERED near Grace while she set up the hammock. She used the tent as a tarp for a roof.

One hammock. Two people.

Events were progressing nicely.

"You were peeking as he showered, Darling."

"So were *you*," Grace fired back.

Constance chuckled. "Well, yes—who wouldn't admire those broad shoulders and muscular chest? Yum, yum."

"You know, he's *also* a renowned photographer—dedicated to bringing the world the truth in pictures."

Beneath them, Wade watched Grace work, but he was out of earshot. He couldn't safely join her in the tree yet, since Grace only had one harness.

"Yes," Constance murmured, high above him. "Well, the brains are the bonus to the brawn."

"Maybe the brawn is the bonus to the brains," Grace retorted.

Constance waved a hand in the air. "*Toe-may-toe, toe-mah-toe,*" she paused, "and you *like* him." She jabbed a finger at Grace.

She rolled her eyes, tying one end of the hammock off. "Of course I *like* him. He's smart, adventurous, good-natured, and—yes—attractive." Her eyes narrowed. "I find it interesting—and no coincidence, I'm sure—that you picked someone my age and *single* for me to rescue."

Constance beamed a smile. "You asked for an adventure. You know I never underdeliver."

"No, Constance, you certainly do not."

Constance frowned. The conversation had been focused nicely on Wade, and then she'd inadvertently reminded Grace of the wishes with that last statement.

"Can I do anything?" Wade called up to her.

"Open the MREs," Grace suggested. "We'll eat."

Grace turned back to Constance. "You realize we have a logistical problem here, right? I brought one tent—which is now our roof and protection from getting rained on all night—and one hammock. That's now the only bed."

Constance grinned and batted her excessively long lashes. "I don't see that as a *problem*, Darling."

"One person can sleep in the hammock and the other strapped to the tree," Grace considered, "but I still only have one mosquito net."

Constance poked out her bottom lip as she clicked her nails together. "I can see only one logical solution."

"Of course you can." Grace finished securing the ties at the other end of the hammock.

"Remember to sleep on his right side. The hairline rib fractures are on the left."

Tonight, romance under the stars.

Tomorrow, flee from impending danger.

CHAPTER 7

*A*s Grace and Wade ate the food, sitting on a log beneath the hammock, they discussed their families. Grace was an only child, while Wade had an older sister. Grace lived in upstate New York, while Wade mostly lived wherever the next job took him. She enjoyed the casual exchange and how easily they conversed.

Chewing a spoonful of MRE, he asked, "How did you discover Constance?"

"Are you saying you're a believer now?" Grace playfully nudged him with her elbow.

"I'm saying some of the things you've known are uncannily accurate, so I don't know what to believe."

Grace nodded, feeling confident enough to speak about it. "I discovered her lamp while I was a medical student," she explained. "I bought it and took it home to my dorm room. When a genie seemingly popped out, I freaked out. Lucky for me, my dorm roommate could see ghosts, too—she explained to me how they work."

"How they work?"

"Some people see and hear them," Grace nodded. "Some only hear them. Some ghosts have a stronger presence than others. Some can see the future or glean information from people."

"And some grant wishes?"

Grace sighed. Wade wasn't going to forget about the wish thing.

Not that she minded. He seemed pleasant enough to talk with so far. Why not divulge her past to a stranger? It seemed fitting, as the sun set over them in the depths of this Colombian jungle.

"Not *real* wishes per se," Grace explained. "Since Constance can see the outcome of any set of intended actions, she can tell someone which course of action to take to achieve that '*wish*'."

"Like studying harder to pass an exam? Or like entering a particular set of numbers to win the lottery?"

"More like the latter."

Wade's brows shot up. "Wow. Okay, then—so what was your first wish?"

"Probably what half the twenty-two-year-old women of the world want. Love."

"You wished for love?" His tone was more awe than incredulous.

"I did—and Constance made it happen. I positioned myself in the right place and at the right time—for Mr. Wrong. He and I fell madly in love before actually *knowing* each other. It was all passion and no substance, and as simmering passion went as flat and stale as day-old champagne, we both discovered how little we had in common."

Grace took a drink of water. "Or rather, I found out how dishonest he'd been about who he was—not that I was entirely truthful, either. I never mentioned Constance, for example." She sighed. "Anyway, the divorce proceeded with haste. Not painless, but quick. I was devastated at the time. Young and divorced, and so terribly naive."

"That's brutal. I take it Constance's predictions only go so far."

"Yeah. They're short-term predictions, since longer outcomes inherently rely on so many more variables."

"I'm guessing wish number two had nothing to do with love?"

Grace chuckled. "You are correct. I was twenty-four when I cast the second wish. I went for money this time. I was in medical school, living off Ramen noodles, and staring at a quarter of a million dollars in student loans."

Wade winced. "Lottery numbers?"

"That probably would have been smarter. Unfortunately, my request was a little vaguer. I just wished for money—and nothing shady about how it came to me. Constance led me to Daniel, and the true love I'd been looking for with my first wish."

Grace took a deep breath. "He was a practicing physician. Together, we lived frugally and paid off my loans. We were on a path to financial independence by the age forty-five. I'd thought that was the extent of it—wish granted. Two actually, because I had love back in my life."

She massaged her temples.

Wade placed a hand on her shoulder.

"I'm sorry, Grace. If it's too painful…"

Actually, it was the opposite. The more she talked, the more a weight lifted from her chest. "It's painful," she admitted, "but I think I'm past due for sharing. You're the first to hear the true story." Grace took another deep breath before explaining. "A car hit Daniel while he was out riding his bike. He died, and he left a trust fund. It's a fund I never knew he had, and he left it all to me. That—and a life insurance policy."

"What are you telling me?" Wade smiled gently. "That I'm eating dehydrated ice cream in the depths of the Colombian jungle with a beautiful millionaire?" His eyes twinkled. "One who just saved my life?"

Grace shrugged. "I guess. But I'd trade all of that money in a heartbeat if Daniel could just come back."

Wade swallowed.

"Anyway—" Grace ran her fingers through her hair "—that was two years ago. Two days ago, I made my final wish." She turned her head, and their eyes met. "I asked Constantine for an adventure, and here I am."

Wade smiled. "I'm grateful your adventure meant you came to my rescue."

"Ah." Grace gave a tsk. "You say that now." She scraped the last bit of MRE from the pouch, avoiding his gaze. "You may revoke your gratitude once you hear the sleeping arrangement."

~

Wade adjusted his body as the sound of rain pattered on the tent above him. Grace lay beside him in the nylon hammock, her head resting on his shoulder.

"Are you comfortable?" he asked.

They'd tried side-by-side and back-to-back; in the end, gravity had made the decision for them. This was the only way to fit two bodies in one hammock without someone ending up in the mud.

"Maybe too comfortable," Grace admitted. "My eyes won't stay open much longer—especially with the sound of the rain overhead." She shifted in the hammock—to the point that Wade wondered if she was inadvertently snuggling up to him. "Did you know you're incredibly warm? It's like you're my personal bedwarmer. I got chilly last night because this hammock doesn't hold any heat."

Wade smiled in the darkness.

Hmmm. The woman bold enough to launch a solo rescue mission in the guerrilla-infested Colombian jungle fell to nerves rambling in the arms of a man? He felt flattered.

He kept his voice low as he spoke. "You know, we all wish for things in life. Some come true and some don't. Bad things happen when we make mistakes, and bad things happen even when we don't. Sometimes, good things happen when we make mistakes." He let out a deep breath. "My point is—I hope you don't blame yourself, or your ghost, for every bad thing that's happened to you or the people you love. It sounds like you live life to its fullest extent, and that in and of itself is remarkable."

Grace's fingers found his in the dark, tentative at first, then settling as if they'd done this a hundred times.

He hesitated, feeling her pulse flutter against his palm. Darkness made people brave—or foolish. He lifted her hand and brushed his lips across her knuckles, a gentle press of warmth in the cool, damp air.

Her breath hitched. Then their joined hands relaxed back onto his chest, right over the steady thump of his heart.

So, maybe she had money, and maybe she had a genie. Wade couldn't offer Grace anything spectacular, but it seemed that what she needed more than anything was comfort—that, he had an abundance to offer.

She let out a contented sigh as she relaxed into him. Soon, her breathing became slow and rhythmic.

As he listened to the steady fall of rain overhead, he pondered the complexities of this woman. He'd seen many things on his global travels, but nothing that would make him believe in ghosts. Until now.

He had no explanation for how someone with no military training could infiltrate a rebel cell in the depths of a foreign jungle—and rescue him just three days after his initial abduction. Those were impossible odds—unless you had a genie in your pocket.

He'd have to process all of this later. Tonight, he needed rest—and tomorrow, they needed to be at the rendezvous to meet that plane.

While he hoped the trouble was behind them, he wouldn't rest easy until he left the country behind.

JUAN'S wet and deflated men ambled back into camp empty-handed. They hadn't found the Americans. He and his team had until noon tomorrow to do so—otherwise, he'd have to pay that pilot and then seize the *gringos* from him.

Tonight, though, Juan needed everyone to rest. They'd resume the hunt fresh at daybreak.

One way or the other, Juan would have his prisoners by tomorrow. This time, he'd make sure they weren't left unguarded. He'd also strip-search them for tracking devices, since he couldn't fathom how this American woman could have found the man she'd rescued—if they even were traveling together, which he still didn't have official confirmation of.

Juan brought his cross pendant to his lips and kissed the gold crucifix. Tonight, he'd pray to the patron Saint Rose of Lima. She'd understand his need. Rose had dedicated her life to helping her community—just as Juan was trying to do for his own.

The sale of drugs, the kidnappings, and the extortion were merely a means to an end. Life had become so much more complicated since Rose's era. Selling needlework and flowers, like she'd done, wasn't going to cut it in the 21st century.

But if all proceeded as planned, Juan would soon have his captives. Then, he could squeeze them financially dry, and let the jungle finish them off.

He needed the ransom money and hoped to take them alive. Of course, if the photographer and the physician died trying to escape, his organization could simply use that as an example of what happened to capitalist pigs when they came to Colombia.

CHAPTER 8

Grace woke to the rowdy squawking of Capuchin monkeys clinging to a nearby tree. She started to stir, but froze when she felt a muscular body resting beside her. She'd been so deeply asleep that she'd forgotten she wasn't alone.

Lying beside her in the hammock, Wade smelled like the little bottle of citrus soap she'd brought with her but mixed with his own scent of sage. She turned her head to look at him. In the dim morning light, the dark whiskers of his square jawline were visible. She smiled at the sight of his wavy hair gone wild in his sleep.

Lips curled at the edges, Grace began to move her hand off his firm abdomen.

At her movement, Wade stirred. He turned slightly in the hammock and tightened his hold on her. Grace's body responded to his heat and touch, flooding her with a warm sensation in her core that made her heart beat faster.

She stiffened before reassuring herself this was probably an entirely normal physiological response. After all, she hadn't slept—in any sense of the word—with a man in two years.

"Wade?"

When he wriggled against her, she bit back a groan.

"*Wade?*"

His eyes flickered open. She gave him a moment to remember that he was in a jungle, sleeping with a stranger, in a hammock swinging twelve feet above the ground.

When his dark blue eyes finally blinked with registration, Wade grinned rather than letting her go. His eyes lit with desire.

Swallowing back her physical response, she tried not to think about how their bodies were separated by nothing more than a couple of layers of thin clothing.

"I need your help getting out of the hammock," she said.

"Sure. What can I do?" He moved his hands down to her waist as she sat up.

"There's no graceful way to do this," she warned, "and I need to pee. So, put your hands wherever you need to in order to hoist me out while keeping me from falling back on top of you."

"That doesn't sound too difficult."

When Grace shot him a look over her shoulder, he chuckled.

As Wade hoisted her up, she reached outside the mosquito net for one of the dangling ropes. At the same time, she extended a foot across to a nearby branch.

When the swing of the hammock started to pull her away from the tree, Wade gave her a firm push on the buttocks, launching her across the gaping chasm until she was safely standing on the thick limb.

"That was *not* intentional," Wade called out to her, holding out the hands he'd cupped her backside with.

She laughed. The touch had been brief and accidental, but her heartbeat punched upward like she'd been shocked. "It's okay. I needed the boost." She smiled as she slipped into the harness.

Seemingly encouraged by her reaction, he grinned. "Full disclosure, though, I might have enjoyed it."

She arched an eyebrow at him and attempted to suppress a grin as he smiled wryly at her. Feeling his eyes on her, Grace lowered herself from the tree.

"I think you enjoyed it, too," he called after her as she descended.

She didn't look up, but she felt warmth spread up her neck and into her cheeks and ears.

CONSTANCE WATCHED THE EXCHANGE, rubbing her hands together with greedy delight. Her plan seemed to be working after all, and fortunately the weather was cooperative.

In addition to her ability to see into the future, if Constance focused properly, she could also stir a little wind, move a few clouds or fog, and even disrupt electrical currents. All were very minor except in rare circumstances.

Although she'd had nothing to do with the rain and mudslide, the such romantic detour was a delightful bonus. Now, more urgent matters took precedence. The cute couple still needed to make it to the airstrip to escape this jungle.

Airstrip. Ha! Some might be more inclined to call a strip of pasture land, and it was still a fair distance away.

Back up in the tree, Grace and Wade worked together to untie the ropes, hammock, and tent. After they'd untied everything, the two of them descended the tree, one at a time, using the harness and ropes.

Constance enjoyed watching them work together. She hadn't yet informed Grace that the hunt for Wade Rawlings was well underway. Their initial search had taken the guerrillas down Grace's decoy path, which had given Grace and Wade a good head start—until the mudslide.

Now, the pair were behind schedule. And this morning, the Colombians were broadening their search and strategically including every means of extrication from the jungle, including the local airstrips.

Grace needed to arrive at the rendezvous point on time and use her green smoke flare to signal the pilot that he was safe to land his tiny, single-engine casket—er, *plane*—to extract them. If he didn't see the smoke signal at the agreed upon time, the pilot had been ordered to circle the landing strip just once before leaving.

If he left, Grace and Wade were as a good as dead. Without a plane, there'd be no leaving the Colombian jungle, and they wouldn't be able to outrun the guerrillas for long.

Constance fanned herself with her hands as she floated toward Grace.

"You two need to get a move on."

"Trouble?" Grace raised an eyebrow as she rolled up the hammock. Across the clearing, Wade rolled up the tent.

"I'm worried the Colombians will reach the airstrip before you do," Constance explained.

"Well, will they?"

Constance drew her lips in a straight line. "I can't tell." She couldn't see *everything*.

"Okay—we'll move faster."

"What trouble?" Wade asked.

Constance noted he didn't seem unduly perturbed about Grace communicating with an entity he could neither see nor hear.

Grace turned to him. "Constance says your captors are advancing on our airstrip. It's going to be a race to the finish line."

She began packing supplies faster as she spoke, fashioning the harness into a back strap and securing the tent, blanket, and hammock to it. She deftly secured the equipment. Constance had been with Grace on her many hiking trips—some peaceful, domestic excursions and others with danger hot on her heels. The dangerous ones had only been in the last few years—ever since Daniel's death. Each had been more dangerous than the last, and each had required increasingly faster packing skills.

Well, if Grace was determined to tempt fate—perhaps to join Daniel sooner than destiny had intended—Constance could at least try to counter that by using her powers of perception to keep Grace alive; and hopefully rediscover her passion for life.

Wade finished packing the backpack and slung it over his shoulders. "We good?"

Grace nodded, cinching the harness. "Ready."

Constance took the lead, and the three of them began the trek.

. . .

WADE KEPT up with the brisk pace set by Grace. As he hiked, he thought about what a weird trio they made: A photographer, a physician, and an imaginary ghost dodging armed guerrilla fighters. There were worse ways to spend the night in a jungle than holding a competent and beautiful woman, but the impending threat of their pursuers kept him from truly enjoying the moment.

This wasn't Wade's first brush with danger. He'd been on a chopper from Kabul to Ghanzi—photographing the ravages of war—when enemy fire riddled the chopper. The helicopter had been forced to land in Taliban-controlled territory, and for two days Wade snuck through hazardous mountains and arid desert to reach safety.

At least the jungles of Colombia were prettier.

He tried to quell his nagging worry over the dwindling probability of escape by staying observant of his surroundings. "I wish I had my camera," he lamented. "The exotic plants and wildlife are breathtaking."

"Maybe you can come back after this and take more pictures of the Amazon. Just take a different route back home next time." Grace held a cluster of vines aside for Wade to walk past.

"My equipment's gone." He sighed. "No photos means no payment —and no payment means no way to buy replacement equipment."

They trudged through the jungle in silence. He hoped his complaint hadn't sounded like an invitation for her to offer to buy him new equipment. He'd figure something out when he got home.

Eventually, Grace broke the silence. "I'm sorry about your crew. Even if I'd arrived sooner, I don't think I could have done anything for them."

"Please don't apologize. We were in the wrong place at the wrong time. I'm nothing but grateful you arrived when you did."

Grace snorted. "Don't thank me yet."

"I *am* thanking you." He laughed bitterly. "Accept it. Even if they beat us to the plane, you did everything you could." He reached out and touched her arm softly, adding, "So, thank you, Grace."

She turned and smiled. "You're welcome."

As she resumed walking, he followed closely behind and worked up the courage to ask, "When we're back home, maybe I can buy you a drink sometime?"

An inexplicable flutter buzzed in his chest. Did he just ask her on a date?

This woman clearly wasn't even operating with a full deck of cards—not with the whole imaginary ghost friend thing. So, why did he feel nervous about her response? Why was his heart counting the beats as the seconds ebbed by? Grace was an attractive, fit, and intelligent physician—despite the paranormal delusions. She was also apparently rich. Yeah. She was out of his league, and that made him nervous.

"Sure," she answered casually. "We can reminisce about that time in the Colombian jungle over a glass of Guinness."

"Yeah," Wade chuckled humorlessly. His initial relief that she'd agreed was quickly replaced with confusion. Reminisce? Did she just transform his asking her out into something platonic? He'd have to remedy that.

"Wade."

He stopped suddenly—but not before almost running into her.

She turned to face him, and their bodies were almost touching.

"We're two miles out," she warned, "which means we need silence from here to the airstrip."

He nodded—even though what he really had the urge to do was pull her into his arms and fit their bodies together like they had in the hammock.

Get a grip, Wade.

Normal people didn't make out in a jungle.

Then again, normal people also didn't follow a ghost through the aforementioned jungle, and normal people probably didn't risk their lives photographing the beauty enveloped in danger in that same jungle. Or equally hazardous places elsewhere across the world.

Clearly, there was nothing normal about either of them.

Before he had a chance to do something stupid about it—like lean in for a kiss—Grace resumed walking.

Slow your shutter speed, Wade. Some rich chick with a reckless side doesn't want your cheap hands all over her.

As soon as that thought escaped his mind, he knew it was unfair to Grace. She'd never behaved in any way to suggest she thought herself better than him. Not to mention, out of all the people in the world she could have used her resources to help rescue from danger, she had chosen *him*.

CHAPTER 9

Grace motioned for Wade to crouch, dropping down to her knees herself. The two of them remained hidden under the cover of the lush jungle ferns, but through the foliage, she could make out the clearing ahead where their landing strip was located.

The Cessna they were trying to rendezvous with was parked at the end of the runway, engine off.

"Dammit." She hissed out the word.

On the other side of the fern, Constance began chewing her translucent nails, staring at the plane. She was clearly as concerned as Grace was.

Wade crouched so close behind Grace that he bumped elbows with her beneath the cover of the ferns. He followed her line of sight.

"I see the plane. What's the problem?" he asked.

Easing the harness off her back, she gave her shoulders a rest. "The pilot wasn't supposed to land—not without my flare signal."

"But he's here now. We have a ride out, right?"

Grace shook her head as a lump formed in her throat. How did she tell Wade she'd failed him?

She rubbed her temple. "If he landed and parked on this strip, that means he's working for the Colombian fighters."

"You're sure that's our plane?"

"I'm sure." Her mind raced. What were their options now?

Turning to her ghostly friend, she said, "Constance, if I try to negotiate with them, will they accept payment and let us go?"

Constance's eyes fluttered as she focused on the future and the outcome if Grace followed a specific course of action.

"I'm not letting you do that," Wade interrupted, but neither Grace nor her ghostly genie listened to him.

"No, Darling," Constance warned Grace. "If they seize you, they'll never let you go. And Wade won't survive."

Grace swallowed and took his hand. "I should have made a backup plan."

Her gaze snagged on movement by the plane. "Wait, I see the pilot. Constance, can you tell what he's saying to the guy with the AK-47?"

The two men were smoking, but she was too far away to hear them—not that she'd be able to understand them, anyway. Her Spanish was still a work in progress and better suited to asking a patient to stick out a tongue than understanding an exchange between two sketchy villains.

Constance accepted the task, though, and vanished.

That left Grace alone with Wade. She looked down at their hands, only now realizing she'd intertwined her fingers with those of the handsome photographer. When she started to pull her hand away, he clasped it with both of his.

"I'm sorry," she said, still staring at their joined hands. "We can keep hiking north until we reach a town, but we'll run out of food in a day."

He cupped her chin and brought it up until they were making eye contact. "You got me out of that pit, Grace. I thought I'd die in there. If you managed that, I know we'll get through this, too—together."

She nodded, staring into those warm blue eyes and full lips framed in stubble.

She was so close to him, kneeling in the ferns, that one small motion would bring her close enough to sink her fingertips into his thick, black hair. The air grew quiet as the leaves faintly danced around them.

"So," Constance's shimmering apparition reappeared in a puff of blue smoke—very genie-like.

Startled, Grace pulled back from Wade and released his hand. "Constance!"

"Oh, damn." Constance looked back and forth between the two of them with a wry smile. "I interrupted something, didn't I? Was there magic in the air? Were you going to kiss him, you saucy vixen?"

"*No!* Knock it off. What did you hear?"

"They're contemplating why you're late. One of them suggested checking the river, so two men are hiking down there while the other two stay here. Two more are retracing their steps back to camp."

Grace relayed everything to Wade.

"Two here." His brows furrowed. "I'm not sure we can take two armed men."

"Even if we could—then what? I can't fly a plane."

"I can," he shrugged. "I mean, I'm not a pilot yet, but I've logged forty hours of flight time—and another forty on the simulator."

She stared at him, wanting to kiss him even more this time.

He shrugged, his cheeks turning red. "I did so much remote travel and learned a lot from pilots over the years, I decided to work toward getting my recreational pilot certificate. Single-engine planes I can do. Helicopters? I'm not so good at them yet."

"Okay." Grace beamed. "We have a pilot."

"I can take out the two men," Constance said.

Grace turned to her, astonished. "How?"

"You know I was responsible for the plague of locusts in Capua in 203 B.C.?" She paused. "Well, not *directly* responsible—the swarm was coming anyway. My jinn 'magic' merely directed it where it should go."

Grace stared. "Constance, this isn't the time for your ancient war stories."

"Darling, everything is the time for my ancient war stories."

Grace growled in frustration when she wanted to snarl. "You're going to distract them with bugs?"

"Something like that. Move closer to the plane, and on my signal, get to it and take off."

"Oh-kay." Grace's voice dripped with skepticism. "We need a long enough distraction for us to start the plane *and* take off."

"Darling, I never underdeliver."

Grace exhaled—whether from relief or rising fear, she wasn't sure. She turned to Wade and held up her index finger. "One moment. I'll be right back."

As she walked several steps away from him, Constance followed.

She turned to the genie as she hovered alongside her in a cloud of blue smoke.

"Listen," she told Constance, "I appreciate that you feel like you have to fix everything, but when my wishes went south, it was on me."

Setting a fast pace, Grace tried to piece together her thoughts into something cohesive, but not hurtful. "Your abilities have limits, Constance," she warned. "I'm not faulting you for that. I'm the imbecile that jumped out of a plane over Colombia." She clasped her hands together. "What I'm trying to say is: You could make things worse than they already are."

Constance scowled.

Grace kept on, ignoring the disapproving glare. "Maybe Wade and I should just give the Colombians a wide birth," she suggested. "We could hike north toward Bogotá." She glanced over her shoulder, back at Wade, who stared intently at the ground as though diamonds were buried there. As though sensing her, he perked up and looked her direction.

Constance's reaction wasn't quite so copacetic. "Make things *worse?*" Constance glowered, rising to her full, rather masculine height.

Grace cringed—not out of fear, but out of recognition that she'd just deeply upset her ghostly friend.

"Is that what I do?" Constance boomed. "I make things *worse?*"

"Now, hang on." Grace's defensive temper flared, but she kept her voice a harsh whisper to avoid giving their presence away to the two nearby armed Colombians.

Constance could roar at the top of a mountain—only Grace would hear her. Grace herself, though, couldn't risk speaking too loudly.

"I don't *blame* you," Grace whispered heatedly. "I'm merely suggesting that *sometimes* things don't turn out the way you predicted they would—and we *need* this escape to be a successful one—our lives depend on it."

Constance scoffed. "*All* of my predictions—my guiding your future —have been spot on. You wanted love? I gave you love. You wanted money? I provided it."

She rolled her heavily lashed eyes. "I *never* underdeliver, Darling? Tiglath-Pileser, King of Assyria, wanted a professional army, and I delivered. The maharaja, Shivaji Bhonsle wanted an empire, and yup, I provided that, too." Her face hardened. "Whatever disaster ensued from some cascade of events later down the line—love lost, lives lost, famine, plagues, pestilence … well, they're your own damn faults!"

Grace clenched her fists. "*Thank you*, Constance." She seethed through gritted teeth. "I'm *well* aware my choices are my own, and that they've ultimately led me to this moment." Grace blinked away angry tears. "Money without love. Possible captivity without end." She turned away, unable to look at Constance anymore.

If Constance was remorseful, she didn't show it. Instead, she seethed. "Oh, don't worry. I'll get you out of this mess—and *then* you won't have to worry about my *interference* anymore."

With that, Constance abruptly vanished.

GRACE SAT DEJECTEDLY on an exposed rock with a view of the plane right on the meager runway, waiting impatiently for Constance's signal. Her stomach rolled, but only part of that was from nerves. Most was feeling like she'd ruined her friendship with Constance.

Whatever Constance's distraction turned out to be, she and Wade would have to make a mad dash for the plane as soon as it started. Grace needed to stay alert; she couldn't afford to be off her game.

Wade sat beside her, keeping his voice low. "They might shoot at us," he warned.

"Yeah, they might." Grace nodded. "But only until we're near the plane. I don't think they'd risk firing at it." She twisted her hands together. She'd never been shot at, which she assumed was the reason Wade had mentioned it; to mentally prepare her.

She'd been near weapons in perilous situations, when delivering medical care. Although danger had been present on several of her adventures, she'd never been the specific target of bullets zipping around her and she wasn't all that keen on starting now.

"Have *you* been shot at before?" Grace asked Wade.

He sat beside her on the small rock and took her hands in his. "I've been in war zones before—where bullets and bombs were real threats —but I've only been directly shot at once." He shifted on the rock. "We were taking aerial photos in Afghanistan, and insurgents shot down our helicopter. It was rough, but I survived with the help of the soldiers I was with. Until I got thrown into that pit, that helicopter landing was the most terrified I'd ever been."

Wade then turned to face her, leaning in to cup Grace's chin with his warm, calloused hand.

"If they fire," he murmured, looking deep into her eyes, "just keep your focus on the objective—get to the plane. No matter what, get to the plane. I'll be right by your side."

She looked into his soft, azure eyes—and, for a moment, she felt transported to a shore, as if gazing staring at a tranquil ocean.

His hand on her chin slipped around to the back of her neck.

She smiled weakly. "So much for my grand rescue."

"You came for me, Grace. You risked your life to traipse through the jungle and pull me out of that pit. I don't care that it was some bizarre third wish from a spirit only you can see and hear. You came for me. And I'm damn grateful you did."

Leaning in, she closed the gap between her mouth and his succulent lips. Finally, he kissed her, and as their lips met, she fully accepted his mouth against hers, feeling his firm fingers pressed into her scalp, holding her in place as he deepened the kiss.

She felt transformed in that moment—as if she wasn't in the Colombian jungle at all, but on a secluded romantic getaway with a charming and handsome man.

Who, *oh boy*, knew how to kiss!

When they finally broke away, he smiled at her with a look of sweet intoxication on his face.

"Gringos! Eschúchame! Levanta tus manos!"

Grace's blood turned from liquid, steamy lava to frigid ice so fast, it felt like it congealed in her veins. Spinning around, she found herself staring down the barrel of an AK-47 as two Colombian guerrilla fighters, dressed head-to-toe in camouflage clothing, glared murderously at her and Wade.

"Levanta tus manos!"

"Okay, okay." Wade slowly raised his hands.

Grace followed suit—glancing around desperately for Constance. The men had snuck up on them so quietly that neither she nor Wade had heard a thing—and Grace hadn't gotten any warning from her spirit friend. She could only hope that meant Constance was preoccupied scheming her plan and hadn't just abandoned them.

CHAPTER 10

Constance absorbed her surroundings. Somewhere deep in the interconnected, biological machinery of the jungle—from a raindrop, to a ruffle of branches as a red-tailed squirrel leaped from tree to tree, to the fall of a petal on the dirt floor—lay the specific path to enact her plan.

If a butterfly flaps its wings in the Caribbean, does it lead to a typhoon in Japan three weeks later?

Constance wasn't sure about the Chaos Theory, but she was intimately familiar with cause and effect. She didn't have three weeks to wait, though, so she needed more than an airborne butterfly.

Constance clicked her long fingernails together, closing her eyes to focus.

Cause and effect.

When she opened her eyes again, the infinite possibilities fanned out before her in luminous colors—millions of threads linking countless actions and reactions.

Wajadtuha!

She found the one path she needed.

Constance floated toward an arrangement of rocks cascading with dripping water. Using the full force of her supernatural powers, she shoved aside the trickle of water to the left.

A small spray spurted off-course—and, in response, a mosquito that had been flying toward the rocks veered sharply right, sending it into the path of a spotted frog. The frog's black eyes tracked the sudden, unexpected appearance of the mosquito before instinctively lashing out it's tongue.

The quick motion caused the broad leaf the frog was perched on to ripple. That ripple shook a nearby spider web, causing an adjacent assassin bug to leap away from the sticky threads. A small lime and blue tanager, flying past at that exact second, caught the assassin bug in its beak before swooping higher.

The bird flew past hundreds of brown moths, all converged on a tree. The moths were startled, and instantly took flight at the appearance of the fast-moving predator. Like a great, brown cloud of smoke, they flowed toward the airstrip—a fluttering undulation of umber-colored, flapping wings.

While all of that was occurring, Constance took similar action within a small, nearby cave—setting a flock of bats bursting from the darkness toward the airstrip. Their course would not-so-coincidently intersect with the moths.

"*Vamos!*"

Wade scolded himself as he and Grace were marched at gunpoint through the jungle. He'd been passionately kissing Grace when he *should* have been tuned to danger and checking his surroundings.

Wrong as it may sound, there were worse times to die than after a kiss like that. Only, he didn't want to die—and he certainly didn't want to go back into the pit, either. He wanted was more of Grace—talking, and kissing, though preferably not in the jungle or staring down the barrel of a rifle.

He promised himself he'd listen to every whimsical ghost story she had to tell if only they could somehow survive this together.

But even as he thought that, he grudgingly admitted that the evidence of her invisible, intangible genie spirit was becoming harder to dismiss. Wade had no plausible, non-paranormal explanation for how Grace had found him in the first place—not to mention how, after becoming utterly lost during the mudslide, Grace had still managed to find the airstrip, despite not having a GPS or map.

The two of them had been waiting on that rock to see what type of supernatural distraction this so-called Constance would conjure. Wade now promised himself that if this genie actually got them out of their current predicament, he'd be transformed from cynical skeptic to wholehearted believer.

For now, though, he needed to think of a plan that didn't involve either him or Grace getting shot.

The jungle thugs led them at gunpoint through thick, prickly branches and into a clearing. Before them stretched the airstrip—at the end of which squatted the white and blue, single engine Cessna 172 Skyhawk that Grace had been planning for them to escape aboard. It was a 1970s model, Wade guessed, probably plaid interior.

"Mira lo que he encontrado," one of the gunmen said as they approached the plane. A tall Colombian man, who carried himself like the leader of the group, turned to acknowledge the words. He'd been talking and smoking with the pilot, confirming Grace's theory that the pilot had betrayed them.

As they approached the plane, Wade recognized a small pile of boxes and bags on the ground—all of his camera equipment!

After the pilot and the leader of the Colombian rebels exchanged more words and a firm handshake, the pilot began to load Wade's equipment onto his plane.

An exchange. Wade understood now.

The leader stomped out his cigarette underfoot, before turning to glare at Grace and Wade. His dark, greedy eyes examined Grace from head to toe—and when he finally spoke to them, it was in heavily accented English.

"American," he sneered. "Rich, white American. Do you have a daddy who will pay for you? *Me pregunto.*"

Grace stood straight and still as a board.

"You look good enough," the man purred menacingly. "Someone will pay, yes?" He reached up and rubbed strands of her blonde hair between two fingers.

"Keep me," Wade snapped. "Let her go."

The Colombian's eyes flashed, and his nostrils flared. He turned and struck Wade's stomach with a lightning-fast punch. Pain and nausea rocketed through his abdomen as he doubled over. The blow would have been bad enough, but combined with his broken ribs, it was agony.

Throughout it all, Grace never moved.

Instead, she turned to the menacing man and looked deep into his murky brown eyes. Despite being his prisoner—despite having two men with guns behind her—Grace's voice was filled with a dark, terrifying confidence.

"Do you have ghosts from your past Juan Landa?" she asked. Then, eyes narrowing, Grace answered her own question. "Yes, you do, don't you? And they're coming for you, Juan. They're coming for you right now." She uttered her threat in a low, coolly even tone.

Juan seemed to falter at Grace's use of his name, and Wade couldn't blame him. The way Grace spoke—the preciseness of her tone—filled even Wade with ominous dread; as if she relayed things no living being could possibly know.

JUAN BLINKED AT THE AMERICAN—WHO, until a moment ago, he'd considered to be his walking, talking, blonde-haired payday.

What ghosts was she referring to? And how did she know his name?

Something in the woman's chill tone sent icy talons sinking into his chest, squeezing his heart. Instinctively, he reached for the gold cross hanging around his neck.

A Brazilian woman he'd once kidnapped had been similarly— eerily—calm when he'd captured her; reciting a curse against Juan in almost exactly the same tone of voice as this blonde American. That woman had made all his men worry about 'spirits' and similar super-natural nonsense throughout the weeks she'd spent shackled in the camp—until Juan himself had grown unsettled. It was during that Brazilian woman's captivity that he'd begun wearing the gold cross still dangling around his neck.

That had been five years ago, and the medallion had apparently served its purpose in protecting him. Juan was confident it would continue to do so now.

But even as he calmed himself, he heard a strange rustling noise from the thick jungle surrounding them. The noise grew ever louder, as something approached them from the depths of the thick foliage.

Behind him, Juan's men turned from the Americans and leveled their weapons at the edge of the jungle, looking both confused and disconcerted by the rustling hum, which seemed to be reaching a crescendo.

Hundreds—no, *thousands*—of brown and grey moths burst from the forest and flooded the clearing. Like a great, fluttering storm cloud, the solid wall of insects swept directly toward them. Juan staggered back as they overwhelmed him, desperately swatting the moths away from his face, hair, and neck. The thick blanket of frenzied, thrashing wings engulfed him—sending him into panic and confusion.

His men were similarly frightened, flailing uselessly at the insects until their nerves cracked and they cried out, ducking and running for the cover of the jungle.

The pilot, meanwhile—who'd been picking up the last of the American's camera equipment—clutched the bag to his chest and ran desperately for the plane in a haphazard zigzag.

This is absurd!

Even as Juan's heart pounded in his chest, he convinced himself that this rogue swarm of insects would pass momentarily—if everyone just kept their wits about them.

The chaos escalated as a hundred bats swooped from the sky, seemingly from nowhere. The swarm of bats speared through the cloud of moths, devouring them and sending the hysterical storm of insects into even more dizzying circles.

Juan's men ran deeper into the jungle, shrieking. He wheeled around as the cloud of insects began to dissipate, but he didn't see his captives anywhere. They'd vanished in the confusion, like ghosts; or as if they'd been transformed into moths themselves.

For a moment, Juan stood firm—and then, heart threatening to burst, the guerrilla leader followed his men into the jungle; fleeing the unnatural swarms of insects and flapping bats.

CHAPTER 11

Grace darted across the clearing with Wade, heading to the plane and dodging the battle royale being fought all around them by the swarm of moths and bats. As she ran, a rippling blue form shimmered into coalescence alongside her.

"Thank you," Grace panted at the familiar spirit now gliding along beside her.

"It's nice to know I still have my mojo," Constance answered, looking pleased with herself.

That she had—but how had Constance managed such a feat? Well, Grace had heard the genie claim to have turned the tide for great rulers once upon a time, when she'd been the formidable jinn Constantine. She'd also learned, much to Constance's chagrin, that as a ghost, she'd never been written into the textbooks or recognized for the pivotal role she'd played.

Grace recognized that role now, since Constance's distraction had let her and Wade reach the other side of the clearing, and the plane. The door of the Cessna hung open, abandoned by the pilot midway through loading his loot.

Wade hoisted Grace into the small plane. When she turned back to offer her hand and pull him in after her, she caught site of the pilot coming into view, running desperately toward the plane.

"Look out!" Grace cried.

Wade spun, dodging the pilot's fist as he launched himself at the pilot, swinging his own punch in retaliation, which landed solidly on the pilot's jaw. The Colombian stumbled backward, and then Wade was on him with another two punches. After the second blow, the pilot crumpled to the ground and stayed there.

Wade turned and hauled himself inside the plane. Grace yanked the door shut as he slithered out of the straps of the backpack and squeezed himself into the pilot's seat.

She wanted to ask him where he'd learned to fight, but she suspected he'd acquired those skills during his days on photo shoots with soldiers in active war zones.

Behind the yoke, he flipped levers and checked gauges. Grace quietly took off her harness and climbed into the co-pilot's chair, careful not to disrupt Wade's concentration.

Constance shimmered into being and stuck her head between the seats.

"I took care of the distraction," she purred. "The rest is now up to your man, Wade. Bats and bugs are one thing, but airborne contraptions are beyond my scope."

Grace bit her lip and nodded.

Wade had told her he could fly, and she trusted him. He'd had faith that a spirit genie would send them a signal, so Grace owed him faith that he could fly them to safety—under threat of captivity from the armed men twenty feet away, in a plane the size of postage stamp, and on an airstrip the size of a stick of gum.

Grace looked at Constance and mouthed the words: "I believe in him."

WADE STARED down the nose of a plane at the runway—which was unlike any other he'd ever seen: Narrow, grassy, and short.

The plane had already been lined up on the runway, since the pilot had clearly been intending his takeoff. There'd be no preflight planning, because they had to liftoff before their moment of distraction passed. Instead, Wade did a quick gauge check—just the essentials. The oil pressure and oil temperature were both in the green.

Bumpy landscape aside, there was no crosswind, which meant one less thing to worry about. However, the warm, heavy air would make it harder to takeoff. At least they were several thousand feet above sea level, so the air density wasn't as bad as it could have been in this tropical climate.

He took a shaky breath. As he advanced the throttle, the engine revved faster and louder.

Because of the short-field takeoff, he held down the brake while applying full power to the prop. He'd set the flaps to one notch to give him maximal lift with minimal drag. While he knew the concept behind a short-field takeoff, he'd never actually performed one except in simulations.

As he released the brake, the plane launched forward. A second later, he glimpsed the airspeed indicator, reading thirty-five knots and rising.

The plane's tires bumped and skipped across the rough terrain. He kept a firm grip on the yoke even as his palms began sweating. As their speed increased, he began to pull back on the yoke—slowly adding pressure as the plane reached fifty-five knots indicated airspeed.

The tree line approached so rapidly that his gut clenched. Sweat broke out down his neck and his heart beat faster—driven by the fear that he might not be able to lift them into the air in time. Even if the wheels left the grass, the nose of the plane could still clip the treetops and hurl the little Cessna back into the jungle.

When he felt the aircraft lifting into the air, he glanced over and saw Grace in the corner of his eye. She pursed her lips tightly, a white-knuckled grip on her pant legs.

Wade pulled the yoke back, and they miraculously cleared the treetops. As they rose higher above the jungle, he lowered the nose of the Cessna and raised the flaps—continuing their ascent more gradually.

"You did it!" Grace leaned over and planted a kiss on his cheek.

Step One complete, Wade grinned.

Now, they just had to fly this forty-year-old plane back to Bogotá —and find out how many laws he'd be breaking by attempting an unregistered landing in a major airport. His ears began to pop, and he leveled out. He'd wanted to climb higher for a smoother ride, but the elevation was already five or six-thousand feet alongside the mountain range. He couldn't go above twelve-thousand feet without oxygen —so bumpy ride it would be.

Gripping the shuddering yoke, he looked over at Grace. "Okay, co-pilot," he ordered, "open up that sectional chart, and let's see if we can figure out precisely where we are over Colombia." If he'd had his phone on him, he could have looked up the terrain view for landmarks, but they'd have to make do with a paper map.

Grace beamed at him, looking cute with the bulky headset she'd fitted over her ears and those thick, blonde bangs touching her eyelashes.

She opened the sectional chart, and they talked through where they'd taken off, identifying landmarks and towns as they flew over them. Wade needed to know the names of the landmarks beneath them in order to accurately describe where he was to Colombian air traffic control.

When they were about twenty miles outside of Bogotá, Wade scanned the cabin. Looking to the pilot's side, he found a worn, yellow piece of paper taped to the bulkhead with the radio frequencies for Colombian airports listed on it.

He first squawked 7700 on the transponder, letting air traffic control know he had an emergency. Then, he tried to remember the sequence for an urgent call. Mayday was for loss of aircraft control or a fire—neither of which they were experiencing—but pan-pan would alert ATC to an urgent issue.

He switched the radio to 119.5 for Bogotá approach. "Pan-pan. Bogotá approach. Cessna two-six-zero-five."

"Cessna two-six-zero-five, this is Bogotá approach." The accent was thick, but Wade felt grateful the global language of air traffic controllers was English.

"Cessna two-six-zero-five. Cessna one-seventy-two, south over Chipque at ten thousand MSL."

"Cessna two-six-zero-five. Proceed Parque Metropolitan Simón Bolívar, maintain ten thousand. Expect right traffic runway five."

Wade glanced at the sectional chart that Grace had spread out for him, taking note of the layout of Bogotá. The park named for *El Libertador* Simón Bolívar would be a good landmark for him to follow. He'd be able to spot the large lake there as they flew over the city.

"Cessna two-six-zero-five. Contact El Dorado tower one-one-eight point two-five."

Wade went through the motions of switching frequencies to 118.25 and contacting the tower. He repeated the pan-pan call, and the tower controller directed him to an open runway.

Grace remained quiet and observant throughout all this, which enabled Wade to fully concentrate on flying and landing.

The landing was a little bumpy, but they stayed in one piece as the wheels of the Cessna made contact with the tarmac. Once safely on the ground, Wade taxied the Cessna as instructed by ground control—to where two white and green police cars awaited them.

As his shoulders relaxed in relief, he couldn't help but feel like they'd jumped out of the fire and into the frying pan.

CHAPTER 12

Grace sat in the interrogation room feeling stiff and tired. She'd relayed her story to the authorities multiple times—obviously omitting Constance's role.

Her ghostly friend had disappeared during the flight and hadn't yet returned. Perhaps she wasn't going to.

Was this the end? Three wishes had been granted, so perhaps now her genie had vanished, never to reappear.

If that was the case, Grace would have quite the adjustment to make. She'd become accustomed to seeing Constance's translucent form—adorned in blue eye-shadow and wearing blue harem-pants—at least once a week for the last ten years.

They'd been friends who'd parted on bad terms—which sucked.

Grace thought of the lamp that remained in her backpack. The Colombian police had seized her backpack on the tarmac when they'd hauled her and Wade in for questioning. Would she even get it back? The radius of the genie's presence spanned a good fifty miles, but Constance was still intangibly bound to that tangible object.

And what of Wade? Was he being questioned somewhere, too? Were authorities comparing her stories to his, to see if they lined up? Grace and Wade would both describe events that mostly aligned—at least once they'd met up with each other. The exception, though, was why she'd come to Colombia in the first place. Grace had given a rather poor explanation to the police—something about seeking adventure and just happening upon Wade. Perhaps he'd be vague about that part as well. He'd have to be, given how coincidental it all sounded.

Except, there was nothing coincidental in their meeting. Constance had foreseen it all.

Had she foreseen their kiss in the jungle, too?

One tentative night in a hammock and one tentative—yet succulent—kiss, a relationship did not make. Both moments were so brief, so hesitant, and so applicable to a single moment in time that surely they promised nothing more.

Grace couldn't fault Wade if he wanted to distance himself from her—an apparently eccentric millionaire who talked to a ghost.

"That's a glum look for someone who survived the jungle."

Grace lifted her head when she heard the familiar voice. Constance reappeared in a haze of blue smoke.

"Constance!" Grace felt relieved, but then she looked nervously around the small room. "Are the cameras on?"

"No."

Grace stood up and stretched. "Thank you for getting us out of the jungle. I'm so sorry I ever doubted you."

She wanted to ask for ideas on how to get out of the custody of the Colombian national police force, where she'd been trapped for several hours. However, she knew she'd used all three of her wishes. Had she used up her friendship, too?

"In about five minutes, you'll be released with all of your belongings." Constance's tone was full of boastful smugness.

"Oh?" Grace raised an eyebrow. "How'd you manage that?"

"It turns out the Mayor of Bogotá can see ghosts, too. It took me over two hours to find someone in the government hierarchy with the gift. I tried the Operate Directorate of the police first, then two military generals, a brigadier general, a captain, the President, and a special forces commando to no avail. Anyway, I might have invoked the fear of wrathful spirits to do it, but I convinced the Mayor to expedite your release. Of course, he had to speak with the police and confirm your background check first."

"Wow. What about Wade?"

"He'll be released as well—especially since I implied you two were a couple."

"Oh-kay."

"Oh, and I *might* have also promised you'd take the Mayor and his niece to a Yankees game next time he's visiting her. She's studying at NYU." Constance widened her thickly lashed eyes. "I suggest you splurge for the Legend Seats."

"I'll be sure to do that."

The spirit's form rippled and started to grow more and more transparent. She was fading away.

"Wait!" Grace called before the genie vanished entirely. "Are you and I okay?"

Constance smiled and waved a dismissive hand. "Of course, Darling. Life's too short to waste time in a state of anger."

Grace gulped. "Is this goodbye? Will I see you again?"

"Is that a wish?" Constance waggled her eyebrows. "Because I hate to remind you, but you're out of wishes."

"It's me," Grace replied, blinking her glistening eyes, "just wanting to see my friend again."

"Well," Constance sniffed, "I suppose I have forever to find my next victim—er, *wish-maker*—but *you* only have a finite time with *me*; what with how short life is, and all." Her lips curled. "I imagine I could *grace* you with my presence a little while longer."

JUAN'S TEMPER burned through him like a hot flare. So hot, he wondered if smoke was swirling from his ears—the same way it swirled from the cigarette clenched between his fingers.

He drove north on National Route 45 toward Bogotá, replaying the insane events of earlier that day over and over in his mind. A cloud of moths had attracted a flock of bats—all of which had descended on the airstrip; impossibly, *perfectly* timed to allow the Americans to make their getaway.

When Juan had first heard the plane start up and the engine rev, he'd thought Sal—the pilot—had decided to leave, having delivered the gringos as promised and taken his loot as payment.

But as the insects—and the swooping predators pursuing them—had finally dissipated, he'd watched the plane accelerate down the runway and noticed Sal lying on the ground.

"I can't believe they stole my plane, *hombre.*"

Now, that same pilot sat in the passenger seat of Juan's Jeep, running his mouth. Juan wanted to slap the man. He certainly wasn't Sal's *hombre.*

"And that crap on the airstrip? *Loco*, man. *Lo-co*. It felt like an act of God." Sal performed the sign of the cross over his chest.

Juan frowned, taking another drag from his cigarette. God hadn't interfered with his plans—but something had. Spirits perhaps? Old curses?

Regardless of whatever supernatural events were working in the couple's favor, Juan couldn't afford to let those Americans get away. They were his payday.

"I just want my plane back," Sal continued. "I wonder if it's been impounded, or something like that—after an unauthorized landing of an unregistered flight to Bogotá."

Fortunately, Juan had contacts in the *Policía Nacional de Colombia.* He learned that the Americans—Gracelynn Kowalski and Wade Rawlings—had both been taken into custody after landing at the Bogotá airport.

His inside man on the police force would try to stall them as best he could, detaining the Americans until Juan could make it to the city. But Juan was still two hours away, because not only did he no longer have a plane, but he'd had to hump through the jungle to reach his Jeep, followed by spending time finding out where the gringos had gone. Only when he'd got word from his man in the police had he started heading north to Bogotá.

Now, Juan had his foot on the gas and all four wheels on the road, driving fast with two of his best men in the back seat ready to help him reacquire his 'assets.'

Even if that American doctor was released from custody, Juan promised himself that she wouldn't get far. She was a rich white woman in Colombia, and Juan knew her name. She'd have nowhere to hide.

CHAPTER 13

fter a warm shower in the comfort of a hotel room, Grace felt incredible. The only thing missing was a night of rest in a real bed—but because her flight home wasn't scheduled until tomorrow, she'd enjoy that final luxury tonight.

Before that indulgence, she needed to meet with the mayor of Bogotá in the hotel restaurant, arranged courtesy of Constance. She adjusted the hem of the dress she'd bought in the hotel lobby, right after checking in. Glancing at the clock, Grace took the opportunity to flop on the couch in her hotel room to relax before she needed to leave.

"Better?" Constance appeared, shimmering into form and hovering above the brass lamp from which Grace had summoned her a decade earlier. After retrieving it from her backpack, Grace had set the lamp on the table so she could stare at it and be reminded of all the enjoyed moments with her genie.

Smoothing the length of her dress, Grace smiled. "Much better, thank you, but I'll be positively wonderful when I'm stateside."

"And your next trip?"

"I'm not sure." Grace eyed Constance. "I'm a little afraid to ask you for ideas."

291

"Hmm—as you should be," the genie mused.

"Why? What are you scheming?" Her lips curved.

Constance crossed her arms and changed the subject. "Why'd you run away from Wade?"

Grace lifted her eyes, staring up at the ceiling. "I didn't run away from Wade. I was released from custody before him."

"You could have waited for him. It's like you're determined to unravel all my hard matchmaking."

"I slipped him a note."

"A note? *Have a safe trip. Look me up if you're ever in New York.* You call that a note?" Constance scoffed.

"Yes," Grace defended herself. "If he wants to see me again, he can look me up."

"That's the absolute worst invitation in the history of invitations. You might as well have written: *'Thanks for the memories.'*"

Grace, no longer having a restrain herself for fear of discovery by gun-toting guerrillas, raised her voice at the genie. "I don't want him to feel *obligated* to see me just because of everything we've gone through together."

"Because you saved his life?"

"*You* saved his life. I was just the tangible matter to your will."

"*We* saved him."

"Yes, fine—but I don't want an obligatory relationship because *we* saved him." Grace sat up sharply and gently rubbed her temples.

"So, you're hiding from him?"

"I'm not hiding."

Constance sighed—as if she were summoning the strength of a saint to endure this conversation. She picked at her long, azure, sparkling nails before smoothing her fingers over her heavily penciled eyebrows.

"Liar, liar."

"I'm going to dinner." With a huff, Grace slipped on her shoes, snatched up her phone, and retrieved her room keycard. She marched toward the door.

JUAN PARKED his jeep outside the decadent hotel. He'd dropped the pilot off at the airport. During the time it had taken him to drive to Bogotá, he'd had his spies in the city get to work locating which hotel a certain 'Gracelynn Kowalski' had checked into.

He entered the hotel armed with a concealed 9mm Córdova and chloroform. Two of his crew accompanied him. Sneaking his prize out of the hotel would pose a risk—but it was far from impossible. The pretty American doctor was small enough to be folded into the trashcan of a maid's cart. Beyond keeping her alive, the woman's physical wellbeing didn't matter much.

Juan and his men knew which floor Kowalski's room was on and took the elevator upward. When the ding sounded, the three of them exited the elevator and stalked menacingly down the corridor toward her room number. As they approached the door, Juan checked the hallway.

Empty.

One by one, they drew their handguns.

When Juan nodded to the man to his right, he stepped forward and brushed a keycard he'd bribed the corrupt receptionist to create for him against the electronic lock.

They heard a 'click'—and then Juan exploded into the room, gun raised.

"Don't move—or I'll shoot!"

Wade had been standing outside the hotel room door, debating if he should knock or not, when he'd heard arguing—a one-sided argument.

He smiled. Grace must be arguing with Constance—about *him*, apparently.

Grace had abandoned him back at the police station, leaving

nothing but a note. Wade had been determined to find her—if she hadn't left Colombia already.

Working off the assumption that she'd want a shower and a soft bed as much as he did, he figured she'd remain in the city for at least a little while. So, he'd checked into his own hotel room and started calling around, making up stories about looking for his missing friend. Knowing Grace was wealthy, he'd started by calling each of the five-star hotels in Bogotá, asking after a Gracelynn Kowalski. When he'd struck out at the first hotel, he also started asking for anyone who'd checked in with the name of Elvis. At last, one hotel confirmed the presence of a guest called Gracelynn Kowalski—and a different hotel had someone with the name of Elvis.

So, which one was his Grace?

Or what if they both had been reserved by Grace?

Wouldn't a savvy world traveler like her check in under a pseudonym? Would she also pay for a second room somewhere else? Under her real name—just in case she'd thought someone might be after her…

Someone like the leader of a vicious cell of Colombian rebel fighters?

He remembered how Grace had laid a false trail for the guerrillas to follow, back when she'd rescued him from that pit. She was always one step ahead—and with that in mind, he decided to try Elvis's room first.

He arrived at the hotel, and the clerk fortunately bought Wade's story about him being her boyfriend—here to surprise 'Elvis' with flowers.

Yet, once he'd arrived and taken the elevator up to her floor, Wade had hesitated outside Grace's room. What if she didn't want to see him?

Maybe she didn't, but he needed to know one way or another if they had something; or if he'd been nothing but a jungle fling to her.

Then, suddenly, the door had swung open, and a startled Grace stood in the doorway with flushed cheeks. She'd stammered out his name.

Grace's golden hair was brushed straight and down, and she wore a bright, red, floral dress. Standing in the doorway, she'd shot a glare over her shoulder, which Wade suspected was directed at Constance.

"Still have your ghost?" He smiled.

"Yes." Flustered, Grace turned back to him, brushing strands of blonde hair from her face. "And she's still putting on a performance."

"May I come in?"

"Yes, of course." Grace stepped aside.

Wade walked in and Grace let the door close behind him.

"Did you get your equipment back?"

"All of it." Wade nodded.

He handed her the bouquet of flowers he'd brought. After she took them with an astonished 'thank you', he held up the note Grace had left for him. "This doesn't work for me."

She licked her lips and swallowed. "What do you mean?"

"I mean: I don't want to wait until New York to see you again—to kiss you again." He stepped forward, crowding her personal space.

Her eyes widened, but she didn't back away from him. Her hands lowered, moving the bouquet out of the space between them.

Leaning closer, his lips hovered less than an inch from hers. He looked from her lips, up to Grace's emerald-green eyes, and then back to her lips again.

"But, just to be clear," he reassured her, "I'm not doing this out of obligation. You pulled me from the pit, but I flew us to safety. We're even."

"We're even," Grace agreed in a husky tone.

She was the one who finally closed the distance, pressing her lips to his. The sweet, succulent taste of them lit a fire inside his heart. Wrapping his arms around her, he pulled her body flush against his and lost himself in the feel of her curves and taste of her mouth.

After several minutes of kissing, they finally broke apart—both breathless.

"Wow," Grace said, exhaling. "I'd continue this—believe me, I would—but I have dinner reservations." She paused, biting her lip. "Care to join me?"

"I'd like that." Wade looked from his jeans and collared shirt to her dress. "But am I underdressed?"

She linked her arm through his. "You're perfect."

CHAPTER 14

Grace entered the hotel dining room with Wade on one side and Constance on the other. They were led to a table where an older Colombian gentleman sat, wearing an elegant suit and a pleasant smile.

Grace extended her hand. "Mayor Carlos Álvarez—I'm Gracelynn Kowalski and this is my friend Wade Rawlings." She turned. "Wade—this is the man who facilitated our release."

She noted Wade's expression of surprise quickly transformed into a smile as he greeted the Mayor with an enthusiastic handshake.

"I'm grateful—and I'm sorry if we caused any delays at the airport with our unauthorized landing."

Carlos waved a dismissive hand. "I think it's all fun and gossip now. What do the kids say? It went *viral*—which I believe means anyone initially put out by the events is now claiming to have been part of them."

Wade chuckled as he pulled out Grace's chair for her. He sat beside her.

The Mayor continued—but this time he addressed Constance—or, to any bystanders, the empty seat which she now occupied. "You'll be relieved to know your scheme worked. Juan Landa and two of his operatives stormed the hotel room that *señorita* Kowalski had booked under her real name just moments ago. The national police have him in custody."

"Marvelous," Constance crooned.

"That's a relief." Grace extended her arm and laid her fingers over Wade's hand, where it rested on the table.

"So," Wade asked, looking back and forth between the Mayor and Grace. "Do you two know each other?"

"No," Grace explained. "Constance introduced herself to the Mayor and explained our situation. He then facilitated our release."

"Oh—so you can see the genie, too?" Wade asked Carlos.

The Mayor smiled. "Yes—but please, let's not go around spreading rumors that the Mayor of Bogotá can see and hear ghosts."

"I wouldn't dream of it."

The waiter arrived to take their drink orders.

"Honestly, I'd love an ice-cold beer," Grace admitted.

"Then, I'd recommend the Monserrate Red Beer," the Mayor offered. "It's a craft beer made right here in Bogotá."

"Sounds perfect."

"I'll have the same," said Wade.

"Make it three," the Mayor grinned.

As the waiter left with a nod, Grace turned to Wade. "The Mayor is going to come to New York next spring for a Yankees game. His niece is at NYU." She paused. "Would *you* like to join us for a baseball game?"

Wade brightened. "I'd like that."

"Finally," Constance rolled her thickly lashed eyes. She then turned them toward the Mayor. "Do you have any idea how exhausting it was playing matchmaker to a reluctant bachelorette? She's *finally* embracing the possibility of a future with this man."

Grace pointedly ignored Constance, continuing to speak to Wade despite her hot cheeks.

"My treat," she promised Wade. "Legend Seats."

"*Now* you're trying to chase him off by reminding him you're rich," Constance snorted.

Grace suppressed an eye roll. She was having beers in a private room in a five-star hotel with the Mayor of Bogotá. She didn't need to *remind* Wade she had money and connections.

When the waiter brought them their beers, they each took a long drink.

"A wise man chooses a woman based on all of her strengths," the Mayor commented, licking the foam from his lips.

"I agree." Wade's words came out hesitantly, because he hadn't heard Constance's part of this conversation.

The Mayor stood. "I know I'd planned to dine with *señorita* Kowalski this evening, but I feel I should leave you two to enjoy dinner alone—and this is *my* treat. This way, you'll have some fond memories of my country, rather than only terrifying ones. And perhaps you'll want to return someday."

Wade stood and shook his hand again. "I look forward to seeing you in New York, Mayor Álvarez."

"I as well, *señor* Rawlings. As we say in Colombia—*que tenga una buena noche!*"

As the mayor walked away, Wade turned to Grace. "Dinner?"

"I'd love dinner."

~

~~SIX MONTHS LATER~~

GRACE SAT across the table from Wade after they'd finished eating. Constance had left them undisturbed for the duration of the meal. Wade had cooked homemade lasagna, enjoyed at Grace's dining room.

This had been just one of the many dates they'd enjoyed since returning from Colombia—but she and Wade had also taken three international trips over the past six months. During each of them, Grace had administered much-needed medical care to underserved communities, while Wade had photographed the poverty or conflict in the region.

They'd made a great team, and Constance hadn't needed to help them out of any more dangerous situations.

The Mayor of Bogotá had visited New York as promised, and Grace and Wade had taken him and his niece to the Yankees game—Legend Seats.

Wade had earned his pilot license in the meantime, and Grace had slowly come to feel the closest to fully healed that she'd ever felt since Daniel's death.

Her life with Wade left her feeling fulfilled each and every day.

Wade rose from the table. "Come with me." His blue eyes sparkled. "I have something to show you."

He took her hand and led her down the hallway to one of the many entertainment rooms. He pushed open the doors.

Within, a hammock stretched between two large palm trees; planted in enormous ceramic pots. The darkened room was bathed in electric green light, which slowly panned and rippled across the walls and ceiling as jungle sounds played from a sound system hidden in the darkness.

She laughed. "What is *this*?"

"A walk down memory lane." He grinned. "Our first night together —minus the mosquitos and the threat upon our lives."

"It's fantastic!"

Wade walked toward the hammock, which was secured only a few feet off the ground. "Come—get in with me."

After he'd clambered inside, Grace eased herself in beside him. She curled her body close to his.

"Perfect."

"Almost." He withdrew a small box from his pocket. As the hammock swung gently to and fro, he opened the box to reveal a beautiful, gleaming diamond ring.

"I love you so much, Grace. You've filled my life in amazing ways and made wishes I'd never even known I wanted come true. Grant this one for me: Marry me."

"I will." Blinking away tears, Grace stretched over and kissed him.

~~~~~

301

~~~~~

HEATHER'S HERO

When Heather's past catches up with her, an unlikely hero intervenes. But when the line between reality and the paranormal blurs, she realizes she's not the only one in need of saving.

CHAPTER 1

Heather strummed her fingers on the steering wheel to Fleetwood Mac's *The Chain*. Outside, pink flowers from Japanese cherry trees danced on a crisp Tennessee spring breeze. A few more blocks and she'd reach the retirement home and begin a fun afternoon of repotting plants with the residents.

A car plowed through the intersection, ran a red light, and crashed into Heather's Honda Accord. Her body tensed on impact, but she had no time to avoid the collision. The sickening sound of crunching metal and shattering glass was followed by the smell of gasoline and burnt rubber.

When Heather opened her eyes, the world around her took a moment to stop moving. She loosened her white-knuckled grip on the steering wheel and blinked at the deployed, side-impact airbag.

Through the shattered windshield, she saw a familiar shape climb out of the car that had hit hers. Black pants, black shirt, and that walk. Her brain tried. to make sense of the impossible. Blake had found her.

Her pulse snapped into a frantic rhythm. For a moment she couldn't breathe—not from the airbag, not from the crash, but from pure, bone-deep terror she thought she'd left behind in another state.

"Hey, man? You okay?" A bystander approached Blake.

As a crowd of bystanders began to gather, Heather's attacker abruptly turned and stalked away from the scene of his crime.

"You need to get out of your car right now."

Heather jolted when a man appeared beside her in the passenger seat. She'd been driving alone, hadn't she?

He was early-thirties with dark hair and sharp, defined facial features—chiseled jaw and ruddy cheekbones. His brown hair and thick eyebrows accentuated a pair of warm brown eyes.

"What?"

"You're leaking oil," he said. "When that ignites and combines with the fertilizer in your back seat, your whole car will go up in flames."

She noticed his clothing—a well-worn, fire-retardant black uniform with yellow reflective stripes. Firefighter. How had he gotten here so fast after the crash? And how had he managed to get *inside* the car?

His sleeve had a circular patch with a raven against a blue sky sewn into it.

The heat in the car intensified.

"Move it, Phillips!" the fireman barked at her.

She fumbled free from her seatbelt before shoving open the driver-side door and clamoring out, dragging her purse with her.

With the movement, she felt pain for the first time since the collision. Her left shoulder throbbed in rhythm with her head. She stumbled to a nearby sidewalk on the corner of Crossland Avenue and Cumberland Drive. As she looked around, she didn't see the firefighter. She didn't see Blake either.

Her car burst into flame, and she gaped at the sudden heat and fire. Ten seconds earlier and she'd have been toast. Where had the man who'd saved her gone? He'd mysteriously vanished.

Suddenly nauseated, she sat on the cold concrete and put her head between her knees.

"Are you okay, young lady? Your head's bleeding. I called an ambulance."

She looked up to see a man in his sixties standing over her with a worried expression. A friendly Good Samaritan, she deduced immediately. She looked down at her baby blue turtleneck, stained with drops of blood from her head wound.

"I'm okay." She'd had worse. Blake had done worse. And he'd probably be back to finish what he'd started.

Heather looked around again. "Where's the fire department?" She didn't see the fireman's truck or hear sirens.

"They should be here soon. The Clarksville Fire Rescue station is just a few blocks away from here. I've got a first aid kit in my car if you want me to clean that up a bit."

"No. Thanks. I need to make some phone calls."

She pulled her phone out of her purse and called her friend Evelyn.

BY LATE AFTERNOON, Heather had arrived home to the cheerful yips of Denver. The large German Shepherd greeted her at the door as his ferocious tail wagged the entire back half of his furry body.

She dropped her purse on the entry table and deactivated and reset the alarm before sinking her fingers into soft fur. Lowering herself to the floor, she let the dog smother her with love.

After the accident—no, *crash*, there had been nothing *accidental* about Blake careening into her car—Heather had watched the fire department drown her car, answered police questions, and turned down an ambulance trip to the ER. She didn't need another trauma evaluation—one more CT scan of her head in her lifetime and she'd start glowing in the dark. Besides, she'd been beaten and bruised enough to know when she needed to take a few ibuprofen and sleep it off.

She hadn't lost consciousness after the crash, which was reassuring. Though maybe she had hallucinated. She'd seen a man in her car when he couldn't have gotten in through the smashed passenger-side door or through the broken windshield. She'd seen the firefighter even though the fire truck hadn't arrived on the scene yet.

"Well, boy," she scratched behind Denver's ears, "if I'm going to hallucinate a fireman who saves my life, he might as well be drop-dead gorgeous."

"Thanks."

Heather startled. She looked up to see the same man standing in her living room with his arms crossed.

She shot to her feet. "How'd you get in here?"

Denver cocked his head to one side, looking at her while not seeming to notice the uninvited guest. Normally, her guard dog was very protective.

"I'm not sure exactly." The man wore a slightly bemused expression and the same black gear as in her car. His black and yellow uniform was different than the grayish-brown gear she'd seen on the Clarksville firefighters.

Backing away, she pressed herself against her front door. "I don't know whether to scream or thank you."

"I don't require gratitude for doing my job, and I'd prefer you not scream."

Something about his appearance seemed odd. She stared harder at him and realized she could see her television on the opposite wall *through* him. She walked closer, inspecting him. Denver followed her before walking right through the man to go lay on his rug in the living room.

Heather shrieked, recoiled back, bumped the table beside the couch, and barely caught her lamp before it fell over.

"Nice catch."

After setting the lamp upright, she backed away toward the kitchen, stammering, "You're a ghost!"

"Seems that way." He frowned.

Did he not know he was a ghost? And since when were ghosts *real*?

"I must've hit my head *really* hard." She snatched a glass from her cupboard and poured herself orange juice from the refrigerator. She glanced at Denver again, who made no response to the sound of a deep male voice in his house.

The fireman looked down at his appearance. "I could be a figment of your imagination, but I *feel* like I'm my own person—in a manner of speaking."

Heather drank the juice, the cold liquid hitting her empty stomach with a revitalizing burst. After a moment, her heart returned to a normal rhythm. "Do you have a name?"

"I—I don't know." His expression changed from confused to deeply sad.

She decidedly didn't like seeing him sad. She preferred playful and bemused over sad.

"What does the raven symbolize?" she asked.

He looked at the patch sewn onto his uniform. "Reckoning. Rebirth. Protection. Guidance. They mean different things to different religions. Sometimes different things in the same religion."

"Okay. Let's call you Rave."

He grinned, his warm eyes radiating amicably. "I like that."

She pulled a container of Ramen noodles from her pantry, peeled the lid back, and added water. She hadn't eaten all day. Maybe some food would put an end to her overactive imagination.

"So, you make a habit of saving women in car crashes?" She eyed him nervously.

"I've rescued a few, though I think I was still living at the time. It's all a little fuzzy."

"Yeah? I can relate." She pointed to the bandage on her forehead. After punching the microwave buttons, she hit START.

"Are you okay?" Rave asked.

"Since I'm talking to a fireman's ghost, probably not. But since you're the best-looking thing in my disastrous life right now and you saved my life, I'm just going to roll with it. I'm not going to look a gift ghost in the mouth."

"Disastrous?" he said, cutting through her attempt to lighten the mood.

"How much of the crash did you see?"

"Just you in the car, the smoke, and the fertilizer."

"And my name? You called me Phillips."

"Heather Phillips. I don't know why I know your name and not my own."

She'd never met Rave. She would've remembered that face and those caring eyes. With all of her prior injuries, she'd never hit her head so hard that she saw a man in her house. Why a fireman? She didn't have a fetish she was aware of. Though, if Rave stuck around, she might develop one. Except, she'd sworn off men after Blake.

"Are you okay?" Rave asked again.

Heather blinked and watched a tear fall into her noodles as she mixed them. "Yeah." She sniffed. "Long day."

"A long day doesn't make a disastrous life."

"Maybe disastrous is too strong. No. It's probably accurate. The man who rammed his car into mine and then ran off is my abusive ex. Apparently he's found me even after I moved cross-country, stayed off social media, and died my brown hair red." She ate her noodles.

Rave stiffened. "So, he's still out there?"

"Oh, yeah, he's definitely still out there."

CHAPTER 2

Rave glanced back at the dog on the rug, who watched his owner with adoring eyes.

Heather said, "I'm safe here. I've got an alarm system. And Denver."

Rave turned back to Heather, who ate her noodles one by one but didn't seem to enjoy them. She had vibrant, wavy dark red hair that was obviously died. Yet it looked good on her and accentuated her vibrant green eyes. Her face was a lovely oval and her lips full and symmetrical. On her forehead were three Steri-Strips over a laceration on her hairline, and Rave wondered how he knew that detail.

The thought of Heather being in danger flared a protective instinct in him, even though she was a stranger. But, then, he was a firefighter and had an inclination toward protecting everyone. Except he couldn't do any of that as a ghost—no extinguishing fires, no administering first aid, no rescuing cats from trees. Well, the latter of those he was certain he'd never done.

"Why is he after you?" Rave asked.

"Blake?" She rolled her shoulders, and Rave instantly knew she had a large bruise on her left shoulder, even though he couldn't see it. "I got away. I damaged his ego. He told me that if I ever left, he'd kill me. I believe he intends to follow through on that."

Rave pursed his lips. Heather may have been talking calmly about the threat on her life, but a small tremor in her hand betrayed her fear.

He looked around her kitchen and living room. It was an efficient house but not warm and cozy. The walls had no photos. The absence of decorations created a lack of personal touch. She may have started her life over after escaping Blake, but she must have suspected he'd find her. She hadn't established a home, just a temporary place to live. Somewhere she could abandoned within minutes.

"What if—" Rave began.

"What about your life." Heather cut in. She went back to the refrigerator and pulled out a bottle of Zinfandel.

My life?

He remembered pieces, like growing up in a happy home—photos and trophies on every wall and mantle. His parents had pictures of him from birth to college graduation. The word *home* snagged in his chest like a barbed hook. He could picture rooms, voices, laughter—but not the address, not the anchor.

When he didn't answer, Heather continued. "If you're not a figment of my imagination, tell me about you." She poured the wine into a glass and took a sip.

"I remember going to a building fire—fully involved." He shook his head. "I worked as a fireman while I finished my bachelor's degree. Then I got my certificate as a fire investigator. I'm climbing the ranks to arson investigator. I'm still a firefighter while waiting for the right job to become available. Something close to home." He scrubbed a hand over his face before continuing. "I don't even know where home is anymore. And, I can't smell right now. I remember the smell of smoke—different scents based on what's on fire. Wood fires are musky and pleasing. Plastic and rubbers are abrasive and acrid. Burning flesh is like tanned leather over a charcoal flame." He hesitated at her stunned expression. "Sorry. That last one was too descriptive."

"It's okay," she said slowly, moving the bowl of half-eaten noodles to the sink. "I'm doubt I could have conjured those descriptions from my subconscious, which makes a stronger case for you being a real ghost—whatever that is—rather than a figment of my imagination. So, are you on your way to a fire now?"

He looked down at his gear. "Guess I'm overdressed. I wonder . . ." As his voice trailed off, he imagined himself wearing normal firehouse attire. As he did so, his fire gear disappeared to reveal his uniform slacks and white undershirt.

Heather choked on her wine as she gave a nervous chuckle. "Okay. Maybe you should cover that back up."

"I'm covered. What are you talking about?"

She cleared her throat, her gaze drifting down his chest—a purely reflexive, human reaction—but it burned through him all the same. If he still had a pulse, it would've stuttered.

"This part must be my mind conjuring images. Your white shirt leaves nothing to the imagination. Oh!" She hopped up from the chair and walked to him. "There's another raven."

He watched her inspecting the black tattoo on his bicep. He remembered going to the tattoo parlor with friends—fellow firefight- ers. After tattoos, they'd gone out for beers to celebrate. Hops. Greasy fries. Aerosmith playing on the jukebox. What were they celebrating? Rave couldn't remember.

Heather was close but not touching him, not that she could. "It's very intricate. I don't remember ever having a thing for birds. I don't think this part is coming from my imagination either."

When she straightened and looked into his eyes, she was only inches from his face. He suddenly felt like a fully involved house fire had engulfed him. Who was this woman and why could only she see him?

He took a step back from her. "I'm not a figment of your imag- ination."

Her lips curled in a luscious half smile. "I agree. What woman invents an attractive man who doesn't want her in his personal space?"

He swallowed but didn't know how to respond.

Denver barked once and got to his feet. A second later, the door- bell rang. Rave's shoulder's stiffened as he considered make a move to put himself between her and the door. But he had no substance to stop an intruder.

The canine stuck his nose at the seam and sniffed, tail wagging.

"Relax, Rave. My friend Evelyn is here." Heather walked around him. "She's staying with me tonight in case my head bump turns into a massive head bleed and I need to be rushed to the hospital. Okay, I was being melodramatic. Don't look so worried." Heather deactivated the alarm and let her friend inside the house.

Evelyn handed her a container of homemade cupcakes. "I brought us some comfort food. Edgar has the kids, so I can stay all night."

"Thank you for the cupcakes." Heather set them on the kitchen counter. "And thank you for feeding and walking Denver earlier today."

"Anytime. Who were you talking to?"

Heather shot Rave a look. "Myself, mostly. I think." She waved a hand in the air. "I'm probably delirious."

"Who wouldn't be after what you've been through?" Evelyn tossed her jacket on the back of Heather's sofa. She patted Denver's head as she walked through Rave on her way to the kitchen. She was a good foot shorter than Heather and had straight blonde hair. Her skirt suit suggested some type of professional office or executive work.

"And since when do cars erupt in flames? I thought that only happened in movies?"

"I was carrying fertilizer to Sunnydale."

"The nursing home you visit?"

"Retirement home," she politely corrected. "I was going to repot plants with some of the residents this weekend."

"Oh! Zinfandel!" Evelyn poured herself a glass.

"I really appreciate you coming," Heather added.

The blonde woman waved a hand of dismissal as she sipped her beverage. "Of course. But you can't drink alcohol after bumping your head." She shook a finger at Heather's glass. "You know, when we first compared exes, I thought you had nightmare-of-the-year award, but this is a full-on nightmare-of-the-decade. *And* he got away with it. What are you going to do?"

Heather dumped the rest of her beverage down the sink. The easy familiarity of the two women had Rave suspecting they'd been close friends for a while.

Heather fixed herself a glass of water. "I don't know what to do." She arranged a bag of ice and slipped it under her shirt against her left shoulder.

The women took their drinks and sat on opposite ends of the couch, looking at each other. They launched into conversation about Evelyn's work in real estate before circling back around to Heather's car turned fireball turned junkyard trash.

Rave partly listened and partly dwelled in his own thoughts. Was Heather's danger the reason for his presence? Was he supposed to protect her somehow? He had no physical body to do much of anything. But he could watch out for danger. He'd known and warned her about the car fire.

For now, Heather didn't need him hovering while she enjoyed time with a friend. He concentrated on just fading from view and slowly the room around him began to dissolve into darkness.

Just before he vanished completely, Rave caught a concerned and sad look from Heather.

Maybe she was the reason he was still here.

CHAPTER 3

Heather woke to the smell of her automatic coffee maker. Best. Purchase. Ever.

She stretched and padded out of the room, Denver by her side. She read the note on the counter

> Headed to work early. Pretty sure snoring and drooling are normal for you, so I thought it was medically safe for me to leave. If I'm wrong and you're lying on the floor with internal bleeding, please call me. Better yet, text me when you're awake.
> —Evelyn

Heather rolled her eyes and balled up the note. After pouring a cup of coffee, she texted Evelyn that she was awake. She flicked the note off the counter and into the trash. Retrieving half-and-half from her refrigerator, she added it to her coffee.

"You like a little coffee with your cream?"

"Bah!" She jerked, spilling cream on her hand and shirt.

"Sorry."

Heather glowered at Rave as she snatched a towel and cleaned the mess. The fireman still wore navy slacks and a fitted white shirt over bulging biceps. He was still semi-transparent, still standing in her kitchen like it was the most normal thing in the world. Her world. That was the problem.

"You're back. Okay. It was entertaining at first, but now I'm getting a little spooked."

"No pun intended?" He arched an eyebrow.

"Funny. Have you been here all night?"

"Well, it turns out I don't need sleep. So I watched your perimeter."

"You were guarding me?" A whisper of endearment flickered through her before she dismissed the feeling.

"Yes," he said. "And did you know your neighbor smokes cigarettes with oxygen in the home? It's a fire risk."

"Janet? Yeah, she smokes. I think she's trying to quit." Heather took several sips of coffee, not knowing what to tell Rave. She wasn't going to nag or police her neighbors because the ghost of a firefighter suggested it.

Firefighter.

She felt the caffeine already kicking in. Or maybe her brain was just trained to wake at the taste of coffee. "Maybe you died on duty and that's why you showed up in uniform."

He scowled slightly. "Is that relevant?"

"Well, yeah. Shouldn't we figure out who you were?"

"Why?"

"I read this article once—probably hogwash—but it was an interview with a psychic detective from Georgia. I seem to remember him saying that ghosts linger when they need help moving on."

"You want me to leave?" There was a confusion in his voice that tugged at her.

"Okay. Don't make me out to be callous. I can't handle a ghost in my life—real or imaginary. Why don't I help you find whatever closure you need?"

"What if my closure is helping you survive Blake?"

A warm sensation gave her a twist of panic. Helping him move on meant not letting herself get attached. Still, his focus on her seemed to be a way to avoiding facing his death head on.

"How is that logical if you and I never met before you died?" she asked.

He placed his hands on his hips. "Did you get that from the medium article, too?"

"Don't you want to know if you left behind loved ones?"

"Don't you want to *not* become a ghost like me?" Rave shot back.

Heather laughed. "You realize we're arguing about who should help whom?"

Rave blew out a breath without moving any actual air. "Right. Let's compromise. We'll find out who I was while we figure out a way to stop Blake."

"You escalated from watching out for me to stopping Blake."

"Stopping Blake *is* watching out for you," he countered.

"Watching out for me is *defensive*. I intend to plan where to move next. Stopping Blake is *offensive*."

"Then I want an offensive strategy." He crossed his arms.

Handsome though he was—and adoringly consumed with her safety—she wasn't following anyone's orders. "I'm going to have to hear this strategy before I agree. Meanwhile, I'll investigate you online." She brought her cup of coffee over to the kitchen table where she opened her laptop.

Rave stood behind her, watching.

She searched for firefighters killed in the line of duty. "I don't suppose you could narrow this down by remembering your name? Maybe you at least know what part of the country you lived in?"

"NFD."

"Beg pardon?"

"Nashville Fire Department."

"Ah. You're close to here then." She typed in her search on the keyboard. "Okay. Here's something."

They read the headline together.

NOVEMBER 12. One firefighter was killed and
two injured in a building fire Friday night.
Fire investigators suspect the fire may have
been the product of arson ...

Heather turned and looked up at Rave. He was leaning close, reading the screen with a dazed look in those brown eyes.

Now who's invading whose personal space?

But she wasn't going to point that out because she liked his proximity.

"Ring any bells?"

"Yes." As his throat worked around the word, the kitchen light dimmed, the laptop's fan whined. Grief, apparently, had its own static charge.

The light above the kitchen table dimmed and her laptop screen flickered.

"Hey, what are you doing?" she asked.

He leaned back and looked around. The light and computer returned to normal. "I don't know. Sorry."

"You just keep your supernatural powers bottled up on the inside. No frying my laptop. I need it to make a living." She tried to keep her voice light even though she ached for his loss.

Clicking on the link provided in the article, sent her to another article.

Officer Victor Roberts died in the line of
duty November 11. He is survived by three
siblings. A memorial service will be held on
November 15. The burial will take place at
Grove Cemetery...

"Victor. Is that you?"

"Um, I guess so? This is the only Tennessee fireman death. I definitely recognize that building. I remember going into *that* building."

"Okay. *Victor.*" She tapped a finger to her lips. "Nope. I'm going to leave you at Rave. It can be your ghost nickname." Victor belonged to a life he'd lost. Rave was the one standing in her kitchen.

He nodded but his expression looked doleful.

"How about we visit your grave?" she said softly. "Maybe it will trigger some memories or help with closure. The fire was only five days ago." She wished she could offer the plutonic comfort of holding his hand.

How awful it must be to learn about your own death.

She wanted to reach out and provide some touch of comfort, but that was impossible.

"No," he said firmly. "We agreed to find my identity and that's done. Now, we focus on your safety."

She stood and spoke in a comforting tone. "I think this is what you need. I'm no ghost expert—you're my first. Ugh. That sounded wrong. Anyway, I'm a counselor. People need closure. Maybe ghosts do too."

He crossed his arms. "I'm fine. Dead as of five days ago. But fine."

The kitchen light flickered again.

Heather looked skeptically up at the ceiling lights. "Uh, huh."

Rave was definitely not fine.

With determination, she went to her room, dressed, and emerged with phone in hand. She pulled on a light jacket and tossed a golden scarf around her neck.

"Where are you going?" Rave asked with alarm.

"I'm going to visit Victor Robert's grave. You're welcome to join me." Because he considered himself part of her protection duty, she suspected he would.

He narrowed his eyes at her and stepped closer, towering over her by a half foot. "I know what you're doing."

"I hope so. I'm being fairly transparent. Pun intended." She walked around him, let Denver out to the backyard, and then came to her front door where she peered out, checking for any unfamiliar cars lurking.

Rave stood with his arms crossed, a pose he seemed to favor. "It isn't safe."

"I'm not keeping myself on house arrest. If you're worried about my safety, come with me." She reached for the door.

"Heather—"

The worry in his voice made her stop and stare up at him. When was the last time a man had spoken her name with such husky concern?

Never.

The word from a ghost had echoed louder than the horn outside.

Real ghost or not, he wasn't here to stay. She wouldn't let herself get too attached.

A horn honked, shattering the looming silence between them.

"My rideshare." She extended a hand through him, opened the door, and left.

RAVE STOOD inside Heather's house, cursing her stubbornness. They hadn't yet formulated a plan on stopping Blake, but she was throwing caution to the wind and dashing into the open.

Admittedly, Rave was being irrationally reluctant to learn about the life he'd lost. What if it hadn't been a good life? How could it have been good if he didn't even remember it? How could he not remember having siblings?

What if the road to truth was paved with disappointment?

But he couldn't leave Heather alone. He vanished from her house and appeared in the rideshare beside her. How was he able to sense where she was and simply will himself to her? It felt like following a thread only he could see, tugging him toward her.

Keeping his spirit in pace with the car took some effort and concentration as he kept fading in and out, but he managed. On the forty-minute ride to a cemetery outside Nashville, he watched the buildings and trees as they passed. Early spring in Tennessee was always beautiful. Yellow forsythias were in bloom alongside white magnolias. Redbuds had shed their pink flowers, leaving their heart-shaped leaves visible.

When Heather exited the rideshare, Rave followed. She waited outside the cemetery as the car and driver left.

"Thank you for coming," she said to him. "I do feel safer with you close by."

Rave extended his senses as far out from Heather as he could—no danger, no stalker, no Blake.

"Shall we?" he asked.

Heather nodded and led the way between crypts and gravestones, gravel crunching underfoot. The morning sky was gray and overcast. Ravens perched in looming trees, watching the two of them walk past rows of tombstones. A breeze stirred fallen white petals shed by pear trees.

"You said you used to be a counselor?" Rave asked.

"Yes, student counselor. When I left Blake, I left that life behind. That was five years ago. To maintain anonymity, I write a column under a pseudonym."

"A column?"

"Sort of a Dear Abbey but for parents to ask about school-age kids."

"That's creative. I love going to schools and talking about fire safety with children. They take in everything with their minds as open as their wide eyes. Or ... I did like schools." He shoved his hands into the pockets of his navy slacks.

"If it's any consolation, I miss interacting with kids, too." Heather stopped and turned toward Rave.

"You're a good person, Heather." He stroked a hand lightly over her hair, unable to feel its texture.

His eyes fell on the Steri-Strips over the cut on her forehead. How could anyone harm this woman?

"Lets get to the grave." He forced the words out. Regardless of what his life had been, he could do this one last thing as a ghost: stay with Heather until she was definitely safe.

They continued to wander until they found Victor's grave. Rave stood and stared at the headstone. The ravens, which had been dispersed throughout the cemetery, congregated on the trees and stones near the fallen fireman's grave.

"That's a lot of birds." Heather glanced around nervously.

"Don't fear them. I don't know why they're here, but they're not dangerous."

She poked a finger toward his tattoo with a wry grin. "I think I know why they're here. They're connected to you."

"Are they?"

Her theory sounded plausible. Rave raised his hands and spun in a slow circle. Dozens of ravens took flight and swirled above them like a black, silky whirlwind.

Heather gasped and smiled. "Are you doing this?"

"I think I am." A faint connection linked him to them, like the strings extending to puppets, though the birds' actions felt more like they were answering a request than obeying a command. The more he focused, the stronger the tug.

He smiled back at Heather before having the birds descend and fly around the two of them. They stirred the air and whipped Heather's red hair around her head. With flushed cheeks, she raised her arms in awe and looked transcendent with glowing red hair in a backdrop of black wings and the white flowers stirred into the air by their flapping.

"Keep your arms out," Rave told her.

She held them as ravens landed on her sleeves. She laughed. "Rave, this is amazing!" She looked … free. Not like the careful woman checking locks and alarms, but the version of her he suspected had existed before Blake.

He laughed, too, as the birds flapped their wings to steady themselves. The remaining birds continued to circle above in something like a dance. With a thought, Rave asked the ravens to fly away and they did.

He turned back to the grave. His heart sank as he read the words and stared at the freshly laid grass.

"Heather."

"Yes?"

"That's not me." His voice cracked.

"It's not?"

"Victor was one of my friends and fellow firefighters." Fresh pain washed over him.

"You remember? That's good." Then, she frowned. "Oh, no. I'm sorry about your friend."

Rave nodded grimly.

"So, who are you?" Heather asked.

He gave her a lopsided grin. "I'm Rave."

She rolled her eyes playfully.

"Okay. We read that one person died and others were injured. And I remember going into that building fire. So who were the injured firemen?"

"The article didn't list them. We can dig further online. Or," she tapped a finger to her lips, "if you can remember your friend, can you remember what fire station you worked at?"

Rave brightened. "I do. I'll tell you how to get there." For the first time since dying, he had a solid fact to hold: a building, a station, a place.

BLAKE WATCHED the news for the next twenty-four hours, on the lookout for himself. People were so quick to video with their phones that he could've been captured on the scene of the crash.

The crash he'd caused.

Ramming into Heather's car hadn't been part of the plan. He'd been watching her every move for a week, calculating when he could grab her. She had a lesson to learn. A lesson about faithfulness and obedience.

He was planning her abduction followed by a slow—probably painful—indoctrination into how a wife should behave—love, honor, and *obey*. He'd even rented a remote house for it. But he had to carefully sculpt a plan. He couldn't grab her at her house since she had a security system and an enormous guard dog. Somewhere in her routine of grocery shopping, errands, and lunch with her friend, he knew he'd find a weakness.

But red rage had foiled his meticulous planning. First, his eye began twitching followed by his hands wringing the steering wheel. Before he realized what he was doing, he'd gunned through the light and plowed into her vehicle.

There was a certain satisfaction in seeing her dazed and bleeding. She lived—which was good because she didn't deserve a quick death. Still seething and crackling with anger, he'd planned right then to kill her and be done with it. He would drag her out of the smoking vehicle and beat her to death. She deserved at least that much.

But it was too public. People were gathering around the crash site. He'd been forced to flee. At least no one caught him on camera, based on the news footage he watched.

Now, Heather knew he'd found her. That part of the surprise was ruined. No matter. He'd still find a kink in her armor—a moment when her guard was down and he could teach her those lessons.

CHAPTER 4

Heather stepped out of her next rideshare at Rave's fire station. The two-story brick building stood on an acre of manicured land. Out front, the American flag waved in the spring breeze.

She hesitated a moment and stared.

"Are you okay?" Rave asked.

"Um, yes. I was realizing that I'm traveling around town, helping a ghost solve his mystery. This is all more than a little surreal."

"We can stop if you're uncomfortable."

"No! I want to solve the mystery of my ghost hero's body-spirit dissociation." She marched inside the firehouse.

A young, muscular black woman met her just inside the door. "Afternoon, ma'am. Can I help you?"

Heather hadn't considered what she might say when she arrived. "I heard about the tragic building fire."

"Yes, ma'am. We flew the flag at half-staff for that. We just raised it back today." The firewoman wore navy slacks like Rave and a navy t-shirt with "NFD" on it.

"I'm sorry to hear about the loss. Can I make a donation?"

"That's not necessary," Rave told her, but she ignored him.

"Absolutely," said the woman. "Here's a brochure with the links and how to donate. We take checks, too."

Heather took out her phone and lined up the Q code. It took her to the website, and she made her donation.

The woman beamed at her. "Thanks for that. I'm Johanna Smoot."

"Rookie of the year," Rave added with a grin. "She's a heck of a firefighter."

"Can I show you around the station?" Johanna offered.

"I'm Heather. I'd like that."

She walked over to one wall where a photograph of men and women in dress blues hung. "These are photos of our team," Johanna said.

Heather's eyes roamed the faces in the picture. Rave pressed in close, looking with her. "That one." She pointed at Rave.

"Oh, that's Logan Roundhouse." Johanna stuck her hands in her pockets. "If you were reading about the fire, you might have heard about Logan. He was injured. Chief's been checking on him every day and says he's stable."

"Stable?" Heather inspected other photographs on the wall.

"Yeah. A falling beam in the fire knocked him down. He's been at Vanderbilt ever since. In the ICU." Johanna added the last few words in a soft voice.

Alive. Rave was alive at a hospital!

"Oh, wow," Heather murmured. Gooseflesh prickled her skin, as she tried not to turn to Rave so they could discuss what this meant. Only she could see Rave, and she'd alarm Johanna if she started talking to him.

Heather saw a framed clipping of a newspaper article and photo of Rave—er, Logan—and other firefighters at a local elementary school. Another photo showed Rave standing beside a bald man, bigger and bulkier than him.

Rave shifted beside her. "That was Victor. Except we all called him Buster."

A caption under the photo read: Victor "Buster" Roberts and Logan "The Raven" Roundhouse.

"The Raven." Heather stared at Logan's brown hair and brown eyes in the photo. The photo hadn't captured the depths of those compassionate eyes.

"We all get nicknames around here," Johanna said.

Heather swallowed. "Is he married?"

"Nah. I don't think he was even dating at the time. He worked a lot."

Rave said, "I was paying off student loans, working my way toward arson investigator." He spoke the words slowly, as if remembering details as he verbalized them. "I dated some, but I didn't want anything serious until I could support a family as an investigator and not the crazy shift work of a fireman."

Johanna continued. "Nicest guy though. Give you his kidney if you needed it. That one there," she pointed to another picture, "is Logan and the chief."

Heather turned to the woman. "Thanks for your time. I'm heading out now."

"Thanks for the donation, but are you sure you don't want to see the fire trucks? Everyone comes to see the fire trucks."

"No thanks. Maybe next time." Heather's phone chimed with a text message.

She left the building and read her message. Next, she used her phone app to request another rideshare. As she stood out in the open, she checked the lot and street for unfamiliar cars.

"Where are you going?" Rave asked.

"First, I need to have lunch with Evelyn. We already arranged this a week ago. After that, we're going back to Nashville—to the hospital."

"You want to see me in the ICU?" he asked hesitantly.

"Well, yeah. I mean, I have a million questions. If you're not dead—which hallelujah there—why is your spirit outside of your body? I don't know anything about the paranormal, but that doesn't seem healthy. Do you need to be in the same room to reconnect?" She rubbed her temples. "And it helps me know this isn't all in my head."

～

"Do you need help going to pick out a new car?" Evelyn asked.

Heather tugged at strands of bright auburn hair. "There's no point getting a new car until I go where I need to go."

"So you're moving on?"

"He found me. I don't know how. I thought I was careful, but there are always electronic records. It took him five years, but he found me. Maybe I can buy myself another five years." She thought about Denver never seeing his favorite park again.

"It seems like the justice system ought to protect you better."

Slices of uneaten pizza squatted on their table in Caprigios Pizza parlor in Clarksville. The food smelled delicious, but Heather's mind was busy racing from Rave to Blake to how to move again.

"It's my word against Blake's, and I don't have any proof. They're going to look for the car that hit me, and if they found him, he could be charged with a hit-and-run. But Blake's smart enough to not drive around in a car registered in his name."

"Where will you go?" Evelyn asked, dipping her straw up and down in her ice water as she drowned a wedge of lemon.

"I'm not sure yet. But when I do know, I'm not going to share that with anyone."

"So goodbye is goodbye forever?" She stared at her drink.

"It has to be. I'm sorry. Goodbye is permanent." Heather could call and text Evelyn from a new number, but their relationship wouldn't be the same. "I really enjoyed our friendship—you took me out of the dark place I was in when I first had to start all over. I hope you know you're my hero." Her smile wobbled, just for a heartbeat, before she smoothed it away with a sip of water.

Evelyn snorted. "Just a friend, not a hero. As far as I can tell, you're the hero of your own story. You managed to extricate yourself from a dangerous situation when you left Blake. Then, after suffering a head injury you had enough wits about you to get away from your car when it was on fire."

Heather picked at a piece of pepperoni on top of her pizza. "Still, the last five years would've been a lot harder without a friend like you."

"I'll help you pack. I mean, I want you to stay, but I understand your dilemma. If anything changes or if you need help, you know where to find me and how to reach me."

"I do, thank you. I also have a favor to ask of you. Can you give Denver and me a lift to Vanderbilt University Medical Center?"

"Sure. Is tomorrow morning okay? I have the kids this afternoon. Is somebody sick?"

"I don't know. I'm going to check on a friend. Tomorrow works great. Thanks." Heather took a bite of pizza.

Evelyn sat up straighter and picked up a slice of pizza. "Okay, now that the serious stuff is out of the way, we need to talk about the latest gossip with Prince William and Princess Kate."

Heather smiled. She wasn't particularly emotionally invested in the royal family, but she enjoyed Evelyn's enthusiasm, and the conversation would be a welcome reprieve from her nagging worry about starting a new life.

"We definitely need to talk about that."

RAVE FOLLOWED Heather inside her house after the two women finished lunch and Evelyn drove Heather home.

"Sorry about lunch. There wasn't really a way to include you in the conversation." She gave Denver a robust greeting in the form of behind-the-ear scratches.

"It's okay. I've never been a fly on the wall at a ladies luncheon. It was a new experience for me."

Heather poured a glass of wine.

"Wine in the afternoon?" Rave teased.

"Yes. We're celebrating. You're alive. This is great news." She took a sip of wine before retrieving cardboard boxes from her hall closet.

She placed one on her counter beside a stack of newspapers. "So, Logan Roundhouse, tell me about yourself."

"I like Pina coladas and getting caught in the rain." He smiled.

"Ah! He has a lighter side." She pulled a ceramic mug from the cupboard and began wrapping it in newspaper. "So, you're happier knowing you're actually alive."

"Part of my somber mood was worry over you. That's still a problem."

She gestured to her boxes and she took another sip of wine. "I'm dealing with my problem. Pack and vanish into the night." She added, "Once you're put back together again."

"You make me sound like Humpty Dumpty."

"If the shoe fits. You both bumped your heads." She shrugged and winked at him over her shoulder. "Okay. Out with it. More about you —other than that you blush when a woman winks at you."

"About me." He sighed in feigned irritation. He enjoyed spending time with Heather even when she teased him. Maybe especially when she teased him. But he could tease back. "Is this the school counselor emerging?"

"Could be. But remembering more about who you are might bridge the connection of body to spirit."

"I grew up right here in Clarksville, so that must be why I was drawn to your car wreck. I played baseball—Clarksville Wildcats. My parents still live here on about thirty acres outside of town. We had horses and pigs and chickens—more of a petting zoo than an actual farm. After high school, I took a year before college to backpack Europe."

"Really? That must have been fascinating."

"I wasn't in a hurry for more schooling at a desk so I opted for cultural enrichment. I kept a list of everywhere I want to go back and visit again. After that, I was four years at Tennessee State."

As Rave told Heather about his past, his mood stayed light. Talking to her felt therapeutic, and he wondered if students felt this way in her presence.

He stopped talking when he noticed Heather had stopped packing.

She stared at the box of packed kitchenware.

He thought about what she'd said: *Pack and leave.* And what she hadn't said: *Just like last time. Just like all the other moves she'd made in foster care.*

"You don't get attached, do you? Not to places, things, or people?"

She swallowed. "The one time I let myself get attached, the man turned out to be obsessively possessive. I don't want anyone else to be in danger because of me."

"You're referring to Evelyn?"

"Anyone. But, yes, right now, Evelyn."

He moved closer to her. "What about *your* past, Heather? Maybe we should discuss that."

He was piecing himself together while she was carefully taking herself apart.

She sealed the filled cardboard box with packing tape and started on another. "Oh, no. This is your spiritual therapy session and your youth sounds mostly happy. Besides, the more we talk, the more you seem to remember. For me, foster care was not a happy place. Trash bags instead of suitcases. Leaving behind budding friendships. Haven't you heard people become therapists in part to learn to handle their own problems? Well, that was part of it. That and hopefully giving kids in troubled families some support they needed."

"You miss it."

"Denver needs a walk."

DENVER WAGGED his tail as Heather fitted his harness.

"Blake's still out there somewhere." Rave frowned his disapproval of her venturing into public.

Heather refused to be contained. "Yes, but Denver and I need to stretch our legs. Besides, Blake is afraid of dogs. Dogs and heights. I'll be okay on a walk with my four-legged friend."

She was out the door and walking at a brisk pace as Rave followed, glancing around in all directions. She smiled to herself, enjoying the fireman's protective nature.

Truthfully, she wasn't as cavalierly dismissive of danger as she let on. She was always looking over her shoulder. She'd spent five years fearing the day Blake would find her. But she'd promised herself long ago that hiding inside four walls wasn't living. She wouldn't give Blake that type of power over her.

"That's the Customs House Museum," Rave commented.

"Ah. More memories." She looked at the unique building of stone and brick with its steep tiled roof. She scanned reflections in store-front windows, but no one followed her.

"I remember the 1999 F3 tornado that ravaged downtown. It's when I knew I wanted to become a fireman and help people. I was here and helped rescue efforts during the 2010 flood and another tornado that hit in 2018."

"Wow. I picked a natural disaster haven to live in. It's a beautiful town. I guess getting rebuilt a few times adds character." She kept walking, feeling like she was a counselor again—taking someone for a therapeutic wander down memory lane.

"There's a lot of character. A lot of history—Trail of Tears, Civil War, the Lillian Theater, later named the Roxy Theater. It was the backdrop for Sheryl Crow's song *All I Wanna Do*."

"And it's a growing city. Every day I feel like I see new construction."

"Yeah, it's not small-town America anymore."

"It still has that down-home feel though."

Rave looked around. "Yeah, it does." He stopped and turned toward her. "You're bringing back my memories. I can't thank you enough." He extended a hand and then seemed to remember she couldn't hold it and pulled it back.

She wanted to hold his hand, too. Doing so would physically confirm the emotional connection she was forming with him. Perhaps it was better she couldn't touch him. With Blake on the prowl, she wouldn't be in Clarksville much longer. She didn't need to add heartache to the list of baggage she'd carry with her to her relocation destination.

Rave saw her safely back home. He shuffled his feet as she lingered by the door. She'd had dates that had less awkward goodbyes.

"See you tomorrow?" She was reminding him of the hospital trip with Evelyn.

He nodded.

If it had been a date, she might have told him what a nice time she'd had or how she was looking forward to seeing him again. Since he was a ghost and their time was limited, she opted for a simple. "Goodbye, Rave."

"Goodbye, Heather."

As she closed the door, a car rolled slowly past, and she had an eerie feeling of someone watching through those tinted windows.

CHAPTER 5

The next morning, Rave sat quietly in Heather's kitchen while she dressed and prepared for the day. She wore her usual blue jeans, this time paired with a plush lavender sweater. After an insufficient breakfast of coffee and an orange, she put a harness on Denver that looked different from the one she'd used yesterday.

Rave inspected the stitching on Denver's brightly colored harness. "Recreational Therapy Dog."

"Yup. Denver goes with me to the retirement home once a month."

Rave scratched his chin. "We're going to a retirement home?" He thought they were going to the hospital.

"Nope. As promised, Evelyn will take us to the hospital. Denver here is our ticket to your ICU room. They won't let me in because I'm not family, but I might get away with recreational therapy. Most places want you to register with them—paperwork and a prolonged process. I'm going to just walk in and see how far we get. You, Logan Roundhouse, need recreational therapy."

"That's better than lying," he said.

"Yeah." She chuckled. "It'd be a little awkward if I claimed to be your fiancé no one knew about."

"Why would you do that?"

She clasped a leash onto the dog's harness. *"While You Were Sleeping?* You've never seen the Sandra Bullock movie?"

He gave her a blank look which earned him an exasperated shake of her head.

"Never mind," she said.

Outside, Evelyn honked her horn.

Rave rode in the back seat with Denver as Heather rode beside Evelyn. The women talked about the latest political scandal as Rave tried to pet the German Shepherd. His hand went unnoticed through the animal, though once he thought he made an ear flicker. He liked dogs and always thought of getting one of his own. However, fire station shifts were twelve to twenty-four hours—not conducive to owning a pet.

After Evelyn dropped them off at the medical center, Rave followed Heather into the hospital as she held Denver's leash. She walked to the front desk receptionist.

Heather gave the woman a warm smile. "I'm visiting the ICU. Well, I'm tagging along. He's visiting the trauma ICU." She gestured at Denver.

The woman looked down and instantly warmed to the animal. "Oh, how wonderful."

"Can you remind me which floor it's on?"

"Tenth floor. Elevators are down the hall on your left."

"Thanks." Heather walked quickly, her thick-soled winter boots making no sound on the patterned linoleum floor. "This place is enormous."

Rave's mind tried to process the spinning world around him. Initially, he thought he was the ghost of a dead man. Yesterday, he learned he was the spirit of a living man. Today, he was going to see himself in the hospital. But, why in the world would his spirit leave his body? Was he near death? He wasn't sure he wanted to see himself on his deathbed.

Heather apparently did. She moved with the grace and speed of a panther, boarded the elevator, and pressed the already lit button to the tenth floor three more times.

"It's already lit," Rave pointed out to her.

"I know. I'm nervous. If I screw this up, I lose my one chance to see you. Maybe save you."

The strangers on the elevator cast skeptical glances at the woman talking to herself.

When the doors opened to the tenth floor, Heather walked to the ICU reception desk. The young man behind the desk had eyes only for the dog.

"Look at that handsome German Shepherd! I love it when ya'll visit."

"This is Denver. And he has a sweet spot for firemen, so when he heard about Logan Roundhouse, he practically brought his leash to me." Heather winked at Rave.

"Oh. That's adorable. It's such a sad story. He's down in room twelve. Let me give the nurse a heads-up in case they're doing a procedure or bathing."

Heather wriggled her eyebrows and turned to Rave. *Bathing,* she mouthed.

He felt his cheeks flush before he turned away from her. Heather and Denver waited as Rave paced.

A moment later, a gangly man in blue scrubs approached. "The therapy dog. He's adorable. Come on back. This one needs some extra furry lovin'."

They followed the nurse, whose badge said *Philippe,* down the hall and into the ICU room. Philippe leaned on the doorway and ushered Heather and Denver into the room.

Rave stared at his body in the bed.

"Is he any better?" Heather asked.

"Well, sweetie. This is only my first day with him, but the doctors think he's doing well. After his induced medical coma—you know for the brain swelling—he's shown signs of improvement, and recovery is expected. All of his reflexes are strong. As soon as he decides to wake up, he'll be able to get that breathing tube out."

"Wake up?"

Philippe shrugged. "They're not sure if maybe the medications are taking a long time to wear off. There's nothing on his brain MRI to indicate why he'd be slow to wake. No permanent damage."

Rave's heart raced—*no permanent damage*. Was his life salvageable then? But how? He'd been reluctant to face himself because he feared the worst. For the first time since realizing he was a ghost, he felt something like hope.

"Okay. Thank you," Heather said to the nurse.

"If you need anything, I'll be next door with another patient."

When Philippe left, Rave and Heather gaped at Logan. He was attached to wires and cords snaking everywhere. A monitor on one wall displayed his vital signs. He looked like a victim, not a hero.

Denver approached and wriggled his muzzle into Logan's hand.

"Hey, I can feel a tingling sensation in my hand with him doing that." Rave rubbed his hand.

Logan didn't move.

"Your torso really is that muscular."

"That's your first thought?" Rave chuckled.

"Well, I thought initially you were a hallucination, then you were a mystery to solve, and I tried not to think about how I was talking to an attractive man—er, ghost. Next, I wondered if maybe I was the one in a coma after my crash, and I was inventing this whole thing, which I guess is still a possibility. So, yeah, rather than dwell on the eerie supernatural bizarreness of all of this, I'm taking a moment to appreciate your body." She sat down in the chair beside Logan and rested her hand on top of his, which rested on top of Denver's head.

Rave felt the tingling sensation grow stronger in his hand.

"You don't have any burns," Heather commented.

"Our fire-retardant gear is pretty effective. Firemen seldom get burned. Usually blunt force trauma gets us—as I'm evidence of." He walked around to the opposite side of the bed and watched Heather watching him. He hated seeing himself looking fragile—dependent on tubes for breathing and nutrition. But having someone worried at his bedside made him feel cherished in a way he never had been from a woman.

Heather stroked his hair. "You saved my life, Rave. Even in a slumber, you're saving lives. That's some kind of hero."

"Considering I wouldn't have found my way back to my body without you, maybe you're the hero."

She smiled. "We saved each other."

"Agreed. So how does this work? How do I get back in my body?" He was eager now that he knew his health was good and a beautiful woman of flesh and blood awaited on the other side of the supernatural threshold.

"True love's kiss?" She batted her eyes and laughed.

Trust Heather to turn life-and-death into something that made him want to grin.

She shrugged. "I've no idea. Why don't you try to lay down and see if you can merge or stitch back together?"

He moved toward Logan but hesitated. "Heather, what about Blake?"

"You still trying to protect me?" She grinned.

"Yes."

"Well, you can do that better if you're solid rather than a spirit."

She bit her lip, and Rave wondered if she worried the same thing he did.

"If I don't remember any of our time together, please come find me. Introduce yourself. I'd want to get to know you," he said.

She nodded but stared at Denver rather than Rave. With her gaze diverted, he didn't believe she felt committed to seeking him out.

No attachments.

Rave lay down, trying to align spirit and body. He felt a jolt, like static electricity that felt more like rejection than rejoining.

He sat up. "Now what? True love's kiss?"

"Ha! I'd kiss you but we only just met."

"Who are you?" a voice spoke from the door.

. . .

HEATHER BOLTED OUT of her chair and spun toward the door.

Rave stood. "Mom. Dad."

A man and a woman stood in the doorway.

Heather's mouth went dry. "I'm Heather Phillips. I'm . . ." She wrung her hands looking for an exit and trying to remember what her cover story had been in the first place. She couldn't lie to Rave's parents. "I'm a friend. But I'm done visiting. I'll let you two have your time with him." She picked up Denver's leash and tried to ease around the pair of them.

"We wouldn't push aside a friend of Logan's." His mother walked to the bedside and stroked her son's cheek.

"How'd you two meet?" his father asked.

Heather heard the slight desperation in his voice—like he needed some happiness amidst the anguish he and his wife had been going through. Heather knew that tone from parents she'd counseled over the years.

She slowed her hasty retreat and lingered by the exit. "He's my hero. Saved my life."

His mom's face brightened in surprise and delight as she sat by the bed. His father stood beside her. They waited silently for her to continue.

"I was in a car accident, and Rave saved me. If he hadn't gotten me out of my car, I would've died in the fire."

"Rave?" his mother blinked.

"Ah, yes. My nickname for Logan."

The woman smiled. "He always liked ravens. He said they were his spirit animal. Some people think they're an ill omen, but Logan always said they were intelligent birds of insight."

Rave watched his parents with a tortured expression. "And they connect the material world and the spiritual world."

"I think his spirit animal is watching out for him," Heather told his parents.

His mother nodded. "Perhaps. But I always think of the Edgar Allen Poe poem—*And his eyes have all the seeming of a demon that is dreaming.*" She shuddered.

"The deeper meaning of that poem is that you can't hold onto things that you love forever or it will consume you. The man in the poem couldn't let go of his lover and so his soul would be lifted *nevermore*," Rave explained to Heather.

Heather kept her gaze focused on his mother. "I prefer the raven Tearsica Brooks writes about. Her birds are pure of heart and devoid of judgment. Like the Rave I know."

His mother placed a hand over her heart, and his father put an arm around her shoulder to comfort her.

"I like that very much," the woman said.

Heather had gotten that information from one of her smartphone searches during her many rideshares.

"I like that one too," Rave said.

His father patted the dog. "Logan was always bringing home stray animals we had to find homes for."

"And wanted to be a firefighter since kindergarten."

A shadow of a bird darkened the window, and Heather bid them politely farewell so they could have time with their son

RAVE SILENTLY WAITED with Heather for her ride. Seeing his parents' distress tore at him more than seeing his body lying in bed. Heather had been sweet to give them the hope and encouragement they seemed to need.

Evelyn drove Heather back home. The two women talked about the house Evelyn was helping a client close on and all of the drama revolving around the home inspector's findings.

Rave rode with them and stared out the window—the world outside passing him just as it did while Logan slept in the hospital bed. He'd never regret being a fireman; the first fire truck he saw at the age of six on a preschool tour had been love at first sight. He'd helped a lot of people over the last decade. And he made a new family with his coworkers. They ate, slept, played cards, lifted weights, trained, and bonded all under the same roof.

Then the building fire call came from dispatch, a 10-61. Victor hadn't survived. Rave had, but he'd become somehow disconnected from himself in the process. And he didn't know the remedy for his predicament.

To add to the confusion, he'd met a remarkable woman whose life was shrouded in danger. At least he understood their connection now—she lived in his hometown of Clarksville, where he'd been wandering when the crash had happened. The incident drew him to help her.

If he woke and didn't remember her, he couldn't help her. If he woke, weak from his coma, he might not be able to help her even if he remembered. He wondered if his own reluctance to rejoin his body was the reason the reunion hadn't worked.

When they arrived back at Heather's house, Rave didn't follow her inside. "I'm going to take a walk."

"Sure. Okay." She let herself and Denver inside and closed the door.

The alarm system beeped—deactivated and reactivated.

With Heather safe inside her home, Rave whisked himself back to his hospital room, where his parents still watched over him. His mother sat beside his bed, where Heather had been, and his father sat in one corner, staring out the window.

"A woman came to visit you today, Logan. And she's a looker. Probably a firecracker with all that red hair, but maybe a firecracker and fireman are the right combination."

Rave shook his head with a smile. It would be just like his mother to see a woman holding her son's hand and jump to conclusions.

"She only said she was a friend," his father pointed out with an amused tone.

"Her eyes said she was more. Besides, he's all work all the time. The last girl he brought home was—what—prom fifteen years ago?"

His father rolled a pen in his hand, and Rave wondered if he was missing his pipe. "He's had relationships. He's told us about a few of them."

"No one he thought well enough of to bring home to meet us."

"Honey, meeting a woman in his hospital room doesn't qualify as bringing a woman home."

His father's attempt at levity would have been well accepted under different circumstance. Instead Rave's mother bristled.

She sniffed. "Well, it might be the closest thing we ever get."

Rave felt sorrow well inside of him. "Oh, Mom. I'll find a way to come back. I promise. And you can meet Heather. If she agrees, I'll even bring her home for dinner."

His father went over to her chair and wrapped his arms around her. "I'm sorry, honey. I didn't mean to upset you. She seemed like a sweet woman. I bet they've had some happy moments. Maybe Logan is still getting to know her before he brings her home."

His father stood and patted Logan's shoulder. "We're very proud of you, Son. You know your mother has that scrapbook of articles of all the people you've helped. It's only half full, so you come on back to us because your work here isn't done yet." He reached for a tissue at the bedside and dabbed his eyes.

Rave let his own tears fall.

BLAKE POPPED a couple of oxycodone pills in his mouth and washed them down with soda. His back ached from the long hours doing car surveillance. Now that Heather knew he'd found her, she was probably making plans to bolt again.

He couldn't let that happen.

He had to keep the tail going so he wouldn't lose her. But she was being erratic. His appearance had altered her routine—probably as she made arrangements to pack up and move.

But what arrangements would take her to a cemetery, a firehouse, and a hospital? Was she coming unraveled?

Could she have the common courtesy to come unhinged in a way that made tracking her easier rather than harder?

All her rideshares buffered her. He didn't want witnesses when he reclaimed what was his. And the odd locations meant he didn't get downtime from his never-ending surveillance.

His hands cramped on the wheel. Rolling his neck, he felt each vertebra pop. He followed that with a twist of his back, then cracking of his knuckles. Soon he'd use those knuckles on her traitorous face.

Soon.

Soon he'd find the opportunity. She'd get careless, and then he'd pounce like a tiger.

CHAPTER 6

*H*eather threw herself into her writing. She had enough experience with emotional turmoil that she knew how to manage it. After a year of therapy following her divorce from an abusive man, she'd learned how to function even when her life became taxed with unsolved problems—no, *challenges*. She knew, as a counselor, that the word *challenge* possessed a positive connotation over *problem*. She knew how much to distract herself with writing and when to cut through the anxiety with the endorphins of exercise.

She hadn't, however, learned how to trust a man again. The few relationships she'd had since Blake had been fun and physical, but she'd never dispensed her address, phone number, or last name. She maintained no social media accounts.

Now, the perfect man had floated into her life—literally. Honest and honorable. And he'd never lay a hand on her in anger, and not because he couldn't touch anything. The problem—er, *challenge*—was that she needed to help him get his life back. She didn't know if that life of tangible solidarity included her or not. The fireman knew her secrets—those skeletons in the closet were enough to deter any man.

If the fear of a vengeful ex didn't make a suitor run, the stigma of a "battered woman" might—the ill-conceived notion that such a woman was dysfunctional either from mental health issues or trauma.

Damaged goods.

And maybe Heather was. But she'd never met someone who traveled life unscathed. Everyone had scars. And scars were a sign of healing—a sign of strength. Somehow Rave didn't seem put-off by her scars.

But that didn't mean he'd want a relationship when he woke up.

Rave could reconnect with his body and either not remember her or not want to associate with her at all. The uncertainty of the future hovered over her like a black cloud. She was going to need more therapy when all of this subsided.

Heather was on her elliptical machine when Rave reappeared.

"Knock. Knock," he said.

She smiled. "'Suddenly there came a tapping, as of someone gently rapping, rapping at my chamber door.'"

Rave chuckled. "I promise I'm not here to haunt you like Poe's raven."

"No," she agreed. "I've really enjoyed your company."

"How'd your writing go?" he asked.

"Two articles. How'd your personal time go?"

"Good." He slipped his hands into his pockets.

"Any trouble in the periphery?" she asked.

"No, but it occurred to me that I should see a picture of Blake so I can commit his image to memory and know who to be on the lookout for."

"I didn't keep any photos, but we'll look online." She wiped a towel across her forehead. "We were married for six months. In hindsight, I should've seen the signs—telltale moments of possessiveness. Hints that he thought I should quit my job when we were married or that I shouldn't do as many activities with friends. But I was young and he seemed so much wiser."

She slowed her speed to cool down. "I also didn't have any family. I think that made me overeager to create one of my own and pretend the flaws in him were cracks rather than craters. Whatever the case, the first time he struck me I vowed would be the last. It wasn't, but I still left and filed for divorce. His text and emails became more threatening—all great to use in court, but wreaked havoc on my psyche.

"I moved from place to place—shelter to shelter. When the papers finalized and I got half his worth—not because I'd earned it but because I needed it to disappear—I cashed out and did just that. Disappeared. Here we are, five years later, and he's found me. Time to disappear again. Too bad I don't have enough saved to move to the Caribbean."

Rave didn't smile. He calmly listened while wearing a concerned scowl. "You said you didn't have a family. Foster care. "

"I don't know who my parents were. I figure they had no use for me, so I have no use for them," she said.

His jaw clenched. "You've had a rough life."

Heather stepped off the elliptical machine and gulped water from her bottle. "I've got a job I enjoy, a pet who adores me, and a roof over my head. I don't have any use for pity, either from myself or anyone else." She looked at Rave. "Until today. I felt a twinge of self-pity when I saw your parents beside you in the ICU. So much love."

What would it be like to have a family unit like that?

"When I made the comment about the raven, I was afraid your mom might hug me."

Rave gave a slight smile. "She's been known to do that."

"I probably would've cried."

"Would that be so bad?" he asked softly.

She regarded Rave. She'd bet he was the type of man who'd hold a woman and just let her cry—no questions asked—until she was ready to talk. "No. I guess not."

She left the small room—her home office and gym combo. "I'm going to shower, fix dinner, and then you and I are going to watch a movie."

"We are?"

"Yes. We need distraction and happiness. And since you can't change the channel, it'll be a romantic comedy. *While You Were Sleeping.*"

He grinned, chocolate eyes sparkling. "I could always disrupt the signal."

"Yes. Apparently your supernatural talents include electrical disturbances and raven summoning. Anything else?"

"I think I can sense danger. At least, when you're in danger."

"Useful. I'll be back." She closed her bedroom door.

RAVE SAT on the couch beside Heather while she flipped through on-demand platforms to find the movie she wanted. They'd talked through dinner about where each of them had grown up. She'd touched on some of her foster-home days. The conversation had seemed to flow effortlessly.

"So, what do you do for fun when you aren't rushing into fires and saving lives?"

"Rescue cats out of trees," he joked. "No, honestly, I like playing the guitar—sort of a holdover from high school and college band days. You also can't grow up near Nashville and not have music be a part of your life. I like playing and watching most athletic games—basketball, baseball, soccer. What about you?"

"I like listening to music, though I have no inherent talent myself. But I would enjoy listening to you play. I liked biking before I became a recluse. Nothing cleared my mind like twenty miles of open road."

Rave pulled his gaze to the television as he tried not to envision Heather in tight bike shorts, leaning forward, muscles flexing as she peddled.

"As for watching sports," she continued, "I like anything noncontact—tennis, ice-skating, golf. I can do baseball, too."

"Golf?" He turned back to look at her.

"There's something very soothing when the announcers talk quietly as the athletes take their shots. It's therapeutic."

"Maybe I should start watching golf. When I get my body back, or when my body gets my spirit back, we should go to a baseball game. Go see Nashville Sound play."

"I'd like that."

"Can't bike there though, so we'll have to do a separate bike trip. And," he added, "because you live near Nashville, there are a hundred great places to go listen to music."

Heather smiled at his planning future dates with her, but the expression didn't reach her eyes. She was a guarded woman—like she wanted to share his optimism but couldn't help but worrying about the future. Even if he did wake up and if he remembered her, he wondered if she'd stay in Tennessee to be with him. No. She wouldn't risk putting Rave in danger. Well, he needed to convinced her he was willing to take that risk.

Rave rested his hand on top of Heather's. He wanted to know what she felt like, wanted to feel her warm skin and smell her scent. Maybe strawberries with all that flaming red hair.

His hand sunk into hers, but the sensation was different than other matter he passed through. Her essence had a faint tingling warmth.

When he looked into her eyes, he tried to read her expression— part surprise, part ... something else.

"What does it feel like?" he asked.

"Like champagne bubbling lightly on my skin."

He grinned.

She licked her lips as her cheeks flushed. "Movie?" she asked dryly.

"Movie."

They lapsed into comfortable silence during the movie. Toward the end, Heather fell asleep on the sofa with Denver on the floor nearby. Rave wished he could pull a throw blanket over her. Watching her sleep, he wondered what a kiss with those sweet, pink lips would feel like.

Beeping jarred him, and for a moment the smell of sterile plastic filled the air. He had the sensation of lying on his back, fluorescent lights overhead. Was this his time to reconnect? Back to his body or was he being summoned to the light?

He wanted to say goodbye to Heather, but if he could get back into his body and wake up, he'd never have to say goodbye. Unless he didn't remember any of this when he woke. But she'd come introduce herself. Right?

Another beep, sharper, and the pull toward his own chest tightened.

~

HEATHER WOKE to Denver's cold nose. She patted him gently on his head, rolled off the sofa, and let him into the backyard.

"Rave?"

No answer. The house felt oddly hollow without his presence.

She recalled he'd said time was harder to keep track of as a ghost. He'd show up eventually, and when he did, she'd share her next plan to help Rave repair the connection to his body.

As she dressed, blue jeans and a cream-colored sweater that accentuated her auburn hair, she contemplated her next new life. Maybe a quiet coastal town in Maine. She'd miss Evelyn, but she had Denver. At least she'd designed her job to be mobile.

After these few days with Rave, she wanted to fantasize about a life that including watching movies on the sofa with a man she adored. She shouldn't entertain such dangerous hope. She let herself picture it anyway—him warm and alive beside her—then slammed the door on the image before it hurt.

Waiting on another rideshare, Heather checked the street and debated bringing Denver. The driver might not appreciate a large dog in the forty-minute ride to Nashville. She had to go alone and take the risk to help Rave.

During the ride, she considered her need for a new car, but there was no point buying a new one until she moved. Maybe that was how Blake had found her. She'd finagled her driver's license under a different address, but she couldn't do anything about the state. Perhaps at her next location she'd forgo getting a license altogether—move to a place she could bike everywhere she needed to go.

She exited the car, tipped the driver on her phone app, and stood outside the chain-link fence that surrounded the industrial building—what was left of it. The metal frame structure still looked two-thirds intact, but most of the walls had been incinerated. Staring at the monstrosity of charred and twisted metal, she wondered how Rave had managed to survive a cave-in.

She imagined the appearance of the fully involved structure with flames rising high into the sky and black smoke billowing like an angry storm. Then Rave and his team arrived, black gear with reflective stripes glowing by the light. They hoisted yellow air tanks onto their backs and bravely entered the hazardous building.

Looking around, she still didn't see Rave. Nearby lots were empty and only the distant hum of machinery filled the air. There were no houses and few cars populating the area.

Her plan to try reconnecting him with Logan by returning to his place of injury could only be tested if Rave showed up. She tugged on the lock loosely connecting the two chain-link fences.

Locked.

There was a DO NOT ENTER sign, but Heather didn't want to walk among the wreckage anyway. She only wanted to get Rave here to see if the place of his injury could help him reconnect with his body.

But where was he?

BLAKE SAW HIS OPPORTUNITY. When Heather's ride drove off, she was alone. She stood outside a chain-link fence that encircled what was left of an incinerated building. Her red hair tossed lightly in the breeze—ridiculous and long.

The woman he'd married—the woman who belonged to him—had been a short-haired brunette. Conservative. Proper. Her current appearance would be one of the many things he'd fix when he got his hands on her.

Her back was to the road, so he eased his car closer on the curb. He glanced up and down the street. The closest pedestrians were a few blocks away on either side. If Heather got a scream out before he abducted her, they weren't near enough to help. They also weren't near enough to see his license plate.

His hands shook slightly when he put the car in park, and twisting out of the seat made his back pain flair.

Heather was still oblivious to his presence. He smirked.

This was going to be easy.

CHAPTER 7

Rave wasn't sure where he was when he sensed Heather in danger. Somewhere peaceful and cosmic. Like floating among the stars.

He wasn't sure where he was … warm, weightless, drifting toward something that felt like home—until a spike of terror, not his own, speared through the haze. Snapping to alertness, he pulled his apparition to Heather's location.

She stood by a fence, staring at a dilapidated building. He could see the back of her head. Behind her, a man approached in menacing strides.

"Heather, duck!" Rave screamed.

Blake swung a balled fist—intending to punch Heather in the back of her head. When she ducked, his fist landed in the fence. He snarled as he pulled back his bloodied knuckles.

Heather turned to see her attacker, and all color drained from her face. She backed away, but the chain-link fence kept her from retreating to safety. Her hands fumbled behind her as though willing the lock to free itself. As she pushed against the fence, the two halves bowed.

"Between the fences," Rave said. "Can you fit?"

She crouched beneath the padlocked chain and forced one shoulder between the two hinged halves. Then her head.

Blake's expression turned from anger to surprise as he seemed to realize Heather wasn't trapped. He lunged for her, his hand closing around her ankle as she forced her body sideways through the small gap, tearing her sweater and scraping the skin on her arms.

She screamed as she fell back and Blake yanked on her leg. Rearing her free leg back, she kicked the pole edge of the fence. It sprung forward, striking Blake in his face. He recoiled, grabbing at his bloodied nose.

Heather scrambled back on her hands and butt. Her chest rose and fell in gasping breaths as she stared at her attacker.

"On your feet, Phillips!" Rave commanded, by her side now.

Blake couldn't fit through the fence as she had, but it would only take him seconds to climb over it.

Heather pushed to her feet and dashed toward the wrecked structure.

Rave searched the premises as Blake struggled over the fence. What could he use to stop this madman? There were chunks of concrete debris and loose rebar—none of which Rave could wield.

Blake must have formulated a similar plan because he snatched up a three-foot-long piece of rebar after he cleared the fence.

Rave looked desperately up and down the street. A few gawkers were approaching—probably lured by the sound of Heather's scream. They were pulling their phones—some calling for help and others taking video. No one was moving to help the woman fleeing for her life. No one could get to her before Blake did.

Rave rushed to Heather's side, flying through the air. "Watch out!"

She spun but not fast enough. Blake had hurled the rebar at her from a distance like throwing a javelin. She took the blow to her shoulder and back. It knocked her to the ground, but she rolled and sprang to her feet.

Dang, she was tough.

She began to climb.

Rave looked up, following the path she would take. Eventually, she'd run out of places to go—that was if the building remnants didn't collapse first.

He floated up to her.

"Blake is afraid of heights," Heather told Rave as she panted from the effort of the climb. "He won't follow me."

Beneath her, Blake began the climb. The blood on his face enhanced the rage in his eyes.

Rave frowned. "His desire to harm you seems to have superseded his acrophobia."

When Heather reached the highest she could go—about five stories—she stopped to catch her breath. Her hands, covered in soot, dirt, and rust, clung to the beam.

Blake continued to climb. "I'm going to kill you!"

When Rave saw the fear and desperation on Heather's face, his anger soared. Heat flooded through him like a backdraft in a building fire. He clenched his fists, furious at his inability to help her.

When he spotted a raven perched on one of the beams, an idea gave him hope.

"Heather," Rave softened his voice and pointed, "walk to that vertical beam and hold on to it."

In order to walk where he directed her, she'd have to cross a beam only four inches wide.

"But there's nothing to hold on to while I cross," she protested.

"I know. One foot in front of the other. Try to imagine you're just walking on the curb of a sidewalk. It's about that wide. You can do it."

"Okay. Okay."

With legs trembling, Heather took slow, shuffling steps. Rave was certain he felt his heart pounding all the way across town in his hospital room. At last she reached the other side and clung to the pole.

"Ha!" Blake cackled. "You've got nowhere to go."

"Neither do you," she snapped.

"You shouldn't have left, Heather. You don't break a marriage vow to your husband."

"I'm pretty sure cherishing someone doesn't involve punching them!" she hollered back.

Blake glanced down at the long drop below before easing himself onto the horizontal beam, holding his arms outstretched for balance. "It does when you don't obey."

"You lost, Blake. I'll never obey, and we'll never be together."

"Then I guess we're a cliché: 'til death do us part." He was halfway across the beam.

Rave called on everything he had to command the ravens who'd been quietly gathering around the building ruins. They swept into the air before diving toward Heather. As they encircled her, they formed an impenetrable barrier between her and Blake.

The rational choice—the sane choice—would have been for Blake to back off and leave Heather alone. Instead, he advanced, swatting at flapping black wings as they whirled protectively around Heather.

Blake's balance faltered before his footing slipped. Screaming, he lost his balance and fell five stories into the concrete chards and rubble below.

Rave closed his eyes. Blake's obsession had led to his own demise. "Nevermore."

Rave entered the flurry of the ravens, and his apparition was swept up in their small tornado. His world turned black before bright light struck his eyelids. He blinked his eyes open to the sensation of a painful, stiff body on a firm bed.

HEATHER KEPT her eyes shut tight as her arms and legs shook. Wings flapped as the birds circling her—protecting her. Although she'd heard Blake's screams fade and then vanish, she didn't dare move. Her fear hadn't yet subsided.

"Heather?" Rave's voice was a whisper in her ear, audible over the sound of flapping wings. "You're safe now."

And the air went still and silent.

Heather opened her eyes. The ravens flew away, black angels speckling a light blue sky. Rave was gone. She blinked away tears.

"Hey, lady! Just hang on. The police and fire department are coming."

She looked off to one side where a group of bystanders stood just beyond the chain-link fence. All she could do was hold on. She didn't trust her legs to carry her back across the beam or down from this height.

Moments later, sirens filled the air.

Heather eased herself lower so that she was seated on the horizontal beam while still clinging to the vertical one.

"Are you hurt?" a policeman called to her.

"No." Even as she answered, she remembered the beam hitting her shoulder. Nothing ice and ibuprofen couldn't fix.

"Hang on. We're going to get the fire truck as close as we safely can and get the ladder up to you."

"Okay." That sounded good. She'd sit here and rest and let the cavalry come to her.

The rescue team took time to cut the locked chain on the fence, direct the fire truck around debris, and then raise the ladder. While that was being arranged, the police covered Blake's body and raised a barrier of police tape around the scene.

She recognized the firefighter who climbed to meet her. "Just another cat out of a tree?"

Johanna gave Heather a puzzled look. Too bad. Rave would've laughed at Heather's joke.

"You're the woman who came by the station," Johanna said.

Heather looked at the long, extending ladder and fire truck below. "I guess I get to see the fire truck up close now," she joked, even though her voice still quaked.

Johanna gave her a warm smile. "You're going to be just fine. Let's get you out of this tree."

CHAPTER 8

*H*eather had her freedom back.

After her feet were on solid ground, she'd endured police interviews. She'd gone back to the beginning to explain everything. Her voice sounded distant even to herself as she gave the police the facts. Trauma training kicked in; she compartmentalized, packaged, delivered.

Fortunately, the events on the building didn't require much of an explanation; bystanders had videoed the entire event—her running, then climbing for her life, and finally the miraculously protective ravens intervening. With everything in evidence, Blake's death was ruled an accident.

Rave had saved her life.

When the interview was over, she called Evelyn and updated her on what had happened. Loyal friend that she was, she offered to come over and spend the night. Heather declined; she needed rest—and that ice and ibuprofen. Maybe an epsom salt bath. Solitude was going to do more for her recovery overnight than keeping company.

A single black feather clung to her sweater when she undressed. She placed it on her nightstand, unsure why it steadied her.

That night, she fell asleep as soon as her head hit the pillow, an icepack still against her shoulder. She'd had the briefest time to wonder where Rave had disappeared to. She hoped his disappearance was a reconnection to his body and not the alternative.

HEATHER WOKE the following day and busied herself with work and paying bills. She took Denver for a long walk and contemplated buying a new bike. There were so many things she could do with her new freedom.

By the afternoon, Rave hadn't returned. She checked news websites, but no one had reported the death of a firefighter. She hoped his absence meant his spirit was back where it belonged.

She could go back to the hospital, but she didn't think the recreation therapy card would play again. And if Rave was alive but didn't remember her . . . well, that would be awkward. Worse, she wasn't sure her heart could bear knowing it.

Instead, Heather focused on making mental notes of all the public things she could do in the absence of a stalker. She would keep busy. She considered looking into local school counselor jobs. But first, she and Denver would visit the retirement home tomorrow and finally pot those plants with the residents.

Maybe she could give him time to heal and find a way to serendipitously meet him and recreate those sparks. She would have to get past her fear of rejection first.

THE DAY AFTER RAVE WOKE, he was well enough to move out of the ICU. The day after that, he was proving to the physical therapist that a head injury and a week of slumber hadn't slowed him down.Although sometimes, in the quiet of his room at night, he swore he heard the soft beat of wings.

During the day, he was on a mission.

"Look at you!" his mother cried with delight as she entered his room. She looked well rested and infinitely less distressed than she had when he'd been unconscious. She set a box of chocolates down on his bedside table.

"Hi, Mom. The doctors say I might be discharged tomorrow."

"Oh, fantastic!" She hugged him.

He relaxed into the bliss of human contact. She'd hugged him several times every day since he'd awakened, and he enjoyed every one of them.

"Did you find a number?" he asked hopefully. He flexed his fingers. Last week, he couldn't lift a cup of water. Now he could button his jeans.

"Your friend must be unlisted, dear. I couldn't find a number for Heather Phillips."

Of course, with everything Heather had been through, she'd be unlisted. She had worked hard to stay under the radar. Although, now she wouldn't have to.

"And I knocked at the address you gave me, but no one answered. She must have been out. Do you want me to try again?"

"No. Thanks, Mom. I'll reconnect with her later."

Why hadn't she come to the hospital to check on him? He'd known from the local news that she had made it safely down from the ledge. Did she not want to see him?

Rave—and he'd come to think of himself as Rave even after he'd woken—could speculate that maybe a woman didn't want damaged goods. He was a man who'd suffered a severe head injury, and she might assume he'd have a lasting debility. But Heather wouldn't be deterred by such things.

Still, the absence of a visit puzzled him. He needed to get discharged and see her.

HEATHER WALKED the Clarksville Greenway with Denver. This was the same trail she'd walked him on dozens of times, but it felt different. The springtime leaves seemed brighter, the air crisper. She didn't have to give herself her usual periodic assurances that Denver would alert her to danger and keep her safe. She could walk and relax.

Relax.

Even Denver sensed her change in demeanor and wasn't as hyper-alert as usual.

Denver's ears twitched. He spun, sniffing and wagging his tail.

"Denver? What—?" Heather turned to see Rave walking down the trail towards her.

He wore a gray cotton shirt, black leather jacket, and blue jeans. He walked toward her through a tunnel of spring green, sunlight catching in his brown hair, every inch of him unmistakably, beautifully alive.

"Rave!" She started toward him, hesitated, and then decided she would toss caution to the wind. He'd gone through the trouble of finding her after waking from his coma; he deserved unrestrained emotional excitement from her.

She dropped Denver's leash and ran to Rave. He opened his arms, and they embraced.

"You're alive and in one piece," she marveled.

Solid muscle met her arms—warm, real, breathtaking. She hadn't realized how starved she'd been for this: connection that didn't slip through her fingers.

"I can say the same about you."

She reveled in the feel and smell of him. Oak and wood musk.

"You saved my life." She buried her face in his neck.

"I can say the same about you," he repeated.

She pulled away and looked quizzically up at him.

Rave caught her chin in one hand and rested his other hand on her hip. "You helped me find my way back to my body. If you hadn't dug deeper to discover my identity, I might have been a spirit indefinitely."

She grinned. "Okay. We're a couple of heroes."

Denver nudged a cold, wet nose into the conversation. Rave dropped a hand down and pet her dog.

"Three heroes," she amended. Denver had saved her years ago through canine love and companionship.

Heather stretched to her tiptoes as Rave bent to meet her halfway for a sweet, succulent kiss. She felt both the solidarity of it and the way his touch made her feel light as a raven's feather. When they broke away from the kiss, Heather was both breathless and hungry for more.

"Do you remember... all of it?" she whispered.

His thumb brushed her cheek. "Every moment, Heather."

"You know what I'd like to do?" Rave wriggled his body closer.

"What's that?" she smiled, enjoying how well they fit together.

"I'd like to pop a bag of popcorn, sit on your couch together, and watch another cheesy romantic comedy with you. I'd even watch *While You Were Sleeping* once more."

"Hmm. I think we'll watch *Just Like Heaven.*"

Rave bent down and kissed her again.

She kissed him again, feeling—for the first time in years—not hunted, not haunted, but lifted. Light as a feather. Free.

CHLOE'S CUPID

Third time's a charm. Or is it? Can Chloe and Zack finally tie the knot with the help of ancient ghost of love?

CHAPTER 1

Chimes filled the air with gentle music as Chloe walked into the dimly lit Busy Broomstick. The smell of jasmine incense filled the air. Twinkling golden lights lined the periwinkle walls and dark mahogany shelves. Rows of labeled bottles were stacked together in bright pinks, purples, and blues.

As Chloe's eyes adjusted to the lighting, she read the labels of aromatherapy scented jars on one row—lavender, vanilla, peppermint, passion fruit, and more. The next row had similar fragranced lotions, and the next had matching scented candles.

The opposite wall held spell books with gold lettering and faded spines. A potpourri of ingredients surrounded them—dried fruits, nuts, mushrooms, herbs, and flower petals.

She paused. This was ludicrous. She should turn back around and leave this store. But she was desperate.

"Can I help you?" a woman asked.

Chloe faced the woman behind the counter. "You're Rose? Emma's aunt?"

"Ah, you must be Chloe." Rose wore a long, purple cotton dress, embellished with lace and sequins. The lightweight material was ideal for a California summer. Her dark braided hair contained purple feathers, and her eyes were rimmed in midnight black eyeliner with dark, smoky eyeshadow.

Chloe straightened. "Yes."

Rose walked to the front of the store, locked the door, and flipped the OPEN sign to CLOSED.

"Let's sit down and discuss your dilemma." Rose gestured to a pair of high-back, velvet cushioned chairs.

Chloe sat, tucked a strand of brown hair behind her ear, and clasped her hands in her lap. She fidgeted with the seam of her baby-blue yoga pants.

Rose glided to a table and dispensed hot tea from a large insulated thermos into two small dainty cups with pink flowers and gold fleur de lis. She handed the cup to Chloe.

"Thank you." Chloe sipped. Chamomile. She probably shouldn't drink something that might make her sleepy first thing in the morning, but her nerves appreciated the soothing, warm liquid.

Rose gently sat and crossed one leg over the other. Her relaxed demeanor helped calm Chloe's angst.

"Now, how can I help?"

Since Emma had referred Chloe to the Busy Broomstick, Chloe would see this through. She could back out at any time, she reminded herself.

"My wedding is a week away," Chloe began.

"Congratulations."

"My *third* wedding."

"Oh, my."

"To the same man." Chloe sighed, turning the cup on its saucer in her hand. "See, we've been engaged for two years. We planned to have our first wedding in Hawaii—destination and island paradise all in one—but the Kīlauea volcano erupted. For our second attempt at marriage, we opted for a ski lodge—no danger of volcanoes, or tropical storms. But, unfortunately, I got appendicitis. *Whoosh*—off to the hospital for emergency laparoscopic surgery. At least all the guests had travel insurance for that one."

"You're worried about the third attempt," Rose said, nodding sagely.

"Yes. I mean, I know third time's a charm, but I'm at my wits' end here. We're staying local for the wedding, but Zack travels for work. He flies back tonight, so what could possibly go wrong? Right?" Chloe gave a nervous chuckle before taking another sip of tea. More of an undignified gulp.

"What did you have in mind that I might be able to do?" Rose smiled warmly.

"I don't know." Chloe didn't even know what Rose *could* do. Her friend, Emma, had said only that her aunt dealt with the supernatural and maybe could help. Chloe wouldn't be here if she wasn't so desperate to make the wedding happen.

She continued, "I have no idea what you're capable of doing or how it could possibly help. I'm willing to be put in a hypnotic trance if it would help me to stop worrying. Maybe you have tarot cards that would predict our happily ever after—not that I'm naive enough to equate marriage with happily ever after. I know relationships take nurturing and work. But getting married has been a wicked hurdle we haven't cleared." Chloe pressed her lips together, determined to stop rambling.

Rose gave her another warm and patient smile. "I don't induce trances or predict fortunes, but I think I can help. I'll make you a tincture of belladonna, rose petals, lavender, rosemary, cinnamon, and cloves. After you drink the potion, you'll be able to see a ghost for seven days."

"A ghost?" Chloe asked, sounding skeptical and trying not to sound rude.

"Not just any ghost. Cupid."

She choked on her next sip of tea. "As in arrow through the heart, Cupid?"

"Yes."

"But you said *ghost*, not mythical creature." She set down her cup of tea on a small table beside the chair.

"Yes. Cupid is quite an ancient ghost. His life was filled with love and loss. Now, as a ghost, he helps others find love—perpetuating the stories about him. But there are several points you need to be aware of if you choose to go through with this. First, you will be the only one who can see and hear him. True mediums who can interact with ghosts regularly are rare. My tincture creates a link that normally doesn't exist. Second, Cupid will only help those with pure intentions—you must love Zack, and he must love you. Cupid doesn't trick anyone. No shenanigans."

"No shenanigans." Chloe nodded. She had zero doubts about the fortitude of her and Zack's love. She only wanted to ensure they actually tied the knot this time.

"Third, you need to have the mental fortitude to handle a ghost in your life for seven days. No mental breakdowns. If you can't handle Cupid's presence, he'll disappear, and so will any help he can provide."

"Help?"

"Yes. And this is important to remember. Cupid can't affect his surroundings—not beyond a few supernatural gusts of wind or flickering lights. But he can see glimpses of the future and guide you to help make your happy day come true."

Chloe felt her skepticism rising along with her heart rate. At least skepticism about ghosts wasn't one of Rose's rules. Chloe locked a congenial smile in place as she contemplated the ludicrousness of taking a potion to see a ghost who'd supposedly help ensure her wedding would take place.

For real this time.

Rose stood, retrieved something from beneath her cash register counter, and returned to Chloe. The strange, elegant woman set a box —ornately decorated in tiny gems and shaped like a miniature treasure chest—on the table beside Chloe's tea cup. After withdrawing a key from around her neck, she unlocked the chest and retrieved a small pink vial from the velvet cushion within the box.

Well, Rose is nothing if not dramatic, Chloe thought.

She accepted the vial. "How much does it cost?"

Rose gave her a pitying look. "For a friend of the family with your bad luck … nothing. I only ask that if you decide not to use it before your wedding day, please return it to me."

Chloe, now standing, stared down at the vial in her hand. "K-k. Thank you for this, and for taking the time to meet with me."

"K-k?" Rose asked.

"It's my slang for okay."

"Ah." Rose led her to the door. "If you have any questions, you know where to reach me. Oh, and don't mind his accent. It's a remnant of the Victorian era, though not as flowery."

Because Chloe had no idea how to respond, she gave a weak smile as she left.

If this potion worked, Chloe could tell Zack and they'd both have a good laugh. If it didn't work, she might never admit she'd visited a mystic for help and walked away with a mysterious potion in her hand.

She wasn't sure what terrified her more—that the potion might work… or that it might not.

AFTER CHLOE LEFT, Cupid sat down in the chair she'd occupied. He leaned back, crossed his legs, and looked at her partially consumed cup of tea. Rose sipped her own tea and acknowledged his presence with a slight nod of her head.

"Do you think she'll drink it?" Cupid asked.

The young woman who'd scurried out of Rose's shop clearly didn't believe in ghosts.

Rose's eyes twinkled through her heavy make-up. "I'm not sure. She definitely doesn't believe in the paranormal, but then they never do. However, she might be desperate enough to try anything."

Cupid strummed his fingers on his blue jeans. He hadn't had an assignment in months, and hoped to have one now, but—"You've given me an easy one. A soft pitch, as Americans call it. I call it a doddle.. She's already in love and already has a wedding date. All I have to do is a little handholding for a few days."

"Is that what you see in her future?"

"No. I haven't looked. There's no point in bothering to look unless she actually asks for my help by drinking the potion." And sometimes looking meant seeing only heartbreak.

"Must be hard to know what the future holds, because her repeated efforts to be married have been met with many surprises."

"If she faces some other disasters in proximity to her wedding, maybe she needn't bother to try." He tossed the words out lightly just to antagonize Rose.

"That's an unbecoming thing for the ghost of love to say," Rose scolded lightly. Maybe she's in danger of giving up," Rose countered calmly, "and she needs a little nudge from a ghost."

"We'll see what she decides—play it safe or into the rabbit hole."

A faint breeze curled the pages of a spellbook.

Somewhere across the city, Cupid sensed a choice was already unfolding.

"So, that's where we're at. Five little days away from finally getting married," Zack said.

The gray haired woman in the seat beside him smiled sweetly. "Quite a story. I do hope it works out for the two of you this time."

When his plane touched down at the San Francisco airport, he felt excitement rise in him. As it taxied, he sent a quick text to Chloe.

Landed. Be home at 8.

"Nothing can go wrong," he told the woman. "We're keeping the wedding local. My fiancée is at home. The plane just landed. The June weather is perfect right now. Everything is set."

Chloe texted back immediately. *K-k.*

He knew she was worried about his travel plans—flying to Dallas and back home so close to the wedding. And rightly so. Their third attempt at a wedding was approaching. They'd made a pact to have no travel plans or strenuous activity the week before the wedding. For him, that meant being cognizant of his work schedule. For her, that meant no vigorous sparring with clients.

Zack enjoyed his job in cybersecurity, but it often meant traveling to the places where his company had been hired. Not everything could be set up remotely when it came to securing data.

Chloe ran her own gym where she taught spin-bike, yoga, and Taekwondo classes. When Zack had met her, she was teaching a self-defense class.

Admittedly, at that first encounter, he hadn't known she was a smart, funny entrepreneur. He'd first noticed her compact body, brunette curls, and dimpled cheeks. She had an adorable smile that crinkled her nose and squinted her eyes.

When he reached Ground Transportation, he withdrew his phone to connect with a ride share. He'd have an hour in traffic so he hoped he'd be able to get more work done on the trip home.

A prickling sensation crept up his neck—the feeling of being watched.

Nerves, he told himself. Wedding-week nerves.

"Zachary Sumner, come with us. Quietly." Two men flanked him on either side.

"What?"

"We have Chloe, and you need to come with us if you want her to stay safe."

"Chloe?" Zack's heartbeat doubled as he tried to process the threat around him.

Even as they spoke, the large men in black fatigues were already leading him toward a parked green Jeep. Were they police? Military?

"Who are you? I need to see some identification," Zack demanded, blood pumping with fear.

"Get in and don't make a scene." One of the men snatched the phone out of his hand.

They had no identifying logos on their clothing. Their darting eyes looked menacing, and they stunk of sweat and cigarettes.

"Chloe?" Zack's voice constricted even as his mind raced with the hostage training he'd had. The training videos he'd watched did nothing to mimic real danger when everything was moving too fast.

But he couldn't let himself be taken. Catastrophic data breaches could be achieved if someone forced him to share the secrets he knew.

When they reached the vehicle, Zack whirled. "Now wait a damn minute. I want to see Chloe right *now*." He couldn't fight two kidnappers, but he could make a public scene.

Large arms from inside the vehicle wrapped around him, pulling him into the fold. A noxious smelling rag—presumably chloroform—closed over his mouth, followed by darkness.

Chloe.

He'd never forgive himself if anything happened to her.

CHAPTER 2

fter a long day of exercise classes, Chloe arrived home and showered. She left the vial in the kitchen so she could avoid looking at it for a while. She dressed in comfy cotton pants with a matching gray shirt and fluffy pink slippers. An advantage to being a fitness instructor was always wearing comfortable clothes.

The exception was when she needed to pitch a gym membership package to a company for their employees. Getting companies to agree to group rates was part of her specialty. She had the 'pep'—as Zack called it. And once people were inside her facility, she could motivate them. The challenge was keeping them coming back. People led busy lives and struggled to carve out time for wellness—even when they had a group discount and twenty-four hour access.

Blending a kale smoothie, she added protein supplements. She practiced everything she advocated with her clients—low carb, no fake sugar, lots of water and tea.

Chloe's gaze fell on the small pink vial on the kitchen counter as she drank her health shake. She checked her watch. Zack would be home in thirty minutes. Everything would be fine. She didn't need hocus-pocus potions.

Her phone rang. She jumped, lunged for it, thinking it was Zack, and knocked over her drink. Thick green liquid spread across the counter.

"Dang it!" She answered the phone and put it on speaker as she fetched a towel.

"Hi, Chloe. How are you?"

"Hi, Emma." Not Zack. Chloe tried to conceal the disappointment from her friend.

"My aunt said you visited her this morning."

"No client-mystic privilege, I see," Chloe teased.

"She didn't tell me what she offered you. Did you do whatever it was she advised?"

Chloe mopped up her dinner, picking up the pink vial and cleaning smoothie off of it. "No."

"What? Why not?"

"It's a *potion*. I don't know if it's safe or not. It has belladonna in it."

"So, you might get sleepy. I'm telling you, Rose has helped a lot of people—and not just lovers."

"I don't know. I feel silly about this whole thing."

"Do it. It can't hurt. Oh, my mom's calling in. Gotta go. And please don't leave your maid of honor hanging a third time. Drink for good luck." Emma clicked off.

Guilt rippled through Chloe. Emma had flown to Hawaii and then to the ski lodge without a word of complaint. What was one little drink?

Chloe finished cleaning and drank what was left of her shake, all the while staring at that little pink bottle. The clock on the mantle in the nearby living room ticked by as the weight of silence hung in the room between her and the potion. She drummed her fingers on the counter.

When she checked the time again, she frowned. Zack was fifteen minutes late. She looked at her phone—no calls or text messages. He could be in traffic. Were it not for their track record close to their wedding day, she wouldn't worry at all.

She phoned Zack, but the call went instantly to voicemail. The pink bottle stared at her. What if something stupid and random ruined them again and she'd done nothing to at least attempt to ward it off? At last, she came to a decision. Worst case scenario was nothing supernatural happened and the belladonna soothed her worry.

She plucked it off the counter, pulled off the cork top, and downed the potion. After downing the surprisingly flavorful drink, she stopped to consider that Rose hadn't given specific instructions—on an empty stomach or with food? In the morning or at night? Maybe it didn't matter.

She waited a moment with bated breath. When nothing happened, she doubled over laughing at herself. "I'm so ridiculous." She wiped at her eyes.

Blinking, her laugh snapped off mid-breath as a translucent figure shimmered into existence before her.

"Hello, Chloe."

Chloe stumbled back, regrouped, and did a roundhouse kick straight through the figure.

"Good reflexes," he said, voice crisp, clipped, and unmistakably London.

"You're … you're a ghost!"

"I am the ghost, Cupid, as requested."

The intruder was a young man—perhaps twenty—dressed in jeans and a t-shirt with a cartoon of a plump red heart with an arrow through it. His skin appeared to be a smooth porcelain without a wrinkle or blemish. No wonder he was sometimes depicted as a baby.

"This isn't possible." Her heart raced as she looked around the kitchen for some type of planted projector.

"Your eyes don't deceive you."

Chloe circled Cupid in a careful, defensive pose. Despite teaching Taekwondo, she'd only ever been in one fight where she'd had to defend Emma from a groping drunk at a dance hall.

"You're trespassing," she said.

"You invited me when you drank the potion."

Chloe swiped a hand into the translucent figure, watching it go straight through Cupid.

The ghost yawned. "I can do this all night. In fact, I can do this for eternity. You, however, are on a deadline, if I'm not mistaken."

Chloe stopped circling Cupid as she glanced at the clock. Zack was over an hour late now.

"I want to make sure my wedding happens without any more disasters."

"Hitched without a hitch. Yes, I heard your entire conversation with Rose—she's such a gem. Don't gape at me—just because you couldn't see me up until five minutes ago doesn't mean I don't exist—in the supernatural sense of the word, of course."

Chloe checked her phone again—no call or text from Zack. "So, can you help me?" Her voice had an edge of pleading desperation.

"Because I can see parts of the present others cannot and some of the future, I have been able to unite many couples over the centuries. Usually, it's the little things—flowers, a perfectly timed gift, making impeccable travel plans." His eyes sparkled.

"What do you get out of it?"

"Comfort. Satisfaction and pleasure in knowing I've united lovers. And it passes the time."

"And you're with me for the next seven days?" she asked.

"Seven days or until I'm no longer needed or wanted. I never overstay my welcome."

Chloe paced her kitchen, trying to process how she was having a conversation with a ghost—or perhaps Rose's concoction was a powerful hallucinogenic.

"K-k. I need to test this."

Cupid rolled his eyes.

"Tell me exactly what Emma is doing right now," Chloe said.

Closing his eyes, Cupid pinched the bridge of his nose. "Your friend, Emma, is on her way to the movie theatre with Nick to see the latest superhero blockbuster."

"What!" Chloe snatched up her phone and speed dialed her friend.

Emma answered.

"Are you with Nick?" Chloe demanded.

"How did you know?"

"I thought we decided he was a jerk and you weren't going to give him a second chance."

"I changed my mind," Emma said.

"By taking him to the movie you and I were going to see together?"

"I'm sorry. You've been tied up with wedding plans. Wait. How did you—?"

"Never mind. Enjoy the show, but don't trust Nick."

"Wait, Chloe—"

But Chloe was already disconnecting the call. She set down the phone as she leaned on the counter and closed her eyes to stop the room from spinning. K-k. She could do this. There was no harm in maximizing her chances of wedding success through utilization of this paranormal encounter to its fullest extent.

Her eyes fluttered open, and she scrutinized Cupid's appearance. "No bow and arrow? No wings?"

He crossed his arms. "Nor am I a god as Roman and Greek mythology would have you believe. I used to carry arrows and a torch —symbols of how love wounds and inflames the heart, but I modern-ized." He gestured at the cartoon heart with an arrow through it on his t-shirt. "I discovered that people of the twenty-first century don't trust young men in togas."

"K-k, Cupid, can you tell me where Zack is?"

"Are you saying you're a believer?"

"I'm saying, I'm less of a skeptic."

"I like honesty. Give me a moment." He closed his eyes again. His face went lax before his brows knitted in together and his lips dropped into a frown. "No, no. This makes no sense."

"What is it? What's wrong?"

"Wait. Give me some context clues right now. Where should your fiancé be?"

"Driving home from the airport. He usually takes a ride share."

Cupid's brow furrowed deeper. "So there's no reason he'd be tied to a chair in a dark room?"

Chloe gasped as she went rigid with fear. "No! What are you seeing?"

"You'll have to excuse me for moment. I need to explore Zack's surroundings to learn more." With that, Cupid vanished, leaving her alone and worried.

The kitchen felt suddenly colder.

Zack was out there somewhere, tied to a chair in the dark.

ZACK WOKE to the obnoxious odor of what he assumed was smelling salts. He recoiled only to feel his arms bound to a chair. He rolled his neck to loosen an ache as his eyes adjusted to a small, dark room with a single ceiling light and heavy curtains over the windows.

He'd been dreaming of Chloe—a vivid re-enactment of when they'd first met.

"Wake up!" a gruff voice commanded.

The awful sulfur smell filled his nostrils again. His eyes focused on a man in a ski mask. Another masked man was a few steps behind him. Were the masks necessary? He'd already seen their faces at the airport.

"Chloe? Where's my fiancée?"

"Alive. For now."

What was the accent? German perhaps. Was he doing business with any German companies? Not recently.

"We need your cooperation, Mr. Sumner, to maintain her safety."

"Cooperation with what?"

"Backdoor access to True Health's medical records. You were the cybersecurity specialist on their team. You helped build their system."

"Why do you want access? Those are people's health records." But Zack knew the answer.

He'd heard the rumors in the tech world that a health conglomerate's database had been hacked. Those infiltrating had held the access to information for ransom—threatening to leak personal health information electronically. *Globally.* Rather than face public disgrace, loss of clients and investors, and ultimate bankruptcy, the company had paid the ransom money to have the data breach sealed by the very perpetrators who'd opened it.

This felt exactly like that—and he was the tool they wanted.

"Your cooperation, Mr. Sumner."

"Let me speak to Chloe. I want to know she's safe." He'd promised no travel this close to the wedding. One last quick trip, he'd argued. One last quick payday. God, what a mistake.

The man reared back and punched Zack in the jaw. Pain exploded through his face as the taste of blood filled his mouth. Lights and stars swam before his eyes.

"Hey!" the other man snapped. "Not the face. And not the hands. We can't risk damaging his sight or his ability to type." This other masked man was dressed in slacks, a button-down shirt, and loafers. He smelled of expensive cologne.

Zack couldn't place the men. He certainly had never met them before.

"Then, why didn't we grab the woman from the start? This guy isn't going to cooperate without coercion," the brute complained.

Through the pain, Zack concentrated on their words. So they didn't have Chloe. Had they lied to get Zack to comply?

"We planned to pick up Mr. Sumner's fiancée at their home while we picked up Mr. Sumner from the airport. Unfortunately, those men were stuck in traffic. But they should have her any moment. She'll be here soon. In the meantime, I'll try to appeal to Mr. Sumner's financial tastes."

Loafers turned toward Zack. :If you can't be bribed, then we'll see how much you value your betrothed."

Zack's stomach sickened. He would cave if they produced Chloe, he knew he would. Whatever they wanted—code written for access to the health records, build a platform to export data, build a website to post the information for their ransom scheme. Any of it in exchange for Chloe unharmed.

But they didn't have her in custody yet, and that gave him a glimmer of hope. She was a petite five-five—all slender muscles from endless days of teaching exercise classes. She also knew Taekwondo.

These men had her beat by size but maybe not skill. And certainly not spunk.

Except, she'd be home alone right now. And the kidnappers probably had weapons.

There was another enormous problem—Chloe loved Zack. If the two men picking her up told her to come or harm would befall her fiancé, she'd accompany them without hesitation.

Zack figured he had maybe a few hours to devise a way for both of them to escape, because if they didn't, these men were unlikely to leave them alive after they got what they wanted.

CHAPTER 3

Chloe paced her kitchen, waiting for Cupid to return. Waiting for a ghost. She shook her head in disbelief.

Seven days.

She only needed him for five. Just to make sure the wedding happened. She wasn't crazy. She was desperate. Desperate times, desperate measures and all that.

Cupid reappeared, looking distraught.

"What's wrong?" Her heart thudded with worry.

"Zack has been kidnapped."

"Kidnapped? I don't understand. Why would he be kidnapped?"

Cupid pinched the bridge of his nose. "I saw... a group of international thieves. They want his cybersecurity skills to break into True Health's data. Ransom, blackmail—the whole rotten lot."

Chloe clasped her hands to her mouth. Zack had said something like this was a possibility in his line of work. There were protocols. She was supposed to go to the police. Her knees went weak. For one dizzy heartbeat she couldn't move at all. Then training and terror kicked in together.

She raced upstairs and began packing. According to the company's safety protocol, she had to leave the house and not return until it was safe. She needed at least an overnight bag.

Cupid watched her frantic motions. "I was going to tell you to pack and leave, but it seems you're already aware."

"Aware? Aware of what?" Her voice was breathless from fear and exertion.

"The thieves intend to kidnap you next to use you as leverage to make Zack comply."

Chloe stuffed jeans and shirts into a bag. "Is he hurt? No, don't tell me. He's alive. That's all that matters." She dumped toiletries in the bag. Still in the bathroom, she put on her work clothes she'd set aside for the following day. Pausing and without making eye contact, she asked again, "Is he hurt?"

"Just scratches and bruises."

Chloe sniffed as she zipped her bag shut. She lugged it to the kitchen where she filled a plastic bottle with tap water. "I have to go to the police."

Cupid scratched his head, not ruffling his perfectly waved crop of hair. "This is all a bit beyond my purview."

"I can't go to the police." Eyes wide with realization, she turned to look at the ghost—through the ghost. "I have no proof he's been kidnapped. I can't tell them a ghost told me, and even though the twenty-four hours missing rule is actually a myth, Zack is only late by over an hour. No one will believe me. And I can't risk his safety by waiting."

Cupid shuffled his feet. "I'm not really qualified to help with this sort of thing."

Chloe snatched her keys, phone, and charger before heading to her car, her mind racing.

Zack has been kidnapped.

She loaded her bag in the backseat of her Prius and turned to Cupid. "Are you coming?"

"I think Rose should find you the ghost of a former police detective or FBI agent or something. I'm the ghost of love and desire—not rudding kidnapping."

"Oh, no you don't. You're not backing out on me. I've got you for seven days. I don't have time to find another ghost. You agreed to help make my wedding happen, and this is part of it. Hop in … or whatever it is ghosts do."

Chloe climbed in the driver's seat, closed the door, and buckled in.

"Ghost of love, not Liam Neeson," he grumbled, but he still flickered into the passenger seat. "Are you always this commanding, then?"

"Instructing," she corrected him. "I'm a teacher, so I'm good at instructing."

She pulled out of the driveway. "Where to?" She was a teacher, but also a doer. She didn't run her own gym by shrinking from her fears. Face them. That's what she taught in her classes … although she would never advise her students to take on a group of kidnappers.

"What do you mean?"

"Where is Zack being held?"

"You're going after him?" Cupid gaped at her.

"Yes."

"In your pink yoga clothes?"

"Yes."

He crossed his arms. "You and what army?"

"Why do you say that? How many are there?"

"Four. And one of you."

"But I have you."

"Take a left here." He waved his hand. "But what if they have guns?"

"We'll need a way to sneak in and sneak out," she replied. She wasn't being reckless, she assured herself. If the situation looked too dangerous, she could at least get proof of his kidnapping and share that with police.

"A spy ghost. What if we find you a former spy?"

"Buck up, Cupid. We're on the clock. Give me the layout of where Zack's being kept."

∾

CHLOE TAPPED her steering wheel while they sat in traffic on Highway 92—on the bridge outside Palo Alto. Nervous energy and worry over Zack rippled through her.

"How'd you become a ghost?" she asked.

"Betrayed love. A broken heart. Proper tragic, really," he said. "There's a medical term for it in modern times—Takotsubo cardiomyopathy—when an emotionally traumatic event causes heart failure. It's not usually fatal these days. It's also uncommon in men, but then I am a hopeless romantic."

"I'm sorry about your heart."

"Ah. That was so long ago. And look at me now—I'm famous, and I help people find love. No piercing arrows involved in the literal sense."

"And you seek nothing in return?" she asked. The conversation helped distract her from her worry over Zack.

Cupid shrugged. "I'm a ghost. I can't do anything with material items. I suppose if I were mean spirited, I could make people leap through hurdles before I helped them, but that's not what love is about."

"How can you help find love? Is it so predictable?"

"I can glimpse the future—see if two people fall in love. But—disclaimer alert—it's up to them to maintain it."

"Have you ever had a request like mine?"

"A kidnapping? No."

Chloe chuckled. "No, I meant two people who love each other but can't seem to tie the knot."

"Twice. One was a man who needed help with the right proposal because his attempts were thwarted by fate. Another was a runaway bride. And there was no chasing her. I can't always give a happily-ever-after..." His voice trailed at the last sentence.

Chloe suspected Cupid was partially referring to a less-than-optimistic outlook on her situation with Zack. She'd fix that. She'd show him how they were meant to be together and the kidnappers were not insurmountable obstacles.

"Zack and I met at a self-defense course."

"Oh? What motivated you to take such a class?"

"I was the instructor."

"Fascinating."

"Yeah, so, we're in my gym, and everyone is dressed in workout clothes, ready to get physical. I try to weave the lecture portions in with hands-on demonstrations. After all, everyone's tired after a long day of work. There are a dozen things they'd rather be doing, so part of my job is to keep the class interesting. Anyway, I notice a man. The *only* man."

"Zack?"

"This guy has a pretty good build, right? Defined arms, flat abs. Tall, dark, handsome. All that and a bowl of whipped cream."

"A bowl of—"

"So, I'm thinking to myself—he's built like that and not wearing a ring while taking a class statistically known to be predominantly filled with women. There's only one reason he's here."

"There is?"

"To pick up women," Chloe explained.

"Ah."

She could envision the event like it happened yesterday as she told Cupid the story. Each person stood on their respective mats—attentive and limber.

She'd already covered a few basic lessons—know your surroundings, don't be distracted, and protect your space.

"Gentleman in the back?" she asked.

He waved.

"Can you volunteer for us?"

He joined Chloe at the front of the room with a surprisingly tentative smile when she'd expected him to eat up the attention.

"Your name?"

"Zack Sumner."

Chloe addressed the group. "Zack is going to be our stand-in demo." She leaned toward Zack. "You signed the waiver at the beginning, right?"

The class laughed.

"I'm just kidding," she chuckled. She leaned closer, dropping her voice to a whisper. "Only half-kidding."

His cheeks flushed.

"Your key attack areas," she announced, circling Zack, "are the eyes, throat, and groin."

Zack's Adam's apple bobbed in an adorable swallow.

"Let's demonstrate that." She took a stance with her back to Zack and one side facing the students. "You grab me from behind, and let's say in this situation we're in a parking garage, so you don't want me to scream. Your hand goes over my mouth."

He wrapped one hand around her in a mock attack where he was two inches from actually touching her. His hand hovered in front of her mouth.

Good-looking, shy, and a gentleman. Maybe she shouldn't have picked on him.

"I can't give you one formula to say—if you're grabbed from behind, do this. The reason is that where you're grabbed and where your attacker's center of balance is will determine your reaction. So we need to go through each scenario. In this one, his hand is over your mouth, like Zack's demonstrating, which means he's going to be pulling you back against him. Don't fight it. You're not stronger than him, so you'll waste energy and probably get hurt in the process. You can't reach his neck or groin if he's pressed against you, but you can reach his—?"

"Eyes," several people said.

"Yes. So, as he pulls your weight back," Chloe leaned back even though Zack seemed too terrified to move and play the part of attacker, "you can shoot your fist—thumb pointed towards his eye— towards your attacker's face. You might not hit the eye, and that's okay. Zack, when you see my fist and thumb coming toward your face, what do you want to do?"

"Back away, duck, or spin away."

"Exactly. Show me."

As she bent her arm at the elbow and brought her thumb jerking toward his eye, he took a step back and twisted slightly.

"Good. Pause right there. Now, class, maybe you hit him in the face or eye and now he's standing like this or maybe he dodged and now you have an opening to his—?"

"Groin."

"Yes. Now it can be a chop with the same arm or a grab, squeeze, and pull down."

She took him through several other demonstrations without ever touching each other as Zack dutifully played the role of the attacker while simultaneously not comfortable with the idea of attacking. She'd expected him to work the crowd a little bit, but he was surprisingly reserved. Had she misjudged his intentions?

When they finished, she asked everyone to give him a round of applause before dismissing the class.

As students packed their belongings and filed out, she approached Zack. "What brings you to a self-defense class?"

"I was mugged. I'm not so upset about the money, but it felt like such a violation of my humanity. I didn't like feeling helpless."

"You don't look helpless." She caught herself looking, really looking for the first time at his trim physique. She started to wish he had touched her during the demonstration but quickly dismissed the thought as unprofessional.

"Having a good weight and cardiovascular routine doesn't mean I know how to defend myself."

"True. And it takes courage to both realize that and come to a class like this."

He grinned. "I didn't know I'd be the only guy."

"I hope you'll come back. I promise not to put you on the spot like that again."

"I don't mind being part of a demonstration. I just didn't want to be the violent offender."

"K-k. Next time, we'll reverse roles and see how much you remember from tonight's lessons."

An impatient horn blared behind them. Chloe checked her mirrors, heart lurching, half-expecting a green Jeep with masked men.

Nothing—just a BMW riding her bumper. She exhaled and adjusted her grip on the wheel.

"Was it love at first sight?" Cupid asked.

"Um. No. Is that really a thing? I can see it with shoes. But people?"

"It can be. It doesn't replace the work needed to remain together."

"Duh." Chloe went to nudge Cupid's arm with her elbow, but it went right through him. She threw her head back and laughed—part humor at her bizarre situation and part nerves at driving into the unknown.

CHAPTER 4

Zack sat alone in the dark room, thinking about his future wife. He recalled the unconventional start to his and Chloe's relationship. It had been perfect. Just perfect. It fit Chloe and her unconventional personality.

He'd started taking self-defense classes not only because he'd been mugged—a frightening and infuriating moment where he'd frozen and given the mugger what he'd wanted without even considering putting up a fight—but also because Zack had heard rumors in the cybersecurity world about thieves not having their own hackers and so kidnapping people to do their bidding. Someone with Zack's computer skills could be an asset to someone with dubious intentions.

When he'd returned the second night to self-defense class, Chloe had showed students how to free themselves from several different holds with the attacker standing behind them. But she didn't once call on him to be the victim as she'd said she would do. Instead, she rotated through different women in the group. He'd learned a lot, but he was a little disappointed she hadn't used him for one of her demos again.

He lingered after the lesson to ask Chloe about the change of plans, waiting in the line of women who talked with her. He watched this social butterfly answer questions from defense, to offensive fighting, to health and nutrition. Her light and bubbly personality was in contrast to the depth of knowledge she possessed about overall personal wellness.

By the time he reached the front of the line, he'd forgotten what he'd originally planned to discuss.

"So, magnesium for leg cramps?" he asked, having overheard the last several conversations.

"Yeah. You can get it through leafy vegetables, fruits, and nuts. Or my favorite—dark chocolate. But sometimes you can take a supplement."

He made a mental note to pick up magnesium next time he was grocery shopping. He seemed to cramp on heavier workout days and a banana wasn't cutting it. "Cool. How'd you get into fitness?"

"I could claim it was my really cool older sister who's a doctor, but it probably was the crush I had on my high school gym teacher."

Zack chuckled.

He'd later learned that Chloe not only owned the gym he was standing in, but three others around town. Wellness instructor, Taekwondo first-degree black belt, and entrepreneur.

She bit her lip. "Look, I know I said we'd swap roles in the demo today, and then I benched you, but I felt bad putting you on the spot last time."

"I didn't mind." He picked up his gym bag and slung it over his shoulder. "I'll be here next time, if you need a victim."

She tilted her head to one side and grinned. Zack left before his flirtatious tone could sink in and the moment turn awkward. He didn't look back as he left. He didn't want to know if her grin had widened or slipped into a frown. He'd find out next week, and by that time, he'd work up the courage to ask her out.

A pipe groaned somewhere in the old house, snapping Zack back to the present. His wrists throbbed against the restraints. He forced himself to breathe evenly.

And yet… remembering Chloe steadied him.

"ARE you always this energetic or only when your fiancé is in trouble?" Cupid asked.

"Always," Chloe answered without hesitation as she tapped her fingers on the steering wheel. "I learned the word *exhausting* at a young age because my parents used it to describe me to other parents. 'We love little Chloe, but she's *exhausting*.' And they'd draw it out as if it had six syllables. Don't get me wrong—they love me. But I was a late in life surprise baby, so my energy level combined with older parents was hard on them. Of course, now that I'm thirty three, independent, and running my own business, they can sit back and enjoy. I'm referred to as *jubilant* rather than *exhausting*."

Cupid chuckled. "And what about Zack? Does he enjoy this energy?"

"I assume so. After all, he still wants to marry me. He's three years younger than me so maybe that's why he doesn't find me *exhausting*."

"Indeed? He's three years younger than you?"

"Yeah, we didn't know that until after our first date, but I already liked him by then. Besides, women live longer than men—maybe we all ought to be picking younger men." She glanced in the rear view mirror for tails.

"Brilliant. Sounds like you've got it all figured out."

She narrowed her eyes at him. "Are you mocking me?"

He raised his hands as if in self-defense. "Not at all. I'm enjoying your *jubilance*. It's very refreshing. This entire experience is quite different from the longing-to-love-whilst-languishing individuals who call on me and imagine that love will fix all of their problems."

"Well, this time, we're fixing love rather than it fixing us."

"Bending it to your will," Cupid mused.

"You bet your heart-tipped arrow. Zack and I tried playing love's game—peaceful wedding planning and anticipating our union. Now, I'm taking the bull by the horns."

"If anyone has the needed tenacity, I believe you, Chloe, are that person." His tone was light, but she sensed the worry beneath it.

As she took I-580W, she passed a billboard for the latest action movie with the hero looking buff and ready to fight. She recalled another class Zack had attended. She'd dressed one of her personal fitness instructors in a padded suit and had the students form a line. One by one, they'd moved through the line, made a punch or kick into the padding, and walked to the back of the line to do it again.

"We're all taught at a young age—no hitting, no biting, no scratching, no throwing things. When you're in a situation with someone who means you harm, those rules go out the window. You do what you need to do to get free and get safe. This exercise is to get you less uncomfortable striking someone so that if a crucial moment to your survival arises, you don't hesitate because you're a decent person programmed since childhood to play nice in the sandbox. Defending yourself doesn't make you a bully or a violent person."

Chloe broke into the line. A redhead stood at the front—Barbara, Chloe recalled her name.

"Now, you're going to kick Rick between the legs."

"What?"

"I assure you, he's well padded. We've been doing this routine for five years."

"Um, okay." Barbara took a ready stance but didn't kick.

Chloe addressed the class. "The good person in you would never do that to a man. The woman—or man—defending herself—or himself—might have to." Chloe turned back to Barbara. "Go ahead."

Barbara kicked. Rick didn't flinch. Some of the other women gasped and others chuckled, but the momentum picked back up and all of the women took their turn—some shy and some with a bit of telling aggression.

Zack stood at the front of the line. "Maybe I'll skip my turn."

"Because you're a guy?" Chloe asked.

"Yeah. It doesn't seem right." He eyed Rick warily.

"Ever seen *Butch Cassidy and the Sundance Kid*? Guys kick other guys when they need to. Remember, your actions are for self-defense."

"Since we're talking movies, you know *Casino Royale*—the James

Bond movie? I'm picturing that awful torture scene. I was physically ill watching that."

"Look at Rick. He's fine, ten kicks later."

"And he looks like a decent guy. Probably wouldn't hurt a stray dog."

"K-k." She took a step back from Zack. The purpose of the exercise was to push people out of their comfort zone, but Chloe wouldn't push too far. "Next up?"

The lesson continued. At the end, Chloe had everyone relax on their mats and deep breathe.

When the class was dismissed, Zack approached. "Great class."

"Thanks. I feel like I put you on the spot again."

"We're good." He smiled. "Would you be interested in grabbing a bite to eat?"

"K-k. I'm going with a group of friends to Fuki Sushi. Do you want to join us?"

Noticing the part-startled, part-disappointed expression on his face, Chloe realized Zack had been referring to a date. "Oh, you meant just you and me."

"Well, a group is fine, too. In fact, with you being a black belt, maybe a group would be safer for me to start with."

She chuckled since he was making reference to one of the safety-first rules she'd covered in class—getting to know someone before dating them alone.

Zack had joined her that night with her friends and proved himself very amicable. Three days later, they went on a real date.

"You know, this isn't quite what I do in guiding a love life," Cupid muttered, bring her attention back to the present. "Most people just need help picking a proposal spot."

She tightened her white-knuckled grip on the wheel. "I'm not most people."

~

ZACK TWISTED his wrist against his restraints. How much time had passed? It was hard to gauge, but he hadn't made much progress in his escape plan. His kidnappers still hadn't produced Chloe. He took that as a good sign.

He thought of the first date he and Chloe had gone on. She didn't want a long, drawn out meal, so he'd opted to take her to Red Java's House. After dinner, they'd strolled along The Embarcadero strip of piers.

"Tell me more about cybersecurity. What do you do exactly?" she asked.

He took a chance and reached for her hand. They walked side by side as he felt the warmth from her slender fingers. Her body language remained relaxed, and he wondered if she felt the same zinging chemistry at their touch as he did.

"Cybersecurity is all about protecting online data from being compromised. I safeguard files and networks, and install firewalls. Then, I show medical centers how to create security plans and monitor for internal and external threats."

"Very cool. Sounds pretty intense," she said.

"Not really. It's a lot of code. Long hours at a desk."

"Oh, you could get one of those hinged desks so you can alternate sitting and standing."

"I might look into that." he said.

"And I could show you some stretches you can do at work during your breaks."

The idea of Chloe stretching had Zack forgetting the discomfort of lower back pain. "You own gyms. You're funny and energetic. I have to ask … you are actually single, right?"

She laughed. "Yes, I'm single. Let's see … Bobby said I was too high energy. Justin got mad at my suggestions for healthier eating. I mean, the guy was a walking junk food munching machine. He may have been built like Chris Hemsworth, but it's going to eventually catch up to him. And, most recently, Antonio didn't want a woman who could beat him in a fight."

"Was he planning on fighting you?"

"No, but when he learned I was a black belt, he excused himself from the relationship. Oh, this is way more information than I should be sharing on a first date. Which reminds me, Jim said I shared too much."

She started to tug her hand back, but Zack didn't let go. "I like it. I deal with data. You're giving me a data download. Besides, cybersecurity is all about protecting secrets, so I like being with someone who isn't secretive. Also, I like health and high energy. As for beating me in a fight, I'd spar with you anytime and enjoy watching you land me on my backside over and over and over."

She laughed, tucking a strand of dark brown hair behind her ear. He saw a faint blush of her cheeks by the light of the lanterns lining the dock. She looked up at him, blue eyes vibrant from her rosy cheeks.

"Where can I take you on date number two?"

Chloe stopped and leaned on the railing.

Zack followed her gaze out over the ocean. The salty breeze blew through his hair as gulls flew low, looking for their next snack.

"The Zone."

"The laser tag place?" he asked.

"My niece's birthday party is there on Saturday, and the rest of my calendar is full until the following week. And I don't want to wait that long to see you again."

"Laser tag it is."

Chloe bit her lip. "It'll be a rambunctious bunch of twelve-year-olds cracked out on pizza and soda."

"It'll be fun."

Zack had had so much fun, especially watching Chloe fully embrace the role of warrior aunt. With her grace and agility, no one got a shot on her while Zack spent most of his time with his lights alarming that he'd been hit.

A door slammed somewhere in the house and Zack flinched.

What he wouldn't give to be playing tag with Chloe right now instead of tied to a chair, fearing for their lives

CHAPTER 5

"Are you okay?" Cupid looked at Chloe who'd fallen uncharacteristically silent. The night was taking unexpected turns for him, but the ordeal was much harder for her.

"The only fight I've ever been in was over before it started. Emma and I were at a dance club. She was dancing her heart out, and I was drowning in sorrow over missing Hawaii. Zack was out of town on business. Anyway, so this chunky guy with some 1990s boy-band hair waving in the breeze gets all gropey."

"Gropey?" Cupid asked.

"Yes. It's totally a word, and if it isn't, it should be. So, I'm already in a bad mood with two drinks on board."

"Honestly, I'm incapable of picturing you in a bad mood," he mused.

She was so relentlessly chipper. But she also had a protective streak, evidenced by her rush to rescue Zack and now this story which sounded like she was going to rescue Emma.

Chloe gave her most severe scowl, but Cupid only laughed.

"Do go on," he said.

"I stormed onto the dance floor and got in his face. 'My friend obviously doesn't like your frisky fingers, buddy, so get it under control.' Gropey tells me to mind my own business while Emma gets sheepish. 'It's okay, Chloe, let's just go.' But I'm not about to let the situation diffuse, because *it's not okay*. 'Say you're sorry,' I tell Gropey. He smirks and replies back with 'You're just jealous.'"

Cupid listened with captured interest to Chloe's retelling of the events and the way she changed her tone from Gropey's lazy, deep slur to Emma's high-pitched damsel-in-distress.

"'Lay a hand on me, and you'll find out just how *not* jealous I am.' He moves to push me away with one hand because—let's be honest—I was crowding him and picking a fight. I intercept his hand, twist his wrist, and bring him to knees. Emma gasps, and by this time, the dancers are turning into gawkers. 'Say you're sorry,' I tell him again. 'I'm sorry. I'm sorry,' he says, though that's the PG version of what he actually said. As we left, he called me crazy."

A horn blared behind her when she drifted a little in her lane. Chloe corrected, heart pounding, then finished, "As you can see, the entire event unfolded in a completely rational way."

"Completely rational," Cupid replied dryly in that British way that meant the opposite.

When Chloe fell silent again, Cupid stared out the car window at the dark summer sky speckled with stars. What had Rose gotten him into? Of course she had no idea Chloe's situation would become so dangerous.

He was way out of his depth here. He felt the weight of everything in the couple's life riding on his ghostly skills. Normally, if he didn't succeed, two people didn't end up together. Such an outcome could be blamed on the intricacies of finicky love. In Chloe's and Zack's case, a failure on Cupid's part could result in one or both of them harmed or worse.

Chloe's spunk, honesty, energy, and obvious love for Zack had instantly endeared her to Cupid. The ancient ghost desperately wanted to give her the outcome she desired and seemed to deserve.

Much of Cupid's worry came from their heavy reliance on his ability to see the future. The future held thousands of possibilities, each dependent on a chain reaction. They could misstep anywhere along the way and alter the outcome they had hoped and planned for.

Cupid silently vowed to do his best—for both Chloe and Zack.

Failure didn't just mean a broken heart this time—it meant broken bodies.

ZACK TRIED to gauge how much time had passed when his captors came back into his room. Two hours perhaps. He hadn't succeeded in loosening his bonds. Mostly, he was sore and bleeding now.

"Is your fiancée sleeping around?" Brute asked.

"No."

"She's not at your home. Where else would she be at night? A friend's house?"

"You think I'm going to make this easier for you?" Zack laced his voice with venom, even as he felt rising hope that they wouldn't snare Chloe.

She could be any number of places—Emma's house, the movies, her parents' house. She was also probably frantic with worry with the wedding so close and then him not home on time. By now with no communication from him, she would've checked her app to try to track him on his phone, and—assuming his kidnappers had turned it off—she might even already be asking the police to help her. This close to the wedding and the fact that he always called or texted if he was going to be late, would spur her into action.

But would the police do anything other than ask her the same question the kidnappers had asked him: could your fiancée be sleeping around. Of course not, but they might not take her concerns seriously.

Or... she could have already made that assumption and be out looking for him. But she'd never find him. That was a good thing—he didn't want her anywhere near these monsters.

Loafers pulled out his phone and began typing with his thumbs.

"Actually, you *are* going to help us. If she isn't cheating on you, then she'll respond to a little SOS text message."

"What?"

"We obtained both of your mobile numbers weeks ago. Cloning phones is far easier than hacking a multilayered security system."

"No!" Zack yelled, squirming in his chair. If they had cloned his phone, then the text message Loafer's was writing to Chloe would appear to come from Zack's phone.

The man left the room, chuckling and typing. Brute snickered as he followed behind his partner in crime.

Zack tilted his head back, cursing. He had to escape. His ropes hadn't loosened enough to free his hands. When they were free, he had only one exit from the room and no idea the layout of the house. There were at least two kidnappers—both larger than him—and his only weapon was the chair he sat on. He hadn't seen any guns yet, but that didn't mean they weren't armed.

Five days until their wedding. Five days. All he wanted to do was live a blissful life with his effervescent wife, Chloe. Were they destined not to achieve a union?

He recalled their last failed attempt. They'd been packed and ready to fly to the mountains. That night Chloe had complained about an upset stomach. The next morning, she looked pale.

"Honey, maybe we should get you checked out," Zack suggested.

"I'm okay." She loaded her carry-on into the car. "Probably something I ate. It'll pass."

He didn't want to argue with her, so he hefted their suitcases into the trunk, watching her try to hide the abdominal pain she obviously felt.

On the way to the airport, Chloe gasped and grimaced. "This might be bad."

Zack never slowed as he changed routes from the airport to the nearest hospital. The ER did CT scans and told them she had appendicitis before she was whisked away to surgery.

Zack remembered wiping tears from her eyes as she lay on the gurney. "I'll be right here when you wake up."

While she was in surgery, Zack had called her family and cancelled the wedding.

She went from laproscopic surgery in the OR to the recovery room to a hospital room bed. The surgeon told Zack that if she'd been on a plane with a ruptured appendix, Chloe would have had to have emergent open abdominal surgery. She added, "You probably saved her life."

The next day, Zack was by Chloe's side when she woke. Her smile lit his world.

"Can I get you anything? Juice? Another pillow?"

She took his hand in hers. "A rain check on the wedding, I guess."

He kissed her hand. "You know I'm devoted to you even without the legal documentation that declares it. I'll put the ring on right now. I'll get the hospital chaplain to make us official."

Chloe chuckled but shook her head. "I am not getting married in a hospital after surgery. I probably look hideous."

"You're the most beautiful woman I know."

She snorted. "Love really is blind."

To prove his point, he leaned over and kissed her. The kiss was slow and sensual. When he pulled away and looked into her eyes, he saw that he'd stripped away her sadness, pain, and worry.

"Wow," she said, a little breathless, and wrapped her arms gently around him.

The memory blurred under the harsh reality of the dim room and the bite of rope around his wrists. Would he even get the chance for a third attempt at "I do"?

As they continued their drive, Chloe realized she'd spent a lot of time talking about herself. She didn't know much about Cupid, and learning about him would both enhance their relationship and distract her from the current crisis.

"What's your greatest match-making success?" she asked him.

"Oh, it's hard to pick just one. Princesses to paupers, they're all rewarding. But this isn't my story. I'm learning about you and Zack."

"Fine, but when this is over, and Zack is safe, I get to hear about the man behind the legend."

"We can do that."

Chloe bounced her left leg as she kept her right on the gas pedal. "Is Emma okay? Did she make it home from the movies?"

"One moment…. Ah, yes. Nick behaved himself."

"Good. How do you do that anyway? Can you find anyone?"

"Almost anyone, and it took hundreds of years to get good at. Not all ghosts can track people."

"Cupid's got skills."

"Tell me about when Zack proposed?"

"Hmm. How do you know I wasn't the one who proposed?"

"I know." He smiled.

Chloe thought about Zack's proposal. "He proposed on the pier. Very romantic. I remember it like it was yesterday. The night was cool but not cold, and salty air swept past us. We walked to the pier where our first date was. Golden lights were strung along the railing. As we approached, hand in hand, a quartet started playing," Chloe said wistfully.

"I'll never forget his words as his hands shook, holding the ring in it's display box. I think you know a man is committed when he's nervous in his proposal. Anyway, he said, 'Chloe, you're the most vibrant and vivacious woman I know. You are the supernova in my life, and I'd be the luckiest man to bask in the light of your life for the rest of mine.'" Goosebumps spread down her arms at the retelling.

"Cupid sniffed and turned to look out the window. "Charming."

"Are you crying?"

"No."

"You teared up, didn't you?"

"Maybe." He dabbed at ghost tears under his eyes. "It was very touching. I'm a romantic, you know. It's why I do what I do—so I can be a part of the special moments in people's lives."

Chloe drove in silence as she thought of when she'd told Emma the same story. Her best friend was a massage therapist. Chloe had first met her when she'd gotten a massage at Emma's day spa. Well, not her spa. Emma hadn't owned her own place yet, but that was because Chloe hadn't yet inspired Emma to work for herself and be her own boss. She kept feeding her referrals from the gym and boosted her business.

The day Chloe told Emma about Zack's proposal, Chloe had been face down on the message table since Emma had insisted pampering herself was the best way to celebrate the happy news.

Chloe grunted from the intense pressure. "Shouldn't this be a relaxing Swedish massage to celebrate my engagement?"

"It would be—" Emma kneaded the muscles between Chloe's shoulder blade and spine "—but you're all knotted up. When was your last massage?"

"I don't know. When was the last time I came to you? Ugh, it feels like my rhomboid's being cycled through a meat grinder."

"You last came to me two years ago for a massage. Are you serious? Has it been two years?" Emma demanded.

"I've been busy," Chloe squeaked out the reply as Emma ran her forearm down her back with such force, Chloe thought her ribcage might crack.

"You need to work more self-care into your routine." She pushed directly on one of the knotted muscles.

Chloe felt the pain shoot deep before radiating outward. "Are you sure this isn't a manifestation of your frustration that I'm engaged and you're not?"

"Hmm. Tempting, but no. I really am doing deep tissue for your sake. You'll thank me later. Now, when are we going dress shopping?"

Chloe's phone chimed, bringing her back to the present. She pulled the car over to the side of the road and yanked the phone from her console.

"It's from Zack," she told Cupid with excitement. She read it aloud, "Ran into car trouble. Can you pick me up?"

"It's not from Zack," Cupid said.

Chloe rubbed her temple, considering the ghost's words. If they had Zack, they had his phone. They could have force him to unlock it, or they could have cloned his phone.

"So … trap?" she asked.

"Trap. They need to use you as leverage against Zack."

"Oh, they'll get me, and they'll be sorry they did."

"I've no doubt." He grinned.

"How do I play this?" She wriggled her thumbs as she held the phone, ready to text back.

"I've no idea." Cupid pointed two thumbs at himself. "Ghost of love, not hostage negotiations."

"Right. K-k. But you can see the future—or parts of it?"

"Yes." He answered hesitantly as though afraid of what she was scheming. "But if you play this wrong, they might put additional, *physical* pressure on Zack to comply."

"Tell me this—is it better for me to send something like 'K-k, I'm on my way'—which I don't think they'll to believe anyway because if your rideshare breaks down, you just get another rideshare and none of that explains a two hour delay. Or, do I creep them out with a different message?"

"Let me look into this…"

Chloe waited while Cupid sat with eyes closed, channeling whatever supernatural things ghosts channeled. In the quiet, she had a moment to contemplate panicking over how she was taking advice from the ghost of love while driving toward a kidnapping and considering a rescue. She swallowed back her worry. Focus now, panic later.

At last, he told her, "Make it creepy. The creepier, the better."

"Excellent." With a maniacal grin, Chloe typed her reply and hit send.

Then she turned to Cupid. "I'm going to need a few more pieces of information from you."

CHAPTER 6

Zack was flexing his legs to keep them limber when Brute burst into the room, eyes flashing beneath the ski mask he wore.

"What the hell does this mean?"

Zack's eyes adjusted to the light on the screen of the phone as he read the text message.

One, two, Chloe's gonna get you.

"Does she know we have you or is she messing with you?" Brute demanded.

"I don't see how she could know you've abducted me. But she wouldn't direct something like that at me. She hates horror movies. She had nightmares from just the *Freddy Krueger* movie trailers as a child."

Loafers entered the room. "Your phone is inactive. No one can trace us here." His phone beeped with an incoming text, and he pulled the phone from his pocket.

As Loafers read the message aloud, Zack thought his face went ashen based on the parts of his face he could see through the eye holes in the mask. He held the phone for the other man to see.

"*Three, four, you're gonna hit the floor.* How'd she get your number?"

Another beep—this time Brute's phone, different from the cloned phone he initially held. *"Five, six, bury you in the sticks."* Brute's knuckles whitened around the phone as he read, like he expected the screen itself to bite him.

Cursing, the men dashed out of the room, slamming the door behind them.

Zack sat under the dim light, wondering how this was possible. Part of him hoped Chloe was orchestrating the percolating of fear through the kidnappers, and that she was arranging some type of rescue. Part of him wanted her stowed away somewhere safe.

CHLOE BURST out laughing as Cupid told her the reaction of Zack's captors. The laugher felt good, though her insides were still churning with intense worry for Zack.

"I thought they might wet their britches," he added.

"I would've liked to have seen their faces."

"Well played, Chloe. Well played. You've managed to thoroughly confuse and worry them. You still need to rescue Zack tonight. Look at me," he shook his head, "I'm helping a woman maneuver a kidnapping. You're a first for me. And that's saying something when you've been around as long as I have."

"You might change your MO after this and join SWAT."

"Certainly not. This is far more adventure and suspense than I want for the next century."

"You've got the skills to be anything you want to be."

"'With great power comes great responsibility.'"

"Huh. I wouldn't have pegged you for a Spiderman fan."

He blinked at her. "That quote is from Voltaire, 1793."

Chloe chuckled at herself. "Well, I never claimed to have any literary knowledge."

Cupid turned to face the road, trying to feign annoyance, but she saw the upturned corners of his mouth in amusement.

"Onward?" Chloe put the car back in gear.

"'*Once more unto the breach!*" Cupid declared.

"Ah, Shakespeare. I know that one."

"Yes, we Brits do love our Shakespeare."

They headed north on I-680, into the night, toward Zack.

CUPID LEFT CHLOE while she drove, and he arrived back at the isolated home where Zack was being held. The cybersecurity expert appeared to be making snail-pace progress on his ropes.

Unseen, the ghost walked through the door into the kitchen. He followed the sound of voices of dissension to the front living room and passed over cables running from one wall to a table near a worn, brown sofa. The table held two large computer monitors attached to a CPU and a keyboard. Beside the keyboard were a pile of ski masks and two handguns—9mm if he had to guess. And Cupid would have to guess because he knew nothing about guns.

He looked back down at the floor. Ethernet wires. The kidnappers must have taken time and planning to set up this location.

Four men were in the confined space. One lounged on the couch, watching a soccer match on mute. Of the three men standing and bickering, one was dressed smartly in a navy suit and loafers. The other two were in black fatigues.

Cupid picked up names as he eavesdropped. The well dressed German was Erik, the large bulky man was Dolph, and the one dipping snuff was Pork.

"We don't have the woman, so we need a new plan," Dolph said.

"The backup plan is we torture the cybersecurity captive. It'll need to be something without much blood loss, and he'll need to still be able to see the screen and type," Erik explained.

Cupid's stomach rolled. This was most definitely not his domain. He was puppy dogs and heart shaped confetti. Not weapons and blood.

"Don't you have tools?" Pork asked Dolph

"I brought what I needed to rough up his fiancé who doesn't need consciousness, eyesight, and fingers."

A wave of nausea pummeled through Cupid at the image of something horrible happening to Chloe. But he didn't want Zack to suffer either.

"We"l look around the house. See what we can use," Erik said.

Cupid decided to do the same. What could he do to derail their plans—or at least delay them? He scanned the living room, eyes falling on the computer and robust trail of wires.

Perfect.

Like most ghosts, Cupid could disrupt electrical systems—trip fuses, dim lights, turn televisions to static, drop internet connections, and even shut off power. He plunged both hands into the CPU. With his full concentration and ghostly force, he shut down the system.

The TV flickered, the lights dimmed for a second, and every man in the room glanced up at the ceiling like it might fall. The effort made him dizzy.

"What the—?" Pork rushed to the table and punched buttons on the keyboard in irritation.

"What happened?" Erik demanded.

"The system shut down. I'll have torestart it."

"If we don't have a computer and internet, our plan implodes," Dolph said.

"I know. I know. I'm working on it. I don't understand what happened."

The disruption was temporary, but Cupid had bought Zack a little time. His ghostly powers may have to come back periodically to continue to disrupt the computer and delay their insidious plans for Zack.

Cupid returned to Chloe as she drove.

"Everything okay?" she asked.

"Zack is still unharmed. We need to discuss our rescue plan."

"I'm ready."

ON THE DRIVE toward Rio Vista Junction where Zack was being held, Chloe and Cupid had talked through three dozen rescue scenarios.

They finally found one which didn't end in flaming disaster for Chloe and Zack. But it did involve fireworks.

"Why is Zack being held at an old house in the middle of nowhere?" Chloe asked.

"I suppose because it's remote but still has internet access. Again, ghost of love, not rescue missions."

"What can you tell me about the kidnappers?"

"They all have criminal records. The leader knew someone who'd pulled off a cyber-heist, so he thought he'd try one. They've been stalking your husband for months, scheming the kidnapping. They set up the house well in advance. My understanding is that they'd planned on taking you and Zack simultaneously from separate locations. Then neither of you could alert the other. But an accident on the bridge caused traffic to back up which prevented the second team from getting to you before you left."

She smirked. "And because you warned me. That shook up their plans."

"Yes. Once it became obvious they weren't going to find you to leverage your well-being and make Zack comply with hacking True Health's database, they went into discussions on another plan." His voice turned dismal.

Chloe swallowed. "Hurting Zack."

Cupid scrubbed hands across his face. "I don't understand this kidnapping nonsense. Why wouldn't they just hire someone to hack a backdoor to the data if they have the money for this elaborate scheme?"

Chloe blew out a slow breath. "It's complicated. And there's no 'hacking a backdoor.' A backdoor is a programmed security flaw—the programmer can *access* a backdoor, but people don't hack into it. Zack wouldn't have built that into True Health's system anyway. The kidnappers would have to have a hacker to attempt a security breach. And hacking is a lot more complex than it seems in the movies. Zack has explained it to me before."

At Cupid's raised eyebrows, she continued, "First, a hacker would have to break through the initial firewall. This only gets him or her as far as the DMZ."

"DMZ?"

"Demilitarized zone. The DMZ consists of health system applications but not sensitive data like patient information. Then, there is another firewall between the DMZ and the patient database. And this firewall would be a different manufacturer from the first—few people would be able to hack both. If they managed to get that far, it's not as though they can just 'copy-paste' the information they want from the server."

Cupid nodded in understanding. "They picked Zack because he set up True Health's security."

"Right. He knows the layers required to get all the way to the data. He doesn't have to 'hack' anything or use a 'backdoor'. He can use administrative access and walk right through the front door. He may even be able to suspend the firewall, get to the server, and copy-paste the data."

Cupid's face fell. "They argued about how to interrogate him in a way that still kept him lucid and functional enough to navigate the internet."

"Are we going to get there before they hurt him?"

"Yes. I caused delays."

"You? What delays did you cause?"

"You've seen me flicker in and out of your car for the last half hour?"

"Yes, I thought maybe that was a ghost thing."

"I've been intermittently disrupting their power and internet access. Because of technical difficulties, they haven't had a reason to start their interrogation."

"You're not a ghost. You're a freakin' angel! No wonder people sometimes draw you with wings."

Cupid smiled. "I prefer 'reluctant hero,' but I'll take angel."

Chloe parked her car and got out for the second stop of the night and the last one before she would reach Zack. She'd first stopped at a convenience store and bought a pocket knife, lighter, and USB cable.

Now, she went inside a shady looking thrift store where Cupid had divined the store owner would be willing to sell firecrackers outside the June 28th through July 6th law in California.

"Hi." She approached the clerk counter. "I'm interested in buying Black Cat Flashlights. The one-hundred pack."

The owner, a gangly man with leathery skin and thinning hair, turned down the volume on the reality show he watched on an iPad. "By law, they don't go on sale until June 28th."

"I'm not a cop. I'm a cash paying customer."

The man ran a tongue along his teeth as he looked her up and down. He quoted her a price.

"That's double what they're worth," Cupid told her.

"That's fine." Chloe produced the cash from her purse but didn't hand it over to the man.

"How much more you got in there?" The man gave her a feral grin. He glanced leisurely around the room as if to convey she was alone with him.

Chloe clenched her teeth. "Not enough for you to get a broken nose trying to take it from me."

His eyebrows shot up but more in amusement than fear. "Is that so?"

She slammed her palm down on his countertop, startling him.

"I'm on a rescue mission! If you don't get your act together and get my firecrackers, I will beat you to a pulp and take them anyway!" She felt her cheeks flush with fury. She didn't have time to waste and meant every word—well, maybe 'to a pulp' had been an exaggeration. One of the rules of self-defense was not appearing meek or helpless. Not acting like a victim made you less likely to become one.

The man backed away from her. "Okay. Okay. They're in the back."

As he left, she turned toward Cupid. "Is he on the level or is he going to come back with a sawed-off shotgun?"

"He's getting your Black Cats only. You've made your point."

She blew out a breath as she tried to steady her nerves.

When the owner returned, they made the exchange—cash for fireworks. And he threw in some poppers for free.

Two minutes later, Chloe was out the door, in her car, and back on the road.

CHLOE PARKED her car a half-mile out from the house where Zack was held captive. At least, according to Cupid, this was the location and the stealth required to approach it. She was putting a lot of faith in a ghost she'd only just met. But she did trust him.

"I'll lead you through the brush to the house," Cupid said.

Chloe didn't move.

"Chloe?"

"We're really doing this? I'm launching a rescue mission?"

His brow furrowed with worry. "We've been over the options. Calling the police will cause delays and potentially a hostage situation."

She nodded but still didn't move.

"What's wrong?" he asked.

"I don't know if I can do this. And if I don't do this, something bad could happen to Zack. If I do this and screw it up, Zack could get hurt —or worse."

"You can do this. You're a black belt."

"Sure. In sparring. I don't actually fight anyone. I teach."

"But you're trained nonetheless."

"Have you ever heard the saying *those who can't do, teach?* Well, that's me. I live in my sheltered, middle-class world where I never actually have to get physical with anyone."

Cupid turned in his seat and placed his hand on hers—through hers. "Today, that changes. Today, you'll storm that house and free your beau. Today, you'll teach those criminals they messed with the wrong fiancée."

For a moment, she imagined him having had a hundred morale boosting moments like this through the centuries, although she suspected they involved summoning the courage to court or propose, not storm a house on a rescue mission.

She took a deep breath. "K-k. Let's do this." She hopped out of the car and slammed the door shut. "I'm ready!"

Cupid lowered his chin to his chest. "Your phone, Chloe. You need your phone to call the police at the right time. And you need the Black Cats to cause a distraction."

"Right." She opened the driver's side door and grabbed her phone and firecrackers.

"We went over the plan," he said flatly.

"I know."

"Thrice."

She stretched her arms and legs. "I'm nervous."

Her mind swam with images of men wearing black with dark ski masks and guns—just as Cupid had described them.

Creeping through the tall grass, Chloe approached the dilapidated single story farm house. The building was as Cupid described—steepled roof, white siding that was peeled and chipped, and weather-beaten shutters. Cooling AC units were jammed into various windows and padded with tacky insulation. They rattled noisily, as if working overtime to cool the house. Electrical wires crisscrossed before diving under the roof. A green Jeep was parked beneath a slanted carport which looked like a strong wind might topple it.

Feeling a little like Macaulay Culkin from *Home Alone*, Chloe laid her traps. Poppers at the front door as well as a trip wire. The wire was actually a ten foot micro USB cable, but was the closest thing to a trip wire she found at the convenience store where she'd stopped. The poppers and wire wouldn't do more than trip and scare the kidnappers, but it was a much needed distraction as part of their choreographed plan.

According to Cupid, there were four men, two of them armed. When she came in with firecrackers blazing, two men would bolt for the front door, one would go to the back door, and the other would check the status of the hostage.

Chloe dialed 9-1-1 on her phone. When prompted to press a number if she couldn't safely speak, she did so. Then, she placed the call on mute.

She crouched outside the backdoor to the house, holding the firecrackers. "You're sure that door will bust when I kick it in?"

"Yes. The frame is rotted, so it will break the wood around the lock but not the lock itself."

"And the keys are on the kitchen counter to the left?"

"Yes. Trust me."

"K-k. Here goes nothing—or everything."

""All for love, then. Off you go." Cupid said with an encouraging smile.

Chloe unmuted her phone, slipped it in the leg pocket on the side of her yoga pants, and lit the roll of Black Cat firecrackers.

Five seconds until detonation.

She kicked in the back door, stepped inside, and hurtled the firecracker stack down the hall toward the living room where two of the men dozed in front of the TV.

Spinning back toward the kitchen, she grabbed the vehicle key just as the firecrackers erupted in what sounded like automatic gunfire.

Two men rushed out of the master bedroom. One streaked past her as she crouched in the shadows. The other spotted her and lunged for her.

Chloe dodged his big arms and jabbed an upper cut into his abdomen. He unleashed a surprised grunt.

Stumbling back, he seemed to rethink his rushed attack. This time, he readied his stance and took a more calculated swing. She rolled into him, curving around the attempted strike, and cracked her elbow into his nose. When he tried to snatch her with his hand, she ducked and glided a safe distance away.

He was bigger. She was faster.

The attacker clutched at his bleeding nose but never took his angry eyes off Chloe.

"Wait for it," Cupid told her. The man lunged for her again.

"Now!"

Chloe reached up, pulled open the freezer door, and let the man collide face first into steel. He crumpled to the floor, unconscious.

One down.

CHAPTER 7

After hours of slow, painful effort, Zack had managed to liberate one wrist from the rope. He used his free hand to untie his ankles, all the while listening for sounds in case his kidnappers returned to the room they were keeping him in. The only noise was the rattling hum of the AC unit and the muffled sounds of a television. If he extricated himself from the chair, he could probably kick out the rusting AC unit and crawl out the window.

Why hadn't they yet tortured him for information? Not that he was complaining. At first, they seemed to be waiting to catch Chloe. When that failed, Zack had overheard bickering among some of the men.

An explosion of noise came from another room. Was that gunfire? Screams followed. Had the police arrived? If so, it sounded like a botched rescue. Or had the men turned on each other? That might not go well for Zack, either.

He struggled to free his last hand but wasn't fast enough before one of the kidnappers burst into the room.

Loafers.

His mask was gone and he held a gun in one hand. Even without the mask, Zack didn't recognize the man as anyone he'd seen prior to tonight, but that didn't mean they hadn't crossed paths in Zack's many travels. Somehow, Loafer's had known Zack's cybersecurity consulting job for True Health.

Loafers' eyes went wide when he saw Zack's free hand. He rushed toward Zack, and Zack remembered his self-defense training from Chloe. He kicked up his free leg, hitting the man in the groin. With an agonized groan, his aggressor fell to his knees.

Another person entered—a petite woman in a pink yoga outfit. For a wild second, Zack thought he was hallucinating.

"Chloe?" He did a double-take.

She looked down at the man writhing on the floor, clutching his injured part. "Well done," she congratulated Zack with a proud smile.

"How did you find me?"

"Explanations later. There are more bad guys out there." She pulled out a small pocket-knife and sawed through his last restraint.

His legs felt rubbery after sitting so long, but he forced them to move as he followed her to the back door. He gawked at the large man, Brute, immobile on the floor. Had Chloe done that? Was she alone?

She took his hand and led him to a Jeep parked outside.

"Their Jeep?" Where was Chloe's ride?

"My Prius is a half-mile away," she whispered. "You'd never make it that far on foot right now, and I couldn't park any closer and give my approach away. We're taking theirs."

"Go, go," she ushered him into the passenger side. "There's one more armed kidnapper."

As he climbed in and strapped on his seatbelt, she did the same. She produced keys, started the car, and threw it into drive.

When a man stepped in front of the vehicle and took aim at them with a handgun, Chloe never slowed. Zack tensed as the gunman faced a choice—fire one round into the Jeep that might hit the driver but not in time to alter the path of the vehicle or save his own life and dodge the Jeep.

The man dove to one side. He still fired a shot, but it went wild.

Chloe let out a yip of terror, but kept the vehicle steady. Zack felt his heart threaten to pound through his chest.

"Are you okay?" she asked him.

"I'm okay." He looked down at his bleeding wrists. "I don't under-stand what happened back there, but I'm okay."

"I won't allow kidnappers to ruin our wedding. That's what happened."

Chloe gripped the wheel with one hand and pulled her phone from the thigh pocket of her exercise pants with the other. She spoke into it. "I'm turning my phone off now. Zack and I will drive to the station." She ended the call and put her phone back in her pocket.

"Who was that?"

"Police dispatcher." She pulled over to the side of the road where her Prius was parked.

When she climbed out of the Jeep, he followed her lead on unsteady legs. She raced around to him and threw her arms around him. Her embrace felt like a homecoming, especially since he thought he'd never see her again. Or worse, he'd see her in the hands of his kidnappers.

"Chloe." He squeezed her tight, relishing the feel of her close to him. "You could have been hurt. They had guns. What were you thinking, running a one woman rescue?"

She looked up at him, tears streaming from her eyes. "You. I was thinking about you. About what they'd do to you to get information. I couldn't trust anyone else to return you to me safely."

He smoothed her hair back from her face and kissed her forehead.

Later.

Later they could discuss this—and how she'd found him. For this moment, he wanted to cherish her. He pulled her back into a tight embrace.

"Did I ever tell you that you're the most amazing woman I know?"

WHEN CHLOE and Zack arrived at the police station, Chloe explained the situation. Sort of. Chloe told authorities she'd tracked Zack through his phone when he didn't come home. When questioned about why she didn't notify police, she explained that he was only late getting home and it was too soon to file a missing person's report. As soon as she reached where he was, she called the police. But since she couldn't see inside and suspected Zack was in imminent danger, she couldn't wait for their arrival. So she detonated some robust fireworks she found outside the house—definitely not purchased illegally by her--and went inside to rescue him.

She didn't like lying, and the police didn't seem completely satisfied by her explanation, but her *exhaustive* personality seemed to wear them down. The police informed the couple that the kidnappers were in custody when they released Chloe and Zack with a cautionary, 'we'll be back in touch.'

Explaining events to Zack on the way home was a different matter. She couldn't lie to Zack.

They didn't arrive back at home until daybreak.

Chloe tossed her keys on the counter, and Zack bolted the door.

She turned to him as she kicked off her sneakers. "Do you want the sane version I told the police or the bizarre, mind-bending truth which involves potions and a ghost named Cupid?"

He grinned. "I can't fathom how you found me. The police said you said you traced my phone, but these creeps were no amateurs. They wouldn't have left my phone on except briefly when they texted you. And how did you text their phones?"

She gave him a sheepish grin. "You're a logical man. My explanations will not be based in logic."

"I'm exhausted, and everything seems surreal. I think if you told me you rode a unicorn with a leprechaun on your shoulder to come to my rescue, I'd just accept it." He reached over and held her hand. "Let's get home, get some sleep, and tell me all about potions and Cupid tomorrow."

As Zack led her toward the bedroom, Chloe glanced over her shoulder.

Cupid leaned against the doorway, arms folded, watching them with a small, satisfied smile.

Six days left, she thought. Plenty of time to make sure they actually got to "I do."

CHAPTER 8

Chloe stood in her dressing room, white gown flowing around her. Her hair was pinned up away from her face, and she wore teardrop diamond earrings.

Emma dabbed tears away from her eyes with a tissue. "I can't believe this is finally happening. And all because Aunt Rose loaned you a ghost for a week."

"I'm glad you believed my story. I lived through it, and I'm still not sure I believe what happened." ." A week ago she'd been pacing her kitchen, staring at a potion bottle like a lunatic. Now she stood in a gown, a ghost at her shoulder, and her entire world intact.

"Once you've seen half the bizarre things Aunt Rose does, ghosts don't seem so farfetched. And Cupid of all ghosts! Maybe he can play match-maker for me next."

Cupid appeared beside Chloe, an admiring look on his face. "I've come to wish the bride well on her special day. And what a beautiful bride you are."

"Emma, Cupid is here. Can you give us a minute so I can say goodbye?"

Emma blinked at the empty air beside Chloe—empty to her,

anyway—and smiled. "Tell him I said hi." She gathered up the hem of her pink maid of honor dress and slipped out the dressing room door.

Chloe turned to Cupid and smiled. "I wish I could hug you right now. This is as far as we've ever gotten. And it's all because of you."

"You don't give yourself enough credit. You're the one who had the tenacity to make your wedding day a reality."

"Will you be there today?" Chloe asked.

"I wouldn't miss it for all the arrows in Robin Hood's quiver."

"And then you're gone?"

"And then I'm gone. Hopefully, the next time a young woman or a young man calls on me for help, it won't be such a dire situation. One nail biting, kidnapping, edge of your seat suspense is quite enough for me for the next hundred years."

Chloe nudged his apparition with her elbow. "I don't know. You might get bored."

"Love is many things, but never boring."

"Thanks again."

"Go get your beau."

A few minutes later, Chloe stood at the back of the church, arm-in-arm with her father. Soft light from stained-glass windows warmed her shoulders as she walked.

He patted her forearm. "Today's the big day."

"For real this time." Chloe couldn't stop smiling.

As the music played, her father escorted her down the aisle. She was surrounded by both her and Zack's family and friends. Rose was in the crowd with Cupid sitting beside her. Rose winked at her, and Chloe wondered if Cupid had told her much of what had happened. Emma stood near the altar with the bridesmaids.

Then, Chloe's gaze fell on Zack, and at long last, they said their vows.

Zack danced with his mesmerizing, beautiful wife with her silken brunette hair and white dress. She looked like a princess. She was always beautiful in her exercise clothes, but today, she looked exquisite. Her entire body glowed from head to toe—his supernova.

Chloe had given an outlandish tale of how she'd rescued him the other night. She'd chatted on about a ghost and setting traps, but it all seemed impossible. And yet, he had no other explanation.

She'd even gone so far as to prove she was omniscient through Cupid by having Zack hide things in the house from her and having her 'ghost' tell her where the items were. So odd. But he'd always liked her quirks and her spunk. What mattered more than mythical creatures, was the end result. He was free, they were safe, and they had said their vows.

Chloe had been in charge of choosing the music. For their first song, she picked Sam Cooke's *Cupid*. Zack didn't need anyone to strike him or Chloe with an arrow of love like the lyrics suggested—that had already happened years ago, but the song was soothing and perfect anyway.

Of course, as long as he was dancing with his wife, Chloe could've picked any song, and it would still have been one of the happiest days of Zack's life.

As the music wrapped around them, Zack tightened his hold on his wife. Cupid could retire for all he cared—his work here was done.

Chloe was his forever.

<<<<>>>>

IN BOXED SETS

Romancing the Spirit

INDIVIDUAL BOOKS

Romancing the Spirit Series #1
Sadie's Spirit / Willow's Windfall
Cassie's Chase / Phoebe's Pharaoh
Vanessa's Valentine / Autumn's Angel
Romancing the Spirit Series #2
Carol's Christmas / Allison's Alibi
Gracelynn's Genie / Michelle's Miracle
Heather's Hero / Chloe's Cupid
Romancing the Spirit Series #3
Sabrina's Storm / Jenny's Justice
Stella's Star / Gigi's Gift
Phoenix's Phantom / Fiona's Freedom

THE CHRISTMAS COLLECTION

DEAR READER

If you enjoyed this book and want to know about future releases by CB Samet you can CLICK HERE (or visit www.cbsamet.com) to sign up for my mailing list! I promise I won't spam you. I only send an email when I have a new book released, giveaways, or special discounts. And I'll never sell your information. You can also unsubscribe at any time.

You can also connect with me on all major social media platforms below.

I also sell signed paperbacks through Etsy.

If you enjoyed this story, kindly let others know by posing a brief comment on social media or leave a review where you purchased it.

Thank you for reading,
CB Samet

OTHER BOOKS BY CB SAMET

Looking for more romantic suspense with more action and sizzle? How about with an urban fantasy twist? Check out my supernatural adventures...

The Shadow Guardians Trilogy

Urban fantasy Norse Mythology Adventure

Get *Raven's Flight, a prequel novella* for FREE. In my newsletter, you'll learn about me, special discounts, and new releases.

Raven's Flight, prequel novella

Raine Down, Book 1

Rosalyn's Run, novella

Storm Surge, Book 2

Anka's Orb, novella

Sky Fall, Book 3

Olympian Awakenings Trilogy

Urban fantasy Greek Mythology Adventure

Grab the prequel exclusively HERE.

Stone Hearts

Winds of Destiny

Flame and Shadow

Box Set 3

The Rider Files

Romantic Suspense Thrillers

Meridian File / Masters File / Box Set 1

McMillan File / Maltisse File / Box Set 2

Storm File / Sullivan File /

Sharp File / Sizani File / Box Set 4

Rivera File / Rucker File / Box Set 5

Richmond File / Redwood File / Box Set 6

Atlas File / Angel File / Box Set 7

Buy 4book box sets direct from author and save 10%

Payhip. Use code E152M0GZG4

~

The Dr. Whyte Adventure Novels

Thriller Series

Black Gold

Whyte Knight

Gray Horizon

~

Love action/adventure and strong female leads in a fantasy world? Check out my other genre:

The Avant Champion Fantasy Series

The Avant Champion: Rising

Malakai: An Avant Champion Origin of Malos Story (prequel)

The Avant Champion: Honor

The Avant Champion: Ashes

Brothers' Bond: An Avant Champion Malakai Story

The Avant Champion: Conquest

Isabel: An Avant Champion novelette

The Avant Champion: Redeem

ACKNOWLEDGMENTS

This series would not have been possible without the support of so many people. My husband, first and foremost, has provided feedback on every novella. He supported me with the time and encouragement I needed to write. I also have other fantastic beta readers who took the time to read and provide feedback.

Next, is my team of professionals. I have a team of editors who always adds a layer of polish. The book cover designers for this series created some breath-taking covers I never tire of looking at.

Lastly, are my readers. My review team takes the time and effort to comment on the quality of my work so that new readers will find me. Other readers take a chance on a writer new to them and dive whole-heartedly into the series.

www.ingramcontent.com/pod-product-compliance
Lightning Source LLC
Chambersburg PA
CBHW031609180726
48284CB00005B/1462